THE LORDLESS CITY

BOOKS BY MATT KARLOV

The Unbound Man
The Lordless City

THE LORDLESS CITY

BOOK 2 OF THE UNDYING LEGION

MATT KARLOV

IMAGO MUNDI PRESS

THE LORDLESS CITY

Maps of Kal Arna by Maxime Plasse
Map of Spyridon by Misty Beee

Interior Art by Amy Brym

Cover by Damonza.com

Published by Imago Mundi Press
Sydney, Australia
www.imagomundipress.com

ISBN 978-0-9925701-4-9 HB
ISBN 978-0-9925701-5-6 TPB

Typeset by Imago Mundi Press

First Printing

*This book is dedicated to my mother, Merike Karlov,
to whom no amount of words can do justice*

CONTENTS

ACKNOWLEDGEMENTS

My thanks to Amy Brym, David Karlov, Lisa Jeffery, Linda Taimre, and Abigail Nathan, each of whom contributed to the development of this novel. Further thanks are due to Amy Brym (again), Misty Beee, and the team at Damonza.com for providing the artistic pieces that turned the final book into something special. Thank you to my outstanding proofreading team: Karl, Merike, and Lisa. And once again, special thanks to my wife Anthea for her support and encouragement across the entire process of writing this novel.

GULF
OF SABAH

Nara

Afin

Ormande

Am

J E R V I A

PEKRATA

Cort

Dakin

Sadurne

JERVIAN

PROTECTORAI

Levente

Ma

Farica

CRYSLE
BAY

Taborri

MIRCOR
BAY

Kiarnon

Lake
Viho

Chayle

Telanon

Talasi

BEL HENNA

STILLWATER
BAY

S A P P H I R E   S E A

Natane

Yenene

PLAINS OF H

Safak

Sanam

Menefir

KHARJIK EMPIRE

BAY
OF ZEVA

Veda

Isra Water

Namir

Manelin

S E A

PLASSE
2014

ENDLESS SEA

Nalbaye

Cathal

SPOKARLE
BAY

Highview

Eastcliff

oras

Acton

Reidor Forest

EAST
MELLESPEN

Safrabor

Garran

Scarpton

Ormos

Uros

Djella

Domokos

Hyace

Nirel

RADOMER
BAY

PAZIA

Bosck

Zeanes

GISLEAN PROVIN

Rondossa

FREE

Shandrel

N

BAY
RACHA

Tresa

Illith

Neysa

Anstice

CIEIES

Fanon

Spyridon

Panin

Damara

Acantha

STORMS

THE FREE CITIES

(FORMERLY CORIDON)

Scale in Leagues

0   22   44   66

⊚ Great City   ○ City   • Town   ······ Roads

RADOMER BAY

N

SEA OF STORMS

Uros
Domokos
Hyace
Bosck
Rondossa
Pircassel
Storn
Hanfort
Gravesend
Illith
Borronoy's Crossing
Tresa
Anstice
Neysa
Miller's Wharf
Poet's Corner
Fanon
Rullo
Lissil
Spyridon
Vorsa
Morran
Panin
Zonta
Jorth
Lagon Cove
Damara
Garansen
Acantha

Elin River
Nerm River
Tenette River

PLASSE 2014

THE FREE CITY OF
SPYRIDON

1. Ebck's Boarding House
2. Quill Schoolhouse
3. Rhothe's Bar
4. Low Market
5. Arandra's Shop
6. Four Hands of the All-God
7. Army Command Post
8. Goldsmiths' Row
9. High Market
10. Trattas Estate
11. The Library
12. Arandra's Lookout
13. Onsoth's House
14. Clade's Suite
15. Lasavis' Workshop
16. Spyridon Mint
17. Hesea's House
18. Construction Office
19. Barracks

Anstice

Port Gate

Agratha

REEE
2019

Dramatis Personae

In Spyridon, among the rulers

Feren Skaratass, Conservator of the Library, member of the city circle
Onsoth, special assistant to the Conservator
Piator Pronn, army commander, member of the city circle
Hesca Matharan, army subcommander
Cas, a soldier
Zann, a soldier
Mistress Agli, a trader, member of the city circle
Dathreos, a priest, member of the city circle
Ernst, a craftsman, member of the city circle
Prince Urjo, member of the city circle
Arnol, his driver
Sandrine Velle, moneyer to Spyridon

In Spyridon, among the ruled

Clade, a sorcerer, formerly of the Oculus
Yevin, a Library scribe
Druce, a broker of services
Mock, his assistant
Taroqul, a construction foreman
Burr, his assistant
Charle Trattasi, a trader
Ral Garvan, a trader
Morrus, his driver
Osco Lasavi, a stained-glass maker

Yasa Lasavi, a stained-glass maker
Leff, a ditch-digger
Wil, his son
Old Jess, an elderly woman
Jak, a stray dog

IN NEYSA

Eilwen, a trader, formerly of the Woodtraders Guild
Den, a perfumer, Eilwen's brother
Irilli, his wife
Vess, their daughter
Orval, their son
Triv, Orval's friend
Ria, a trader
Fosclaw, city governor, of the Oculus

IN THE WIDER WORLD

Arandras, master of golems
Tereisa, his wife, deceased
Tiy, one of his golems
Mara, a swordswoman
Jensine, a sorcerer
Lurso Lutt, a smuggler
Kep, a fisherman
Azador, a god, associated with the Oculus
Rathzange, an Oculus sorcerer
Nezhar, a sorcerer of the Hungry Men
Sehv, an elder of the Hungry Men
Havilah, Spymaster of the Woodtraders Guild, deceased
Laris, Trademaster of the Woodtraders Guild, deceased

What Has Gone Before:
The Unbound Man

Arandras Kanthesi is a linguist and translator who makes a living as a scribe for Spyridon's illiterate poor. Though once a researcher for the *Quill* — an influential organisation of sorcerers and scholars that holds a keen interest in the relics of the ancient Valdori Empire — Arandras became embittered toward his former employers after the death of his wife, *Tereisa,* in a bungled attempt by parties unknown to ransom her for an artefact held by the Quill. When a misdirected message written in the same hand as the ransom note for Tereisa chances across his desk in Spyridon, Arandras resolves to discover its origin.

Eilwen Nasareen is a trade factor for the *Woodtraders Guild,* one of several mercantile organisations servicing the Free Cities. Unbeknown to her colleagues, Eilwen once betrayed a Guild ship to a clandestine band of sorcerers known as the *Oculus,* resulting in the death of almost everyone aboard. Wracked with guilt but unable to confess, Eilwen now hunts members of the Oculus with the aid of a black amber egg that enables her to identify her prey. On her return to Anstice from a trading assignment, Eilwen is summoned to meet with *Havilah,* the Guild Spymaster. Eilwen is convinced that her secret has been discovered, and indeed Havilah admonishes her to stop killing; but to her surprise, the Spymaster then offers her a job as his adjunct. Though unsure how much Havilah knows or suspects of her original betrayal, Eilwen accepts the new position.

Clade Alsere is the overseer of a small Oculus outpost in Anstice. Like all Oculus sorcerers, Clade has been bound somehow to *Azador,* a being regarded by the Oculus as a god and capable of riding the senses of anyone bound to it. Clade wishes to free himself of Azador and leave the Oculus, but he must plot his escape in secret or risk a traitor's death. When Clade's adjunct, *Garrett,* reports his failure to retrieve an old Valdori urn critical to Clade's plans, the bad news is compounded by Garrett's refusal to take responsibility for the mistake — a sign that his trustworthiness is diminishing.

Arandras is not only a scribe. He is also one of a small group of friends who seek out ancient relics and sell them for profit. Another member of the group, *Mara,* returns to Spyridon from one such journey with a small Valdori urn and an unlikely tale of a Quill expeditionary party murdered by unknown assailants dressed in black. The urn is sealed and bears a series of images and a strange inscription that Arandras cannot immediately translate. Arandras, Mara, and the other two members of the group, *Druce* and *Jensine,* find the circumstances odd but do not consider them a reason to delay selling the urn. However, when Arandras begins making enquiries of potential purchasers, he finds more interest than he expects and decides not to let the urn go just yet.

Meanwhile, Arandras learns that *Yevin,* the scribe who was the intended recipient of the misdirected message, is presently abroad. While investigating Yevin's activities, Arandras discovers that *Narvi,* an old friend from Arandras's Quill days, has moved to Spyridon. Arandras visits Narvi, who reveals that he recently dispatched a Quill team to retrieve a Valdori urn, but the team has not yet returned. Narvi has borrowed books from Spyridon's Great Library to research the urn — books that were also recently borrowed by Yevin, suggesting a possible link between the urn and the misdirected message. Arandras considers telling Narvi what he knows, but his distrust of the Quill is too great and he remains silent.

Resolving to make a fresh start in her new position, Eilwen buries the black amber egg. One of Havilah's field agents — now one of Eilwen's subordinates — complains that somebody else in the Guild is encroaching on one of her sources. Eilwen investigates and discovers that messages are being passed between the source and *Kieffe,* an elusive fellow member of the Woodtraders Guild. After several days, Eilwen manages to locate a room apparently being used by Kieffe but marked in the Guild records as allocated to Havilah. Unsure who to trust, Eilwen breaks into the room herself, but she is too late: the room is bare and Kieffe lies dead on the floor.

Clade's plans to rid himself of Azador are further complicated by the arrival of *Councillor Estelle,* a member of the Oculus's governing body, and *Sera,* a former student of his. Despite the growing risk of detection, Clade manages to sneak away from the Oculus compound to meet Yevin, who has travelled to Anstice with information Clade requires in order to construct a binding that will allow him to escape Azador. Clade begins to develop his spell, but he is interrupted by Garrett who reveals that he has been speaking with Councillor Estelle about his activities as Clade's adjunct. Fearful that further discussions might lead to Estelle guessing Clade's secret, Clade kills Garrett.

Arandras is visited by Narvi, who has learnt of his deception. Ashamed, Arandras recounts Mara's story to Narvi but refuses to sell him the urn. Arandras's own research at last bears fruit: though the urn is clearly of Valdori make, it is fashioned in the shape of a spirit ossuary, a ritualistic object unknown to the Valdori. Convinced that the urn is somehow connected to the misdirected message and therefore to Tereisa's death, Arandras rejects his friends' demands that he sell it, prompting Druce and Jensine to renounce their friendship with him. Arandras confronts Yevin, who has returned to Spyridon, but the scribe refuses to answer his questions. With nowhere else to turn, and against his better judgement, Arandras accepts Narvi's offer of Quill assistance to solve the riddle of the urn.

Arandras, Narvi, and Mara travel to Anstice, where they enlist the aid of a variety of parties: *Fas,* a senior Quill sorcerer who is keen to discover who killed the field party sent to retrieve the urn; *Bannard* and *Senisha,* Quill researchers assigned by Fas to assist Arandras and the others; and *Isaias,* an independent dealer in maps and artefacts. But it is Arandras who makes the breakthrough. The inscription on the urn is found to describe the resting place of an army of golems — near-mythical warrior constructs created by the Valdori — suggesting that the urn itself is the key to discovering them.

Eilwen is interviewed about her discovery of Kieffe's body by the masters of the Woodtraders Guild, including *Laris,* the Trademaster, and *Caralange,* the Guild Sorcerer. Havilah believes that one of the masters is preparing to forcibly seize control of the Guild, and Laris and Caralange seem the obvious candidates. Eilwen's efforts to re-trace Kieffe's movements lead her to an importer's warehouse, where she makes a shocking discovery: a shipment of cannons, the first of several, has been ordered by the Guild on behalf of an unknown party.

Councillor Estelle places Clade on trial for Garrett's murder, a charge Clade denies. To avoid being sent back to the Oculus head-quarters in Zeanes, Clade tells Estelle that he is close to locating an army of golems. Estelle gives him leave to continue his efforts, and Clade succeeds in tracking down the mercenary captain dispatched by Garrett to retrieve the urn, who claims that the urn may have now found its way to Anstice.

Arandras and the Quill research team succeed in opening the urn, only to find that it is empty. However, the inside of the lid bears a sequence of numerals soon recognised as location coordi-nates used by the Valdori. Everyone is thrilled by the discovery — everyone but Arandras, who cares less about golems than the still mysterious association between the urn and his wife's murderer. But there is worse to come. With the location of the golems all but revealed, Fas decides that Arandras's continued presence is neither needed nor desired. Fas rescinds the Quill's offer of assistance and expels Arandras from the schoolhouse.

Eilwen comes to suspect that Kieffe was killed by sorcery and attempts to gain access to his remains. However, she is surprised by Caralange who forces a bag over her head and drags her away, seem-ingly confirming his guilt. Shut away in a dark room, tied to a chair, Eilwen feels her old bloodlust return as she vows to bring Caralange down. However, when he returns to interrogate her, it emerges that he too is hunting for the traitor within the Guild and that *he* sus-pects *her.* They reach a tentative understanding, and Eilwen gains a new lead: a sorcerer and assistant to Caralange by the name of *Orom*.

Moved by regret for leading Sera to join the Oculus, Clade reveals his disaffection to her. She is shocked and refuses to accept his account of Azador's true nature, but neither does she reveal their conversation to Estelle. Out of options and running short of allies, Clade contacts a double agent he has secreted within the Quill: the researcher, Bannard. When they meet, Bannard attempts to kill Clade out of resentment for the treachery Clade is forcing him to commit. He fails. Clade reasserts his dominance over Bannard and learns that the urn is indeed in Anstice, in the possession of a man whose wife Clade killed, and that the Quill are close to locating the golem army.

Arandras visits Isaias and places a deposit on the only map Isaias has which shows the location referred to by the urn's coordinates, emphasising that he is not to reveal the map's existence to the Quill. Then, at Mara's suggestion, Arandras visits the city registrar where he finds documents written in the same hand as both the misdirected message and Tereisa's ransom note. The documents carry a name — Clade Alsere — and an address that leads Arandras to the Oculus compound, where he sees Bannard emerge. Bannard confesses his duplicity, but Arandras cares nothing for Bannard's betrayal of the Quill. His only interest is Clade, who he now knows to be responsible for his wife's death.

Eilwen follows Orom to a meeting with the Trademaster, Laris, where she overhears proof that Laris is the traitor within the Guild. Orom departs, but Eilwen stays and learns more: Laris not only intends to kill Havilah, but her plans are already underway. Eilwen rushes back to the Guild compound, but she is too late: Havilah lies dead on the floor of his office. Shattered, Eilwen succumbs to her bloodlust. She digs up the black amber egg. When Laris returns later that night, Eilwen confronts her and learns that she is working with the Oculus, the same band of sorcerers that Eilwen has been hunting. The combined effect of Havilah's death and Laris's revelations push Eilwen beyond her breaking point, and she kills Laris.

With a Quill expedition to retrieve the golems imminent, Clade prepares to follow them with a team of his own. Only one obstacle remains: Councillor Estelle, who wants the golems for the Oculus.

Clade manages to seal Estelle in what is effectively a sorcerous coffin: a way of killing her without attracting Azador's attention. He gathers his team, and they wait for Bannard's message signalling the Quill's departure.

Arandras devises a plan to lure Clade out of the city and use one of the golems to exact his revenge. He returns to the Quill, demanding a place on the field team for himself and Mara in exchange for the map showing the golem's location. Fas agrees, but insists on accompanying Arandras to retrieve the map from Isaias. Confronted with a group of hostile Quill, Isaias misunderstands the situation and refuses to produce the map. Only when Mara takes it upon herself to threaten Isaias's cat does he finally yield.

Their destination at last revealed, the Quill set out, accompanied by Arandras and Mara. Clade and his team follow, their presence known to Arandras but not to the Quill leadership. And behind them all comes Eilwen, drawn to the Oculus team by the black amber egg and thirsty for blood.

The trail leads to a cavern within a lakeside cliff, where Arandras and the Quill discover a vast company of golems, all apparently dormant. Arandras succeeds in binding the golems to his control, infuriating Fas and the Quill, who storm outside only to be ambushed by Clade. Most of the Quill are killed, and the few survivors are taken prisoner, Narvi among them. Clade enters the cavern with what is left of his team, and finds and subdues Arandras and Mara. Eilwen witnesses the battle and follows the Oculus into the cavern, but she is caught and imprisoned along with the others.

Finding the golems already bound, and discerning Arandras's contrary nature, Clade dumps Arandras outside the cavern with instructions not to interfere, in the hope of prompting Arandras to voluntarily exchange the golems for the lives of his colleagues. He interviews Eilwen, a discussion that is cut short by the arrival of Azador. To Clade's surprise, Eilwen can sense Azador's presence just as he can, thanks to the black amber egg — an object normally used by the Oculus as a sensory locus for Azador, but in this case damaged in such a way as to allow the bearer to sense Azador. Once the god has left, Clade returns and is able to persuade Eilwen that Azador is her enemy, one she shares with Clade himself. He asks her to kill the rest of his team — their Oculus loyalties and the pressure of Azador's presence make them a liability now that the Quill have been disposed of — and Eilwen agrees.

Outside the cavern, Arandras agonises over what to do. At last he decides to offer the golems in exchange for the lives of Mara and Narvi. But on encountering Eilwen at the cavern entrance, he changes his mind, realising that he cannot surrender such power to people as callous as her and Clade. He talks his way past her and finds Clade partway through a spell — one that will free him from the sorcery binding him to Azador by transferring it to one of the golems. Arandras prepares to kill Clade in payment for Tereisa's death, but at the last moment recognises that in doing so he would become no different to Clade. He relents and allows Clade to complete his spell.

Arandras finds Mara, Narvi, and another Quill still alive and helps them from the cavern, then returns to lead the golems out. Eilwen watches him go, standing guard over Clade who has lost consciousness after completing his spell. When he awakes, Clade finds Azador gone, but at a price: his right hand and forearm are now withered and useless. Unbowed, Clade resolves to find a way to build on this victory and drive Azador from the Oculus.

THE LORDLESS CITY

PROLOGUE

The phoenix is more keenly sought than any living creature. No sight is more auspicious, for good or for ill. No portent grants courage or snatches it away like that of a phoenix on high.

Does it know as it spreads its wings that the sight will embolden the observers below, that armies will march, that cities will be destroyed and monarchs overthrown? What instinct causes it to swoop, to climb, so that it will be glimpsed as the sun edges the horizon and not a moment before or after?

Perhaps this work of mine is vain, an idle speculation on events governed by those we least suspect. Perhaps our true masters are neither kings nor gods but these birds reborn in flames.

— Tiysus Oronayan, *Histories,* Second Volume

O N THE DAY BEFORE THE spring equinox, Nezhar stopped eating.

Small trees and scrappy, half-stunted bushes covered the slope on which he sat, extending past the creek at the hill's base and out along the flat where they gave way to fields, paddocks, and orchards. Beyond the farms and plantations rose the city of Spyridon, the earthen tones of its tiled roofs peppering the city's own hill beneath the grand red-stone library at its summit. A new wall surrounded the city, little more than a narrow grey band from this distance, its angular, star-shaped lines all but invisible.

For now.

Hunger curled through his gut, low and insistent. Nezhar took a mouthful of water from a half-empty skin — enough to fool his body into thinking itself fed, if only for a moment. Food was not something he took pleasure in, but he missed it when it was gone, that was for damn certain. But such was the price of belonging to the order known as the Hungry Men. The clue was right there in the name.

This is the last time, he thought as his stomach discovered his deceit and growled its displeasure. *One final job before I walk away.*

He stood, brushing leaves and twigs from his trousers, and trudged back up the hill. The first few days were always the worst. It was pointless to seek calm while his body maintained its truculent demands for sustenance. Only when it resigned itself to privation would he be able to begin the long, slow process of preparing for his task.

Ducking his head, Nezhar stepped inside the timber lean-to — an abandoned forester's shelter, or so he assumed, as the firepit out the front had been half-overgrown when Nezhar stumbled across the site several days ago. He'd cleared away the opportunistic shrubs and grasses, killed the spider he'd found ensconced in a corner of the lean-to, and dug a privy hole a dozen paces away in what he guessed would be a downwind direction, though that was unlikely to matter after today. His gear now rested against the wall beneath the dead spider's web: a lantern and oil, a shovel and a hand-axe, a whetstone, a coarse woollen blanket, a writing slate, and some pre-served fruit and dried meat for when it came time to break his fast.

He pulled the small axe free, its smooth handle fitting easily in his grip. He'd been given it by Sehv, the old waterbinder who had sponsored his admission to the Hungry Men, on the morning of his departure for his first assignment eight years ago. "Whatever you do, stay warm," Sehv had said in his breathy wheeze. "You'll be no good for anything if you die of chill." Nezhar had accepted the gift with his customary nod, but in truth he'd found himself unexpectedly moved by the elder's gesture. Unlike most of their small order, Sehv had truly embraced their ascetic origins, spurning all but the barest of essentials and refusing his share of the gold his work brought in. If the day had not already been noteworthy, Sehv's suggestion that Nezhar might benefit from another possession would surely have made it one to remember. He'd left with the axe dangling from his belt, the bump of its bound head against his leg reminding him with each step of the trust that Sehv and the other elders had placed in him.

He'd brought the axe with him on every job since. Its head was now notched along the top and bottom, and a long scratch in the handle marked the time the summer before last when he'd used it to fend off a wildcat that had chanced across his camp. Aside from the unwelcome visitor, that had been one of his simpler jobs: a straightforward weakening of the keystone in a bridge, timed to coincide with the passage of a carriage carrying the client's sister and nephews. As it turned out, one of the boys had survived the plunge into the rocky flume, albeit at the cost of his leg. Nezhar hadn't cared. The Hungry Men were paid to perform a specific action, nothing more. The outcome of that action and the success or failure of the client's broader enterprise lay beyond the scope of their agreement.

And it would be the same this time. Despite the difference in scale, this was just another job, same as the bridge and the one with the three-eyed gargoyle and all the others. Except once this job was done, he'd have enough coin to set himself up for good.

Axe in hand, Nezhar left the rough shelter and made his way uphill. He'd discovered a fallen eucalypt nearby, its tangled roots erupting skyward as though grasping for the sun. The wood had dried enough to make it difficult to split, and Nezhar had spent hours hacking at the thick branches, keen to build up his store of firewood before the weakness of his fast set in.

He crouched beside the fallen tree, hefting the axe and grimacing at the anticipatory twinge in his shoulder. This was the part he hated most, these first days when one was neither travelling nor at home and the absence of civilisation became painfully apparent. There was nobody out here to tend the fire or serve him cheap ale, no comfortable chair into which he could sink at day's end. Right now he even missed his last whore, that freckled Jervian girl whose incessant giggling he'd found so irritating at the time.

It would pass, of course. It always did. A week from now, he'd be basking in the silence as though he'd been born to it. And when the job was done he'd be gone, free to empty his fat purse in whatever city he chose. But none of that made the present moment any easier.

Gritting his teeth, Nezhar raised the axe to strike — and paused. The ground here was equal parts rock, grass, and dirt; his own tracks around the fallen tree were clearly visible. But there, in a soft patch of dirt just beside the trunk, was a mark that hadn't been there the day before.

Nezhar frowned and leaned closer. A paw print, and one he didn't recognise. Smaller than the axe head, but more than large enough to hold Nezhar's interest. He stood, glancing around uneasily. Further uphill the slope steepened, culminating in a high, rocky outcrop — an unlikely site for a den. Birds fluttered overhead, chirping complacently. The air held the scent of leaves, and earth, and the faint metal tang of his axe. Nothing seemed out of place.

Yet the print remained.

He scowled at the mark. Small grooves above the pads indicated the presence of claws, but the shallowness of the print meant the creature had been walking rather than running. *Looks like some sort of dog. Nocturnal, perhaps?* Whatever it was, it hadn't seen fit to disturb him yet. Perhaps, if he stayed out of its way, it would be content to leave him alone.

Besides, it was too late to find another site now. His fast had already begun. This location, with its clear view to Spyridon several leagues away, was perfect for his needs. And once he'd collected enough firewood, he'd be able to hunker down in his lean-to and leave the rest of the hill to whatever creatures called it home.

His belly growled. Stretching, Nezhar put the print out of his mind and turned his attention to the fallen tree.

This job, then I'm done.

The axe bit into the tree, the sound echoing down the slope. Again, and again.

PART 1:
THE DANCING GIRL

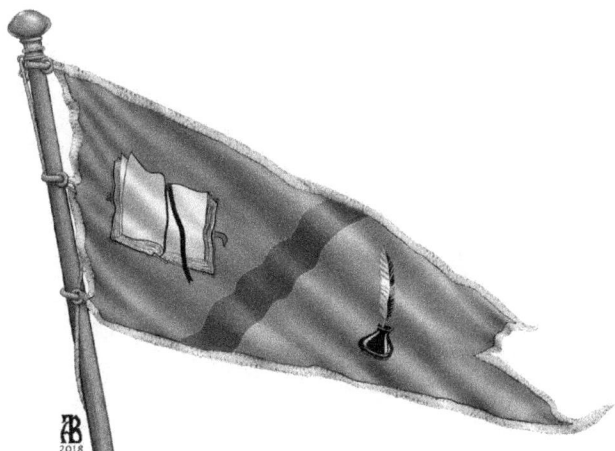

CHAPTER 1

Behold the wonder and the terror wrought by the gods: that they
bestow upon us a spark of the divine and place us in a world that
has no regard for it.

— Attributed to the ancient Valdori sorcerer Korozel

ARANDRAS CLIMBED THE SANDY RISE, hugging himself to
keep warm, and looked out at the stricken ship wallowing
in the dark, moonlit water. Waves rolled over the submerged
hull in an endless quest for land, their passage barely shifting the
three protruding masts. Torn sailcloth still hung from one of the
beams, black against the stars, its listless flapping audible only in the
gaps between the booming breakers.

"Bad night for it," Mara said as another wave crashed onto the
beach. "You sure you don't want to wait for that swell to die down?"

Arandras grunted. "It'll be fine." Dawn would lighten the horizon in little more than an hour. Calling off the salvage now would
mean waiting another day, and Arandras had no desire to spend any
more time on this inhospitable stretch of coastline than he had to.

"If you say so." Mara shrugged. "I'll keep our esteemed employer
company while you and the boys do your thing."

She vanished into the night, leaving Arandras alone with the sea,
the ship — and the golems.

They stood in a cluster just above the shoreline: eleven in all, each
taller than a man by at least a head, their moonlit forms blending

with the ground so that they seemed like statues carved from rock. Most had their backs to Arandras, but one stood sidelong with its head turned toward him, its eyes glowing orange-yellow in its shadowed face.

Of all the wonders wrought by the ancient Valdori, golems were the most wondrous of all: constructs of earth and sorcery created to serve the Empire, to fight its enemies, and above all to survive. So successful had their makers been that the golems had outlived the Empire itself, concealed underground for millenia until discovered by Arandras and bound to his service. There had been hundreds upon hundreds hidden in the cavern beside Tienette Lake and he'd bound them all, defying not only the Quill but also another who had come in pursuit of legendary soldiers: Clade, the murderer of Arandras's wife.

Arandras had led them out — all but one, left behind to allow Clade to rid himself of a strange discorporate being he'd called a god. Then Arandras had sent them into the great lake, entrusting them to the murky depths until he could decide what to do with the overwhelming find. After much trial and error, he'd separated a group of three dozen, which he'd brought with him as he journeyed first to Lissil and then elsewhere in the Free Cities, travelling only at night and hiding the golems by daylight in dry gullies, abandoned barns, or any other place that presented itself. He'd soon realised that even thirty golems were too many to reliably conceal, and so he had culled the group further to the current eleven and secreted the rest in a derelict well a day's walk from Lagen Cove, each golem standing on another's shoulders, the one at the top holding a stone lid above its head to seal the well shut.

In the months since, Mara's discreet enquiries in the moneyed districts of several cities had turned up an eclectic collection of individuals in need of extraordinary services, a surprising number of whom were willing to hire unknown, self-described sorcerers to perform the task, so long as payment was deferred until the job was done. They had politely declined anything that seemed likely to attract the attention of local authorities, but the remaining jobs had kept them more or less occupied throughout autumn and winter. They'd hauled red sandstone from the quarries near Spyridon to

Rull on the eastern coast in little more than a week. They'd burned down a forest and cleared the blackened remains from the grounds of a property belonging to the Morranese First Minister. They'd dug a moat around an old fortress in one night for a retired mercenary captain who'd bought it as a home for her stolen bridegroom. And now they were here, salvaging a questionably legal merchant's ship before its cargo of silks, wines, and exotic foods were lost to the waves.

Arandras started down the rise, stepping carefully to keep his balance on the soft sand. The golems stood motionless, but Arandras could feel their presence at the edge of his mind, faint but unmistakable, like a single strand of hair brushing against his skin.

Golems, he thought, directing the Old Valdori word at the assembled group. *Are we being watched?*

No. No. We are alone. We are unseen. The responses streamed back in the same ancient language as his question, merging and overlapping, each golem responding as though no other was present.

Satisfied, Arandras turned to the golem that stood side-on to the others. *Tiy. Enter the water and examine the ship. Tell me what damage you see.*

With a sound like stone grinding against metal, the golem strode into the sea.

Arandras followed its progress, watching as the water rose from hips to chest to neck until there was nothing to see but the shadow of a head moving across the reflected moonlight. He'd noticed this particular golem on the first journey to Lissil. Unlike the others, its hands were empty of weapon or tool, and its body was carved with the appearance of fine clothing instead of armour. Its face, too, seemed subtly different: the features were slightly smoother, with a keenness to its expression that suggested an alert, intelligent disposition. Arandras had dubbed the golem Tiy, after the Kharjik historian Tiysus, and had been pleased to find that it willingly responded to its new name. Though the concept of rank was irrelevant among golems, Arandras found it hard not to think of Tiy as the captain of his little band.

Damage. The gravelly drone sounded in his head, curling and twisting from one syllable to the next. *A hole in the starboard bow. A hole in the starboard hull. A broken rudder. Scores along the starboard hull. Scores along the port hull. Broken masts. Broken sails. Broken ropes —*

Stop. Tell me about the holes.

There was a pause. Arandras squinted at the ship and thought he saw a shadow rounding the stern.

A hole in the starboard bow, half a hand long. Water within; rocks without. A hole in the starboard hull amidship, two hands long. Rock within and without.

How deep into the ship has the rock penetrated?

Another pause, shorter this time.

Unknown.

Arandras exhaled sharply. Marvellous though they were, the golems had some frustrating limitations. Whenever a golem was less than completely sure about something, it would say only that the answer was unknown, with no distinction between matters that were entirely inaccessible and those that could reasonably be guessed. There was, Arandras had learnt, an art to asking questions that would yield the information he sought.

Can you and the other golems here free the ship from the rocks?

The response was immediate. *Yes.*

Arandras turned to the others still standing on the beach. *Golems, enter the water. Position yourselves around the ship and prepare to lift it ashore.*

They moved as one, marching into the sea with a grinding rumble and barely slowing as a wave curled over their heads and dashed itself against the sandy shore. A chill gust picked up the salty spray and flung it into Arandras's face, and he pulled his woollen jacket tighter around himself. No doubt Mara had joined their client at his campfire by now, perhaps with a fortifying — and fortified — drink in hand to compensate for the weather. Arandras gritted his teeth and peered into the night, willing the golems into position.

Golems. Are you ready?

Yes. Yes. I am ready. Yes.

Lift the ship free by its keel and carry it ashore. Set it down above the tideline.

For a moment it seemed that nothing happened. Then the ship

jerked upward, timbers groaning as water cascaded from the hull. There was a sudden snap and the ship lurched higher again, its aft mast breaking off and toppling into the sea as it began to move slowly landward.

The golems deposited the ship halfway up the sandy rise. It was a sleek, well-proportioned craft: large enough to carry a sizeable cargo, but small enough to manoeuvre past reefs and slip into coves, its present misfortune notwithstanding. A smuggler's ship, and no mistake. Water still streamed from the deck and the gaping holes in its hull. Part of the name painted on the stern had broken away, leaving only the beginning and end: *Inter... ...ation.*

Arandras nodded in appreciation. *Thank you.* Mara would have laughed at the thought of offering the golems his gratitude. Grand as they seemed, they were, of course, mere devices, with as much capacity to resist his orders as a hammer had to resist its wielder's swing. But it seemed right, somehow, to acknowledge his debt. *Return to the shallows and move south along the coast until you have rounded the point and can no longer see this location. Ensure that your footprints remain hidden by the water.*

They set off immediately, filing down the beach and turning in the direction of the point. Then one of them halted.

Arandras frowned. *Golem?* The construct stood motionless, its hands empty by its sides. *Tiy? Why have you stopped?*

For a long moment the golem said nothing. Then it seemed to stir.

A relic. A girl, dancing.

There was another long pause. At last the golem lifted its head and began to follow the others.

What? Arandras stumbled after it, sliding down the sandy slope. *What does that mean? Why did you say that?*

Tiy strode on and made no response.

Baffled, Arandras prepared to call it back. But the eastern sky was already brightening. Mara was waiting, as was their client. No doubt he would want to see the raised ship as soon as there was light, and the golems needed to be out of sight before he arrived.

Arandras cast a final, bewildered glance at Tiy's receding back. Then he turned and stomped up the rise toward the campsite.

~

Their client was less pleased to see Arandras than he expected.

"Here he is at last, eh? The grand sorcerer?" The man waved off Mara's calming hand and gestured angrily at Arandras, bug-like eyes bulging above a pointed beard. "Tell me, sir, have you conjured away the sea that I might stroll among the shells and fishes and board my ship?"

Arandras blinked. "The sea is the sea, Lurso. Your ship, however —"

"Pah!" Lurso spat, narrowly missing Arandras's boot. "Your dark friend has been stalling me, *sorcerer*. Believe me when I tell you I know the signs. Well. Lurso Lutt is not one to stand idly by while a pair of clam-brained charlatans rob him blind. I am going to see my ship, and I am going to see it now."

With a final scowl, the smuggler stalked past Arandras toward the beach.

Mara cleared her throat. "All good?"

"Sure," Arandras said, glancing sourly after Lurso. "Lifted it off the rocks as smooth as you like."

She gave a bright grin. "Reckon we should be able to squeeze another ten percent out of him after that little display. Pangs of conscience and all that."

"You put a high value on a smuggler's conscience."

"You think?" Chuckling, she started toward the ship. "Let's find out."

The stars were fading by the time they reached the shore, the patchy clouds reddening in anticipation of the approaching sun. Lurso was nowhere to be seen; but as they drew closer to the ship they heard the thud of something heavy hitting the hull, then a voice engaged in a rapid count.

"Your cargo's all there, Lurso," Arandras called. "Nothing's been in there but seawater."

"And that pesky rock," Mara murmured.

There was another thump and a clatter, and Lurso emerged onto the steeply slanting deck. Grasping a rope, he lowered himself gingerly to the rail, clambered over, and landed heavily on the sand.

"Well." He looked from Mara to Arandras, a smile playing

around his lips. "It seems Lurso Lutt judged correctly when he hired you. My thanks to you both for retrieving the *Conversation*."

Arandras raised his brows, torn between amusement and derision. *A moment ago we were charlatans. Now we're proof of the fool's discernment.* "The *Conversation*, you say? An unusual name for a ship."

"The *Interminable Conversation*, yes," Lurso said happily. "Named for my first wife, the Gatherer keep her." He reached into his shirt and withdrew a folded envelope, which he held out. "Your fee."

Arandras broke the seal and withdrew a heavy sheet of paper, embossed with the seal of the Artisans' Bank of Acantha and inscribed with no fewer than five signed names, ordering payment to the bearer of thirty-five luri — the agreed payment, no more. He passed the bank note to Mara.

"Very impressive, I must say." Lurso circled the ship, taking in the deep tracks left by the golems on their way to and from the water. "I would be fascinated to know how you achieved such a remarkable feat."

"No doubt," Mara said, her tone injured. "First you call us thieves, now you ask us to reveal our secrets. We might be forgiven for feeling less than appreciated."

"Pah. That envelope is appreciation enough."

Arandras gave Mara a sidelong glance. *Nice try.* "Tell me, Lurso, does the phrase 'a girl dancing' mean anything to you? Is there something on board matching that description, perhaps?"

Lurso shook his head distractedly. "Not that I know of. What does that have to do with your methods?"

"Nothing. Just a question."

"Humph." Lurso shot Arandras a glare, then visibly gathered himself. "I don't suppose your talents extend to the conveyance of cargo? I have wagons on the way, but they seem to have been delayed."

"I'm afraid not." Mara held up the envelope in a gesture of farewell. "A pleasure doing business with you, Lurso." She caught Arandras's eye and together they turned, heading south toward the point.

"But what am I supposed to do with my goods?" Lurso asked with growing alarm. "You can't just leave it here at the mercy of whoever happens past!"

"Oh, I wouldn't worry," Mara called back over her shoulder. "After all, Lurso Lutt is not one to stand idly by while he's being robbed!"

They proceeded down the beach to the fading sound of Lurso's imprecations, the sun inching higher over the low hills to their left. The arrival of dawn had done little to warm the air, and Arandras walked with his jacket pulled tight as the waves pounded relentlessly ashore, one eye pinched shut against the low sun.

Thirty-five luri. It was a handsome sum, roughly twice what he might have earned in a year as a poor-quarter scribe back in Spyridon. And today it was something more: the final amount he needed to settle his debt to Druce and Jensine. The urn that led him to the golems had belonged to them as much as to Arandras and Mara, but in his single-minded pursuit of Tereisa's killer he'd claimed the urn for himself, refusing to either sell the artefact or buy out the others' shares. A belated payment was better than none at all, and though Arandras knew better than to expect coin alone to mend the relationships, it would at least be a start.

"What was that back there about a dancing girl?" Mara said.

"Huh? Oh. Just something Tiy said."

"As in 'bring us some dancing girls'?" Mara laughed. "The boys are finally getting restless, eh? Who'd have thought it'd take so long?"

"Not like that." Arandras had explained more than once that the golems used the term "sisters" to refer to each other as often as they did "brothers", but apparently it amused Mara to call them "boys" — not that they were either, really. "It was odd. They were walking away and then Tiy just stopped, stared at nothing for a bit, and out came this strange comment."

"Sounds to me like he's just feeling homesick."

"Very funny. I suppose you think they were throwing parties in that cavern every other night before we showed up."

"What, you didn't see the empty beer barrels in the back corner?"

The sand disappeared as they neared the jutting promontory, the ground becoming rocky and harder to traverse. A narrow track cut inland, offering a path up the slope and across it to the other side. Mara led the way, climbing the hill with long, easy strides, Arandras following more slowly.

"There they are," Mara said as Arandras crested the hill beside her. The golems stood knee-deep in the water below, concealed from shore by a rocky outcrop but clearly visible both from above and from sea. "Our very own private work gang." She caught the look on his face and chuckled. "I'm sorry. Would you prefer 'military squad'?"

Arandras folded his arms. "That's not funny."

"Yeah. I know." Her laughter faded, leaving an odd expression of amused apology.

He cleared his throat. "Right, then."

"Right." She opened her bag and retrieved Lurso's envelope. "Say hello to the others for me," she said, holding out the folded paper. "Only maybe wait until you've smoothed things over, yeah?"

"I will." Arandras grasped the envelope, then hesitated. "Come with me," he said suddenly, and Mara raised her eyebrows. "I, uh… I'd appreciate the company."

Mara considered Arandras, a cheeky glint in her eyes. "Tell you what," she said. "You go sort things out with Jensine and Druce. I'll find us some business in Neysa, like we agreed. When you're done, come find me and maybe we'll talk about keeping company."

"What? I just meant…" But Mara was already turning away, re-arranging the contents of her bag and pulling the buckle closed. Arandras coughed uncomfortably. "Are you sure Neysa is a good idea? The place was invaded not six months ago. Weeper only knows what it's like up there."

"Relax." Mara looked up from the bag. "The dust should have well and truly settled by now, leaving an abundance of wealthy, frustrated citizens in need of our services. What's not to like?"

Arandras frowned and made no response.

Mara hoisted the bag across her shoulders, checked her cutlasses, and nodded in satisfaction. "See you in a few weeks," she said. "Don't lose any of the boys while I'm gone."

"A few weeks." Arandras raised a hand in farewell. "Try not to get yourself killed."

Mara matched his gesture with a bright smile. "Oh, you won't be rid of me that easily."

She held his gaze for a moment, then turned and walked away, striking inland toward a road that skirted the base of the small hills nearby. Arandras watched her go, their conversation echoing in his ears. She'd been teasing him, that was all. He was certain of it. Almost.

With an effort, he pulled himself back to his surroundings, and the task that lay before him: finding Druce and Jensine. Druce was still back in Spyridon, as far as Arandras knew, but Jensine had apparently relocated to somewhere near Acantha, a coastal city beyond Lagen Cove to the southeast. *Jensine first, then.* Depending on the weather and how hard he pushed himself, he might be there in four or five days.

But first he needed to find somewhere for the golems to spend the day. He yawned, the night's exertions catching up with him at last, and scanned the countryside for some place to hunker down. A promising clump of trees stood away to the south, a short distance in from the shore. With luck, there would be space enough within to hide them all until dusk.

Arandras started down the other side of the promontory. Waves boomed ashore, spraying water high into the air. He pulled his jacket tighter, sliding on the loose rocks, and extended his awareness past the end of the point toward the waiting constructs.

Golems, follow me.

~

Eilwen sat at a table for one on the chocol house balcony, elbows tucked in to avoid jostling her neighbours on either side, and congratulated herself on her foresight as she surveyed the harbour below. Crowds thronged the quayside plaza: merchants and labourers, pimps and preachers, children perched on their parents' shoulders for a better view. Two rows of hastily-erected timber barricades ran through the heart of the crowd, protecting a narrow lane joining the docks to the city. It seemed half the citizenry of Neysa had turned out to see their new governor arrive, and though their mood still seemed more curious than violent, an uncertain tension lingered in the heavy, malodorous air.

The ship they'd all come to see was still some distance away, its prow jutting directly toward them as it navigated the wide canal that linked Neysa to the sea. The angle made its progress difficult to judge, but Eilwen guessed they'd be waiting for another half hour before the ship reached its assigned berth in the centre of Neysa's huge port. She stirred her chocol and took another sip, grimacing at the overly strong taste of cinnamon in the creamy, bittersweet drink. No doubt she could have found better at dozens of other establishments in Neysa, but none of those would have offered the view she sought.

She'd arrived in Neysa that morning, sore from days of travel, to find the square inside the gates strangely quiet. A passing porter had consented to explain in exchange for a few duri. Five months after the shock conquest of Neysa by a hitherto unknown faction known as the Oculus, the occupying general was at last preparing to hand over the city to an Oculus governor who would be arriving by ship that very afternoon. No public ceremony or observance was planned, although — and here the porter leaned close — the Oculus had established a protected route from the docks to the city hall, which many were taking as a sign of trouble and an excellent reason to spend the day at home. If Eilwen was smart, she'd find a room somewhere out of the way and not venture out until tomorrow.

For a moment, Eilwen had considered taking the man's advice. Her brother Dennet and his family lived on the south side of Neysa, well away from both the docks and the city hall. But Clade had sent her here to discover as much as she could about the Oculus position — and where better to start than with the arrival of the city's new administrator?

A scuffle broke out on an adjacent pier and someone fell into the water, prompting a chorus of laughs. Eilwen scanned the crowds, taking in the dock workers guffawing around a tapped keg, the cluster of acolytes clad in the unadorned robes of the Weeper, the youths perched on low ledges protruding from the harbourmaster's tower. Most of those present seemed to hail from the city's lower echelons. Certainly she could see no delegation of leading citizens gathered to welcome the arriving ship. From what she'd heard, the conquering Oculus had taken a surgical approach to Neysa's occupation, placing their own people in key roles but otherwise leaving the city largely undisturbed. Exactly how the Oculus had secured

their position amid the tangle of influence wielded by Neysa's leading families was a mystery, but Eilwen had expected to see at least
a token welcome by those wishing to curry favour with the new
power.

She reached for her bag and pulled out a small wrapped bundle.
With a quick glance around the balcony to assure herself that no-
one was paying her undue attention, she set the bundle on her lap
beneath the small table and peeled back the lambskin wrappings,
revealing the black amber egg within. She drew a breath, bracing
herself, and closed her hand over its smooth, black surface.

A harsh rhythm swept over her, complex and insistent, like the
throb of a wild, multi-chambered heart. She exhaled slowly, willing
herself to calm, and the confused pounding resolved into half a doz-
en different pulses: two from bound sorcerers, the others channelled
through tokens like hers had once been, each emanating from a
different position in the crowd. Beneath them lay a thick murmur
of more distant beats, too many to disentangle, their source directly
ahead of her: the ship in the canal.

The beast within her stirred, lazily opening a slitted eye. She
froze, waiting for the surge of hunger that usually followed. But
the throbbing of the egg remained unchanged: rough, visceral, yet
without the obsessive ache that so often had driven her to kill. Eilwen released her breath. It seemed the endless hours she'd spent
under Clade's guidance learning to discipline her unruly thoughts
were starting to pay a return.

She sat forward and surveyed the harbour once more, studying
the positions in which she sensed an Oculus presence. A pair of
thin pulses denoting two token-bearers rose from the pier beside
the governor's designated arrival point — perhaps those soldiers in
Neysan teal and silver waiting in line before a pastry merchant? Two
more came from the other side of the barricade, where the angle of
the sun made it difficult to narrow their location further. Another, this one a sorcerer's pulse, emanated from the cleared dock itself, where a team of four armoured horses stood hitched to a heavy,
high-wheeled carriage. The last, however, seemed to be positioned
behind — no, atop the harbourmaster's tower. Eilwen studied the
covered platform, wondering which of the three figures might be an

Oculus sorcerer. Two had their backs to her, their attention on the approaching ship, while the third scanned the crowds, his gaze skipping from point to point. For a moment his eye caught hers, and she blinked and looked away, bending her head to her chocol and taking another sip. When she glanced back, the man had already moved on and was looking to her right toward the city hall.

That's the one. Every sorcerer of the Oculus was bound to Azador, a so-called god who could at any time choose to use that sorcerer's eyes and ears as if they were its own. Azador wasn't here yet — the egg would tell Eilwen if that changed — but the sorcerer in the tower had evidently been placed as a vantage point from which to view proceedings.

No ceremony. No greeting. A sorcerer watching from on high, with another in the crowd below. She frowned in suspicion. *They're expecting something to happen.* Maybe the Oculus hoped to take advantage of the governor's arrival to draw out whatever resistance still lingered in Neysa and extinguish it in as public a setting as possible. Or maybe she was jumping at shadows, seeing plots and schemes where none existed.

A shout near the docks pulled her from her thoughts. The ship had reached the harbour and been flung a line that was even now being fastened to the capstan. As a team of sailors hauled on the massive wheel, the ship slowly began to swing around, timbers creaking in the slight breeze, until at length its rope fenders bumped against the side of the pier.

Eilwen squinted at the ship. Three sailors dropped the ship's massive gangway into place with a crash, prompting a loud whinny from one of the horses on the dock. The thick tangle of pulses emanating from the ship began to move, and Eilwen gripped the egg tighter as an expectant murmur ran through the crowd. Her heart pounded in her chest, filling her with its mad rhythm. But no, that wasn't her heart, that was the egg...

The presence settled over the harbour like a fetid cloud, invisible yet suffocating: Azador, the so-called god of the Oculus, come to see its servant take charge of its new city. A rush of hatred rose within her in ghastly counterpoint: the beast, awake at last, murder in its gaze. The sorcerer in the harbourmaster's tower would die first. He was staring at her right now, the god behind his eyes, but a dagger in the heart would close those eyes for good. Then she'd kill the two soldiers who bore Azador's tokens…

No! Eilwen pulled back and slammed her free hand against the edge of the table, but the pain of the blow barely registered beneath the beast's lust. She struck the table again, heedless of the gasps of her fellow diners, and reached for the pain like a drowning swimmer flailing for a rope. But Azador and the beast filled her senses, leaving no capacity for such mundane concerns as physical discomfort. *Not enough. It's not enough…*

Eilwen turned her fading volition to her other hand, willing her crabbed fingers to open. *Let go. Please just let go.* The egg slipped in her grasp, falling to her fingertips; then, blessedly, it dropped from her hand into the lap of her travel-worn trousers.

Her awareness of Azador and the Oculus winked out like a lamp. The beast howled its displeasure, battering her with its rage, demanding she take up the egg and commence her work. But she could feel the bruise in her hand now and she latched onto it, drawing its pain around her like a protective cocoon. The beast's hammering grew weaker, muffled by the welcome ache. Breathing heavily, she wrapped the egg in its covers and slipped it back into her bag. *Not today.*

Eilwen opened her eyes. Her neighbours had drawn back and now eyed her askance, but she ignored them, her gaze fixed on the scene below. A knot of soldiers in teal and silver hustled down the gangplank and onto the pier, the figure at their centre almost completely obscured. The soldiers parted at the carriage and Eilwen caught a glimpse of a lean, grey-haired man. He paused on the step, taking in the massed crowds with a sour glare before ducking his head and stepping into the carriage.

A keg tumbled through the air, flames flickering at its end, and smashed into the dock just in front of the carriage. Fire and black pitch sprayed across the stones as a second barrel heaved into view and crashed beside the first. A soldier slammed the carriage door closed and barked an order to the driver. Then the kegs began to belch gouts of black smoke, and the screaming started.

Shit. Eilwen pushed herself to her feet and picked up her bag. As she slung it over her shoulder, the heavy carriage burst through the smoke and hurtled away into the city. A section of the crowd shoved against the wooden barricades, drawing shouts from the soldiers, and Eilwen turned and began threading a path toward the stairs at the rear of the chocol house. She descended as quickly as she dared, hissing at the pain in her bad leg, her bag bumping at her side.

The proprietor looked up at her approach, his jowls wobbling. "What's happening out there?"

Eilwen dropped a coin on the counter. "Does this place have a back door?"

The man's brows rose. "Maybe."

Something thudded against the wall outside. Eilwen slapped a second coin beside the first. "Yes or no?"

The proprietor scooped up the coins. "Behind the stairs," he said, gesturing sideways with his head.

Eilwen nodded. "What's the best way to the Ashtree district from here?"

"Depends. You want to go around that barricade or over it?"

There was another thud, and someone began to rattle the front door. Eilwen turned away. "Forget it."

The short passageway behind the stairs opened onto a small alley. Eilwen hopped through the muck as the cries of fear and anger at her back shifted to outright panic. Beyond the alley lay a road, narrow but paved. People scurried past, some glancing behind them, others pulling their companions along, but all heading in the same direction. With her bag held close to her side, Eilwen joined them and slipped into the city.

❦

It took Eilwen more than an hour to find a way around the blocked-off section of road. The beast grudged every step from the harbour, gnawing at her with the obtuse insistence of a spoilt child. She ignored it as best she could, focusing instead on the chafing at her waist where a goatskin belt rubbed against her skin. Guided by Clade, she'd tried an exhaustive array of measures to control the beast's urges, but simple pain had turned out to be the most effective. The discovery had been a relief. Finally, something that worked.

The barricades ended at the city hall, a wide, squat building that looked more like an overlong warehouse than the city's seat of government. Large flags at each corner displayed the coiled sea serpent of Neysa in silver on teal. In truth, the building was larger than it seemed. Much of the structure lay below ground, and there were rumours that the lowest levels had been built by the Valdori themselves to conceal some long-forgotten secret. Eilwen had scoffed at the stories last time she'd been in Neysa, but now, having seen the golem cavern beside Tienette Lake, she wondered if there was truth to them after all. Perhaps the Valdori had once housed some of their inhuman soldiers here before the Calamities and the Empire's fall.

She rounded the building, glancing sidelong at the sparsely-windowed facade. A fresh timber scaffold at one corner rose to encompass a jagged hole in the wall and roof, though the work site was currently empty. It was surprising how few Neysan buildings seemed to have sustained any damage in the recent invasion. Had the Oculus victory truly been so swift? She slowed, gazing up at the punctured wall. Havilah would have known how to read this. Except the Oculus, through Laris, had got to him first.

The beast growled deep in her belly and Eilwen broke off her train of thought. *Gods, just let the man rest.* Yet the memory of her mentor was not so easily released. Those few weeks working with Havilah seemed now like a homecoming of sorts, fleeting but precious. She hadn't been able to put words to it at the time, but she could see now that the Spymaster had offered her a way out, an escape from the tangle of pain and blood in which she'd become ensnared. Then he had died and the path he'd opened had closed over, leaving her with yet another wound and a beast that knew only one remedy for such hurts.

She reached beneath her clothes and cinched the goatskin belt tight, hissing at the protest of her raw skin as she drove the beast down.

Her brother's house was situated near the southern edge of Neysa on a wide, gently curving avenue that followed the line of the outer wall. Several of the blueberry ash trees for which the district was named could be seen on the grounds of the larger homes, their pale flowers peeking out from behind spear-shaped leaves. Eilwen halted before a crimson-panelled house, smaller than its neighbours but still large enough to boast an upper floor and a private stable at the side. *Not bad. Not bad at all.* She'd heard that Den had taken part-ownership of his ageing master's perfumery, but she hadn't imagined the rewards would be so quickly apparent. *Good for you, Den.*

She was still taking in the polished beams and worked filigree beneath the eaves when the door opened, revealing a tousle-haired youth of perhaps fourteen summers. He looked at her with wary curiosity, then blinked. "Aunt Eilwen?"

"Orval?" Eilwen laughed. "Gods, look at you. You're twice as tall as when I last saw you."

"Eil?" Den appeared beside the boy, as big and rumpled as ever. She barely had time to step forward before she was engulfed in his embrace. "You're alive. Thank the gods."

"What?" Eilwen said, but the word was muffled by her brother's shoulder. She pushed him away. "Of course I'm alive. Why wouldn't I be?"

"They told us... oh, the hells with it. Come here." And he pulled her into a second, tighter hug, his chin over her shoulder and his blond goatee scratching the back of her neck. "Irilli!" he called from somewhere behind her ear. "Eilwen's here!"

He released her at last and bustled her inside, sending Orval ahead of them to find his mother. The entrance hall opened onto a sheltered courtyard that appeared to serve as the central room of the house, its centrepiece a small garden filled with roses, orchids, and other fragrant flowers. A new dining setting filled one side, the table, chairs, and washstand all made of the same heavy redwood. A tablet bearing a Gislean religious motto stood on a cabinet along the opposite wall: Irilli's, Eilwen guessed, unless she'd managed to convert the rest of the family since Eilwen had last visited. Beside it, a set of stairs led to an upper balcony where further doors could be seen.

Irilli emerged from the rear of the house, drying her hands on a cloth. "Eilwen," she said, smiling slightly, her long earrings bobbing as she crossed the room. "What a pleasant surprise." She offered a polite embrace, which Eilwen returned in kind.

"I'm glad to find you well," Eilwen said. "What about Vess? Is she here?"

A shadow passed over Irilli's face, and Eilwen thought she saw weariness in the other woman's eyes: not directed at her or her question, but the kind of deep exhaustion that had become so close a companion that it was barely noticed. Irilli turned away. "Not just now." Confused, Eilwen glanced at Den, who shook his head slightly. *Later,* the gesture said, and Eilwen tilted her head in acceptance. No doubt her niece's whereabouts would be revealed soon enough.

Den cleared his throat. "How was your journey? Did the street closures cause you any trouble? We didn't bother opening the perfumery today, what with the governor's arrival." He spoke on, filling the room with friendly, meaningless chatter, just as he had as a child when their father reeled in late at night, sour liquor on his breath. Eilwen found herself slipping easily into the supporting role even as she wondered who exactly Den was trying to calm. Irilli, certainly. Orval too, perhaps. And Den himself...?

"It's a lovely house," Eilwen said, glancing back at Orval. Whatever had just been smoothed over didn't seem to have distracted him from his curious appraisal. As Den launched into a fresh discourse about their dwelling, Orval caught her eye, his expression hardening in resolve.

"So what happened to you, anyway?" Orval said.

Eilwen blinked. "I'm sorry?"

"The Woodtraders told us you died, only they wouldn't tell us why or how. Except one of them said you betrayed the Guild and —"

"I didn't betray them," Eilwen snapped. A memory flashed and was gone: *Havilah lying sprawled on the floor, his outstretched hands just short of the door.* She took a breath. "And obviously I wasn't killed." All three of them were looking at her now, waiting for her to continue. "It just... wasn't safe for me there any more. So I left."

Den nodded easily, as though her feeble explanation was entirely sufficient. "What have you been doing since?"

"Trading," Eilwen lied. "Mostly out west, near the Kefiran border. But now" — she spread her hands — "I'm here."

There was a pause as they took this in. Then Orval rolled his eyes. "Whatever you say," he muttered, and slouched away.

"Forgive him, please," Den said. "He's at that age where manners matter less than… you know."

Truth, Eilwen mentally supplied. "Of course."

"You will stay with us while you're in Neysa, yes?" Irilli said, her polite expression restored as though nothing had troubled it. "Herev knows we have the space."

"Thank you, you're very generous," Eilwen said. "Really, I don't mean to be a bother. Just put me in with the horse if you need to."

"Horse." Irilli sniffed. "The farthest any of us travel most weeks is Den's shop. What would we want with a horse?"

Eilwen cursed inwardly. *Gods, how many of their sore spots can I blunder into in my first hour?* But when she caught Den's eye, he was smiling.

"Now, dear, every house that was worth looking at came with a stable," Den said, draping his arm across Irilli's shoulders. "You know that." Irilli sniffed again, but this time Eilwen caught the undercurrent: this was an old disagreement rendered safe by long repetition, its expression now almost a form of affection. Den steered Irilli into the neighbouring room, throwing Eilwen a wink as he passed. "Eil can have the front loft while she's here. The spare pallet's already there. We'll have the room ready for her in no time."

Eilwen released her breath. This, at least, she understood. Aside from that brief time with Havilah, she'd been alone since the *Orenda*. But here in her brother's house, even with secrets yet unspoken on both sides, she felt it once more.

Family. A place to belong.

How had she survived so long without it?

Gods attend, I won't make that mistake again.

CHAPTER 2

Conformity is valued by those who find it easy, promoted by those who find it convenient, and scorned by those who find it empty.

— Vissbronaumi, *On the Tragedies*

CLADE DUCKED INTO THE NARROW alley and spun around, his good hand sliding toward his boot and the dagger concealed within.

A heavy wagon rumbled past the alley's mouth, stacked crates swaying unsteadily on its back. A Library scribe scurried in the other direction, grey robes flapping in the stiff sea breeze. A large, misshapen dog loped along in the wagon's wake, tongue lolling and ears up. Clade crouched in the alley's shadow, the dagger's hilt sweaty in his palm, waiting for his pursuer to step into view.

The woman didn't appear.

A merchant house courier ambled past, then a smelter's boy pushing a handcart of copper ore, and Clade eased his grip on the dagger. Perhaps he'd just imagined he was being followed. He'd spotted the woman with the pale hair and crimson scarf first in Spyridon's artisan district, not far from the rooms he was currently leasing, and again as he began to climb the hill in the city's heart. The second time he'd caught her eye for just a moment, and something in her bearing had set his back itching for a wall to put behind it. The narrow alley had been the next best thing. But now... nothing.

He straightened, clumsily tucking the withered claw of his right hand back into its trouser pocket. The impairment still rankled, despite the escape it had purchased. By ripping out Azador's binding with the same spell that claimed his hand, Clade had hidden himself so successfully that now, in his eighth month as a fugitive, he had yet to see a single Oculus agent lift a blade against him in retribution.

Nor, it seemed, would he see one today. Wherever the woman had gone, she was no longer visible on the street. Still watchful, but taking care to keep his movements easy and unforced, Clade emerged from the alley and resumed his climb.

The buildings in this part of the city were a mix of ages and designs, from recent constructions boasting oversized timber frames and red-brown tiled roofs to those in the Coridon style, many of the latter built with the red sandstone local to Spyridon. Aside from the prevalence of sandstone and the ungodly slope, Clade could almost have imagined himself in an unfamiliar district of Anstice. Yet where the other Great Cities projected a settled assuredness, the relatively young city of Spyridon possessed both vigour and a faint sense of insecurity, as though unsure it deserved to rub shoulders with the might of Anstice, the ingenuity of Rondossa, or the scheming wealth of Neysa. Clade found it energising and tiring all at once.

He rounded a bend, the buildings parting for a moment to give a glimpse of the Arcade running around the crown of the hill. Yevin's shop would be there, just below the Library proper. Clade had seen it several years ago, shortly before taking up his post as Overseer in Anstice. *A poky little place half buried in the hill, as I recall. All that height and no view. What a waste of elevation.*

A tingle across his skin gave Clade pause. *Anamnil.* Not close enough yet to negate his sorcery, but near enough to feel. That alone wasn't unusual: anamnil was a popular enough accessory among the fearful rich for whom price was no obstacle, and Clade often caught a hint of it in the passage of an ornamented yet heavily-armoured carriage, particularly in the wealthier districts. But no such vehicle was visible now, just the regular traffic climbing toward the Library or descending from it...

... and there, only a dozen paces behind him, the woman with the crimson scarf.

They locked eyes. The woman's face tensed in recognition, and Clade cursed. Then she shoved past a pair of elderly Kharjik men and began sprinting up the hill toward him.

Clade plunged across the road, narrowly avoiding an oxcart as he cut into a roughly-paved side street that pitched downward at an alarming angle. A recessed doorway beckoned and Clade scrambled into it, flattening his back against the heavy timber door.

The prickling sensation intensified, and a moment later the woman burst into view, arms flailing to keep her balance. As she passed the doorway, Clade stepped out and swept his boot into her feet. With a screech, the woman fell into a headlong dive down the cobbled slope.

She hit the ground face-first, a blade skittering free of her grasp as she slid downhill. Clade leapt on her back, ignoring the biting pain of the anamnil as he shoved her head to the ground. They skidded sideways, the woman twisting and snarling as the pair of them crashed into a row of broken barrels beside the road.

Clade slammed the woman's wrist to the ground and pinned her other hand beneath his knee. "Who sent you?"

"Who do you think, you fucking traitor?" the woman spat.

The anamnil's stings covered his body like a blanket of nettles. "You're not a sorcerer," he managed. "So you're not Oculus. What are you, some assassin they sent to do their dirty work?"

To his surprise, the woman gave a savage grin. "You know nothing."

Clade's skin was screaming. *Cloth, cloth, where could it be? Could be anywhere.* His gaze lit on the crimson scarf. *Could be...* He grabbed the scarf with his good hand, ripping it free and flinging it down the street. Immediately the stinging eased. *Thank the gods —*

But as he reached again for her wrist, the woman squirmed up and around, her elbow catching Clade in the throat. He reeled back, coughing, and the woman scrambled to her feet. From somewhere on her person she produced a knife and levelled it at his face. "Die, traitor."

She lunged and Clade rolled sideways, the knife striking the cobbles behind him. A section of broken barrel lay in the street before him and he grabbed it awkwardly, swinging it around as he turned to face his attacker. It connected with a hollow thwack, and he looked up to see the woman cursing and snatching after the knife. He stood, holding the chunk of torn wood as a makeshift shield as the woman recovered the blade and extended it toward him once more.

"Not looking good for you, is it?" the woman said, glancing at his crippled limb. "One hand, no weapon. Nowhere to go."

"Oh, I'm not going anywhere," Clade said. The anamnil was only a whisper against his skin now, the scarf blowing down the street. He fixed his thoughts on the broken plank in his hand and began to construct a binding.

The woman smirked. "You must have known this was coming. Nobody betrays the Oculus and lives. If it wasn't me, it'd be someone else, and the end result no different."

A crowd of onlookers was beginning to form a short way uphill. Clade ignored them, his attention fixed on the growing binding. "You got that last bit right."

"You made a good fist of it, I'll give you that. What is it, eight months? Nine? But here we are." She gestured with the knife. "Put that down and I'll make sure it's quick. You're not going to get a better offer."

Clade smiled. "No need for that." And he threw the plank at the woman's face.

For a fraction of a heartbeat, Clade saw the woman's eyes widen in realisation. Then he spun about, tucking himself into a ball, and triggered the half-finished binding.

The plank burst apart, peppering his back with shards of wood. Gasps sounded from the gathered onlookers, and several cried out in dismay.

After a few moments the shower eased, and Clade turned back.

The woman lay sprawled on the street, two long fingers of wood protruding from her eye and cheek, smaller fragments scattered over her face. Her fingers twitched once around the knife then lay still.

Clade stooped and made a hurried search of the body. The woman had strapped blades along each limb, and several to her torso; but aside from the knives, she seemed to be carrying nothing but a small coin pouch on her belt. Clade spilt its contents to the ground. Strangely, there was no locus, just an assortment of copper bits and lengths plus one or two silver scudi… and a peculiar steel disc with a hole punched through the middle, larger and thinner than any Free Cities coin. One side was covered in an abstract design, and the other bore a single glyph, perhaps a letter from another language. Frowning, Clade slipped it into his pocket, then glanced back at the silver scudi —

A shout sounded from up the hill, followed by the crash of something against the wall behind him. Clade looked up. The crowd had grown and several were now shouting angrily, gesturing at him to clear off or simply hefting rocks. Murder, it seemed, could be tolerated, but any subsequent interest in the victim's coinpurse was apparently a bridge too far.

A rock whizzed past his head, and Clade snatched up another plank from the broken barrel. He brandished the plank, then tossed it in a high arc toward the crowd. Shrieks split the air, followed by the sound of a scuffle; then the plank clattered to the ground, unbroken, and Clade turned a corner and was gone.

∼

Eleven.

Clade strode out of the clothier's shop, wrapping the second-hand Pekratan-style greatcoat about his angular frame. The northern fashion was uncommon in Spyridon, but not entirely unknown: in his time here Clade had seen a handful of others sporting similar heavy, oiled coats with wide collars and more buttons than any garment truly required. With luck, it would go some way toward separating him from whatever the onlookers might recall about the sorcerer who had killed a woman in broad daylight.

Eleven kills now by his own hand — or, in point of fact, hands. This was the first since his escape from Azador, the first since his right hand had been rendered useless. And he'd not even learnt her name.

The wild energy was fading, leaving a shocked indignation in its wake. *The bitch tried to kill me.* If he'd failed to spot her on the street, or if those barrel timbers hadn't been right where he needed them, she'd likely have succeeded. He swallowed, wincing at the pain in his throat where her elbow had connected. *Hells take you, bitch, with my regards.*

At least this death would be untainted by regret.

The lane cut across the hill's slope, giving Clade a view of the southern coast and the edge of Port Gallin, once a town in its own right but now effectively an outlying district of Spyridon. The harbour itself lay just out of sight, but Clade could see a square-rigged caravel tacking south and east, perhaps on its way to Neysa or another of the eastern cities, perhaps heading for the island of Pazia and the Oculus base in Zeanes. Perhaps, if his assassin had succeeded in her mission, she'd have been aboard now, slipping away before whatever passed for justice in the city could catch up with her — a problem which, by virtue of her death, now fell to him.

Well. If his admittedly half-hearted effort at disguise failed and the authorities managed to track him down, he would answer any questions they might ask. He had been attacked in the street and defended himself. Yes, he was a sorcerer, and yes, he had used his gift to defeat his attacker. Who wouldn't? Of course, he had no idea why anyone might wish him killed — but happily, his attacker was dead, so that should be the end of it, yes?

He rejoined the main road a few blocks above the side street where he'd been attacked. A black carriage bearing the royal insignia — a scarlet crown and wreath above a fanciful horned beast — rattled downhill, likely bearing Prince Urjo to whatever drinking house he'd decided to visit today. The man was little more than a figurehead, as Clade understood it, with the bitter wit to match his diminished station. Real power lay with the city circle, and although Urjo was known to grace the circle with his presence when it pleased him, his counsel was said to be customarily ignored by the circle's other members.

A staircase at the top of the road opened onto the wide, dark-granite gallery of the Arcade. Small shops lined the inner side, most built partway into the hill, while the outer side offered an impressive view of the lower city, the many-pointed defensive wall, and the farms and orchards beyond. Clade followed the Arcade's course around the brow of the hill, past the printers, typesetters, and traditional scribes in their rented shops. Food merchants and other street vendors roamed the gallery, calling their wares and filling the space with a mixture of scents. A half-Jervian woman shoved a particularly garlicky bowl of chopped eel in Clade's direction, the sauce slopping over the rim and narrowly missing his sleeve. He sidestepped the offering with a scowl, and the woman shrugged and thrust the bowl at a Library student passing the other way.

Yevin's shop lay almost at the end of the Arcade, a narrow room set deep into the hill, its immediate neighbours not shops but stairs on either side leading up to the Great Square and Library. The door stood open, and Clade paused on the threshold, peering inside.

The scribe sat on a stool in the front part of the shop, his back to Clade and a book open on the table before him. A heavy writing desk filled the end of the room, its glass-shielded lamps dark. The air smelled of old paper, new ink, and freshly tanned leather.

Yevin turned a page, the thick paper rustling softly. "In or out is fine, but please don't block the light," he murmured.

Clade strolled inside and perched himself between the unlit lamps. "Saving your coppers for something?"

"Only tomorrow's breakfast." Yevin placed a marker in his book and looked up. The grey in his hair had spread further since the last time Clade saw him, but the crease of his faint smile was just the same. "Clade. Nice coat."

"You think so?"

"Sure. Brings out the colour of the bags under your eyes."

Clade shot him a look. "Very funny."

Yevin gestured in appeasement. "You don't look great, Clade, that's all I'm saying. As a friend." The scribe's eyes flicked for a moment to Clade's withered hand, which had partly slipped out of its pocket. "But you're not the one saving up for breakfast, so who am I to talk?"

"Not great is fine," Clade growled, jamming his hand back into place. "Right now, I'm happy with upright and unpunctured." The scribe gave a questioning look, and Clade shook his head. "Don't ask. Your message said you had something for me?"

Yevin stood and reached for the door. "Let's light those lamps."

An old sparker lay atop a sheaf of unbound pages, its handle worn and its white opal tip smudged in a manner that spoke of numerous visits to the Quill to refresh the binding. The light it produced was weak and grudging, and Clade had to hold it to the lamp's wick for half a dozen heartbeats before it finally caught. As he turned his attention to the second lamp, the scribe seated himself behind the desk and opened a drawer.

"Here," Yevin said, passing a single page across the desk. Lines of neat, dense writing filled the top of the page, terminating in an ugly series of inkblots. "Yes, it's a mis-copied page. No, it's not mine. Don't ask how I got hold of it. Just read."

Clade scanned the lines. The account began mid-sentence, its grammar faintly antiquated.

... try as we might, the monstrosities pay us no heed. We speak to them in their own tongue, as the emperor's inquisitor insists is necessary, yet nothing we say can move them. How much longer must we wait? Their commander's bones have adorned the high tower for more than a month...

"'Monstrosities.'" Clade glanced at Yevin. "Golems?"

The scribe nodded.

"Where is this from?"

Yevin leaned back in his chair. "Somewhere in the Library, a scribe is copying this book right now. A chronicle, or at least a fragment of one, written by a Yanisinian courtier about their attempts to repel the increasing aggression of the Valdori."

Clade stared. "What kind of attempts?"

"I don't rightly know," Yevin said. "They were clearly trying to turn the golems back against their masters. Even if they failed, I imagine the manner of their failure might tell you much."

"No doubt," Clade muttered. The detail about tongues was demonstration of that. For some reason he'd never thought about what language the golems might understand. "When can you get me a full copy?"

"Ah." Yevin's satisfied expression slipped a little. "I can't."

"Excuse me?"

"This isn't just another dusty tome someone turned in for the Bounty. Conservator Skaratass had the Library go looking for this one."

Clade narrowed his eyes. "Why?"

"Why do you think? Everyone wants to know about golems now."

"Everyone wants...?" Clade shook his head. "Did I miss some grand announcement?"

"Of course not. But everyone's heard the rumours. Everyone who matters, anyway." Yevin shrugged. "Maybe the Conservator believes them, maybe she doesn't, but so what? Important people want to know more, and some of them have a great deal of coin at their disposal."

Oh, that's just wonderful. Over the past few months, Clade had further refined the spell that had freed him from Azador, smoothing out the imbalances that had claimed his hand. Yet without the disciplined spirit of a golem into which to transfer the binding, his spell was useless. And without the spell, he had nothing — no beacon to hold out to others who might wish to leave the Oculus, which meant no way to recruit anyone to his cause and no hope of ever challenging Azador, let alone driving the god away and restoring the Oculus to its true purpose: as benefactors and restorers of the lost Valdori Empire.

The hard fact was that he needed some golems of his own. Eventually that would mean tracking Arandras down. For now, it meant learning whatever he could in the hope of finding a way to wrest control of the constructs from their master. Wealthy competitors for that knowledge would only complicate his task.

Clade reached for the small pouch on his belt containing Yevin's fee and made a show of weighing it in his palm. "Tell me you've got a lead."

Yevin's slight smile returned. "I've got a lead," he said, and stretched out his hand.

Clade gestured for Yevin to continue, but the scribe merely looked at Clade and waited. At last Clade exhaled heavily and jerked the pouch open, emptying its contents into Yevin's outstretched hand. "Well?"

Yevin gave the lengths and bits a cursory glance, then dumped them into a desk drawer. "The transcription is being supervised by a man named Onsoth. Used to be one of those people who'd pester you if you hadn't paid your membership, that sort of thing. Now he's Special Assistant to the Conservator, meaning he does whatever she tells him to do."

"So he's her adjunct."

"If you like."

"Can you arrange an introduction?"

Yevin laughed. "Me? Gods, no. Onsoth wouldn't know me from a wheel of cheese. And that's fine with me, I might add."

"But you know him?" Clade said. "Enough to point him out on the street?"

"Certainly, if the opportunity presents." Yevin considered him for a long moment. "When was the last time you saw a show?"

"Excuse me?"

"There's a satirists' puppet show up in the Square. Day after to-morrow, about an hour before sunset. I'll be there. You're welcome to join me."

Clade frowned. "What does that have to do with Onsoth?"

"Hour before sunset, Clade. Could be that at some point we'll see Onsoth heading home for the day. If we do, I'll point him out."

"Ah. Set in his ways, is he?"

"No idea," Yevin said. "I've seen him go past a few times after a show. More often, I don't. But who knows? Maybe you'll be lucky."

Clade folded his arms. "So, what? You want us to stand around pretending to take in a damn puppet show on the off chance On-soth happens past before it gets too dark to recognise anyone?"

"Pretend? Of course not." Yevin grinned. "Those puppets are good."

~

Arandras arrived at the deserted village with a sigh of relief. Five nights of leading the golems south by starlight and five days of try-ing to sleep in ditches, caves, and other makeshift hiding places, had left him sore and annoyed at Jensine for dragging him this far south. Lursa, too, was not without blame: the man's bank note was redeem-able only at the Artisans' Bank of Acantha, meaning that Arandras would have had to visit the city sooner or later even if Jensine was still living sensibly in Spyridon. A pouch of gemstones would have been far more convenient, but the merchant class seemed to prefer the use of promissory notes and similar instruments for transactions of any value. It was true that the notes were useful for some purposes — such as removing the temptation for a middle-man to award himself an undisclosed fee — but in Arandras's view, the trouble of converting them to actual currency outweighed such benefits.

The village was one of several in the area that, though abandoned, still retained most of their buildings. Arandras had heard mention of a plague in the region several years before he'd come to Spyridon, and when he and Mara decided to further reduce the size of their golem squad, the derelict hamlets of the southern Free Cities had been among their first ideas for a hiding place. This particular village had been rejected as a site for long term storage, partly because of its close proximity to Acantha and partly because the available space was divided between three separate cellars. But it would be the perfect spot to leave the smaller group of golems while he ventured into the city itself.

Arandras was almost at the first house when he realised something was wrong. The building was gone, transformed into a heap of scorched bricks and blackened timbers. The next house along had similarly been reduced to rubble, and the one after that. Arandras sniffed the night air, but there was no smell of smoke. Whatever disaster had occurred here seemed to be long over.

He continued down the overgrown street, the golems tromping behind him, and scanned what remained of the village. Any number of things might have happened in the months since he'd last been here: a winter revel gone wrong, perhaps, or a fugitive burned out by his pursuers. The walls of several outer buildings remained more or less intact around debris-jammed interiors, but in the middle of the village entire structures seemed to have gone up in flames, leaving little more than a charred patch of earth where each had once stood.

Arandras drew up in the village square. Despite the surrounding devastation, its central monument remained intact: a five-sided obelisk that rose to twice Arandras's height, the symbols carved into its sides largely hidden in the starlight. Arandras had seen similar columns elsewhere, though not often. They were Valdori in origin, or so the Quill believed despite their inability to match most of the symbols to anything else left by the Empire. The obelisks were

distributed about Kal Arna in a sparse, seemingly random arrangement that led some to speculate they'd originally been linked in
some vast, ancient sorcery. Arandras had never given that theory
much credence, though tonight, with the village a silent ruin on
every side, he could see how such tales might gain hold.

He smiled. If fear or superstition caused people to give the area
a wider berth than usual, that was all to the good. His gaze settled
on a shadowy structure a short distance from where he'd entered: a
shale-stone affair whose walls still stood close to two storeys high.
He moved closer, the golems following in double file, their eyes glittering red and yellow and white in the darkness.

Golems. Arandras gestured to the house. *Clear a path to the cellar.
Disturb as little of the wreckage as possible.*

The golems set to work immediately, using swords, spears, and
maces to lift and carry the debris as if the weapons were extensions
of their own limbs. Arandras had no idea where the cellar door in
this house was, but the golems seemed able to deduce it from signs
invisible to him. Before long they'd formed a corridor through the
front door to the rear left corner of the house, where a wide trapdoor
opened to reveal a long, dirt-walled room. Nodding his approval,
Arandras unlooped the strap of his bag from Tiy's shoulder and
directed Tiy to stand apart from the others.

Golems, enter the cellar and remain there until I return. They started toward the trapdoor and Arandras turned. *Tiy, close the trapdoor
once the others are inside. Return the wreckage to its previous position
so that the path is obscured. Stand above the trapdoor and remain there
until I return.*

By the time Tiy was done, the stars were fading and a pale
smudge was starting to form on the eastern horizon. Arandras examined the scene. The marks on the ground where the debris had
rested showed that something had happened, but the house itself
seemed more or less undisturbed. It was good enough. If everything
went well, they would only be there for one night.

Stifling a yawn, Arandras kicked at the dirt in a half-hearted attempt to erase the signs of their activity. *Redeem the damn note, pay
Jensine, and maybe sleep in a bed for the first time since, what, midwinter at least.* Then to Spyridon to find Druce. Then more of the same,

tramping across the countryside, raising ships and hauling stone...

The sun peeped over the horizon and Arandras shaded his eyes. Was this his life now? He'd left his scribe's shop not only to find Clade but also because it had begun to feel too small. *Other people's words,* Narvi had called it, and he'd been right. Yet somehow he'd ended up right where he'd started, only with tasks instead of words: directed by others, paid for by others, meaningful to others, but not to him.

Soon he would settle his debts to Jensine and Druce. Then he would be released from obligation, in possession of a golem army, and free to do... what?

The question hung, unanswered, unanswerable. Arandras blew out a breath. *Later. I'll figure it out later.*

Squinting against the sun, he slung his bag across his back and turned south toward Acantha and Jensine.

∼

The Artisans' Bank of Acantha was a squat brick building with lozenge-shaped windows, each either barred or boarded up or, in several cases, both. Two uniformed thugs flanked its iron door, one with an array of knives hanging from his belt, the other armed with a single massive club. Disreputable as the building appeared, it did not look out of place on the wide harbourside street, which was home to no fewer than eight establishments with guards of some sort outside their doors. Unlike on Goldsmiths Row back in Spyridon, the guards here seemed to have little interest in maintaining anything more than the most cursory discipline. Several sat around a makeshift table throwing dice; others amused themselves making catcalls at attractive passers-by; while at the end of the street, two watchmen on opposite sides of the road seemed to be engaged in a ferocious contest of stares. Arandras took in the scene with wry amusement as he approached the door. *No wonder Spyridon governs Acantha and not the other way around.*

The best that could be said for the bank's interior was that it was clean. But the staff, in contrast to the hired muscle outside, appeared both motivated and passingly capable, and when Arandras presented the note to a middle-aged woman behind a counter, it took no more than a quarter hour for her to verify its authenticity, complete whatever paperwork was required, and invite him to a private room where the coins were counted into a fresh lambskin pouch and handed over. He left the bank with the pouch secured to his belt where his arm could brush past it with every other stride.

Most of Acantha was spread along the shore, wedged between the Sea of Storms and a blasted expanse of slag and rock dating back to Valdori times: a league long and a hand wide, as the saying went. According to the histories Arandras had read, Acantha had been little more than a village at the time of the Coridon Republic, autonomous in all but name: a port frequented by those who found the Republic's fondness for regulation constraining. The town had grown after the Republic's fall, and its pride had grown with it. As the five Great Cities established their dominance, Acantha had dug in, resisting their encroachment and branding itself the last truly free port in the south.

Eventually, might had won out, and Spyridon had planted its tome and inkpot banner above Acantha's city hall. From time to time, some slight or injustice would rouse the city's rebellious spirit, and Spyridon would be obliged to send in the infantry and squash it once more. The last such uprising was said to have coincided with the plague that emptied dozens of villages in the area and had been quelled by Piator Pronn, then subcommander of the Spyridon army. Since then, it seemed, the city's recalcitrance had subsided. The red-and-grey-clad soldiers seemed to go largely unnoticed by the general populace, and appeared content for the most part to ignore the locals in turn. Perhaps, Arandras thought, Spyridon had grown weary of the cycle and settled on a policy of benign disregard: so long as Acantha continued to pay the appropriate tribute, its master would consent to leave it more or less alone.

He strolled down the main street, taking in the sights: a heavy trading hulk edging into port with a bearded figurehead scowling down from its prow; a tall bronze statue of some worthy figure of the past, her identity long since lost to the corrosive effects of time and bird shit; a grand three-storey tavern, already bustling despite the early hour, its upper balconies festooned with several women and smooth-cheeked men in various states of undress. Street urchins threaded their way through the traffic, and these Arandras glared at as they passed, letting it be known that he was nobody's mark.

Jensine's house stood at the edge of town, one of several sharing a spur of land that jutted into the sea. She'd moved shortly after the break-up of their group, leaving Mara a message with details of her new address. There'd been no such message for Arandras; nor, in truth, had he expected one. *How could I trust you again?* Jensine had said, and even through the fog of his own obsession Arandras had dimly sensed the weight of her words. Each of them had found in each other fellow pilgrims fleeing the abuses of personal and institutional power. Arandras's betrayal had struck at the heart of what they'd had in common.

Squaring his shoulders, Arandras knocked on the sun-bleached door. The houses here were little more than shacks, notable only for their location. A small window beside the door had been partially covered from the inside. Shading his eyes, Arandras peered past the edge of the curtain but could see only darkness.

"Looking for someone?"

Arandras turned to find a wrinkled Kefiran man in loose trousers and a fisherman's smock squinting suspiciously from the neighbouring house. "In fact, I am," he said. "Is Jensine about?"

The old fisherman gave Arandras a calculating look. "Who?"

"Jensine Meyron. A little younger than me, maybe a little heavier. Auburn hair. Ring any bells?"

"Oh, her." The fisherman scratched his stomach and gave a pained hiss. "Barely here a month before she upped and left. Said she missed *trees*."

"Do you know where she went?"

The man glared. "No!"

A girl poked her head out from behind the fisherman's door. "Village called Salie's Rest," she said. "Or Sadie's. Something like that."

"Get back inside, minx!" the fisherman howled, and the girl rolled her eyes and disappeared behind the door.

"Well," Arandras said. "Thank you."

The fisherman cocked his head. "I could show you," he said. He scampered closer and Arandras stepped back, his hand covering the pouch on his belt. The fisherman noted the movement and gave Arandras a toothy grin. "Got something for her, yes? Maybe you'd have something for Kep if he showed you the way?"

"Grandpa! Leave the poor man in peace," the girl called from inside the house; but Kep, if that was the fisherman's name, paid her no attention.

Arandras frowned. "Tell me where this village is and I'll give you half a duri."

"Duri? Pah!" Kep's expression turned sulky. "No good with directions. Road this and hill that. I'll have to show you."

"Thank you, no, that's really not necessary —"

"In fact, I'm heading there right now. Been years since I last saw Stalie's Rest —"

"Stalie's!" said the girl. "That's it! Up near Lagen Cove —"

"Shut it!" Kep treated the house to a malevolent glare. "No-one asked you!"

And that, Arandras judged, was as much information as he was likely to get. "Sorry to have bothered you, friend. I'll be on my way."

Inexplicably, Kep brightened. "Of course! Quite right. Yes." Nodding and smiling, he scurried back into his house, the door crashing shut behind him.

With a sigh of relief, Arandras turned and began retracing his steps back into the city. Stalie's Rest. He hadn't heard of the village before, but that didn't mean anything. *Shouldn't be too hard to find. Head north to Lagen Cove and ask around...*

Footsteps approached from behind, rapid and uneven. Frowning, Arandras glanced around to find Kep panting for breath, a satchel slung across his shoulder.

"Off we... go," Kep said, lack of breath turning his grin into a sort of pained grimace. "No need to... worry. Kep will... steer you straight."

Weeper save me. Arandras glared, but Kep seemed not to notice. The fisherman settled into a half-trot, satchel bumping against his hip, his thin hair blowing in the breeze.

"Won't this... be fun?"

CHAPTER 3

The ancient clans of northern Mellespen worshipped idols of white granite, each as tall as a man. The godlaw permitted these figures to be displayed only when fully upright; and so, when the need arose to move an idol elsewhere, a sack was placed over its head to shield it from the mocking gaze of those who might otherwise glimpse it prone in the arms of its subjects.

Though the worship of such effigies has long since died out in that region, echoes of the custom persist in local discourse. Should you find yourself among the towns north of Spokarle Bay, it will not be long before you hear someone describe their preparations, whether grand or mundane, as "bagging the god".

— Eneas the Fabulist, *One Hundred Truths and Ninety-Nine Lies*

EILWEN SAW LITTLE OF DEN after her arrival. He spent most of each day at the perfume shop, leaving as the sun rose and not returning until after dark. In his absence, Irilli treated her with unfailing politeness, but nothing more. It was clear that Eilwen had blundered into some awkward family situation, but Irilli refused to acknowledge that anything was amiss, and despite her curiosity Eilwen had little desire to press the issue.

On the second day, she cornered Orval at breakfast and asked him about Vess: where she was, what she was doing, and whether Eilwen might see her. Orval was non-committal, saying only that Vess had moved out and wasn't expected back, and offering a mute shrug when pressed for specifics. Eventually, Eilwen had given up, not sure if the topic was connected to the family's tension or if Orval was simply at that age where communication of any kind seemed excessively taxing.

In any event, she had little time to ponder the mystery. Clade had charged her with uncovering the details of the Oculus position: their number, their disposition, how they maintained their grip on the city, even their level of interest in Clade himself. Besides that, Eilwen had her own set of questions awaiting answers, and her own erstwhile colleagues she needed to avoid. The Woodtraders Guild had a sizeable outpost in Neysa that often hosted visitors from Anstice, and Eilwen had no desire to catch their eye.

After some thought, she settled on a former rival as her first port of call. Ria Sonn had been a trader for the Three Rivers Trading Company at the time Eilwen was assigned to represent the Woodtraders in Neysa. Despite being younger than Eilwen by several years, Ria had beaten her to four significant deals before Eilwen notched her first victory with a memorable trade involving an abandoned goat farm, a whisky still, and three crates of Tri-God idols for the chief arbiter's excessively religious father-in-law. The ensuing rivalry had lasted eighteen months, until Ria was caught in bed with her superior's husband and summarily dismissed from her post.

Unhappy at her treatment at the hands of Three Rivers, Ria turned to Eilwen, feeding her information that had enabled her to win several major deals for the Woodtraders. In return, Eilwen nudged a selection of supply contracts Ria's way, giving her the income she needed to establish herself as an independent trader. Then Eilwen's role shifted, taking her from Neysa to Spyridon and the southern cities, and she and Ria had lost contact.

Ria's office was located in the city's western side, on a street facing the heavily-trafficked canal that served as Neysa's lifeline to the sea. She was sitting on a porch chair when Eilwen arrived, a stack of papers in her lap and a tall mug by her side. As Eilwen climbed the steps to the porch she looked up, brows raised beneath her shock of dark hair, her lips twisting into a familiar wicked smile.

"Look what the cat dragged in," she said, eyeing Eilwen as though sizing her up for a suit of clothes. "Still kicking, are you?"

"Always," Eilwen returned with a grin of her own. "Rumours to the contrary notwithstanding."

"So I see." Ria stood, and they clasped arms. "Let me get you a drink."

"No, no, it's fine." Eilwen took in the scene. "So this is how you bring in the scudi now? Sitting on the porch, watching the world go by?"

"Damn right. You should try it." Ria gestured to a second chair alongside the first. "Though if you want to make a go of it, you'll have to look further afield. Reckon I've got the arse-sitting market in Neysa cornered."

"If you say so." The chair was slightly lower than was comfortable, and Eilwen sat awkwardly. "Pretty sure I could give you a run for your money."

"Doubt it," Ria said cheerfully. "From what I hear, plenty of folks at the Woodtraders would be a lot happier today if you'd spent more of your time sitting around. What in the Gatherer's name happened over there?"

Eilwen shrugged. "Tell me what you've heard and I'll fill in the gaps."

"Gaps? Ha. I've heard half a dozen different versions, and every one of them has more gaps than story." Ria settled into her chair and stretched out her legs. "Some paint you as a turncoat, working for Three Rivers or the Crimson Sails, or even the Mathematicians. They reckon you offed half a dozen good honest Woodtraders before either being killed yourself or running back home to your master. The rest have you as some sort of heroic guardian, single-handedly defending the Guild against the gods only know what." She chuckled. "If I had to guess, I'd say the Guild leadership is split down the middle. Some of them want to pin whatever went down on you, either because they believe it or because it's convenient. The others won't have a bar of it. Throw in the fact that several of them are jockeying for position in anticipation of Vorace's retirement, and you've got about as big a mess as you can imagine. The Woodtraders' sales are in the latrine, and likely to get worse before year's end."

Eilwen stared. "Gods." She'd known that the deaths of Havilah and Laris would disrupt the Guild, but she'd thought Ufeus would at least be able explain what had happened to the surviving masters. *Did I misjudge him? Was he part of it all along?* But there was no way to know, just suspicion and guesswork, and none of it would bring Havilah back.

"So." Ria leaned forward, a glint in her eye. "You want to tell me what really happened?"

Eilwen tried to assemble her thoughts. "It's kind of a long story."

"I've got all morning."

Slowly at first, Eilwen began to recount the events leading up to Havilah's death, starting with her transfer to the Spymaster's department on her return to Anstice. She remained silent about her own history with the Oculus and the *Orenda,* focusing instead on her work to identify the traitors within the Guild and her eventual discovery of Laris's plot against Havilah. When she reached the part about returning home to find Havilah dead on the floor of his office, an unexpected lump rose in her throat and she paused, embarrassed.

"I'm sorry," she said, swallowing hard. "I thought I was past this."

Ria eyed her speculatively. "He really meant that much to you?"

Eilwen's brow furrowed at Ria's tone; then she barked a laugh. "Not like that. No. He just..." She trailed off, her voice going soft. "He trusted me. That's all."

"So what did you do?"

Eilwen shrugged. "I killed Laris," she said. "And then... I left."

Silence settled over the porch. A mid-size galley made its slow way down the canal, heading for the sea. A tall, black-skinned woman strode past in the opposite direction, blades swinging at her hips. She glanced sideways at the porch and then away again.

At length, Ria spoke. "Well, if you were looking for a way to split with the Woodtraders that leaves my tiff with Three Rivers completely for dead, I'd say you found it."

"Yeah," Eilwen said. "That was definitely the plan."

"What have you been doing since you left?"

Eilwen blew out a breath. *Killed some Oculus, saw some godsforsaken half-living Valdori statues, and took up with a murderous ex-Oculus sorcerer.* "This and that."

"You must have had something tucked away, though," Ria said. "A little nest egg funded by the Woodtraders whether they knew it or not, am I right? Enough to set yourself up with something new?"

Eilwen looked away, not sure whether she felt insulted at the suggestion that she was a thief or ashamed at her lack of foresight. "No."

"Oh, Eilwen. I forgot how... wholehearted you are."

"Enough about me," Eilwen said. "Tell me what happened here. How much do you know about these Oculus?"

Ria didn't respond at once. "Less than you might imagine," she said eventually. "As far as anyone can tell, they came in by boat and landed just outside the city. Next morning, surprise! Several thousand mercenaries from Mellespen with a couple hundred cannons sitting outside the gates."

"Neysa has spies, doesn't it? Someone must have known they were coming."

Ria snorted in derision. "Neysa's soft. Oh, the rich boys and girls like to play at their intrigues, but it's all just posturing. Nobody around here has had a real enemy to worry about in decades. In any case, the Oculus already had people inside the city. On the second night of the siege they opened the gates and that was that."

The audacity of it was barely believable. "Surely there's been resistance?"

"Some, yes, but mostly at the beginning. It's more or less died off now."

"But how...?"

Ria's grimace seemed tinged with grudging admiration. "The Oculus executed the archon and the few dozen people who actually ran things. Chopped off the head, cut out most of the city's sorcerers, but left everything else intact. Same chain of command, same everything, only now it's the Oculus giving the orders. And if someone lower down doesn't like it, well, they get the chop too."

"And nobody's doing anything about it? No-one's trying to pull together the soldiers outside Neysa, take the city back?"

"If they are, they're not doing it here," Ria said. "The Oculus know, Eilwen. They always know. Nobody can tell how they do it, but if you're plotting something, they always find out. And when they do..." She drew a finger across her throat. "A few people in the early days managed to get their hands on some of those black lumps they use as pass tokens at the city hall. Word is that they walked in as easy as you like, got politely shown to a side room, and then got a knife between the ribs. Every single one."

Pass tokens? The black amber egg lay wrapped in lambskin beneath Eilwen's linen shirt, a soft weight against her side. It made sense, of course. Azador could see and hear through any locus it chose. *Except mine...*

"Besides, for most people life's not much different," Ria continued. "There's been no increase in taxes. The harbour's still open. Everyone's still free to carry weapons if they want to. And most of the damage from the attack has already been repaired. Hells, a lot of people didn't much like the archon anyway. Right now it's just like one bastard's replaced another. So what?"

Eilwen dragged her thoughts away from the black amber egg to the conversation at hand. "And Neysa's tributaries?"

"Your information's likely as good as mine," Ria said. "I heard a few of the northern towns declared themselves independent after the local garrison commanders went native. Maybe the Oculus will leave them alone. Maybe they'll bombard them back into submission. Hells, maybe the Gisleans will cross the border and beat the Oculus to it. Nobody has a Weeper-damned idea where this is going to go."

"Gods." *Change is coming, Eilwen,* Laris said in her memory, and she shivered. Had the traitorous swine known what she was playing at? Maybe she had, and she just hadn't cared.

Ria rediscovered her mug and took a draught. "You ever hear the story of how we got this canal? It used to be the Tienette River, believe it or not. Story is that a few hundred years ago, Anstice and Neysa started poking at each other, and after a while Anstice came out here and laid siege. There were no cannons back then, of course, and their commanders started getting impatient. Eventually one of them came up with a bright idea."

"Divert the river," Eilwen said.

"You got it. Weeper knows how long it took them, but they did it. Dug a new course all the way to the coast to try and starve us out. We deepened the riverbed once the fighting was over, built the locks, turned the whole thing into a canal." Ria gestured expansively at the watery thoroughfare before them. "But ever since, Anstice has controlled its own sea link. No more Neysan fees on Anstice's goods.

No more threats of blockade if Anstice doesn't play nice. And now Anstice is the biggest city in half of Kal Arna."

The scent of Ria's cider caught the faint breeze, awakening Eilwen's thirst. She leaned back in her chair. "So did Neysa turn back the siege?"

"Who in the hells remembers? A few decades later the Coridon Republic came along and gobbled everyone up anyway." Ria stifled a belch. "Point is, that's where we are now. Soon as armies start marching around the countryside, everyone goes slightly insane. People start doing crazy things. Divert-a-river style crazy. And when the dust finally settles, those preposterous, unimaginable feats that'll be felt for the next thousand years? Suddenly they don't seem so crazy after all. Suddenly they just seem... inevitable."

Like bringing about the fall of the Woodtraders? Eilwen pushed the thought away. The Guild might be on its knees, but there was no reason to think it wouldn't recover. *And besides, that was Laris's doing, not mine.*

"So, how much do you need?" Ria said abruptly.

Eilwen blinked. "I'm sorry?"

"Money. How much?" Ria downed the last of her drink. "That's why you're here, right? I mean, apart from one-upping my Three Rivers walkout and gossiping about our new occupiers, obviously."

"In fact, no. But thank you."

"Huh. Just the gossip, then?"

Eilwen stood, the black amber egg shifting slightly at her side. "It's been more helpful than you know."

Ria arched an eyebrow. "Leaving already? You sure you don't want that drink?"

"I can't stay." Not if she wanted to avoid any further questions about her current activities and future plans. She smiled and glanced pointedly at Ria's chair and mug. "Don't work too hard, now."

"Never fear," Ria said, returning the smile. "And you try not to kill anyone before we next catch up, all right?"

Eilwen shivered, turning away as the smile drained from her face. "Never fear."

∾

As Eilwen began the trek back to Den's house, she felt the beast stretch within; not hungry, not yet, just reminding her of its presence. She reached beneath her clothes for the goatskin belt, then paused. There was nothing demanding in the beast's posture. Nothing that required discipline. It was simply there.

Eilwen released her breath. Perhaps she had finally turned the corner. It was weeks now since she'd come anywhere close to losing control, not counting the near-disaster a few days ago, and even that episode seemed better in retrospect than it had at the time. There had been Oculus right there, unmasked by the egg, and she'd been fine. Only the arrival of Azador had tipped her over the edge — and still she'd managed to find a way back. She raised her hand, examining the fading bruises where she'd struck the table. She'd endured the full fury of the beast and come out the other side. Surely the worst was now over.

A hand grabbed her by the shirt and slammed her against a wall, knocking the wind from her lungs. A Kharjik woman loomed over her, eyes as bright as her skin was dark, her face contorted in a scowl. "What in the hells are you doing here?"

The beast hissed, caught between resistance and submission to a stronger foe. Gasping for air, Eilwen reached for the hilt of her dagger. "Have we met?"

The woman batted Eilwen's hand aside. "Where's your friend?" she demanded. "Clade. Is he here too?"

Eilwen shook her head, surprised. "He's not... my friend."

The woman gave her a searching stare, then grunted and released her hold.

Glaring, Eilwen smoothed her shirt. The woman before her was tall, her black hair tied in a ponytail down her back, a cutlass hanging from each hip. "I saw you on the street."

"Just now, yes. While you were sitting on the porch. But we've met before, haven't we?"

"We have?"

"Perhaps you recall a cavern," the woman said, and smiled slightly at Eilwen's flinch. "And the cells beneath it? Or maybe you didn't see me. I certainly got a good look at your face when that bastard took you past, back up to the... what was that term the Quill used?

The First Legion?"

There was no need to ask who *that bastard* was. "You're one of Arandras's friends."

"Very good," the woman said. "And you still haven't answered my question. What in the hells are you doing here?"

The beast growled, its courage returning now that the physical threat had diminished, and Eilwen allowed its displeasure to bleed into her words. "Nothing that would interest you."

"Is that so?" the woman said. "Tell me, is it coincidence that you happen to be here just as Governor Fosclaw settles in?"

"Yes," Eilwen snapped. "What's it to you? Are you working for the Oculus?"

"Me?" The woman laughed. "Hardly. Are you?"

"No!"

"But you did help Clade murder all those Quill."

Eilwen shook her head. Only Oculus had died by her hand. "No," she whispered.

"Well, then." The woman tilted her head, considering. "Does that mean we have a common enemy?"

"Oh, no. Heard that one before. Not interested."

"Are you sure? If you're going to be poking around too, then we should at least try to reach some sort of understanding, if only to avoid stepping on each other's toes."

"Keep your toes out of my way and I won't step on them."

"My name's Mara," the woman said. "And I apologise for my rough manner earlier. But I'm really very curious about Governor Fosclaw and his colleagues. I'd quite like to know what they talk about all day in the city hall. I'm more than a little interested to know why they're here at all." She spread her hands. "Is there any overlap between my interest and yours? Or are you simply here for the fragrant harbour air?"

"Your interest?" Eilwen retorted. "Or his?"

"Who, Arandras?" Mara laughed. "I do have a life of my own. Or is that why you're here — because Clade sent you?"

Eilwen looked away, scowling. "You know nothing."

"I'm pretty sure I just told you that," Mara said. "And it seems you don't know much more. Am I wrong? Please tell me if I'm wrong."

All at once, the situation fell into place. The threats, the cutlasses, the needling about Clade — that was all distraction, intended either to throw her off-balance or to prove Mara's hostility toward the Oculus. This was just another trade negotiation, and she knew now what Mara was bargaining for.

Eilwen smiled. "You're wrong," she said.

"Really?" Mara spread her hands. "Care to fill me in?"

"After being shoved against the wall and accused of collaborating with the Oculus? Not particularly."

"Accused? Hardly. That was just a question."

"If you say so." Eilwen stretched her neck. "So what is it you're suggesting? You want us to investigate the Oculus together? I mean, I can see what's in it for you. Inside knowledge of the Oculus, both from my own experience and, uh, past association with — what did you call him? The *bastard*. But I'm not entirely clear on what I get out of it." She shrugged. "I work alone, Mara. I like it that way. Forgive my bluntness, but what's in it for me?"

Mara gave an amused grin. "My cutlasses make a compelling argument, don't you think?"

"Not really," Eilwen said. "Any partnership would require at least a measure of trust. Blades would be an entirely unsuitable substitute."

"Just so. But that's not what I meant." Mara's grin broadened. "I don't know what work you're used to, but I'm guessing it doesn't normally involve sneaking into heavily-guarded buildings filled with people who'll slice you open the moment they realise you're not supposed to be there. And I'm almost certain you've never been discovered in such a place and had to fight your way out." She patted a cutlass hilt. "I have."

Eilwen's brows rose. "A moment ago we were talking about a partnership. Now we're breaking into, what, the city hall?"

"Do you want to find out what they're up to or not?"

"Perhaps I do," Eilwen conceded. "But I also want to keep my head attached to my shoulders."

"Which is precisely my point. With my assistance" — Mara sketched a short bow — "you'll be able to do both."

Eilwen gave her a long look. "You expect me to believe that if we were discovered in there, you'd risk your life to get us both out?"

Mara's grin faded. Her gaze found Eilwen's and held it. "Once we reached an agreement? Yes, I would."

Eilwen took a breath. Mara's sincerity was either impressively genuine or even more impressively feigned. "I suppose you have a plan to get inside."

"Not yet. Do you have any ideas?"

"Never mind that." Eilwen folded her arms. "Look, if we're even considering this, we'll need some ground rules. Anything either of us learns is shared with the other. Anything we acquire is divided equally. And if we can't agree on a way in, we walk away and forget the whole thing."

"Absolutely," Mara said. "There's just one thing I'd add to that list."

"What's that?"

"We tell each other our names."

Eilwen exhaled. It was a reasonable request, but something in her resisted. The beast, perhaps, seizing the moment to express its lingering displeasure at Mara's treatment. Or perhaps this was the other part of her, the part that had come to recognise first steps down dangerous roads and feared where this one might lead. Yet that was all it was: one step, nothing more. If she didn't like where it led, she was under no compulsion to continue.

She extended her hand. "Eilwen," she said.

~

"Dua-na," Clade muttered, his finger marking the word on the tattered yellow paper. The afternoon sun slanted in the rear window of the poky bookstore, casting an elongated shadow of his finger across the book's facing page. "Breath. *Dua-na.*"

He paused, holding the two words in his mind, one Yaran, one Old Valdori, and drawing a link from one to the other; like sorcery, almost, except this particular construct existed solely in his thoughts. *Dua-na.* Breath. *Dua-sol.* I breathe. *Dua-sen.* I breathed.

Dua-el. I am breathing.

Clade turned the page, carefully smoothing the mottled paper beneath his slender fingers. He'd found the bookstore tucked behind an upmarket spicery, several streets down from the Arcade. The fragrance of sumac and sesame filled the shop, combining with the smell of musty tomes to spark an unexpected reminder of Clade's childhood: sitting on the floor of his mother's study, every wall given over to shelves of books, reading by the light of a cheap candle as the aroma of his father's cooking slowly permeated the room.

He'd been fourteen when the Oculus took him away from that house and the tiny village in which he'd grown up, and twenty the day he returned, a freshly bound sorcerer of the Oculus. He'd ridden into the village to find half of the buildings destroyed and most of the fields overgrown — victims, he learnt, of one of the petty bandit gangs that had long plagued sections of the coast and had now begun to move inland. His mother had died in the attack, though not before driving off enough of the bandits with her rudimentary sorcery to spare at least part of the village. His father had survived but had taken a blow to the head and no longer recognised his son.

Clade had sat with him for the better part of a day, making futile attempts to connect with a stranger whose drooling incomprehensibility Clade found only slightly less terrifying than his familiarity. Eventually he'd saddled his horse and ridden away, leaving the man to the care of a battle-scarred neighbour. His father had been killed as surely as his mother, save only for his physical body. There'd been nothing left for Clade to do but mourn them and move on.

"Can I help you?" asked a wheezy voice in Clade's ear.

Clade started, and the book slipped from its finely balanced perch atop his withered hand and tumbled to the floor. He scooped it up with his good hand and favoured the elderly bookseller with a glare. "Still looking."

"Tch." The bookseller peered at Clade from beneath a mess of white curls. "Drop it again and you'll be paying for it on your way out."

She hobbled away. Clade exhaled silently and flipped back to the page he been studying. "*Seli-ho,*" he murmured, sounding out each syllable in turn. "Button. *Seli-ho.*"

He'd learnt a decent amount of Old Valdori during his training, though it was years since he'd last made use of it. The language had two distinct grammatical designations: gender, in which objects were classed as masculine, feminine, or neuter; and form, in which objects were classed as natural, created, or abstract. *Dua-na* was feminine and natural; *seli-ho* was masculine and created; and they and the other seven combinations each had subtly different rules of usage and declension. Clade had picked up the rules without too much difficulty, but remembering the classifications for each noun had been a nightmare. Just why anyone had thought it a good idea to divide the world into nine arbitrary buckets lay beyond his comprehension.

The old woman reappeared abruptly at the end of the aisle, and only a lucky grab with Clade's good hand saved the book from a second fall. "If you like lexicons, I have several in Kharjik," she said, indicating a collection of tomes in her arms. "Two from the Old Valdori, one from Yanisinian. That last is by Tiysus Oronayan himself."

"No," Clade said. "Thank you. This one will do."

The bookseller's eyes brightened. "Three sculundi."

"You mean scudi." The bar-shaped sculundi was worth twelve of the tiny silver bits. "I could fill an entire shelf for three sculundi."

"Printed books, yes, but this one is not printed. Harder to find. More expensive."

"I'll give you one and three for it," Clade said.

"Two sculundi."

"One and six."

"One and ten." The bookseller gave a wheezy cough. "Last offer."

Clade scowled. "Fine."

Beaming, the woman waggled her finger at the counter in the shop's rear corner. "I will join you in a moment." She shuffled away and Clade strolled to the counter, watching as she returned the rejected volumes to their shelves with evident care. His mother had had a similar way with books, he recalled, although any resemblance between the two women ended there. It was she who had taught him to read, there in her study with her shelves and shelves of books. She'd had a way of correcting without criticising, something Clade had taken for granted until he joined the Oculus and discovered how rare it was.

His father had been more demanding. "That's not right," he'd say when Clade fell short in whatever he was being taught. Splitting a log, sharpening a knife, cooking a meal — the words were a constant refrain with every activity Clade set his hand to. On the day he came back to the village, it seemed those were the only words his father had left. No matter how patiently Clade tried to explain their relationship, his father just shook his head and said, "That's not right."

Clade had moved the conversation to his mother, hoping to trigger some memory in the man's addled mind. One of the other villagers sat with them for a while, telling Clade about the attack and what his mother had done. "She killed five of the bastards, if you can believe it," the villager said, her admiration plain. "Five!"

His father had looked up at that, brow knitted in confusion. "My Rena? Killed…?"

"Five of them," the villager repeated, patting his father's arm. "She was very brave."

His father had screwed up his face, as if comprehension might come from sheer force of will. Then, after a frighteningly long pause, he'd sagged back, shaking his head. "That's not right."

"So," the bookseller said as she shuffled behind the counter. "Learning the old speech, are you? Or teaching it to someone else?"

Clade shrugged. "Perhaps." He picked through his purse, withdrawing coins one by one and placing them on the counter. "One and six, was it?"

"One and ten," the woman returned. "And you needn't fret, I'm not one to tattle about a little unlicensed tutoring."

"Glad to hear it," Clade said as he finished counting out coins. "Because there's nothing to tattle about."

The woman peered at the coins for a moment before sweeping them into a drawer. "As you say."

"Splendid." Clade looked up to take his leave, but his gaze fell on the wall behind the counter where a long nail jutted from the wall, its length adorned with half a dozen holed metallic discs. He looked in his purse, fishing for the object he'd taken from his would-be assassin. It was the same: wide and flat with an interlocking pattern covering one side. "Excuse me," he said. "Those discs you have hanging from the wall. What are they?"

The bookseller glanced behind her. "Do you mean the Bounty tokens?"

Something clicked in Clade's memory. "The Spyridon Bounty?"

The woman gave a windy chuckle. "You're not from around here, are you?"

"So... each of those represents a book presently held by the Library for copying?"

She nodded. "They won't be interested in your lexicon, if that's what you're thinking. I applied for the Bounty on that very book not two years ago, but they already had a copy."

"I see." So the woman who had tried to kill him had a book on deposit with the Library. That was... odd. What kind of assassin spent enough time in one place to rent out a book for copying?

The kind who was short on money, perhaps? Maybe she'd just needed some quick coin and never intended to reclaim the volume. Or maybe something else was going on, and he'd just found a thread on which to tug.

The bookseller's words settled in Clade's thoughts, and he looked up in realisation. "So instead of spending the better part of two sculundi just now, I could have visited the Library and studied a copy of this book for nothing."

The woman smiled sweetly, fingers waggling in a gesture of farewell. "Happy reading."

⁓

Tucking the lexicon into a greatcoat pocket, Clade stepped out of the shop into the late afternoon sun. *Happy reading, indeed.* But it wasn't as though he only wanted to browse the lexicon once and then move on. Hours of study would be required to prepare for communication with the golems. Far easier to do that with his own copy than on repeated visits to the Library — and that was assuming they would make such a book available to a non-citizen like himself.

It was a perfectly convincing argument for a three-scudi book. But for one approaching two sculundi...

Clade shook his head. It was done now, and the afternoon was growing late. Yevin would be expecting him.

The streets were full, a roughly equal number of people seeking to move up the hill as down. Clade allowed himself to be drawn along the ascending stream, following the flow up to the Arcade and from there to the Great Square. A large crowd was gathering before an odd structure: a raised platform surmounted by a timber frame, from which hung thick black drapes. A group of red-hatted men and women stood at the front of the audience, a bare-headed man in their midst, and it took Clade several moments to spot the scarlet sash worn by the man and the glint of silver in the hats of his companions. This was Prince Urjo, Clade realised, surrounded by his gaggle of flunkies, here to take in today's offering from the satirists. Curious, Clade angled through the crowd for a better look.

"There you are!" someone called as Clade passed a patch of lawn, and he turned to see Yevin waving from beneath a maple tree. "Come stand on the roots and you'll get a better view," Yevin said, edging sideways to make room. "Hush, they're about to start."

The curtains atop the stage abruptly drew back, revealing a rod puppet of a sharp-faced woman dressed in grey, the figure recognisable even to Clade as Conservator Skaratass of the Library. It bobbed a curtsey, then turned and wiggled its bottom at the crowd, which laughed in approval. The puppet straightened in mock-alarm and scampered off-stage to be replaced by a puppet version of Urjo in the company of three others, each representing another member of the city circle.

The show that followed was equal parts slapstick and political wit, with the puppets arguing about the still-unfinished city wall while engaging in farcical pursuits and cheerful violence. Puppet Urjo was treated with no more deference than the others, at one point losing his trousers and being chased across the stage by a trio of broom-wielding soldiers. It seemed to Clade that the real Urjo enjoyed those moments no less than the rest of the crowd, flicking coins onto the stage with an exaggerated flourish, his loud calls of "Bravo!" audible even over the general noise.

At last, Puppet Urjo and the rest discovered Puppet Skaratass hiding with a pig in its trough, whereupon half of the group hailed the pig as an oracle of the Tri-God while the other half noted that it was past time for dinner and voiced an interest in roast pork. A general melee ensued in which the pig managed to adorn itself with the clothing and accoutrements belonging to each member of the circle: Puppet Skaratass's grey robe, Puppet Piator's sword, the merchant's scales belonging to Puppet Agli, and so on. The curtain fell on the pig lifting its trotter above the huddled, naked leaders, to the cheers of the crowd.

Yevin raised his hands in applause, and Clade clapped his good hand absently against his thigh, amused but also more than a little surprised. Anstice had had its share of comic performers, many of whom would direct a little light mockery at the archon from time to time, but Clade had never seen so biting a performance given in so public a venue. But then, none of the ruling elite in Anstice would have dreamt of attending a show like this. Urjo's patronage and approval of such displays no doubt altered the calculation both for performers and for others on the circle.

"I told you they were good," Yevin said, smiling broadly as the crowd began to disperse. "You should have been here a few months ago when they put on the Neysan Follies — revised in light of recent events, of course. Had the crowd in stitches."

Clade shot the man a glance, but Yevin was still gazing happily at the stage. Clade had never mentioned his former masters to the scribe, instead presenting himself an independent sorcerer with invitingly deep pockets, an interest in rare texts, and a few pardonable eccentricities. "Isn't anyone worried by what happened to Neysa?"

"A few probably are. But you know what Neysa is like. The politics, the endless games." Yevin's tone suggested a world of Spyridoni contempt that Clade could only guess at. "Honestly, where else could something like that happen?"

Clade let the matter drop. "Does Onsoth ever attend these shows?"

"Not that I've noticed." Yevin stepped down from the tree root. "He's not exactly known for his sense of humour."

"What is he known for?"

Yevin shrugged. "Not a great deal, really. Like I said, until recently he was just another collector making life hard for folks who fell behind on their dues. Guess he must have caught the Conservator's eye."

"What, you mean she and Onsoth are... together?"

Yevin burst out laughing. "Hardly. The Conservator's *lady* friend would have a great deal to say about that."

"Oh. Then how did he become Special Assistant?"

"Your guess is as good as mine." Yevin glanced at the Library entrance. "Honestly, there's no telling when he's going to come out, or if he's even in there today. What do you say we call it a day and... huh."

"What?"

"Seems you're in luck." Yevin pointed. "There, you see? The one with the swagger."

Clade looked in the direction of Yevin's gesture. Like many others, the man was clad in Library grey, but his posture would have befit the heir to the Kharjik throne. He strode toward the lower end of the Arcade, halting before a pastry vendor. The man reddened and tossed his head, then snatched up a pie and shook it in the vendor's face. His grating voice rose above the noise of the crowd, his words indistinct but his displeasure plain.

"My thanks," Clade murmured, moving out from beneath the tree before Yevin could respond and circling around to avoid catching Onsoth's eye. With a final curse at the cowering pastry vendor, Onsoth bit into his pie and resumed his path, Clade trailing behind as he descended to the Arcade and then to the main road that led down the hill.

After a while, Onsoth turned south, heading toward the new estates that filled the narrow strip of land between the base of the hill and the cliffs at the sea's edge. The hill was steep here and the road switched back and forth, and as they descended the slope Clade found himself slipping further behind, catching only a glimpse of his quarry at each turn before the next obscured him once more. Reining in his frustration, Clade crossed to the outer side of the road and looked over the rail. Ahead, Onsoth rounded the turn into the section below; and as he did, Clade breathed deep and opened his mind to the sorcery around him.

For a moment, nothing seemed to change; then, as Clade concentrated, objects began to press painfully against his awareness like jagged pebbles beneath bare feet. Someone pushed a handcart past him down the road, the sorcery that hardened its wheels grating in its crudity. Somewhere above him a strongbox ascended the hill, the rough binding on its lock scratching beneath his temple as it moved. Clade narrowed his eyes, focusing on the figure of Onsoth as he neared the point directly below Clade. Surely a man with Onsoth's level of self-regard would feel the need to carry some small, sorcery-enhanced item on his person…?

There it was. A knife of some sort, small by the feel of it, its binding designed to preserve not its edge but its shine. Gritting his teeth, Clade latched on to the prickly spell and hurried down the road in pursuit.

He'd developed the trick several months ago, inspired by Eilwen's use of the black amber egg to detect Oculus bindings. If he extended his perception as though searching for Azador, then shifted it just so as if preparing to examine a binding, he found that he was able to make himself aware of whatever sorcery happened to be nearby. But where a single binding might feel warm or cool, rough or smooth, or any of a hundred different things to his questing mind, reaching out to multiple bindings seemed only to give him pain. He'd conducted several experiments to get a sense of what he could do, but he'd never before tried it in earnest.

He skidded around a turn, almost losing his feet. The knife continued to swing back and forth below him, taunting him with its pace and the knowledge that soon it would pass beyond Clade's range of awareness. Grimacing, Clade broke into a half-jog, alternately accelerating whenever the slope abated and then slowing again to regain his balance.

The knife stopped. Clade eased to a walk and scanned the area. At the end of the next turn a timber bridge branched off to the southwest, the walkway spanning a cleft in the hill. A pair of Kefiran road preachers had planted themselves in the middle of the bridge, blocking Onsoth's path, and were now apparently enquiring as to the state of the Library man's soul. As Clade drew closer, Onsoth shoved one of the Kefirans aside, sending her stumbling against the rail and striding past.

Once more, Clade moved to follow; but as he crossed the bridge he saw Onsoth turn and approach a modest house, where he paused for a moment before pushing the front door open and disappearing inside. Clade slowed, concentrating on the knife. It moved deeper into the house, then stopped — set aside, perhaps, unless Onsoth had come to a halt.

Disappointed, Clade released his focus on the knife. This must be Onsoth's home. No welcome was evident, suggesting he probably lived alone — not surprising given his temperament, but unhelpful all the same. A partner might offer all sorts of interesting avenues for flattery and manipulation. The fewer a man's connections, the more difficult it was to forge a new one.

He turned away, retracing his steps over the bridge. The Kefiran had regained her feet, and she and her companion looked up at Clade's approach. "Well met," she said, tucking a curl of greying hair behind her ear. "The All-God's favour be upon you."

"He can keep it," Clade said as he brushed past. Gods were the same as anyone else. They only offered their favour if they thought they could gain something in return.

Which, now that he thought about it, might not be a bad plan.

A favour for Onsoth. Something sorcerous, perhaps. Surely such an offer would at least be enough to gain him an audience.

And once he found an opening, anything was possible.

CHAPTER 4

The better part of the world's ills can be traced to this singular cause: that we mistake our peculiarities for generalities, and vice versa.

— Daro of Talsoor, *Dialogues with my Teachers*

NOTHING ARANDRAS SAID COULD PERSUADE Kep to leave him alone. The old fisherman bumbled along beside him, cheerfully oblivious to any suggestion — not to mention repeated outright statements — that his presence was anything less than welcome. "This is the way," he would say every hour or so, gesturing northward as if there were some confusion about which direction the road was taking them. "I'd know it anywhere. Straight ahead, that's what we want."

And straight ahead they went, or as straight as the road would allow, until dusk fell and Arandras found himself with a new predicament.

"You stay on that side of the fire, you hear me?" He fixed the fisherman with as forbidding a scowl as he could muster. "Get too close and I'll drag you back to Acantha by your ear."

Kep blinked across the campfire as if he knew very well that Arandras was bluffing. "Had my dog with me last time. Lucky dog. Lucky the dog." His voice turned wistful. "Come night, me and Lucky would lie together. Stay warm."

"Well, I'm not your Weeper-damned dog, and I'm quite warm

enough, thank you." Arandras stretched out on the patchy grass and tried to ignore the chill breeze. "Go home, climb a tree, or if you absolutely must, sleep right where you are. Just don't come this side of the fire."

Grumbling, the fisherman lay down, shifting and scraping and eventually falling still, his slow, wheezing breaths just audible above the soft crackle of the dying fire. Arandras gazed at the stars, one arm resting on the pouch containing Jensine's gold, and tried to convince himself that it was safe to sleep.

It was unsettling to find himself in the company of a stranger with neither Mara nor the golems nearby. He'd become accustomed to giving little thought to his own safety, and the need to consider it again felt jarring, even in relation to an old fisherman who seemed more peculiar than threatening. *This is normal,* he thought, pressing his eyes closed and trying to conjure a yawn. *Most people have to deal with this all the time.*

Sleep, when it came, was fitful, and Arandras awoke feeling stiff and unrefreshed. The morning began as the previous day had ended, with Kep volubly steering them in the only direction available and Arandras striding ahead in the hope of temporarily forgetting the fisherman's presence. Fields and farms had covered the coastal fringe outside Acantha, but now the road cut through forest. Bulbous-trunked bottle trees, tall hoop pines, and spreading eucalypts combined to cast their path into shade, several of the latter already sporting small cream-yellow flowers. The undergrowth was light for the most part, but it thickened into tight knots often enough to make Arandras glad Tiy and the others weren't there. Even out of sight, the noise they'd have made hacking through bush and scrub would have announced their presence as surely as marching them down the road.

"This way, yes," Kep said, and Arandras strode on for half a dozen paces before he realised the fisherman had stopped. Kep pointed down a cartwheel-rutted track, grinning like a child that had just found a hidden sweetmeat. "Stalie's Rest. Not far now."

"And how far is that, exactly?" A weathered post stood at the junction, but if it had ever borne a sign naming the road or the village at its end, Arandras could see no trace of it now. "An hour?

Another day?"

"Pah. How should I know? Will we run? Crawl? Fly?" Kep shrugged as if all three were equally likely. "Tempting the gods is fools' business. Kep sticks to what he knows."

"Is that so?" Arandras folded his arms. "Then perhaps you can tell me why you're so eager to join me on this little excursion. Seems to me you must *know* there's something at the end to make it worth your while. What might that be, hmmm? That half-copper I promised you?"

Kep scowled. "Half a duri was for directions, not for sharing your road and guiding your steps."

"You're right. I didn't promise you anything for that." Arandras stepped closer. "So what's your game, Kep? You do this a lot? Lead some poor sap of a traveller somewhere out of the way, maybe to some friends of yours who'll lighten my pockets and give you a little something as a finder's fee? Is that it?"

"Oh!" Kep's hand lashed out and slapped Arandras across the cheek. "You think... You dare... Oh!" He tottered back, face filled with outraged disbelief, and raised an accusatory finger. "You are a rude man!"

Arandras rubbed his stinging cheek. "That's not an answer —"

"How do I know what *you* are about, rude man? Perhaps you are leading *me* to some friends, yes? Perhaps you will throw rocks at me for sport. Perhaps you will open my throat and leave me in a ditch. You do not tell me who you are; perhaps this is so that I will have no name to curse with my dying breath. Yes?"

"All right, you've made your point," Arandras said. "But I still don't see why you were so keen to drop everything and come north."

"Oh?" The fisherman glared. "And why do you want to see Jensine, then?"

Arandras hesitated. Kep's outrage at the suggestion of theft seemed genuine, but there was no knowing what he might do if he discovered how much coin Arandras was carrying. "She... helped me, once," he began, then stopped. Why even begin to explain himself to this madman? "She's an old friend, that's all."

"Helped?" Improbably, Kep brightened. "Jensine helped Kep, too." He began tugging at the buttons of his smock. "See, it starts here. Just like a tanner's marks, they say, except that it comes and goes and there's not a physic this side of Menefir can do anything about it." Kep pulled open the top of his garment to reveal an angry red rash across his chest and collarbone. "But Jensine gave a bandage that stopped the pain, at least for a while —"

"All right, fine, I get the idea," Arandras said. "You can put that back on now. How clever of Jensine to — yes, all the buttons, please. Yes. Good."

Flushed with the excitement of discovering a shared confidence, Kep shrugged his smock back into place. "And where was yours?"

"Mine? Ah. Mine was really... nothing like that. At all. In fact..." Arandras sighed, stuck out his hand, then thought better of it and pulled it back. "My name's Arandras," he said. "Stalie's Rest is close, you say?"

Kep beamed. "Close, yes." He pointed down the track. "That way."

"That way. Well." Arandras gestured expansively. "Lead on."

~

Stalie's Rest consisted of an overgrown square, a crumbling stone well, and several dozen cottages nestled at the base of a hill. A surly child with the apparent task of herding the village's three pigs offered grudging directions, and soon Arandras and Kep found themselves standing before a narrow log cabin tucked between two massive pale eucalypts, just up the hill from the village proper.

"Hallooo," Kep called, beating Arandras to the porch and hammering on the door with a scrawny fist. "Meyron? You in there? It's your old friend Kep —"

The door jerked open, unbalancing Kep, who pitched sideways and clutched at the jamb for support. Jensine stood inside, hands on hips, frowning at the old fisherman. "Kep? What in the Dreamer's name are you doing here?"

"Guiding me," Arandras said, and Jensine looked up.

She was little changed from when he'd last seen her: slightly less stocky, perhaps, and her rough shirt and trousers somewhat more dirt-stained, but that was all. She folded her arms, her brows rising. "And what," she said, "in the Dreamer's name are *you* doing here?"

Arandras ventured a smile. "Escorting him," he said, pointing a thumb at Kep. "Apparently."

Jensine tilted her head, eyes narrowing as she considered him. "Is Mara not with you?"

"Not for this. But she says hello."

She nodded slowly. "All right. Come in, then."

Arandras followed a scampering Kep inside. The front room occupied the full width of the cabin and half its length, with an assortment of garden tools bundled in the near corner, a workbench beneath the largest window scattered with smaller tools and utensils, and a stone column in the far wall marking the position of the fireplace in the next room. Jensine dragged a stool out from beneath the workbench and set it across from a high-backed timber rocking chair. "Not much to offer you but water, I'm afraid," she said, as Kep lowered himself cautiously into the chair and began rocking. "Fresh from a brook thirty paces that way. Nothing at all like that swill everyone drinks in Spyridon."

"I want a new bandage," Kep announced. He looked at Jensine expectantly, his brow furrowing when she did not immediately spring into action at his request. "Um. Please?"

"And do you remember what you had to give me the first time?" Jensine said, not unsympathetically.

"He'll pay," Kep pointed at Arandras. "Guide's fee."

Jensine glanced at Arandras, who raised a brow in query. "Three scudi," she said, correctly guessing his question. "And a clean length of cloth for the bandage."

"Can't help with the cloth," Arandras began; but Kep was already pulling a tightly-ravelled roll of undyed linen from his satchel. "Fine," Arandras said, scowling at Kep. "On the condition that you run off home the moment she's done. Understood?"

"Yes, yes." Kep poked out his tongue. "Rude man." He thrust the cloth at Jensine, who plucked it from his hand and glanced at Arandras once more.

"Go ahead," Arandras said, digging in his purse for the required coins as Jensine began unrolling the cloth on the workbench. "The sooner I'm done with him, the happier I'll be."

Arandras had seen Jensine construct bindings on several

occasions during their time working together in Spyridon. Her approach to sorcery was nothing like the calm, disciplined method of the Quill that Arandras had become used to in Chogon. Where a Quill sorcerer might set out his materials, plan his actions, and only then begin the mysterious and wholly unobservable process of building his spell, Jensine flitted from one activity to another, slipping out of her sorcerer's trance to rearrange the cloth or rummage for a knife to trim its end before returning to her spell without the slightest sign of stress. Though her primary discipline was air, she seemed to have an unusual ability to weave sorcery around a variety of materials. The thought of engaging an airbinder to infuse a cloth bandage with sorcery would doubtless have struck a formally-trained Quill sorcerer as absurd — yet it seemed Jensine had not only done it before but done it well enough to be asked to repeat the effort.

She passed her hands over the length of cloth, then exhaled sharply and opened her eyes. "There," she said, rolling up the bandage. "All done."

The cloth looked no different to Arandras, but Kep accepted it eagerly. "Bandage, yes. Kep thanks you." He reached for the top button on his smock, then hesitated. "Could use some help to put it on."

Oh, for the Weeper's sake, Arandras thought; but Jensine just nodded calmly. "Of course."

Looking abashed, Kep unbuttoned his smock. Arandras turned his back, staring fixedly out the window as Jensine attended to the man's dressing. Kep muttered something below his breath, prompting a sigh from Jensine. "Don't worry about him," she said, an uncharacteristic edge to her voice. "He'd be just the same if you stubbed your toe or broke your arm. Stubborn and self-absorbed, that's Arandras."

"Hey," Arandras said. "I'm standing right here."

"There, you see? Even now, he thinks it's all about him."

"That's hardly fair —"

"Ah!" Kep cried. Startled, Arandras spun about — but the fisherman's face showed not pain but blissful release. "Ah," he said again, closing his eyes and tilting his head back. "Good."

Jensine tucked away the end of the bandage and stepped back. The wrapping covered Kep from his collarbone to the top of his stomach, like a vest several sizes too small. He flexed his arms and twisted this way and that, grinning all the while at the ceiling, the unbandaged flesh of his belly wobbling with each move.

"Time for the smock?" Arandras muttered, and Jensine shot him a glare.

"That binding should keep until at least the end of summer," she said. "Come back when it runs out and I'll make you a new one."

Kep bobbed his head. "Thank you," he said. "Very kind. Farewell." He grabbed his smock and glanced at Arandras. "Farewell, rude man." For a moment he looked as though he might say more; then he turned on his heel and scurried out.

Jensine returned her knife to its box and began sorting through the other tools on the bench. "Still making friends, I see."

"*He* followed *me*, Jensine. I never asked him to come — oh, forget it. It's not important." Arandras took a breath. "I just... gods. I'm sorry, Jensine."

"All right." She glanced sideways. "But it's not me you should be apologising to."

"Weeper, I don't mean Kep. I mean Spyridon. The urn. That night in Rhothe's Bar. All of it."

She turned fully at that, studying him closely in the window's angled light. "You're sorry for what, exactly?"

"For..." Arandras swallowed. He'd made a half-hearted effort at preparing a speech, but now that the moment was here he couldn't remember how it started. "I'm sorry for the way I treated you and Druce. Like you didn't matter. Like I was the only one with a stake in what we'd found." He unhooked the pouch containing her gold, held it out. "And I'm sorry for this part of it, too."

Jensine accepted the pouch and looked inside. "You get all this from selling the urn?"

"Not exactly. It's a long story."

She placed the pouch on a small table and seated herself in the rocking chair. "Tell me."

He perched on the stool and tried to gather his thoughts. "I guess you know we went to Anstice. I thought the Quill might be able to tell me something about that writing on the urn…"

Arandras began a rapid account of his time in Anstice, his discovery of the golems, and his confrontation with Clade. Jensine listened closely, her reserve fading somewhat as Arandras told her about the assignments he and Mara had taken up and the experience of putting the golems to work.

"Did you bring one with you?" she asked as he concluded his account of the raising of Lurso Lutt's ship.

"With Kep around?" Arandras shook his head. "They're a day away, give or take. You could come and see them, if you like."

Jensine settled back into the chair with a sigh. "Another time, maybe."

"Why not now?" Arandras said, sparked with a sudden enthusiasm. "One day there, another back, maybe a third if the weather turns. Truth is, I'd be glad to show them to you —"

"And I suppose you can conjure up a convenient guesthouse for us each night, out in the middle of nowhere? No, I'll keep a roof over my head, thanks all the same."

"As you wish." Arandras gestured at the pouch. "In any case, that's for you. Recompense for payments withheld."

Jensine emptied it onto the table and frowned. "That's too much."

"Recompense," Arandras repeated. "Even a moneylender would have given you interest."

"No." She counted out a handful of coins and pushed the remainder — more than half — back to Arandras. "My share of the urn. Nothing more."

"But —"

"This much you owe. The rest is nothing to do with me."

"As you wish." Reluctantly, Arandras recovered the pouch and swept the remaining gold inside. "If you change your mind…"

"I won't," Jensine said. "Give it to some of those clients you used to tell us about back in Spyridon. The ditch-digger and his boy. That old woman who spoke half a dozen different languages. Gods, I can't remember any of their names."

Leff and Wil, Arandras thought, recalling the boy's quiet gaze when he had a question he wanted to ask. *And Old Jess. And Asan the glazier, and that guardsman from Menefir, and all the others.* Most had probably never laid eyes on a gold luri in their life. "I'll think about it," he said.

"You're heading back that way next, aren't you?" Jensine said.

"To see Druce, yes."

"He won't take it so well."

Arandras shrugged. "I guess I'll find out."

Silence fell between them. Arandras scowled at the floor and the window, trying to think of something more to say but finding nothing. Jensine rocked gently back and forth, seemingly content to wait Arandras out. *Narvi would know what to say. Mara, too.* But Arandras, it seemed, had exhausted his store of words.

"Well," he said at last, and stood. "I'm sure you have things to be getting on with. I should go."

Jensine nodded, rising to open the door. "I still visit Spyridon, sometimes," she said as Arandras stepped onto the porch. "Come the end of the month, I'll probably be along to pick up some supplies. Maybe you can introduce me to those golems of yours then."

"I'd like that," he said. "But I doubt I'll be staying long."

"I see."

He took a breath, willing himself to find some words that might bridge the divide, but nothing came. He exhaled heavily. "Farewell, Jensine."

"Arandras," she said, and something in her voice made him look up. "Thank you for coming."

He nodded. "It was good to see you again."

"You, too," she said; and if there was a hint of surprise in her words, at least it told Arandras that they were sincere.

～

To Eilwen's delight, the bath chamber at the rear of Den's house contained a full-sized Coridoni-style tub, complete with clawed feet, a pinion stepping-board, and a beak-shaped fixture from which hung a cloth to pillow one's head. Hauling and heating the water to fill it took Eilwen the better part of the afternoon; but when at last she stepped into the sage-scented depths, steam curling about her ears, her hours of effort melted away into warm liquid bliss.

How long had it been since she'd done this? Too long, that

was for sure. She sank lower, allowing the water to rise to her chin, blinking at its heat against her face. Her bad leg bobbed beneath the surface, the water drawing out its ache until it seemed the limb was not hers at all but some unsensing simulacrum attached to her body. Even the raw, goatskin-chafed flesh at her waist raised only a passing protest before its stinging subsided. With a sigh, she rested her head against the cloth and closed her eyes.

Irilli had seemed pleased at Eilwen's discovery of the bath, though it had been hard to tell through the impenetrable politeness that stiffened her every word. Eilwen had always found Irilli difficult to talk to — she was cool where Den was warm, reticent where Den was expansive — but in the past they'd been able to find the occasional small commonality, little breaches in her reserve through which they could share a real if fleeting connection. But this time Irilli seemed to have retreated so deeply that Eilwen could barely see the woman inside. Had Vess's departure triggered some fundamental break within her? Or had Irilli's withdrawal been the reason that Vess had left?

On a shelf beside her thin pallet in the front loft, Eilwen had found a complete set of *Sermons and Expositions,* the foundational Gislean text consisting of all four volumes of Herev Gis's *Sermons* and seven further books of discussion and interpretation by various early leaders of the Gislean faith. Irilli was Gislean, Eilwen knew, though she'd never been clear on the depth of the woman's conviction. Curious, Eilwen had selected a volume at random and leafed through it. The text was a pre-Coridon translation, filled with archaic terms and patterns of speech, but as she turned the pages one passage caught her eye:

Consider, if you will, the fearsome restraint shown by the All-God with every turning of the sun. We mock Him, we jape about Him, we spit in His face and call it right. And all the while He bides, permitting our every denial, content to wait until we can deny Him no more.

Surely the most terrible gift the All-God ever gave his creatures was the right to be wrong.

The words had lodged in her mind, though not in the way that the writer had evidently intended. All-God, Tri-God, northern fire god — Eilwen had never encountered a one of them. But that *thing* in the caverns beside Tienette Lake, the one Clade had named Azador... whatever it was, god or demon or something else entirely, it had been unmistakably real. And if such a thing existed, what else might also live in the far corners of the world, or in the realms beyond?

The water touched her nose and she pressed her hands against the bottom of the tub, reversing her slow downward slide. Truth was, she'd never given the gods that much thought. Her father had had little to say on the subject, and to the street gangs she'd run with while Den was being schooled, priests had fallen into two overlapping categories: those from whom a sufficiently wretched show might elicit a free meal, and those whose purses might be cut for the same result. When her mother died suddenly a month after Eilwen's seventh birthday, a priest she'd stolen from several days before came to perform her final rites, and he'd scowled at her so fiercely that she'd sworn off thievery for life, a resolution which lasted barely a week.

Since then, she'd had little time for the gods, even finding a kind of comfort in their disregard for her, and hers for them. But there had been nothing benign about Azador, and if the thought of such a creature roaming the world was terrifying enough, the thought that there might be true gods who were content to allow it was even more so. Fearsome restraint, fearsome impotence, or even apathy — every possibility Eilwen could think of filled her with dread.

She was still pondering the matter when she sat down to dinner that evening. Orval was out, as he had been all day, but Den returned home with the sunset as Irilli was serving the food: generous bowls of mutton and apricot tagine seasoned with coriander. He flashed Eilwen a smile as he sat at the table, then cocked an eyebrow at Irilli when he noticed the empty place beside her. "No Orval?"

"Not since this morning," Irilli said in the same polite tone she'd been using toward Eilwen for days. Eilwen wondered if this was another topic with a history of disagreement. "He said he'd be home before dark."

"We can't chain the boy to the house, dear," Den said.

Irilli's expression suggested she wasn't sure chains should be ruled out so quickly. She seemed about to respond, but caught herself with a glance at Eilwen and busied herself with her food.

"He's got a head for numbers, that boy," Den said to Eilwen around a mouthful of mutton. "Leaves me in the dust. But he can't mix a scent to save his life. We've been trying to find someone to take him on when his schooling is done, but so far…" He shrugged.

Eilwen frowned. "The attack?"

"In part. A lot of people are hunkering down and waiting to see what the Oculus will do. Not many want to take on a new apprentice just now."

"And those that do are favouring family," Irilli said. "Even more than usual."

"You could still use him yourself, couldn't you?" Eilwen said. "Give him the books to look after but none of the perfuming?"

"Aye. And if nothing else comes through, that's what we'll do." Den sighed. "Poor lad. All I've got to offer him is a perfumery, and the boy's got a nose like a stone. Irilli's family, well, they've all got their *talents,* but the gods saw fit to deny Rill that particular gift, and Orval too." He took a long draught from his goblet. "Then again, Vess doesn't have much cause to thank the gods either, so who knows?"

Eilwen's brows rose. "Vess is a sorcerer? When did that happen?"

Den glanced at Irilli, who reluctantly put down her fork. "It's not as exciting as it sounds," she said. "The gift has always been weak in my family. Vess's talent only came to light, what, two years ago? She applied to join the Quill, even took the test, but in the end they said she wasn't strong enough."

"Girl still wanted to make something of it, though," Den said with subdued pride. "Found an old fleshbinder out by the docks and convinced her to teach what she knew in exchange for helping around the shop."

"Good for her," Eilwen said. "And now?"

The question hung in the air. Den and Irilli exchanged looks, and Eilwen was reminded of a pair of negotiators trying to decide how much of their position to reveal. "She had to leave," Irilli said. "After the Oculus came. The old woman couldn't keep her on."

Eilwen looked to Den, but her brother seemed reluctant to meet her gaze. "And where is she now?"

"Travelling." Irilli's face was a mask. "Seeing the world."

"Is she coming back?"

There was another, longer pause. At last Den raised his head. "I don't know."

Eilwen nodded slowly, seeing for the first time the pain in Den's regard — pain, and something else she couldn't identify. Irilli gave an unsteady sigh, and Den covered her hand with his.

"Well," Eilwen said. "I won't pry further. But if there's any way I can help, you only have to ask. You know that, right?"

"I know it," Den said softly. "Thank you."

They concluded the meal in silence. Eilwen picked at her food as she turned the conversation over in her mind, searching for some detail that might explain her niece's absence and Den's reluctance to discuss it. But the few facts she knew could be made to fit dozens of scenarios, each as convincing as the next, and every one involving as much speculation as deduction. Yet as the evening progressed she found herself unable to give it up, worrying at the problem like a child at a knot, her thoughts continuing to march in circles even as she climbed the ladder to her bed and lay her head on the thin pillow.

What happened to you, Vess? And where are you now?

⁓

Orval reappeared the next morning just as Eilwen was leaving to meet Mara. He stumbled through the door with barely a glance at Eilwen, his hair and clothes dishevelled, narrowly avoiding a coatstand before sitting heavily on a backless redwood bench.

"Gods, Orval," Eilwen said. "Are you all right?" Orval muttered something indiscernible, and Eilwen turned away at the scent of his sour breath. "Den!" she called. "Irilli! Orval's here!"

Irilli hurried in and knelt before the bench. "Foolish boy," she said, taking Orval's face in her hands. "Where have you been? Come here." She pulled Orval into a tight hug, then abruptly drew back and grasped his shoulders. "Speak," she said as Den stumbled into the hall, still buttoning his shirt. "Where were you?"

Orval swallowed. "It was Triv's soul's-day. His mother gave

him a whole sculundi, and he, uh, bought us some cider." The boy looked appropriately shamefaced, though Eilwen thought she saw a degree of calculation beneath the repentant expression.

Den folded his arms. "Are you telling us you spent the whole night drinking?"

"I only wanted a taste, I swear! But Triv kept filling our mugs, and…"

Leaving Orval to his parents, Eilwen slipped outside into the cool mid-morning air. She'd arranged to meet Mara outside a prominent couturier not far from the city hall — a common meeting place, or so Mara had told her, thanks to the numerous chocol houses and sweetmeat shops in the vicinity. Unfamiliar as she was with that part of the city, Eilwen had been content to accept the Kharjik woman's suggestion. In most cities, wealth and power twined so tightly around each other as to be inseparable; but here in Neysa the administrative and mercantile districts were unusually distant, one clustered about the city hall, the other clinging to the harbour and canal like limpets to a ship's hull. In the past Eilwen had found the separation frustrating, but today it offered an unexpected comfort, reducing the risk of a chance encounter with one of her former colleagues.

In Anstice she'd shunned the Oculus and called the Woodtraders home. Now in Neysa she was avoiding the Woodtraders and seeking out the Oculus. *The gods do like their little amusements, don't they?* That was something that never seemed to come up in the texts, whether Gislean or any other: the jokes played by the gods on unsuspecting mortals to entertain themselves. *Someone really should write that book. I can see it now. Divine Humour — A Study. Chapter One: What makes the gods laugh? Chapter Two: Which god is laughing at me now? Chapter Three —*

"Keep walking," said a voice in her ear. Eilwen started and turned. Mara strode slightly behind, her hand in Eilwen's back pressing her forward. "Don't look alarmed. You're being followed."

"Who is it?" The couturier could be seen half a block ahead. "Should we try to lose them?"

"Follow my lead." Mara steered her to the edge of the road. An alley drew near, the opening barely wide enough to enter. "In there, on three. One… two…"

Mara gave a hard shove and Eilwen stumbled into the alley, the other woman on her heels. After several paces Mara turned, half-drawing one of her cutlasses and cursing as the sheath scraped the wall.

"Do you have a dagger?" Mara muttered, and Eilwen made an affirmatory sound. "Hand it over. Quickly now — wait, no, here he comes…"

Eilwen stood on her toes, dagger in hand, trying to see past Mara but unable to make out more than a glimpse of the street beyond. "Who is it?" she hissed. "Talk to me, damn it!"

"Hush!" Mara crouched at the alley's mouth, her long ponytail flicking back and forth as she watched the traffic pass by. After a long pause she crept forward, poking her head beyond the wall and quickly withdrawing it, then looking out a second time. At last she straightened, sliding the cutlass back into its sheath.

"Well?" Eilwen said.

Mara turned. "Gone. Must have seen me follow you in —"

"Who. Was. It?"

"You tell me." Mara gave a frustrated sigh. "He was short and clean-shaven, if that helps. No? Then I have as much of an idea as you do."

"Fine. Whatever." Eilwen pushed past the taller woman, then paused. "If you're hoping to impress me with your valour, you'll need to arrange something a bit more demonstrative. A knife-fight, maybe. Nothing convinces like blood."

Mara's lips twisted in a half-smile. "Do you think I'm so inept a fraud as to just shove you into an alley and claim you're being trailed?"

"I really couldn't say."

"You don't trust easily, do you?"

"I'm still alive, aren't I?"

"Ha. Excellent point." Mara grinned. "I won't insult you by protesting my innocence. You're going to believe what you choose, regardless of what I say. So I'll tell you what I'm going to do. I'm going to go for a walk past the city hall and see what there is to see. Then I'm going to find myself a cup of chocol and think about what to do next. You're welcome to join me, if you'd like. And if not, I won't trouble you further."

She brushed past Eilwen and strolled away, heading for the couturier and the city hall beyond. Scowling, Eilwen watched her go. If the woman really had staged that little episode for Eilwen's benefit, it would have to rate as the most inept swindle Eilwen had seen in years. But if she hadn't...

Oh, damn it to all the hells.

"Hoi! Wait up!" Eilwen hurried in pursuit, grimacing at the twinge in her knee. "Wait, I say!"

Mara cast Eilwen an amused look as she drew alongside. "What happened? Come over all trusting?"

"Shut up."

The city hall looked much as it had the other day: broad, squat, and adorned in teal and silver. But a new structure now stood a short distance from the main doors — an iron cage, tall as a man and twice as wide, and inside...

Corpses. Eilwen turned away, gagging at the smell of rotting flesh. They lay jumbled on the cage floor, five or six of them, like a ghastly set of life-sized marionettes. A sign had been affixed to the bars, the letters still too distant to read, but Eilwen could guess at their message. These must be the people responsible for the attempt she'd witnessed on Governor Fosclaw's life — or at least, those the Oculus had decided to blame.

"Charming," Mara said, surveying the scene with bland equanimity. "Remind me not to get caught, hmm?"

The main doors to the city hall stood open, admitting all comers — and, Eilwen could only imagine, an unwholesome amount of corpse-scented air — but there was also a smaller set of doors further down attended by a pair of guards in Neysan livery. A richly dressed woman approached, extending her hand toward the guards, and Eilwen glimpsed something smooth and black in her palm. The guards nodded, opening the door just enough to admit the woman before closing it behind her.

"That's quite the hole," Mara said, and Eilwen turned to see her gazing at the timber scaffold and the cavity behind it. "How many rooms would there be behind that? A dozen, maybe?"

"Who knows?" The scaffold was bare of workers, and if any progress had been made in the past few days, Eilwen couldn't see it. "You'd think they'd have patched it up by now."

"I heard they're struggling to find a good source of stone. It's all either too light or too dark. Don't want to leave a big ugly patch to remind everyone how they got here."

"Really?" The stone didn't look like anything special to Eilwen. Then again, she supposed it didn't need to be pretty to be difficult to match.

"Still, the whole city's in pretty good shape, don't you think? There's barely a toppled building to be found."

Eilwen shrugged. "They got in quick. Someone opened the gate for them and it was all over."

"Sure, but then what? Looting, pillaging, burning down buildings? That's what soldiers do, right?" Mara spread her arms. "So where is it?"

Frowning, Eilwen considered the question. *Havilah would have noticed that the moment he arrived. Gods, I wish he were here.* "You said they don't want to remind people of the attack. Sounds like a good reason not to burn everything down."

"Maybe." Mara surveyed the building. "You been in there yet?"

"No." In fact she had, many years ago as a Woodtrader, but she could remember almost nothing of the visit.

"That side is the public area. Above-ground floors only, mind. This side is restricted, as are all the underground levels. There are a few interior doors between the two halves, but they're all guarded, same as the one out here."

"And where do we go once we get inside?"

"No idea. The archon's office was on the top floor, but they might have moved things around." Mara grinned. "Exciting, isn't it?"

"Not the word I'd have chosen," Eilwen said. Yet that wasn't entirely true. The planning, the assessment of ways in and out — it wasn't so different from some of her own ventures of years past, with a blade in one hand and the black amber egg in the other. She studied the doorway, the guard, the people wandering in and out, her gaze flicking from point to point with a focus she hadn't felt in months. *Open street. Plain walls. Nowhere to hide. Shadowy at night, though. And the moon will be on the other side until midnight, making the shadows deeper —*

"Seen enough?" Mara said.

Eilwen shook herself and nodded. "Let's find some chocol."

Mara led them a short distance to a chocol shop consisting of half a dozen outdoor tables and a tiny, windowless room. They sat at the endmost table, the rear of the city hall just visible over Mara's shoulder.

"That hole's our way in, I reckon," Mara said once the server was gone, blowing at her steaming cup to cool it.

"Really?" Eilwen said. "Maybe that's what they want. Offer an entry point that's too good to pass up and have a squad of heavies on hand for anyone who takes the bait. Even if it really is just about the stone, they'd be stupid not to guard it."

"You got a better idea?"

"In fact, I do." Eilwen took a breath. "I have a pass token," she said softly. "One of those black eggs the Oculus give out. Show them that and they'll let us right in."

Mara's brows rose. "You sure about that?"

"Pretty sure." Whatever method the Oculus used to identify stolen tokens would almost certainly be useless with hers, subverted as it was by the sorcery that had sunk the *Orenda*. "If something goes wrong, they might eventually figure out we were there. But I wasn't planning to stay in Neysa anyway."

Mara cocked her head. "This isn't just you, is it?" She nodded back up the street at the city hall. "The way I heard it, Clade put a lot of effort into freeing himself. Why keep nosing around and risk them catching up to him again?"

Eilwen raised her eyebrows and took a long drink of chocol.

"Right." Mara gave an easy chuckle and sat back. "Can't blame me for trying."

"Best not get distracted," Eilwen said. "I'm told there are stalkers about. Wouldn't want to miss a chance to show off with those cutlasses of yours."

"Oh, I wouldn't worry." Mara drained her cup with a smile. "Once we get inside, I'm sure there'll be plenty for both of us."

First Interlude

To the gods, all truths are tautologies.

— *Wisdom of the Pekratan Sages,* translated by Hila Sen

O N THE TWENTY-FIRST DAY AFTER he stopped eating, the roof of Nezhar's shelter collapsed.

Nezhar was relieving himself into the privy hole when he heard the sudden crash behind him. He jumped, spraying his piss wide, and turned just in time to see the last few beams settle atop the heap of broken timbers. Dust puffed up from the bare space before the firepit, its slow drift down the hill the only movement in the abrupt silence that followed.

Shit. Nezhar buttoned his trouser flap and stared at the ruined lean-to, dismay pooling in his gut. *Shit, shit, shit.*

A bird cheeped tentatively from a nearby tree as Nezhar crouched beside the wreckage. The roof was almost entirely gone, and though the walls still stood, one now tilted inward at an alarming angle. Nezhar's few possessions lay buried within — including, he realised with a curse, the small hand-axe.

Scowling, Nezhar selected a beam and gave it a tug. The timber shifted with surprising ease, sliding off the heap and coming to rest at his feet. He stooped and picked it up. The beam was long, its far end a mass of bristling splinters, its weight in his hands implausibly light. He tossed it aside and it struck the stones around the firepit, folding in two with a sharp crack — and from the break, half a dozen white larvae fell wriggling to the ground.

He drew back in disgust, cursing yet again. Woodworms. He'd noticed a small amount of rot in one of the lean-to's walls, but somehow he'd missed the worms. Or maybe it wasn't so surprising. He had heard that here in the east, woodworms often went undetected for years before abruptly making their presence known. Sorcery was the best defence against such infestations — a basic binding could be arranged by any of the reputable timber merchants, but clearly that step had been skipped in this case.

Nezhar turned back to the wrecked shelter with a grimace. A thick branch lay half-buried in the heap, its fall from an overhanging tree no doubt the catalyst for the collapse. Here and there, more larvae could be seen writhing among the broken timbers or flopping to the ground where they gathered in pale, fleshy puddles. All he could do now was clear away the wreckage and reclaim his supplies; and so, reluctantly, Nezhar reached for another beam and pulled it free.

Fortunately, the hollowed wood proved easy to dispose of. Only the fallen branch was heavy enough to pose a challenge; but by then Nezhar had cleared enough of the debris to reclaim his axe, which he used to cut the branch into more portable pieces. The lantern he found smashed in the corner, and with it one of his waterskins; but his packet of food, thank the non-existent gods, remained intact, its wrapping tight enough to defy the three larvae that had fallen atop it. Nezhar flicked them away, his lips curled in revulsion as they joined their fellows squirming blindly on the hard-packed dirt floor; then, setting the food safely out of reach on a shelf that had survived the collapse, he picked up the shovel and began scooping the tiny creatures into the firepit.

By the time he finished clearing the shelter and built up the fire it was close to noon. Exhausted, he lowered himself to the ground, sipping from his one remaining skin as the larvae crackled in the flames. He'd need to examine what remained of the lean-to, see if the worms had spread into the walls. But that could wait. Right now, he needed to rest.

After the first few days, his body had become accustomed to the fast and ceased the worst of its complaints. He'd experienced headaches for a time, but they too had passed, and in their wake had come the early signs of the clarity toward which his fast was directed. It was days now since he'd felt hungry. Sehv had likened the experience to holding one's breath until one's lungs burst, only to discover that one could breathe underwater after all. But Nezhar had never been one for swimming. To him it seemed more akin to what the priests kept babbling about but were unable to see when it actually appeared before them.

Transcendence.

Transcendence came in numerous forms, and Nezhar was familiar with several of them. Sex was the method of choice for many, though its effects were frustratingly short-lived. Sorcery offered some an alternative path, but its bliss also lasted barely a moment before vanishing on the breeze. Some abandoned themselves to food and drink, the pleasures of which Nezhar could no longer truly appreciate. Others claimed to find ecstasy in worship, or in battle, and though Nezhar had little experience with either and in fact viewed each with a similar degree of disdain, he had little reason to doubt such claims.

But fasting... fasting was different. When he denied his body food for long enough, his appetite simply shut down. Unshackled from its demands, he became capable of a focus and discipline far exceeding anything he might normally achieve. It was as though, for a few days or weeks, he was no longer simply Nezhar of the Yenenese, eater of food, one more animal mindlessly prolonging its own existence. Instead, he became Nezhar, sorcerer of the Hungry Men, one who no longer bowed before the world's brute realities but shaped them according to his will.

It wouldn't last. Eventually the hunger would return, telling him that his body's reserves had been exhausted and he must now eat or die. Only then would he open the packet of food and begin the long process of rebuilding his strength. But before that he would complete the task he had been given — and then, with belly and purse filled once more, he'd be free to follow his desires wherever he wished.

Lost in his thoughts, he must have dozed off. The next thing Nezhar knew it was dark, his mouth was dry, and his bladder was full again. Stifling a groan, he raised himself onto his elbows — and froze.

An animal crouched only a few paces away, about the size of a large dog, snuffling at the pile of wreckage beside the now-cold fire-pit. As Nezhar watched, it pushed a broken timber away and sniffed at the ground beneath, then raised its head in apparent disappoint-ment. It half-turned, stepping into the moonlight to reveal low ears, a narrow head, and a series of stripes extending from halfway down its back to the end of its stiff tail.

A stripe-backed wolf. Nezhar shifted involuntarily and the crea-ture swung around, pinning him with a dark-eyed stare. He stared back, fascinated and terrified in equal measure. His axe lay where he had left it beside the firepit, closer to the wolf than it was to him. Around him lay only twigs and leaves — nothing large enough to fend off the creature if it became hostile.

The wolf padded closer, sniffing audibly in the still air. Nezhar watched its approach helplessly, his limbs seemingly locked in place. Then the wolf stopped, ears twitching; and a moment later it turned, its tail brushing Nezhar's boot before it loped away in the direction of the creek.

Nezhar let out a ragged breath. The creature disappeared behind a tree and he lurched into motion at last, scrambling across to the firepit and snatching up his axe. The weapon trembled in his grip and he dropped to a crouch, allowing the axe head to rest against the ground.

No shelter. One waterskin. And now a bloody stripe-backed wolf in the neighbourhood. Nothing was worth this, not even the momentary power of the non-existent gods. Some decent sex and a bit of ordinary sorcery were all the transcendence Nezhar required. Once this job was finished he'd be done with the Hungry Men, and there was nothing on earth or sea that could change his mind.

CHAPTER 5

When you conquer a city, be sure to enter it first by the breach in
its walls, not by its gate. You are no invited guest visiting for tea.
Do not allow your new subjects to mistake you for one.

— Giarvanno do Salin I, *My Son*

MORNING FOUND THE GREAT SQUARE emptied of the
crowd that had flocked to the satirists' edged humour the
day before. Clade strode unimpeded across the sandstone
and granite plaza, his path curving around the central fountain and
its surrounding patches of lawn and maple trees. The black drapery
of the puppet stage was gone, leaving a simple raised platform on
which two grey-clad debaters appeared to be disputing the reason
for the Coridon Republic's fall. Several dozen of their fellow Library
workers looked on — including a pale-skinned woman whose features were partly obscured by a cream parasol held by a servant at
her side.

Clade paused, craning his neck for a better view. Feren Skaratass,
Conservator of the Library, was said to enjoy the debates that took
place on her doorstep, and in this case it seemed the rumours were
true. The woman looked to be in her fifties and stood die-straight,
her gaze flicking between debaters like a hawk's. As Clade watched,
one speaker reached a stumbling conclusion and Feren shook her
head with an audible snort.

An image of Puppet Skaratass poking her head out of the pig's trough came to Clade, and he turned away with a chuckle. Maybe Yevin had been right. The satirists' show had proved a welcome if brief distraction from his cares. *I should do that more often,* he thought as he crossed the remainder of the square to the Library's high doors. *Let it all rest for a while, even if it only lasts an hour.*

The narrow foyer opened to a small enquiry room on one side and the much larger reading room on the other. Clade selected the former, approaching an open desk and placing the Bounty token he'd found atop it.

The man behind the desk nodded in greeting. "You wish to collect your volume?"

"If you please," Clade said.

"Let me see if it's ready." The man picked up the disc and stood. "If you give me a title, it'll be easier to find — ah." He broke off, peering at the glyph on the reverse of the token.

"Is there a problem?" Clade said.

"No, no problem." The man held out the token in an oddly deferential gesture. "My apologies for the delay. Please, follow me."

Frowning, Clade returned the disc to his coinpurse and followed the man out of the enquiry room to the far end of the foyer, where a staircase rose behind a varnished, waist-high gate. Beside the gate stooped a grey-clad man who peered at Clade and his companion through thick, wire-rimmed spectacles as they approached.

"Who's this, then?" he rasped, huffing a sour breath over Clade's face.

"This man has a standing invitation," Clade's companion returned frostily, with a subtle emphasis on the last words.

The attendant straightened as far as he could. "My apologies." He fumbled the latch open and the younger man ushered Clade through. "Take the stairs to the top and turn left. Look for the first set of double doors on the right side." He gave a slight bow. "Enjoy your visit, sir."

The gate swung shut. Clade climbed the stairs, the plush carpet swallowing his footsteps, and tried to make sense of what had just happened. It seemed the man behind the desk had been expecting to fetch a book until something about the token's glyph had changed his mind. Clearly, this particular token was not like the others. Did that mean the assassin was somehow connected to the Library?

Was he about to walk into the rooms of someone who'd helped her try to kill him?

Well, so much the better if he was. There was no anamnil here, or at least none that he'd detected yet. Whoever he found at the end of this trail was damn well going to give him some answers.

The stairs opened onto a richly panelled landing on the seventh floor. Clade followed the leftmost hallway to a pair of slender mahogany doors. He knocked — a discreet tap to match the plush surroundings — and waited.

An annoyed mutter sounded from within the room; then the doors swung open and a man's scowling head poked through the gap. "Who in the hells are you?"

Clade blinked in surprise. "Onsoth?"

"No, I asked who *you* are," the man snapped back.

"I... seem to have acquired a token of yours," Clade replied.

Onsoth scowled. "What token?"

Clade fished the steel disc out of his coinpurse and held it up. "Look familiar?"

Onsoth studied the disc, then Clade. "Where did you get that?"

"That's exactly what I want to talk to you about."

"Is that so?" Eyes narrow, Onsoth jerked the doors open. "Five minutes."

Clade inclined his head and followed Onsoth inside, the doors swinging shut behind him. The office was even larger than Clade's had been back in Anstice: high-ceilinged, with a huge blackwood desk positioned before a window that stretched the length of the room. Stone gargoyles sneered down from above a cold fireplace at a row of chairs along the opposite wall. Half a dozen glassed lamps added their illumination to the daylight streaming in from the window, the combined light giving the thick burgundy carpet the appearance of fresh blood.

Onsoth leaned against the desk and folded his arms. The man's mouth was unfortunately wide, the effect exaggerated somehow by his close-cropped hair and persistent scowl. He studied Clade with suspicious eyes, the fingers of one hand tapping in broken rhythm against his elbow. "Well?"

"What was her name?" Clade asked.

"Whose name?"

He should have approached the subject more gradually, taken the time to test his conjectures before launching an accusation. But there was something about Onsoth that rubbed him the wrong way. "The woman you sent to kill me."

The tapping of Onsoth's fingers stopped. "I have no idea what you're talking about."

"Really? Guess where I found this token?"

"Why don't you tell me?"

"On the body of a *woman who tried to kill me.*"

Onsoth folded his arms. "And who are you, exactly?"

Clade hesitated. But if Onsoth really had aided the assassin, he'd have already heard Clade's name; and if not, revealing it wouldn't change much. He fixed Onsoth with a close look. "My name is Clade."

Onsoth's face revealed nothing. "Did it ever occur you, Clade, that you might not have been the only one targeted by this killer of yours? You plucked that token from a dead body. Perhaps that woman did the same."

"So you admit it came from you? And that it's not an ordinary Bounty token at all, but... what? A visitor's token for someone you've invited to see you?"

Onsoth reached out a hand, but Clade made no move to deposit the disc into it, and eventually Onsoth shrugged. "I have several such tokens," he said. "I won't know if that's one of them until I examine it."

"It led me here, didn't it?" Clade moved to fold his arms, then remembered that his withered hand was tucked into his greatcoat pocket and aborted the action. "Who do you give these things out to?"

"Associates," Onsoth said blandly.

"And why would someone want to kill one of these *associates?*"

"Who knows? Why would someone want to kill you?"

"You tell me."

"To be honest, you're pretty annoying. Maybe the last person you pissed off didn't have my patience." Onsoth smirked. "Come, now. You're seven floors up in the Great Library. Do you think you'd have any chance of walking out of this building if I truly wanted you dead?"

Clade drew a long breath. Perhaps Onsoth had been involved in the attempt on Clade's life — but if he hadn't, Clade risked destroying any chance of using the man to get to Yevin's book. He reached within, walling off his outrage and tucking it away. It took longer than it should have — in the wake of his successful unbinding, he'd allowed his discipline to slip — but the old muscles were still there. *Above all, control.*

He looked up. "Perhaps you're right," he said. "Perhaps I should take this to the guard and see what they make of it."

Onsoth glared at Clade for a long moment. "Fine," he said at last. "As it happens, I have only one token out at present. You're looking for Hesca Matharan."

"And who is this Hesca?" Clade asked.

Onsoth continued as if Clade hadn't spoken. "Look for her at the Four Hands of the All-God. It's a massage parlour to the southwest. Tell her that your news is as ink spilt on sand. If she's there, you can ask her what she did with my token. And if she's dead…" Onsoth spread his hands.

Clade raised his brows. "You're giving up your associate, just like that?"

"There's no pleasing you, is there?" Onsoth scowled. "Go to the Four Hands. Or don't. I don't care where you go, so long as it's away from here."

"But who is this Hesca —"

"Did you not hear what I just said?" Onsoth reddened and waved angrily at the door. "What are you waiting for, a kick in the arse? Get the hells out of my office!"

Clade chuckled inwardly. It was remarkable how predictable some people could be. Clade's initial frustration had fed Onsoth's feeling of mastery. Only when Clade regained his calm had Onsoth lost his.

Nodding amiably, Clade turned to leave, then paused at the door and turned back. "A pleasure to make your acquaintance," he said, and was gratified to see Onsoth's scowl deepen. "I'm sure we'll meet again soon."

~

The Four Hands of the All-God looked more like a gaudily decorated gatehouse than a massage parlour. Five stories high, the building straddled a narrow street that branched off the main road linking Spyridon to Port Gallin. Crimson tassels hung from the windows, shifting listlessly in the slight breeze as music played within: tambourines, Sarean horns, and something that sounded like a low-pitched lute. The smell of incense and dried patchouli tickled Clade's nostrils, and beneath it another scent he took a moment to place: the sharp, faintly heady aroma of blended massage oil.

Clade pushed the door open and stepped cautiously inside. The entry hall was a square-shaped room, richly carpeted in mauve and crimson, with dozens of small lamps affixed to the walls. A young man in a pale woollen robe looked up, his ears jutting from beneath his ginger hair. "Ah, sir, welcome. The All-God's blessing be upon you."

"Indeed." Onsoth had said nothing about the massage parlour doubling as a temple, though in retrospect Clade supposed the name should have been a clue. The abrupt readiness with which Onsoth had yielded the information still struck Clade as strange, but there was no anamnil in the immediate vicinity, and the possibility of learning more about his would-be assassin was too good to pass up — particularly if it resulted in leverage over Onsoth himself.

"You are new to the Four Hands, yes?" The attendant folded his hands over his stomach. "We offer a range of services, from intercession with the All-God to the loosening of sore muscles —"

"In fact, I'm looking for someone," Clade said. "Is Hesca Matharan here?"

"Certainly. If you'll follow me."

The young man strode across the hall to a panelled door half-hidden behind a large potted plant. The room beyond was decorated in a similar style to the entry hall, its main point of difference the two armed figures at a small table who seemed to be halfway through a game of tiles. They looked up at Clade's entry, and he saw that they wore uniforms of Spyridon red and grey.

"Good day," said the attendant from the other side of the threshold, and swung the door shut.

The nearest soldier stood, stretching his neck in a leisurely fashion. "Who are you, then?"

"I'm here to see Hesca Matharan," Clade said, abruptly uncertain. "My name is Clade."

The soldier glanced back at his companion, who shook her head. "Not expecting any Clade."

"Sorry, Clade," the first soldier said, his expression anything but. "Why don't you run along?"

Clade looked from one soldier to the other. Clearly, Onsoth had misled him about this place. But there was an opportunity here, if he stepped carefully. Onsoth must have had a purpose in sending him to the Four Hands, and Clade meant to discover what it was.

"A moment, please," he said. "Do either of you know Onsoth?"

The nearer soldier looked blank, but the one at the table scowled. "That prick at the Library?" She spat on the floor. "What of him?"

Clade hesitated. A wrong turn. He cast about for another angle. "Do you work for Hesca?"

The nearer soldier laughed. "Do you work for Hesca?" he repeated in a high, mocking tone. "Look at this, Cas. We've got ourselves a mouse who doesn't even know who he's asking to see."

The woman, Cas, waved in dismissal. "Get him out of here."

"Wait." Clade stepped back, but not quickly enough to evade the meaty hand that closed about his bicep. "Wait! My news is as ink spilt on sand!"

The soldier slammed him against the wall, his mocking amusement gone in less time than it took to blink. He yanked a knife from his belt and drew it back, muscles tensing to strike.

"Stop!" The voice belonged to Cas, but Clade could see nothing beyond the unnamed soldier's snarling face and upraised blade.

"You heard what he said," the soldier growled.

"I heard. So did you. That's an old phrase."

"So someone didn't get the new one."

"And how could that be, when we all have them drilled into us every other day?"

The soldier glared, the knife a hand's breadth from Clade's eye. Abruptly, Clade found himself spun about and shoved face-first into the wall. Someone yanked his arms behind his back, his withered hand catching on the greatcoat pocket before being roughly freed and clamped in a vice-like grip. "What do you want to do with him?"

There was a sound of footsteps, then Clade felt a second pair of hands run efficiently across his torso, sleeves, and trousers. He heard a grunt as they reached his boots and removed his dagger from its hiding place. "The subcommander will want to talk to him."

"You sure that's a good idea?"

"You've got a firm grip, don't you?"

The hold on his hands tightened, and he was turned and propelled toward a rear door. The soldier behind him leaned close, his warm breath tickling Clade's ear. "No funny business, mouse, or you'll regret it."

The soldiers marched Clade down a narrow corridor, then up a flight of stairs and through an anteroom into a tiled chamber. An auburn-haired woman lay prone on a high wooden table, wearing only a twist of cloth about her loins. Beside the table stood two attendants in loose robes, each digging their fingers and thumbs into the woman's scarred back.

"Sorry to bother you, subcommander," Cas said. "This one asked for you by name. Then he said this."

The man holding Clade's arms twisted them up and around, sending pain shooting along his limbs. "Say it," he breathed.

Clade gasped, raising himself to his toes to ease the pressure. "My news is as ink spilt on sand," he managed through clenched teeth.

"Well," the woman said. "That is interesting, isn't it?" She rolled her shoulders and gave a pained hiss. "Cas, the knife. Zann, the door."

"Now, wait just a moment," Clade began.

Again he was shoved backward against the wall, this time by Cas, whose knife abruptly pressed against his throat. "Stay very still," she whispered as her companion released Clade's arms and disappeared into the anteroom, "or lose your craw. Your choice."

Clade glanced swiftly about the room, sorcery already forming in his mind. But the only timber objects were the door at his back and the table in the chamber's centre, and neither gave him a clear shot at the soldier holding the knife. Sighing, he allowed the threads of his binding to slip away. "Understood," he croaked.

"Splendid." The woman appeared entirely unconcerned about either her own near-nakedness or Clade's presence at her back. "What's your name?"

"Clade," he said.

"And mine?"

Clade considered the scarred back. "Hesca Matharan," he guessed. "Subcommander in the Spyridon army, apparently."

"Very good." One of the attendants jammed her thumb beneath Hesca's shoulder blade, eliciting a long groan. "And tell me, Clade," she said as the masseuse added a pair of fingers to the thumb, "what do you think Cas there will do if you lie to me even once?"

Clade scowled. "Nothing at all," he snapped. "I'm hardly going to lie about anything obvious, am I? If I do choose to lie, you won't have the slightest idea that what I'm saying isn't true."

"Oh-ho! *Excellent* answer!" Hesca pushed the attendants' hands away and sat up, swinging around to face Clade. A thick scar snaked beneath one of her breasts and across her belly. Her lips curled in a smile that was half mockery, half challenge. "Then tell me this, Clade-who-reserves-the-right-to-lie. Who sent you here?"

The pressure of Cas's knife at Clade's throat increased ever so slightly. Clade swallowed carefully. "Onsoth, at the Library."

Hesca studied him closely. "Did he tell you to use that phrase?"

"He did."

"And what did you expect to find here?"

"Answers," Clade said sourly. "A woman attacked me in the street and tried to kill me. I found reason to link her to Onsoth, but he denies the connection." Yet the broad strokes of Onsoth's betrayal were becoming clear. The phrase Onsoth had given him was evidently a kill-on-sight code, something Clade had heard of elsewhere as a tool to eliminate unsuspecting sorcerers. He'd been saved by good fortune alone: Onsoth's knowledge of the army's codes was out of date, and the phrase was no longer in use. *Next time I see that bastard I'm going to wring his neck.*

Hesca stood with an amused snort and wandered across to a pile of clothes in the corner of the room. The attendants filed out without a sideways glance, as if a man with a knife to his throat was not even the most interesting thing they'd seen since lunchtime. "It occurs to me that you might not be favourably disposed toward Onsoth just now."

"You could say that," Clade growled.

"Perhaps you're even thinking of doing him harm," she said as she began to dress.

"A damned mind-reader, you are."

"Like you did that woman near the Arcade." Hesca paused in the action of tying her belt. "That was you, wasn't it? I've got half a dozen witnesses describing a sorcerer not unlike you. Tall, hair, hand." She looked him up and down. "Though I must say, nobody mentioned the coat."

"I told you, she tried to kill me."

"So you did." Clothed at last in the weathered, loose-fitting attire of an off-duty soldier, Hesca returned to the table and began pulling on her boots. "But I don't think you're seeing my point."

Clade had no interest in whatever point Hesca was trying to make. "Look, this is obviously not what any of us thought it was. Why don't we rule it off as an unfortunate misunderstanding and go our separate ways?"

Hesca frowned. "Then our business here is done."

"Precisely."

"As you wish." She stepped forward and pressed her own knife to his neck, fixing him with pale eyes. "Clade, as a duly authorised representative of the city of Spyridon, I hereby arrest you for the murder of an as yet unnamed woman four days ago by means of malicious sorcery. Resist this arrest and your life will be considered forfeit. Cas, tell Zann to fetch an anamnil collar. Then have him prepare a cell —"

"Wait. Wait! There's no need for this —"

"Oh?" Hesca cocked her head. "Would you like to re-open our previous topic of discussion?"

Clade gave her as venomous a glare as he could manage with

two blades tickling his chin. "What do you want?"

"Your aid, naturally. But you needn't worry, it won't involve anything untoward."

"Oh, I feel better already," Clade said. "But I don't just mean what you want from me. What in the hells is this all about?"

"Ah." Hesca lowered her knife. "I'll give you the short version, shall I?"

"Please."

"As you may know, Spyridon is governed by a circle," she began, strolling to the side wall before turning and retracing her steps. "The army is represented in this circle, of course, as is the Library. The merchantry, the craft guilds, and the temples each have a presence. So does the governor of Port Gallin, but that post is currently vacant. Oh, and there's Prince Urjo, though that's neither here nor there."

Clade grunted. "Tell me something new."

"Historically, the Library has always been, shall we say, first among equals," Hesca continued. "But it's become clear to many of us that that's no longer in the city's best interest."

"How civic-minded of you."

"Believe it," Hesca said. "That nice thick wall you passed on your way into Spyridon? The Library's been against it every step of the way. First they didn't want it at all. Then they wanted a ring instead of a star, never mind that such a wall would be impossible to defend against cannons. Then they wanted it built around the hill but not the rest of the city. Then they said we should defend Spyridon but leave Port Gallin to fend for itself." She shook her head angrily. "They've been squeezing the circle for concessions at every step, as if the defence of the city were nothing more than a gods-damned bargaining chip."

"Concessions?"

"Doesn't matter. What matters is now they're trying to install your friend Onsoth as governor of Port Gallin. Give themselves an extra voice on the circle. The All-God knows how we'll ever get anything done if they succeed."

"All right." The explanation made a rough sort of sense. "And you want me to what, kill Onsoth for you?"

"It might come to that. But I'd like to avoid it if I can. We're not Neysans." Hesca shot him a glance as if she might pursue the topic further, then turned away. "Onsoth's rise has been... unexpected. A year ago he was nobody. Now he's practically the Conservator's right hand. I want to discredit him. Turn him from an asset into a liability. If Feren cuts him loose, well and good. And if not, that'll tell us something interesting too."

"And what exactly does 'discredit' mean in your world?"

"This link you found between Onsoth and the woman who attacked you. What is it?"

Clade pondered his answer. "She was carrying something," he said cautiously. "Something that could only have come from Onsoth."

Hesca chuckled at his obfuscation. "Do you have this *something* in your possession?"

Clade's coinpurse hung on his belt, as yet unmolested by either of Hesca's heavies. "It's in a safe place," he said.

"I see." She looked at him as though trying to decide whether to press further, then shrugged. "All right. Here's the deal. You're going to turn yourself in. Confess to killing that woman, but claim it was done in self-defence."

"It *was* self-defence!"

"Because you turned yourself in, the first step will be a preliminary hearing, not a full trial. We'll be able to arrange a friendly magistrate. You'll present the evidence of Onsoth's involvement. The magistrate will rule in your favour, let you go, and cite Onsoth. And we'll see what happens."

Clade scowled. "That's it? My reward for cooperating with you is a tour of Spyridon's judicial practices?"

"Did you not hear me? The magistrate will *let you go*. That's better than most street killers get." She smiled. "But no, that's not it. This only works if you walk into the barracks all by yourself and give yourself up. If we arrest you, you'll go straight to trial, and the choice of magistrate will be out of our hands. So let's say, oh, ten luri as an incentive to cooperate. Payable in full *after* your part is done, of course."

"Ten luri," Clade repeated. It was a healthy sum, and there was no question that his purse could do with some replenishment. Yet the prospect of placing himself at the city's mercy ran counter to every instinct he had. Better free and broke than languishing in a cell with anamnil shackles around his ankles and wrists.

"You don't trust me," Hesca observed. "That's to be expected. We've only just met, after all. So here's what we'll do. I'm going to open the door and get Zann in here, and he and Cas are going to take you down to the foyer where they'll let you go. You can walk out that door and not look back. And a week from now, one of two things will happen. One, you'll give yourself up just like we discussed. Or two, I'll tell my people to kill you on sight if they ever see you in my city again, preferably from a distance where your sorcery won't help you." She folded her arms, all trace of amusement gone. "Are we clear?"

Clade glared. "*Your* city?"

"That's right." Hesca matched his stare, holding his gaze until he looked away. "My city."

~

With Kep no longer tagging along and barely a handful of passing travellers on the road, Arandras found himself more alone than he had been for close to a year. It was startling to think how long he'd gone without a break from the company of others; but now, with only the rustle of shy forest animals for company, he drank in the solitude like a parched desert wanderer at an oasis.

Perhaps Jensine had the right idea, making her home in some out-of-the-way village with an abundance of unpeopled wilderness to lose herself in. There had been times when Arandras had imagined a similar life for himself, before the excitement of finding the golems and then the realisation of his debt to Jensine and Druce. But now, that end was within sight and the prospect of a break from the constant activity of the past year rose before him, there for the taking if he wished it.

Rest. The notion seemed wrong, somehow — a violation of some immutable law of nature. Weeper knew that running his scribe's shop had been taxing enough even before Clade's letter had chanced across his desk. To find somewhere peaceful and simply sit still for a while — days, weeks, months, however long it took to stop feeling as though he was running late for his own life — gods, the idea was becoming more appealing by the moment. He could make his way to Spyridon, give Druce the gold he owed him, and then find somewhere to hibernate until he felt ready to rejoin the world.

Mara will think I'm crazy. He pictured her expression, that what-have-you-been-drinking look she saved for moments like this, and smiled. *That's right, Mara, I've got enough ancient Valdori soldiery at my disposal to conquer any city — hells, any land — in Kal Arna that I want, but what I'd really like is to take a nice long nap.*

The road topped a rise, the forest opening out to a grassy plain filled with spring wildflowers. Arandras took a deep breath of perfumed air, gazing out at the riotous mix of yellow and violet, red and pale blue. *Gods, yes, this is what I need. No more running around the Free Cities like a madman's dog. Just this.*

He made camp that night at the edge of the field and lingered the following morning, his relaxed start delaying his arrival at the burnt-out village until an hour past sunset. The village seemed unchanged since his previous visit several days prior, and as he approached the shale-stone walls within which he'd hidden the golems, he felt the familiar spark of their presence at the edge of his awareness.

Golems, has anyone entered this village since I left?

The alien not-quite-voices filled his head. *No. No. Nobody has come. No.*

Arandras peered into the shadowy jumble within the house. A smudge of orange light still marked the far corner: the glow of Tiy's eyes, faint enough from this vantage to almost mistake for candlelight, except that no candle ever produced a flame so perfectly steady.

A breath of wind set the treetops rustling and sent burnt-out scraps skittering down the street. Arandras stepped across to the shelter of a nearby wall, rubbing his hands together in the cool air. *Tiy, open the trapdoor for the others and clear a path out of the wreckage. Golems, as you are able, leave the cellar and assemble on the street.*

A commotion began within the house, as if someone had decided to demolish what was left of the ruin from the inside. Dark shapes shifted in the gloom, some impossible to make out, others large enough to identify as broken beams or chunks of masonry jolting sideways or crashing into piled debris. The orange glow intensified, casting shadows onto the street; then, abruptly, a gap opened in the wreckage and Tiy strode forth like a demon from the hundred hells, its burning eyes the only discernible feature within its hulking black profile. It stood still for a moment, taking in the street, then turned and set to work enlarging the gap by tearing away at a pile of stones that might have once formed part of a chimney.

"Dreamer, Weeper, and Gatherer, protect me." The soft exclamation came from behind him, falling by chance in a brief silence amid Tiy's demolition. Arandras spun about, scanning the darkness for the speaker. A charred ruin rose a short distance away, its walls lower but thicker than those of the house beside him. Arandras crept toward it, circling around slightly to avoid the hidden observer's line of sight. Something moved at the base of the wall, and as Arandras edged closer he heard a familiar voice whispering a mantra. "Dreamer and Weeper protect. Dreamer and Weeper protect."

Arandras gave a disgusted sigh. "Kep, what in the hells —"

Kep shrieked and leapt to his feet. "Stay away!" He thrust a trembling finger in Arandras's direction and began backing away up the street. "Devil! Worshipper of the dead! Come no closer!" He dropped his satchel, cursed, and picked it up again, his outstretched finger remaining directly between him and Arandras as though his life depended on it. "I abjure you! I defy you! I — yeeeeek!" And with a final screech he turned and sprinted into the night, satchel flapping against his thin body.

Arandras started after him, but Kep had already vanished into the surrounding forest. *Well, that's just brilliant.* The idiot fisherman must have followed him from Stalie's Rest, Weeper only knew why, and managed to avoid Arandras's attention all the way here. Not that that was saying much. Arandras had learnt plenty from Mara about living rough in the past year, but he still had only a fraction of her sense for her surroundings. Probably half of the cracking twigs and soft rustles he'd ignored as the movement of some hidden animal had actually been Kep.

And now he was away, running off to the gods only knew where.

Arandras had no idea whether the man was more likely to pretend the encounter had never happened or to blab about it to every passing traveller, and there was no point waiting around to find out. The night was still young. By the time the sun crested the horizon, he and the golems could be far away, leaving no sign of their presence except some rearranged wreckage in one of the ruins.

He turned around. The golems stood in ranks of two in the centre of the street, Tiy motionless at their head. Their pinprick eyes hung in the darkness like a colony of eerily unmoving fireflies. Arandras paused a moment to take in the uncanny sight. Small wonder, perhaps, that Kep had reacted the way he had.

The breeze picked up again, sending chill air across Arandras's face. He took a breath.

Golems, with me. We march north.

He set off, the golems lurching into action behind him with a sound like boulders rolling slowly down a dry riverbed.

~

The land north of the village alternated between untended fields and thick forest. Within the forested areas, it was easy to follow the path they'd made on their way south; but between them were meadows that seemed more rock than soil, and with the moon's light obscured by scudding clouds, Arandras more than once found himself confronted with an unbroken barrier of undergrowth when he reached a field's end. On the third such occasion he spent the better part of an hour searching for their original path before giving up and directing the golems to break a new trail. Better that than have them carry him, no matter the delay. He'd tried riding a golem once in the early days, but its jolting motion had practically jarred his teeth from their sockets and he'd resolved never to repeat the experience.

As the night wore on and the breeze stiffened, Arandras found his mood souring. Kep could hardly have chosen a worse moment to glimpse the golems. It didn't require a great leap to imagine how others might respond to a tale of strange constructs emerging from a ruined house in one of the region's numerous plague-emptied villages. Spreading rumours might draw any number of treasure-seekers to pick over the other villages; and if one of them happened to lever open the lid of a particular abandoned well…

Arandras blew out a breath. *I'll have to fetch them out.* The well in question was more or less on the way, but Arandras didn't relish the prospect of arriving at Spyridon with thirty golems to conceal instead of eleven. He'd probably end up having to hide them in the sea and hope that no freak tide or curious boatman exposed the secret.

The eastern sky was just beginning to brighten when the golems came to an abrupt, grinding halt. Tiy's rough drone sounded in Arandras's head. *A road. Women and men, unmoving. We stop.*

Arandras moved cautiously to where Tiy stood motionless at the head of the procession. The trees ahead gave way to another field, but this time a rutted road marked the transition point, winding along the edge of the forest in both directions. To his left, about twenty paces away, a wagon had been turned on its side and dragged to the road's edge. Half a dozen bodies lay around it, most little more than huddled shadows in the dim light.

"Hello?" Arandras called softly. He crept closer, covering his nose as the stench grew stronger. Memories of another pre-dawn morning returned in force — *Quill and Oculus, sprawled together in death by the rocky shore of a lake* — and he clenched his teeth in an effort not to gag.

Most of the dead were clothed in what looked like the neatly-tailored but unremarkable attire of moderately prosperous merchants. One, wearing a leather jerkin and with a long knife just beyond her outstretched hand, seemed to have taken as many wounds as the others put together. A smaller form lay beneath the wagon's broken yoke — a child of perhaps ten with a single feathered shaft in her back.

This was the work of bandits, probably long gone by now. Arandras was no expert in such things, but these bodies had clearly been decaying for a while. The wagon was empty, of course: a few broken crates aside, everything had been stripped and taken. Even the canvas covering the wagon's upper section had been cut from its hoops, two of which had snapped off and lay half-hidden in the grass.

With a sigh, Arandras turned away. In the growing light, the scene began to give up more of its pitiable details — the rag doll still clutched in the child's hand, its grinning head sticking out from between thumb and forefinger — but Arandras had already seen as much as he needed to. There was no help to be given here, and nothing to salvage, either. The attackers had been thorough on every front.

Unless... Arandras crouched, studying the wagon. Despite having been turned on its side, both axles appeared intact. The yoke was broken, but that wouldn't be a problem for the golems. Come nightfall, they could pull the wagon down the road for a while with Arandras riding in the back. If nothing else, it would give him a chance to rest — and if these back roads continued in the direction he wanted, he might save considerable time.

He returned to where they'd emerged from the trees, the golems still standing in frozen procession. The light had grown enough now to see that the fields stretched further than he'd guessed, all the way to a series of strangely pale hills. The forest behind them might still be enough to confuse anyone who happened to glance in their direction, but that wouldn't last long.

Golems, right that wagon and pick it up, Arandras ordered, directing the instruction to the first four golems behind Tiy. He looked back at the scene and added, *Be sure to tread only on earth and grass.*

The golems tromped obediently to the wagon, but as they lifted it a flash from the hills pulled Arandras's eye. Sunlight now bathed their crests, revealing a series of tiny white squares and rectangles. *Bleachfields,* Arandras realised, caught by the unexpected sight. Yards and yards of fabric — linen, perhaps, or cotton — lay spread across the grass to be whitened by the sun, their presence in turn whitening the hills as the sun rose until the ground seemed almost to be clad in silver.

Something shifted in the forest behind him. Arandras turned to see Tiy step forward, its gaze fixed on the hills. *A relic,* it said, and stopped.

What? Arandras looked from the golem to the hills and back again. *What relic?*

Something sounded in Arandras's head, as if Tiy coughed or cleared its throat. Then, slowly, it spoke again. *A relic. Streams of light. The making.*

Bewildered, Arandras stared at the golem, but nothing in its face or posture seemed amiss. *What does that mean?*

Tiy gazed at the hills and said nothing.

The wagon gave a long creak and Arandras turned once more to see the four golems standing patiently with the wagon suspended in the air between them. He cursed and strode back toward the forest, waving for them to follow. *Golems, bring the wagon back here. Everyone, move back into the forest along the path we made. Stop after fifty paces and we'll find somewhere to camp for the day. Tiy, that includes you.*

They retreated into the shelter of the forest, Tiy joining the others as if nothing had happened. At a hollow concealed by a pair of wide-trunked trees, Arandras made a simple, fireless camp and instructed the golems to scatter themselves through the nearby forest as carefully as they could. The salvaged wagon they left on the open side of the hollow — enough, Arandras hoped, to conceal him if anyone happened to pass by.

Exhausted though he was after more than a day without rest, Arandras found himself unable to sleep. Tiy responded to his questions with silence, just as it had after its first strange mention of a relic. Eventually Arandras gave up and stared at the leaf-dappled sky, thoughts of bleachfields and relics and dancing girls chasing each other around his head until he fell into an uncomfortable slumber.

CHAPTER 6

Never ignore a belly that needs filling or bowels that need emptying. Never offer friendship to strangers or accept it from rogues. And never, ever ask why.

— *A Fool's Advice* (author unknown)

EILWEN PAUSED AT THE EDGE of the street beneath a sculpted stone terrier and glanced down the adjoining alley. *Dog Lane. Twenty-nine paces with a bend in the middle, then out to the Square of Colporteurs. From there, either east to the harbour or northwest to the city gates and the Anstice road.*

She nodded, satisfied, and turned to consider the hulking mass of the Neysan city hall. In the evening gloom it seemed larger than it had in daylight. Though a handful of windows showed the warm glow of lamps or candles, most were as dark as the surrounding street, making it hard to distinguish where the building ended and the night sky began. In Anstice, dozens of streetlamps would have filled the area with enough light to read by, but here only a few feeble lanterns dotted the street like beacons amid treacherous waters.

Which was all for the good, of course. The darker the streets, the better their chances of getting away if tomorrow's raid went sour. Eilwen had committed to memory no fewer than five potential escape routes, though two involved some form of rooftop scramble that she hoped to avoid for the sake of her leg. Ideally they'd walk out the same way they went in, with a smile and a nod for the guards outside the door. But there was no surer way of ending up dead than failing to plan for contingencies, and Eilwen had no intention of falling prey to complacency.

Until tomorrow. She gave the building one last look, then turned for the southern side of the city and Den's house.

Mara's claim to have seen someone following her had been easy to brush off at the time, but Eilwen had found herself returning to the thought several times over the course of the day. She'd set up little traps in the course of her wandering, pausing outside a shop display or doubling back in an empty lane, but nothing had come of it. Perhaps Mara had scared her tail off, or perhaps the woman had simply been mistaken.

She returned to Den's house to find her brother's entire family in the front room, Den and Irilli sharing an upholstered settee and Orval perched on a shallow armchair. They fell quiet at her entry, their expressions strangely guarded. Eilwen glanced from one to the next, but only Den met her eyes. "Didn't mean to interrupt," she said, resuming her course for the loft. "I'll leave you in peace."

"No, stay." Den's smile was strained, though only someone who knew him well could have seen it. "As it happens, we were just talking about you."

"Oh?" Eilwen eased herself into a chair. "Is something wrong?"

"No, no," Den said in the placating tone that Eilwen knew meant the precise opposite. "Look, Eil, you know I'm not the sort to pry into your business. I mean, any time you want to talk, I'm here, but..." He took a breath. "You don't need to explain yourself to be welcome in my house, is what I'm saying. Gods know we've been through enough for that."

"I appreciate that," Eilwen said cautiously. "And you know that if I had a house of my own I'd say the exact same thing to you."

Den cleared his throat. "It's just that things have been a little crazy lately. What with invading sorcerers and the like. You can leave Neysa any time you like, but Rill and Orval are my family as much as you are, and this is their home. You know?"

"Of course," Eilwen said, slipping into her negotiator's posture almost without realising it. "You're responsible for them in a way you're not for me."

"Yes," Den said, the relief evident in his tone. "That's it, exactly."

There was a pause, Den smiling as if they'd come to some sort of understanding. Eilwen spread her hands. "So...?"

"Oh!" Den gave an embarrassed laugh. "Right. So, uh, we need to ask you some things."

"Is that all?" Eilwen sat back, doing her best to look at ease. "Ask away."

Den took a breath. Even now, he seemed reluctant to pose his question. "Why did you really leave the Woodtraders Guild?"

Eilwen glanced at the others, thinking rapidly. Irilli's face was rigid, revealing nothing of her feelings, but Orval's expression held a strange mixture of distance, anxiety, and expectation. Did they know something, or merely suspect it? And what had prompted this conversation now?

"The Guild was betrayed," she said slowly. "Sold out by one of its own masters. I figured out who it was, and I... stopped them."

"Stopped them?" Orval said. "What does that mean?"

Eilwen gave him a hard look. "It means what it says."

Orval swallowed and looked away.

"But I was too late. My own support among the masters was already gone." Her own throat tightened, and she coughed in an attempt to cover it. "I couldn't stay," she said thickly. "So I left."

Irilli stirred, her long earrings brushing her cheeks. "And now?"

"Now?" Eilwen shrugged. "I told you already. I've been trying to start over. Trading where I could, mostly out west —"

"What are you buying?"

Eilwen blinked. "Excuse me?"

"I took your bag up to the loft the day you arrived," Irilli said softly. "It was light. There couldn't have been much more in it than a change of clothes. You're obviously not selling, so what are you buying?"

Eilwen stared at her and said nothing.

"Or maybe you're not in Neysa to trade at all," Irilli continued, an edge creeping into her tone. "Maybe you're here for some other reason. Something to do with our new occupiers, perhaps?"

"Look, I don't know what you imagine —"

"Are you working for them?" Irilli's voice was little more than a whisper, yet somehow it cut through Eilwen's protestations like steel. "Are you working for the Oculus?"

"What? No!" Eilwen surged to her feet. "I am *not* working for them, do you hear me? I'd rather die than take a single copper duri from the fucking Oculus —"

Someone beat on the front door, startling the entire room to silence. "Hello, inside! Open up in the name of the city!"

"Shit." Den scrambled to his feet. "Upstairs, all of you. Move!"

Eilwen followed Irilli and Orval into the courtyard, where Orval scampered up the stairs and disappeared behind one of the doors. Irilli gestured for Eilwen to follow, but Eilwen shook her head and leaned close. "What's going on?"

"No time to explain," Irilli whispered as the door received a fresh buffeting. "There's a closet with a false back upstairs. Follow Orval."

But as Eilwen made to turn, the door burst open and a man stepped through, short and thick-necked, with a grey-haired woman close behind. Both wore Neysan teal and silver. The woman's gaze flicked from Den in the front room to Eilwen and Irilli in the courtyard as though looking for someone, her expression fierce and humourless.

"Gods, I was just coming." Den's back was to Eilwen, but she could hear his sigh of disgust. "You going to pay for that?"

The thick-necked man had the grace to look shamefaced, but the woman turned her gaze on Den like a bombardier swivelling a cannon. "We're looking for Orval Nasareen. Is he here?"

"Orval? No." Den's voice faltered slightly, but he folded his arms. "What's the problem?"

Oculus. The beast rose inside Eilwen, sinuous and throbbing with hate. At the very least, these two were following Oculus orders. Perhaps they were Oculus themselves. *You took Havilah from me,* Eilwen thought, her hands curling into fists. *You took my Guild.*

There was no way on the gods' green earth they were going to take her nephew, too.

"Orval Nasareen, you say?" Eilwen said, striding toward the two Neysans as Den shot her a surprised glance. "Where is he? You've found the bastard?"

The woman scowled. "And you are?"

"Owed a great deal of money." Eilwen matched the scowl with one of her own. "You know where he is? Take me to him."

The woman considered Eilwen for a moment, then turned and gestured to her colleague. "Search the house."

"Oh, yeah, that's brilliant." Eilwen flopped onto the settee and propped her booted feet in front of her. "I'll tell you this for free, lady. I've already found half a dozen hiding places in this house that you and your headkicker would never think to look for. The boy's not here."

The man hesitated, glancing from Eilwen to his companion. Hissing, the woman repeated her gesture, and the man lumbered reluctantly through to the courtyard.

Sighing theatrically, Eilwen leaned back on the settee and glanced around the room. Den still stood near the door, half a pace from the tall coatstand. Eilwen caught his eye, then flicked her gaze toward it, and Den gave a minute nod in response.

"Where are you going to try next?" Eilwen called, twisting to hide her hand as it wrapped around the hilt of her dagger. "I've already checked the local drinking establishments. If I don't get another lead soon, I might have to take the coin out of Ma and Pa here."

The woman said nothing, and Eilwen shook her head scornfully. Her colleague was upstairs now, clomping around on the floorboards like a one-man platoon. Den edged toward the coatstand and Eilwen tightened her grip on the dagger, listening for the cry of discovery that would spring her into action.

Footsteps tramped down the stairs, and the man reappeared in the doorway. "Kid's not here."

"There, you see?" Eilwen said, resisting the urge to sigh in relief. "Told you."

The woman glared at Eilwen, then turned to Den. "We expect to be informed as soon as Orval returns."

"Good for you," Den said. "And I expect to be paid for my door."

The woman sniffed and crooked a finger at her companion, and the two of them strode outside, the door hanging awkwardly on its broken hinge behind them.

~

"What in the hells was that?" Eilwen rounded on Den, whispering furiously as the footsteps receded into the night. "What do they want with Orval? And how do they think they can just march in here and demand him?"

"They can and they do." Den dragged a side-table across to hold up the sagging door. "Welcome to Neysa, Eilwen."

"But why Orval?" She stared at Den, at the exhaustion in his eyes, and exhaled sharply. "Is this what happened to Vess? It is, isn't it? Merciful gods."

The rush of energy that had propelled her performance was fading. Eilwen sank onto the settee and tried to make sense of the situation. Were the Oculus snatching people as a method of forcible recruitment? That might explain why they'd picked up Vess — her sorcery may have been too weak to interest the Quill, but a group like the Oculus might not have the luxury of choice. But according to Den, Orval had no such gift, so why try to grab him too?

Irilli stepped in from the next room, Orval trailing behind, out from the wardrobe or wherever he'd been hiding. The deep weariness in Irilli's eyes and Orval's perpetual withdrawal no longer seemed strange. *If this is their life, it's a wonder they're still standing.*

"When did they take Vess?"

She'd addressed the question to Den, but it was Irilli who answered. "Nine days after the city fell," she said in a low voice, her gaze fixed on something only she could see. "Five months and three days ago today. There were puddles on the ground when she left for work, and the smell of rain still in the air, but the sun was just coming out. I told her to bring me back some apples and cinnamon for the pie I was going to bake."

"Several prominent sorcerers were killed," Den said softly. "Irilli's brother was one of those. But the younger ones were bundled onto a ship that was waiting for them in the harbour. We're pretty sure Vess was on that ship."

"Gods." Eilwen leaned forward. "Den, I'm so sorry. I can't imagine — ah, hells." She straightened, dabbing at her eyes with her sleeve. "The fucking Oculus."

"Yeah." Den sounded utterly spent. "Look, I'm sorry about before. I didn't want to doubt you. I think we all just needed to hear you say it."

"It's fine," Eilwen said. It had been bad enough at the Woodtraders, not knowing which of the colleagues she'd been working with for years might have been lying to her the whole time. How much worse if it were family, and you'd already lost a daughter? "I get it. Really."

The relief in Den's smile was almost enough to set her weeping again.

"What I don't get," she said, "is why they'd come for Orval. Do they think he's a sorcerer too?"

"I doubt it," Den said. "When it became obvious what was happening, most of the remaining sorcerers cleared out. After that, the Oculus left us alone, more or less. But something's changed. The disappearances have started again — not many, but enough for people to start talking. Only it's not sorcerers this time."

Eilwen frowned. "Who, then?"

"Anyone. A journeyman smith. A pair of apothecaries. An apprentice historian."

"A perfumer's son?"

Den gave a helpless shrug.

"What do you think?" Eilwen said to Orval. The boy sat with his knees drawn up to his chin, his remote expression a mirror of his mother's. "Why would the Oculus be after you?"

Orval glanced at Eilwen and then away again. "Don't know."

"Are you sure?" Eilwen sat forward, trying to find Orval's gaze. "Did Vess leave you anything or say anything before she was taken? Anything that might send them looking for you?"

"No."

Or perhaps they want Orval as leverage. The unwelcome thought bloomed in her mind, pulling her attention like brightly-coloured poison. *Perhaps your sister has refused to behave herself, and now they want you as a guarantor of her cooperation.*

She glanced at Den and saw the same thought lurking behind his eyes. Cursing silently, she looked away.

"There's something we need to ask you," Den said. "A favour."

"Of course. Gods, anything."

"Leave Neysa," Den said. "And take Orval with you."

Eilwen blinked. "Take him where?" she said as Orval looked in surprise from one parent to the other.

"Anywhere," Irilli said, the desperation in her tone all the more terrible for its quietness. "It doesn't matter. Away from here." Her hand crept forward, perhaps in unconscious supplication. "Please."

"I, uh… it's not that simple. I have an employer…"

Orval gave a disbelieving laugh. "Really? You're going to pack me off with her just like that?"

"Come here, Orval," Irilli said, standing and pulling her son into a hug. "Your father and I have been discussing this for a while. What are you going to do if you stay? Every time you go outside there's a chance you might never come back."

Den leaned toward Eilwen, half-turning to give his wife and son the grace of moment alone. "You know we wouldn't ask if we didn't have to," he said. "But if you can't do it, better to tell us now. We'll figure out some other way to get him out of the city."

Eilwen closed her eyes. "No," she said. "I'll take him. Gods, Den, of course I'll take him." *And somehow, I'll explain all this to Clade.* "There's something I have to do tomorrow night. Better you don't know what. After that, my business here is done anyway."

"Thank you, Eilwen." Den took her hands. "I won't forget this."

She wanted to demur, to tell him that thanks were unnecessary, but the words wouldn't come. Den squeezed her fingers, his grip painfully tight, as if it was him clinging to her and not the other way around. But the Woodtraders were gone, and Havilah was gone, and what did she have left but family?

"I'll keep him safe, Den," she said. "I promise you."

❧

If there was one thing Clade hated more than an attempt on his life, it was being pushed around like a game piece on someone else's board.

He strode across the Great Square, hair flapping against his neck as he forged a path through the late afternoon crowds. Hesca and Onsoth, the Library and the army — they could all go to the hells together, along with the rest of the city circle. Clade wished them the eternal pleasure of each other's company. *May a thousand midges nibble their ears and their arms be too short to scratch.*

He stepped inside the Library and strode to the end of the foyer. The attendant minding the stairs was the same old man as the other day, and he readily opened the gate to Clade a second time. Clade took the stairs two at a time and was soon standing outside Onsoth's narrow mahogany doors. He knocked, then thought better of it and pushed the doors open.

"Ah!" Onsoth scrambled to his feet, the chair behind his desk tipping to the floor in his haste. "Clade. Did you, uh, find your, um..."

"You cross-grained bastard." Clade stalked across the room, his steps silent on the rich carpet, and planted his fist on Onsoth's desk. "You sent me off to die."

"What? I did no such thing —"

"Bullshit. You set me up, you know it, and I know it too." Clade allowed the scowl to fill his face. "Give me one good reason why I shouldn't just kill you now and take your gods-damned gold."

Onsoth backed away. "It's not here, is it? You think I keep that kind of coin in my desk? I've got maybe five sculundi, if that. Gold for silver, that's a fool's trade."

"A fool is clearly what you take me for," Clade growled. "I wonder how easily this desk shatters? Looks like good strong wood. How far through your body do you think the splinters would get?" He looked Onsoth up and down. "Let's find out."

"No!" Onsoth squawked. He retreated to the window, face twisted in fear. "I'm sorry, all right? It wasn't my idea."

"Really? Whose was it?"

Onsoth opened his mouth, closed it. "The woman," he managed at last. "She approached me. She, uh, wanted to display her talents. I think she was hoping to find an employer."

"And she just happened to choose me at random, did she?"

Onsoth shut his eyes. "She said she'd find a sorcerer. Said it would make for a better demonstration."

It was a lie, of course. The woman had known full well who Clade was. But had she lied to Onsoth, or was Onsoth lying to him now? Clade supposed it wasn't impossible that an Oculus agent might try to lever some advantage out of their assignment. But was

Onsoth really so foolish as to entertain such an offer?

"If what you say is true," Clade said, "why send me to Hesca with that phrase?"

Onsoth opened an eye. "I panicked. I couldn't give you what you wanted, and I didn't know what you might do."

Clade slowly shook his head. *Lies.* The man's bearing was all wrong, his explanation too pat. Something more had passed between Onsoth and the assassin.

But perhaps there was value in allowing Onsoth to think he believed him, at least for the moment.

"Is that so?" Clade straightened. "Perhaps we can come to an arrangement."

"Oh?" Onsoth opened his other eye, his tone more cautious and less hopeful than Clade would have liked. "How?"

"I wonder how Feren Skaratass might respond to news that her Special Assistant has been entertaining demonstrations of murder from potential employees?"

It was a shot in the dark, built on conjecture and supposition after Clade's discussion with Hesca, but it struck home. Onsoth paled. "Now, wait just a moment."

"Maybe next time she's down in the Square for one of those debates you Library people seem to like, I could have a quiet word in her ear, let her know what you've been up to?"

"No, I —" Onsoth swallowed his protest, a sullen resentment creeping across his face. "What do you want?"

Clade smiled. "I'm interested in a book."

"What book?"

"One that you're handling personally, or so I understand. A recent acquisition." Clade leaned forward. "One with a great deal to say on the subject of *golems.*"

Onsoth flinched. "How do you know about that?"

"Wrong question, my friend," Clade said. "The right question is: when do you need it by? And the answer is: how about right now?"

But Onsoth was already shaking his head. "I can't. No, listen to me. I *can't.* That book is the Conservator's pet project. It can't just disappear, not even the copy. Nothing is worth that."

Clade pursed his lips. Onsoth's protestations seemed

disappointingly heartfelt. "All right," he said slowly. "Perhaps I don't need to take it away. Perhaps I only need to read it. It could stay right here in this room."

Onsoth's gaze flicked away. "There'd need to be some conditions."

"Such as?"

Onsoth began ticking off items on his fingers. "No weapons. No pen or ink. No candles, lamps, or flames of any kind. At least two of my people will be present at all times. When you enter the room, you'll be fitted with an anamnil bracelet, not to be removed until you leave —"

"*Anamnil?*"

"Yes, Clade, anamnil! I literally know only two things about you: you're a sorcerer and you're a killer. You'll excuse me if I consider it necessary to take a few precautions."

Clade gave a menacing glare. "You seem to have forgotten the nature of this conversation," he said. "Allow me to remind you. Either you provide me an opportunity to read the book in question — alone, unmolested, and most assuredly without a scrap of anamnil in the room — or I go to your precious Conservator, show her your token, and tell her how you set a murderer loose on the streets of Spyridon."

"I'm not a fool, Clade," Onsoth shot back. "You think I want you blabbing to the Conservator? But that book..." He shook his head. "I can't risk it. I just can't."

Clade scowled, but Onsoth stared back, grimly defiant. *What do I do now? Threaten to kill him?* He'd opened the conversation with that, and it had won him half-truths at best. And if Clade made the threat again and Onsoth refused to bend, what then? If he truly thought himself about to die, Onsoth would shriek bloody murder, guards would come running, and there was no guarantee that revealing Onsoth's treachery would persuade them to stay their hand. Clade could easily find himself fighting his way down seven storeys just to get out of the building. *Even if I made it out, what would I have to show for it all? Not a damn thing.*

"Ask me for something else," Onsoth said. "Whatever it is, it's yours."

"There's nothing else I want," Clade said.

"Please." Onsoth bowed his head. "Anything."

With a muttered curse, Clade turned for the door. "I'll be in touch."

～

Still scowling, Clade left the Library and crossed the Great Square. The satirists were setting up for another performance, but Clade had no appetite for puppets. He pushed through the growing crowd, ignoring the angry looks and imprecations that issued in his wake.

He'd been too hasty. Hesca's threat had gotten to him and he'd reacted without thinking it through, pressing Onsoth too hard and backing the man into a corner. Somehow he'd managed to come away empty-handed not only with regard to the book but also on the small matter of his near murder. On the latter front, Onsoth was clearly hiding something, though Clade found it hard to imagine what. Surely the Library man had better things to do than help kill a visitor to the city, sorcerer or no.

But it was his failure to shake loose even a glance at the closely-guarded book that Clade found most frustrating. Onsoth hadn't denied the book's existence. He hadn't even denied his own access to it. Yet his invocation of the Conservator's ire had defanged Clade's threats, or at least had provided enough cover to resist their logic. At another time or place, the application of suitably intimidating sorcery might have won from Onsoth a change of heart; but such avenues could hardly be pursued where a single cry for help might bring the full force of the Library's wrath down on Clade's head.

An empty cart rattled past him down the hill, the ox at its head doing as much to restrain the vehicle's progress as propel it. Clade stepped smartly into the empty space in its wake, cutting across the street and following its descent away from the Arcade. Whatever was in that book must be priceless, the kind of information that would draw attention from here to the Kharjik Empire. Damn Onsoth, anyway. The man's loyalty, or more likely his fear, stood squarely between Clade and the book, and Clade had just blown his best chance to circumvent it.

Unless... A man like Onsoth would place little trust in his colleagues, the Conservator aside. Chances were that any secrets he wished to hide would be kept well away from his office where the risk of discovery was greater. And if that were so, where else would he keep them but his home — the house Clade had followed him to, which would be empty for at least the next hour or two until Onsoth left work?

Clade retraced his route of the other evening, down the switch-back road and across the bridge, which today was free of preachers, Kefiran or otherwise. Daylight revealed the house to be larger than Clade had thought — still modest compared to its neighbours, but extending further back than he'd realised. The brick and timber construction rose to a red tile roof, and although its narrow front boasted only a single latticed casement, Clade could see a row of wider, maroon-framed windows along the side wall.

He approached cautiously. The house seemed empty. The knife he'd sensed on Onsoth's person was nowhere in range, but Clade thought he could sense other sorcery within, its nature unclear. He knocked at the front door, listening for movement, but nothing stirred. After several moments he tried the handle, but it turned only a short distance before hitting resistance. Locked, as expected.

Moving quietly, Clade ventured down the side of the house. Most of the windows were fixed in place, but the one in the middle sat in a hinged frame secured with a simple wooden latch. Clade studied the mechanism, shading the window with his good hand to get a better view. The latch's bolt was worn smooth with use, the rounded end barely long enough to hold without slipping free, yet its orientation was such that any attempt to force the window open would only strengthen the bolt's position. It was a clever de-sign, difficult to defeat despite its age — except for one gifted in woodbinding.

Clade reached out with his thoughts, wrapping his awareness around the worn latch. It would be simplicity itself to cause the bolt to shatter, just as he had done to the plank the other day. But such an approach would also leave evidence of his passage. The wood of the bolt was dense, smooth-grained, free of prior sorcery — a solid foundation for a small binding, if he could devise one to solve the problem.

Destructive spells aside, sorcery almost never produced spontaneous motion in an object. The object used to ground a binding was the spell's foundation. One could no more use a spell to move its own foundation than one could cross a room by pushing against one's own body. But there was a kind of sorcery, known as an ant jump, by which a fractional movement could be generated at the cost of minor damage to the bound object. Too many such spells and the object would be destroyed; but done once and done well, the damage might manifest as nothing more than a slight internal weakening and so pass unnoticed.

Clade commenced the binding, working as swiftly as he dared. As long as he remained here he was exposed, visible not only from the street but also from the neighbouring house and positions further uphill. The spell filled the wooden pin as he fit one component to the next, sculpting the sorcery to the shape of its container. When it was done he paused to quickly review his work; then, with a last mental flourish, he triggered the spell.

The bolt jerked as though struck by a tiny hammer. Clade peered through the glass, unsure whether the bolt's motion had cleared the latch. He grasped the window frame, gave it a tentative tug... and the bolt slid free, slipping from the latch and falling softly to the floor as the frame creaked open.

Clade clambered inside, gripping the sill awkwardly with his good hand as he swung his legs through before closing the window behind him. He stood in what might have been a dining room if the table in its centre had been larger and boasted more than two mismatched chairs. A frayed nut-brown rug covered the floor beneath his boots, its corner discoloured by what looked to be an old stain. He found the bolt and picked it up. The object was as smooth beneath his fingers as it had looked, its only defect a small hollow halfway along its length. Perhaps it had been there already, or perhaps it was the result of his binding. Either way, it seemed unlikely to arouse Onsoth's suspicions.

He returned the bolt to the latch and headed out to the main hall. A series of open doors revealed a succession of surprisingly empty rooms. Perhaps Onsoth had purchased the house recently and had not yet had time or silver to furnish it? The room at the end of the hall, however, was different. A low bed filled the chamber, the piece wider than the one in Clade's rented suite but boasting only one pillow. Clothes lay piled on the floor beside a large wardrobe. A long, heavy chest hugged the opposite wall, its red wood catching the light that filtered in through the dirty window.

Clade paused. Something was amiss. He let out a breath and opened his awareness to the sorcery around him. Behind him he could sense the binding he'd placed in the window bolt, dormant now but available should he need to use it again. But there was something else as well, closer yet somehow less distinct. He turned slowly, trying to get a fix on its direction. Not the chest. Not the bed.

The wardrobe.

He pulled the doors open. The hangers were half empty, their garments apparently lying in the heap. Beneath the hangers stood an old pair of boots and an even older pair of moccasins. But the floor on which they rested was a full hand's length higher than the wardrobe's base, and an experimental tap produced a telltale hollow sound. Clade smiled in satisfaction. *Found you.*

He removed the footwear carefully, noting the position of each item, and felt around the inside. There was a small hole near the back of the false floor, and when he reached a finger inside and pulled, the floor's entire right half lifted out of the wardrobe. He laid the board flat beside the pile of clothes and cast an appraising eye over his prize.

A flat ceramic box lay half-exposed in the cavity, its lid adorned with swirls of red and purple. Its weight and position resisted his attempts to slide it out one-handed, forcing Clade to awkwardly lever its end higher and jam his clawed fingers beneath so as to grasp it with his good hand. The box tilted as he pulled it out, and he felt something clunk softly against the lower side.

A simple catch held the lid to the box. Clade released it and pulled the lid free.

Pain struck him like a wasp's sting, shockingly unexpected, and he almost dropped the lid. *Sorcery,* he realised dimly as he lowered the lid to the floor and pulled back his exposed senses. The box was designed to muffle the presence of sorcerous objects, but it could not entirely mask them. That was what he'd sensed when he entered the room; and foolishly, he'd continued to reach for the elusive binding, leaving himself wide open to its slap as he unwittingly uncovered it.

As the pain receded, Clade looked within the box — and froze.

A rounded black lump stared up at him, about the size of an egg. A locus of Azador, given by the Oculus to those whom they hired: mercenaries, usually, but in this case apparently a self-absorbed administrator in disturbing proximity to the city's leaders. *First Neysa, now this. What in the hells is going on?*

Clade brushed the locus gingerly to the floor and covered it with one of the moccasins. Within the box lay something else: a flat leather wallet, almost as wide and long as the box itself. He drew it out, laying it open on his lap to reveal a scribe's wallet with pens, ink, paper and sand, and a single partially-filled page written in a wavering hand — an account of a battle, it seemed, between a squad of shock troops and a single defender: an earthen giant with glowing yellow eyes.

The Conservator's book. This must be another copied page from that same source; but unlike the fragment Yevin had shown him, this page was unmarred, not discarded but apparently set aside to be completed later. Could Onsoth be making his own copy? Clade sat back, the implications flooding his mind. If it was leverage he sought, then he had found it in spades. Whatever Onsoth was up to, he was evidently doing it in his own time — otherwise this wallet would be with him at the Library right now. How would Feren Skaratass react to learning that Onsoth was removing her precious book from the Library, perhaps taking it home each night in order to create his own, unauthorised copy?

Yet if the Conservator dismissed Onsoth for his disloyalty, what then? The bastard would run straight into the arms of the Oculus, bringing with him not only his illicitly copied pages but everything he'd learnt as Feren's assistant. Or perhaps Onsoth would find a way to deflect his superior's wrath and stay where he was, and the Oculus would retain the agent they'd managed to position just one step short of the highest level of Spyridon's government.

Clade sat on his heels. This was no longer just a matter of internal Spyridoni politics. Alive, Onsoth was a threat: to Clade, to

Spyridon, to anyone opposed to the Oculus. Dispose of him, and the Oculus would be weakened. And the potential side benefits were substantial. Hesca might well be grateful if he managed to remove Onsoth from her path. Hells, if he played this right, he could walk away with the Conservator's prized book in his possession and nobody the wiser.

Besides, the whoreson had tried to kill Clade twice. He could hardly complain if Clade returned the favour.

But not here. Hesca might indeed thank him, but he couldn't assume that, and if not then he certainly didn't want to create evidence of a second murder to line up beside the first. No, he needed a clean kill and an alibi that would withstand any snooping neighbours who might have glimpsed him outside the house. Yet he required a certain proximity as well, and a chance to collect whatever Onsoth might be carrying before anyone else happened across the body.

An interesting challenge, to be sure. And he already had some ideas.

He closed the wallet and began returning the box and the wardrobe to the state in which he'd found them. For a moment he considered taking the partially copied page with him, but he immediately discarded the notion. There was little to gain by taking the page, but everything to lose. Better by far if Onsoth suspected nothing until Clade was ready to make his move.

And so eleven will become twelve. It was regrettable, to be sure, but neither murder nor regret was anything new. He'd dealt with regrets before, accepted them, and moved on.

This would be no different.

CHAPTER 7

"We few are all that survive," their commander affirmed, heedless of his blood-streaked visage. "We have fought and suffered loss, yet we have prevailed. Why then should we grieve? These are the moments we live for."

— Prophet Samoval the Fourth, *Warriors of the All-God*

EILWEN CROUCHED IN THE SHADOW of a recessed doorway, the wrapped black amber egg in her hand. The Neysan city hall loomed before her, its bulk hiding the moon and casting the street into darkness. Beside her stood Mara, barely visible in the gloom, still as a cat but for the faint tap of fingernails on cutlass hilts.

"Any time you feel ready," Mara murmured, her low tone doing nothing to hide the wry edge to her words.

"Shut up." Eilwen closed her eyes and took a long breath. The goatskin belt shifted with her inhalation, and she focused her attention on the scratch of coarse hair against skin rubbed raw by constant chafing. *This is who I am. This flesh, this body in the world. This, and nothing else.*

Exhaling, she pulled the egg free from its wrappings and closed her hand over it.

A deep throbbing filled her hand and forearm — a complex, irresistible drumbeat comprising dozens of lesser rhythms, all emanating from the building before her. The Oculus.

And there it came, utterly predictable yet no less terrifying for that: the beast, its slitted eyes gleaming at the scent of prey, filling her with a wild, barely controllable hunger. She reached for the goatskin belt and yanked it tight, clinging to the pain over the beast's roar. *This is who I am. Not the beast, not the egg. Only this.*

The beast lowered its head with a grudging snort and the roaring in her ears subsided. Shaking, Eilwen pulled herself upright, the egg still clutched in her hand. "Let's go," she croaked.

She moved out from the doorway, Mara half a step behind. The main entrance had been shut and locked with the sunset, but the smaller set of doors was still lit and flanked by a pair of guards. Eilwen headed toward it, her stride lengthening as her composure returned, Mara's cutlasses clinking reassuringly behind her. By the time she reached the doorway and held the egg out for inspection, her hand was almost steady.

The guard grunted an acknowledgement and moved to open the door, but the other leaned closer, peering at her beneath the lamp. "Don't think I know you." He glanced at Mara. "And I sure don't know you. New, are you?"

Eilwen affected an impatient sigh. "Her, yes. Me, no. Let us in, will you?"

The darkness hid the guard's face, but the leer in his tone was unmistakable. "And what's your business here, if you don't mind me asking?"

"Actually, I do." Glaring, Eilwen raised the egg and gave it an exaggerated turn. "This tells you my business. Open the damn door."

"Now, let's not be hasty," the guard began; but he was interrupted by a shove from his partner.

"Stow it, you fool," the second guard said. He pushed the door open and gave them a sideways nod. "Get inside."

"Thank you." Eilwen stepped briskly through the door into a dim corridor, Mara on her heels. Behind them, the first guard's angry retort was cut short by the door slamming shut.

"Well done," Mara whispered, and Eilwen gave her a sharp glance, unsure if she was being sarcastic. But there was no smirk on Mara's face, only a quizzically raised eyebrow as she looked Eilwen over. "Are you all right?"

"I'm fine." Eilwen slipped the egg beneath her shirt, its relentless drumbeat shifting from her hand to her side. "Which way?"

"Follow me."

The corridor ran only a short distance before joining a larger hallway whose high ceiling seemed to swallow the intermittent lamplight. Mara led Eilwen through a series of turns, one dim passageway leading to another until they rounded a corner to find themselves before a wide staircase. One flight extended upward, another down, with equally little light in either direction.

"This goes all the way to the top floor," Mara whispered, beckoning Eilwen toward the ascending flight. "Comes out just outside the old archon's office."

"Wait." The egg hammered against Eilwen's ribs as though she were surrounded by Oculus; but aside from the guards at the door, they hadn't yet encountered a single person. Gritting her teeth, she opened her thoughts to the relentless beat, turning this way and that like an archer seeking the wind.

A scattering of pulses emanated from the levels above, a mixture of token-bearers and sorcerers. The ground floor seemed deserted, as best she could tell, save for the guards outside. But from below her feet came a wild, relentless drumming, as though the rhythm had been taken up by the earth itself. Token-bearers, all of them, or near enough — and all but a few concentrated at a single point, as if the men and women holding them had been stacked like logs in a cupboard. Baffled, Eilwen focused on the massed beats and tried to ignore the growl of the beast within. *How could so many people be crammed into so small a space?*

"Hey! Eilwen!" Mara snapped her fingers in front of Eilwen's face. "How about we save the meditation for later and get moving?"

Unless... Maybe these were tokens without bearers. The Oculus would have to keep a supply of the things somewhere. *And it would probably be somewhere secure — a place where other sensitive items might also be stored...*

Eilwen jerked her head in the direction of the downward flight. "That way."

"But —"

"You want to see what the archon left in his desk drawers? Or do you want the good stuff?"

Mara frowned. "What good stuff?"

"I don't know. Haven't found it yet, have we?" The beast slithered through Eilwen's belly, turning her reassuring smile into something that felt more like a grimace. "Trust me. Anything worth finding will be down there."

She set off without waiting and heard Mara mutter a curse as she moved to follow. They descended one level, then another, each passageway extending only a short distance before bending out of sight. On the third level down the stairs ended, with a single flickering lantern marking an angled passageway of smooth, fitted stone. Voices echoed from somewhere down the passage, the words too jumbled to make out. Mara drew a cutlass from its sheath, slow and silent as a breath, then repeated the action with the second blade.

Eilwen crept forward and poked her head around the corner. A wall of iron bars stood ten paces ahead and would have blocked their way but for the empty doorway in its centre. The passage behind it stretched away in alternating pools of light and shadow, an uneven flicker in the distance marking the likely origin of the garbled voices. Cool air brushed her face, carrying with it the scent of stone and lamp oil.

"How far?" Mara said, the words barely a whisper in Eilwen's ear.

Clutching the egg to her side, Eilwen squinted down the passage. Its throbbing seemed to fill the chamber, as though the egg were the living heart of some vast, terrifying intelligence. "Close, now," she croaked. "On the left. Maybe half a dozen lanterns down."

A hand gripped Eilwen's shoulder and she jumped, the egg slipping free from her shirt and clacking against the hard floor. As the throbbing eased, Eilwen was spun around to find Mara's face a finger's breadth from her own. The Kharjik woman's dark eyes bored into hers. "Can you do this?"

Eilwen took a deep breath. The egg nudged her boot, out of Mara's sight. "Yes."

"All right." Mara held her gaze. "I lead. You do as I say. Agreed?"

She nodded. "You lead," she said. *For now.*

A wry smile crept across Mara's face as though Eilwen had spoken her thought aloud. "Stay close."

Mara set off in a half-crouch, blades extended before her. Eilwen hurriedly retrieved the wrappings and grabbed the egg, bundling it up as she followed. Even through the lambskin she could feel its pulsing, the beats intensifying as they crept past the iron bars and down the passage. Doors had been placed along the right wall at semi-regular intervals, each of them closed, but the left wall remained unbroken until just after the third lantern where a doorless archway opened onto the passage. Mara paused and half-turned, her brows raised in question.

Eilwen edged closer. An odd symbol had been carved into the stone above the arch, like a sunburst above a restless sea. The space beyond was entirely empty: no furniture, no sacks or crates, only a bare stone floor and, somehow visible despite the darkness, the faint grey smudge of distant walls. She frowned, her hand resting on the wrapped egg. The source of the massed rhythm lay further down the passage, but there was a strange feeling to this chamber, like a barely perceptible scent at once familiar and maddeningly out of reach. Something had happened here, long ago — or no, something had happened *to her* that reminded her of this place…

Mara touched her arm, and Eilwen flinched. Grimacing, she shook off the peculiar feeling and gestured further down the passageway. Mara nodded minutely and moved off, Eilwen following with a surreptitious tug at her goatskin belt. *Stay focused, damn it. Find the stash, take what we can, and get out before —*

A clipped voice cut across her thoughts. "Who in the hells are you?"

A grey-haired figure stood a dozen paces down the corridor: the woman who had come for Orval the previous evening, her Neysan colours discarded in favour of nondescript black. Her expression shifted in recognition and Eilwen swore, fumbling at her belt for her dagger as Mara leapt forward with blades held high.

"Don't you dare," the woman snapped, her expression shifting to alarm as she stumbled backward. "Boys, get out here right now! Aieeee!"

Mara's cutlasses flashed in the lantern light, piercing the woman's chest and lifting her to her toes. Her scream collapsed to a breathy wheeze and she gaped in astonishment. Mara withdrew the blades and the woman folded to the floor, her head striking the stone with a crack. Eilwen hurried up behind, the dagger in her hand at last; but before she could speak, two more Oculus burst into the passageway, one yanking a sword from its scabbard as the other raised an improbably large cleaver.

Mara stepped back, the swordsman — a bound sorcerer, some corner of Eilwen's mind confusedly noted — following her movement as he stepped over the woman's body. The man with the cleaver fixed his beady eyes on Eilwen and grinned.

The beast surged within her, filling her with its terrible, familiar hunger. Yet there was something else there, too. Something new. A question.

May I?

Slowly, Eilwen raised her head. She pointed at the man with her dagger, then mimed pulling it across her throat, slowly, luxuriating in the motion. The beast inside her licked its lips, and she bared her teeth in a savage smile.

The man's grin faltered. Scowling, he raised the cleaver and stepped forward. But the beast was already making its assessment. *A token-bearer. Fat. Long reach. Angry.* It yipped in excitement. *Wait for his swing, then close. Strike for the heart.*

The cleaver sliced through the air, angling sideways toward her jaw. She ducked, stepping inside the blow as the blade whistled overhead and glanced off the stone wall. Her dagger thrust upward, pulling her arm in its wake as it plunged between the man's ribs. He coughed, the momentum of his swing twisting him slightly; then he collapsed, the dagger tearing free from Eilwen's grasp to stand quivering from the man's bloodied chest.

The beast howled in triumph, drinking in the man's choking exhalation. Eilwen dropped to a crouch, dimly aware of Mara's opponent dropping his sword and staggering backward beneath the Kharjik woman's furious assault. She reached for the goatskin belt and yanked it tight, hissing at the pain. *No more,* she thought, pressing down on the beast's celebration. *We kill when we must, but we do not glory in it. Contain yourself, or I will do it for you —*

A vast presence slammed into the corridor, unmistakable despite the lambskin wrapped around the black amber egg: Azador, god of the Oculus. Eilwen cried out, the weight of its rage driving her down, her bad knee twisting as it hit the ground. But a moment later it vanished as abruptly as it had arrived, leaving Eilwen blinking as she struggled to make sense of what had just happened.

Dead. The sorcerers are dead, and there's nothing to see from the token because it's hidden in clothing. She shivered. *So Azador will be looking for others...*

"We have to hurry," Eilwen croaked. She pulled her dagger free and forced herself to her feet, grimacing at the pain in her knee. "There'll be more here soon."

"Nonsense." Mara stooped to wipe her cutlasses clean on one of the fallen Oculus. "We didn't pass a single person on the stairs. No-one to hear the fight, no-one to raise the alarm."

"Listen to me." Eilwen grabbed Mara by the shoulders, the bloody dagger in her hand jutting into mid-air. "They're sorcerers, remember? They'll know."

Mara narrowed her eyes, then turned away with a disgusted sigh. "Great."

They hurried forward. Mara checked each door on the right as they passed, but only two were unlocked, both leading to small rooms piled high with crates and sacks but empty of people. The end of the corridor loomed ahead, a blank stone wall bearing a final lantern; but a second arch had been set into the left wall just before the terminus, this one narrower than the other and fitted with a recessed door bearing a heavy iron lock.

Eilwen halted, the egg pounding beneath its wrappings. "This is it."

"Wait here," Mara said. She jogged back to the dead Oculus, returning a few moments later with a ring of half a dozen keys. The third key she tried produced a soft *snick* and the door swung open, the lantern behind them casting shadows across the floor of the small room.

A deep chest stood in the far corner — the repository of the tokens, Eilwen knew at once. Beside it stood a desk with an array of drawers and pigeonholes stuffed with papers, a pair of unlit lamps hanging from the corners of its high back. A cloth bag had been folded across the back of the chair, and Eilwen grabbed it and began jamming papers inside.

A crack as the chest's lid hit the wall was followed by Mara's surprised hiss. "What in the hells are these? More pass tokens?"

"Sorcery," Eilwen said, sparing only a glance for the massed black eggs. "It's how they know we're here. Close it up, will you? And for the gods' sakes, don't take any with you." She started opening drawers and snatching up their contents: more papers, plus two heavy pouches that clinked enticingly. "Right, let's get out of here."

"Hang on. You don't even know what's in there."

"You want to sit here and sort through them? Be my guest." Eilwen pulled a fat sheaf from the bag and thrust it at Mara. "Me, I'm leaving."

"All right, all right." Glaring, Mara shoved the papers back into the bag and readied her cutlasses. "I lead. You carry."

They left the room and hurried back the way they had come, stepping carefully past the dead bodies and puddles of blood. The pouches settled into a corner of the bag and thumped awkwardly against Eilwen's leg as she half-walked, half-jogged after Mara. She wound the strap around her hand and wrist, her other hand reaching for the wrapped egg pulsing beneath the lambskin. *Not yet.* But she'd need it soon if the Oculus were as alert as she feared —

"Hsst." Mara came to a sudden stop and Eilwen stumbled to a halt behind her, clutching the bag to prevent it hitting the wall. The Kharjik woman turned with a scowl. "Quiet," she mouthed. She turned back before Eilwen could respond and continued down the hall in a silent, graceful prowl, blades extended before her like claws. Eilwen followed, imitating the other woman's gait as best she could and wincing at every scrape of boot leather on stone.

They turned the corner to the stairs and Eilwen heard what Mara must have caught in the corridor: voices raised in anger and confusion, and a faint but regular clanging, the latter too consistent to be anything other than an alarm. Mara paused a moment, then began to climb the stairs, beckoning Eilwen to follow with a crooked nod.

The second below-ground floor came and went, then the first, the commotion above growing steadily louder. They climbed on, Eilwen doing her best to ignore the growing ache in her knee. As they approached the ground floor, Mara slowed, her head cocked in alert. Most of the noise still seemed concentrated above them, though the voices were fewer now, suggesting that the initial surprise had passed — something that might be a good development or a very bad one.

Drawing a breath, Eilwen reached beneath the wrappings and grasped the egg. The pounding of the massed tokens filled her head, but she pushed it away, searching for other, fainter beats. She could feel them scattered throughout the building, moving this way and that, their motion making them hard to pinpoint. *Where are you...?*

"The corridor seems clear," Mara breathed in Eilwen's ear. "We go out the way we came. Leave the guards to me."

Eilwen reached for the beat of the guards. There they were — easier to find than before, which meant... She grimaced. "There are four of them now. Maybe more."

"How do you know —"

Eilwen started. "Up, *now!*" She scurried past Mara to the pool of shadow halfway up the next flight. Mara stared in surprise, then cursed beneath her breath and bounded up the stairs, pressing herself against the wall beside Eilwen.

A pair of guards in Neysan livery crept from the corridor, blades drawn. "Stay here and watch the stairs," one of them hissed to someone else around the corner. The speaker's companion glanced up, and Eilwen felt her heart stutter; then the first guard touched the other's sleeve and gestured, and they skulked down the stairs and out of sight.

Mara pointed up, and Eilwen nodded as vigorously as she dared. *The scaffold it is.* She took a slow, silent step, then another, edging up the stairs, around the landing, and onto the next flight. The egg throbbed in her hand; but none of the other pulses seemed any closer than those just below, and as they made their slow ascent Eilwen felt herself relax just a little, even as her knee began to ache in earnest.

At the top of the stairs they paused. The walls here were panelled wood, with pomanders nestled in small alcoves every few paces. Mara pointed to a door with gilt inlay and mouthed the words *governor's office*, but Eilwen held up three fingers and shook her head. After a moment, Mara gave a reluctant nod and gestured toward a side passage from which Eilwen could already feel a breath of cool air.

They passed a low bench on which a game of dice seemed to have been abandoned. Then they turned a corner and the passage opened out to a three-walled room with no roof. A wooden platform extended into the gap, its flimsy rail looking like it might collapse should either of them sneeze too hard. To one side, the top of a ladder stuck into the air, almost invisible in the gloom. Mara sheathed her cutlasses and hurried toward it, but Eilwen caught her arm.

"Me first," Eilwen whispered. She held up the egg and looked pointedly at Mara's sheathed blades. "This will do more good than those if someone's waiting for us at the bottom."

"Fine," Mara said. "But if you lose that bag, I'll kill you myself."

Nodding as if she didn't care, Eilwen tucked the egg away and slung the strap of the bag across her shoulder. *Don't think about the drop.* She turned around, open air at her back, and grasped the ladder rails in her slick hands. *Don't think about it. Just go.* Heart racing, she gave Mara a final glance and lowered herself over the edge.

Oddly, the dark seemed to make the climb easier. Despite the rickety appearance of the platform, the ladder itself was sturdy and its rungs blessedly even. The rhythm of the climb soon took over, the world narrowing to the wood before her face and the dull ache of her knee until she was barely aware of anything else. When her feet hit the ground, she was so startled that it took her several moments to register the press of a blade against her throat.

"Don't move," someone hissed into her ear as an arm wrapped around her shoulders.

"You're making a mistake," Eilwen croaked. She fumbled for the egg and held it in front of her face where the person behind her could see it too. "I'm a duly authorised officer of the city."

The pressure around her shoulders eased slightly, but the blade stayed put. "Get down here," her captor said, and Eilwen saw Mara drop lightly to the ground. "You got one of those too?"

"Sure," Mara said, stepping out of Eilwen's view. "It's right here."

Something gurgled in her ear and the presence behind her fell away, the knife clattering to the ground. Eilwen spun about to see Mara pulling a dagger from the man's neck. She caught Eilwen's eye and raised a brow. "You were saying?"

"Shut up."

They ran then, Mara leading them along the third of Eilwen's planned escape routes: past the clockmaker's shop, around the corner and down the stairs to the Beggar's Promenade, a short tunnel that cut south beneath a snarl of narrow laneways and emerged near the south-west gates and the Fanon and Acantha roads. Eilwen fell into a shambling half-jog, each step sending a jarring pain through her knee. They passed half a dozen sleeping beggars in the tunnel, and several others whose interest quickly evaporated at the sight of Mara's cutlasses, before emerging in a quiet square dominated by an empty florist's stand.

Her knee screaming, Eilwen collapsed onto a moonlit bench and thrust the bag at her companion. "No more running. Need to rest."

"Not yet," Mara said, her tone low. "We have to get clear of the city first."

Eilwen shook her head. Orval was probably waiting for her right now, but Eilwen found herself reluctant to mention him. "Not leaving. Need to pick up... my things."

"So do I, but it will only take a moment. Get up."

"No." This place seemed as safe as any — they'd hear any pursuit through the tunnel well before anyone saw them. And there was no sign of pursuit just now, which suggested they might just have made a clean getaway. Eilwen shook the bag. "You want to do the honours, or will I?"

Mara glanced back at the tunnel with a scowl, but seemed to reach a similar conclusion. "Fine," she said, taking the bag. "Let's see what we've got."

The pouches came out first, each filled with what looked to be a mixture of silver and copper, each weighing about the same. Eilwen was too tired to count out the contents, and Mara seemed unconcerned at the prospect of a few duerundi more or less, making it easy to agree on a simple split of one pouch apiece. "A pleasure doing business with you," Eilwen murmured as she accepted the pouch, but the quip earned her only a distracted grunt.

Mara pulled a handful of papers from the bag and held them up to her face, turning slightly to catch more of the moonlight. "This one is some sort of stock record," she said, peering closely at the topmost leaf. "Flour, cheese, wine. Ink and lamp oil. That sort of thing." She moved to the next page. "Same again. And here... and here..." Mara looked up. "This is the good stuff, is it? You'd better have grabbed more than the cook's inventory."

Eilwen shook her head. "What else?"

Mara selected another page. "A recruiter's report, maybe?" She paused, then scowled. "It's just a summary. No names, just totals. Four potential sorcerers added in the last month, all marked as candidates — but it doesn't say what for. Nineteen potential fighters, eleven of whom are candidates. Hardly an enlightening detail."

Candidates for binding, perhaps? Eilwen pursed her lips, not wanting to share the thought and get into a discussion of what binding was and how she knew about it. As Clade told it, the Oculus bound only sorcerers. But what if that had changed? That swordsman Mara had killed had been bound to Azador, so she'd assumed him to be a sorcerer, but she didn't think he'd attempted any spell. *Gods, what about Orval?* Was that why the Oculus wanted him? To recruit him to their ranks as... what? An apprentice accountant?

"Wait. Here's something," Mara said, and at her tone Eilwen sat up. Mara flipped to the next page, her expression tightening as she scanned the writing. "Gods."

"What is it?"

"Travel plans," Mara said. "Orders given to mercenaries. They're moving west and south in small groups. Looks like some have a sorcerer to keep them out of trouble. Conceal them as best they can."

"They're planning another attack." *Damn them to all the hells.* "That's why they brought Fosclaw in — to free up the army's commanders for something else."

"Yeah." Mara looked up. "The groups are small so no-one knows they're coming, I guess. There's nothing like a whole army tramping across the wilderness to raise people's suspicions."

"West and south," Eilwen said. "That's Fanon, right?"

Mara's smile held not a trace of humour. "You'd think so, wouldn't you? But it seems our friends have larger goals."

Eilwen shook her head. "Larger goals? Oh, gods. You don't

mean...?"

"Yeah," Mara said. She offered the paper and Eilwen snatched it up, squinting at the letters in the dim light as Mara announced their meaning. "The Oculus are marching on Spyridon."

~

A relic. Streams of light. The making.

Arandras trudged down the broad, recently re-paved road, Tiy's words chasing each other around his head. To his left, the sea lapped at the shore in gentle waves, sunlight scattering off the water like gems; ahead, Spyridon rose behind its new wall like a flower above a bush of thorns, the former all the more beautiful for the presence of the latter. Or at least, that was how an especially civic-minded poet might have described it. In truth, the sunlight dazzled Arandras's eyes, and whatever aesthetic impression the city might have afforded was overwhelmed by the combined effect of his reduced vision and his knowledge of exactly what those streets and buildings looked like close up. He tramped on, content to match his pace to the ox-drawn cart just ahead of him, taking care to stay close to the edge of the road where the risk of stepping in fresh dung was lower.

He'd left Tiy and the other golems before dawn, concealing them beneath the waves off a stretch of relatively barren coastline. In some ways it had been a relief to leave them behind. Hiding out on the road with eleven golems was hard enough; trying to make camp with thirty was more than a little absurd. He'd been fortunate on the first morning to remember the location of a half-collapsed barn that had sheltered all but three through the daylight hours. On the second day he'd used the wagon to block the mouth of a short gully, but in the course of lowering it into position one of the wheels had snapped off and he'd been forced to abandon it. After that his options had dried up, and he'd resorted to laying the golems flat on the ground and covering them with branches. The resulting mounds would have been unlikely to fool a three-year-old, but nobody had chanced by, thank the Weeper, and they'd managed to reach their hiding place outside Spyridon unwitnessed by anyone so far as Arandras knew.

A relic. Tiy had said that the first time, too. *A girl, dancing.* But there had been no girl, and no dancing either, only a holed ship lying on the beach. The second occasion had been only marginally less puzzling: again there had been no relics in sight, and though the sight of bleachfields lit by the rising sun had been undeniably striking, describing the view as streams of light would have been a stretch even for Arandras's imaginary poet. *Maybe that's it. Maybe Tiy's not a fighter at all, but the army's one and only poet-golem. Created by the Valdori to keep all the other golems entertained around the campfire at night.*

The wall loomed higher as Arandras approached, angling out into the surrounding plain like a many-pointed star. Cannons bristled from its length, some pointing over the plain, others directed along one face of the wall. Last time Arandras had been in Spyridon, entire sections of the fortification had still been under construction, but now it seemed the bulwark was all but complete. Flags flew from the towers and bastions at each point of the wall: the tome-and-inkpot of the Library divided by a slash of red, the combination representing the city as a whole. But the battlements were largely empty. Only a handful of uniformed soldiers could be seen standing or walking along the top of the wall, most of whom seemed more interested in their own conversations than anything transpiring outside the city.

The guards at the gatehouse proved similarly inattentive. Two cast occasional glances across the road from a walled balcony above the gateway arch, while four more at ground level stood watching the traffic with all the interest of breakfasting cows. A woman stood a short distance along with her back to the wall, her gaze flicking over the line of arrivals as she took a bite out of an apple. The gates themselves were nowhere to be seen — the massive hinges on either side stood empty, their steel bright and unmarked.

Arandras passed through the short tunnel beneath the wall and joined the stream of traffic following the street's left fork, the one that would allow him to skirt the base of the hill and head toward the poorer districts on the other side of the city. After months on the road, sleeping rough more often than not, his plans for today went no further than returning to his old shop, climbing the stairs, and collapsing into his own bed. Druce could wait until tomorrow.

"Pastries!" called a voice from somewhere ahead. "Fish and pota-to. Carrot and eel. Get 'em while they're hot."

Arandras's stomach growled. For all his travels in the past year, he'd yet to find anywhere that offered eel to compare to Spyridon's. *Weeper, don't tell me I actually missed the place.* But as he approached the food cart, the combined aroma of rich eel and warm crust fill-ing his nostrils, he felt an unexpected sensation rise in his breast: the warmth of reacquaintance with a once loved, all but forgotten comfort.

"And where have you come from, then?" asked the vendor as he accepted Arandras's coin and ran a friendly eye over his trav-el-stained attire. "Mellespen? Chogon? The Gislean Provin, maybe?"

Arandras bit into the pastry, closing his eyes as the sweet taste of eel flooded his mouth. It wasn't as hot as it might have been, and the carrots must have been hiding at the other end, but the flavour was as familiar as it was welcome. He chewed slowly, then swallowed and shook his head.

"Spent some time in Chogon a while back," he said. "But I'm not from there." Arandras lifted the pastry, sizing it up for another bite. "Me, I'm a local."

~

Arandras's shop looked much as he had left it more than eight months ago, save for the mass of unopened correspondence strewn across the floor. It seemed the couriers had resorted to slipping let-ters between the door and its frame, creating a pile invisible from outside that slid reluctantly inward as Arandras pushed the door open. Sweeping the papers to one side, Arandras unlatched the shutters and threw the window open. The dust covering the writing desk and shelves was not as bad as he'd feared, but the pot of ink on the desk had long since dried out, and several new tenants now occupied the ceiling corners in webs of varying sizes.

He collected the letters with a sigh and dumped them on his desk. The pleasure he'd felt at returning to Spyridon was fading fast, trampled by the reminder of how he'd spent most of his time here. *Other people's words, all of it.* Narvi had summed it up better than he could have imagined, and in that moment something had crystallised. His shop and his work here had lost whatever vestigial significance they'd held, and he'd left them behind with barely a moment's reflection.

And now, he was back.

But only temporarily. He'd sleep tonight under his own roof, and perhaps give himself a day or two to become reaccustomed to daylight hours. He'd find Druce, make amends as best he could, and hand over the gold he owed. He'd put out the marked ink-wells that signified the arrival of a message one last time, read the accumulated letters to their designated recipients and tell them all to find a new scribe. Then he'd close it all up and leave once more, rejoin Mara at Neysa, and then…

He perched on the edge of the desk and pulled off his boots, recalling the glint in Mara's eyes at her mention of *keeping company*. Trust Mara to pounce on an opportunity to tease him, even about something so easily misunderstood. He stretched out his legs, spreading his toes within their thick woollen socks. *She wouldn't have meant it seriously, would she? Not Mara.*

Would she?

It was years since Arandras had been married and longer still since he'd courted anyone. In truth, he'd never figured out how the whole process was supposed to work. He and Tereisa had fallen for each other almost by surprise, and when he cast his mind back he found he had no idea how they'd made the step from friendship to something more. There'd been long discussions about the grand poetic lays of the Valdori, he remembered, and not a few evenings spent listening to a trio of Jervian singers at a bar on the other side of Chogon from the Quill Greathouse. Eventually there'd been a conversation, of course, and then a kiss, but by that point they'd spent so much time together that making the arrangement permanent had seemed like the most obvious thing in the world.

Mara was as unlike Tereisa as it was possible to be. To Mara, a book of poetry would be of interest only if it could be sold for profit; and the airy, lilting style of Jervian music shared nothing with the rhythmic chants and thunderous drums of Kharjik tradition. Arandras had attended a performance of the latter several years ago when a Kharjik troupe had visited Spyridon and Mara had dragged them all along to watch. He'd spent the following day feeling as though one of the drummers had taken up residence in his skull, and he'd sworn never to subject himself to that much noise again.

The spider above the door stepped out from its web, then back, then decided to go on after all. Arandras watched it pick its way cautiously across the ceiling. Perhaps he was imagining things. Mara was nothing if not direct; if she had any interest in him, surely she'd not hesitate to say so. For his part, he liked her well enough, and Weeper knew they'd been through more than a few of the hundred hells together in the past year. In truth, Mara was close to the only friend he had left. But he knew better now than to imagine such ties could be deepened without consequence. Losing Tereisa had brought him perilously close to losing himself. Only a fool would invite such risk into his life a second time.

"Hah. Back, are you?" Old Jess stood in the doorway, a faded patchwork blanket wrapped around her shoulders, strands of wispy hair waving back and forth in the slight breeze. "You, ah..." She scowled and switched from Yaran to Kharjik. "Run you out at last of money, yes? Shop open now again?"

Old Jess had been among Arandras's more irregular clients, one whose vocabulary was pieced together from half a dozen different languages. Her primary tongues of Kharjik, Yaran and Jervian occasionally gave way to smatterings of ancient Valdori and Yanisinian dialects, and others even more obscure. At first, Arandras had followed her constant shifts with his replies, but he'd eventually given up in favour of sticking more or less with Yaran, the trade language spoken across the eastern half of Kal Arna. Old Jess hadn't seemed to notice.

"Hello, Jess," Arandras said. "No, the shop's not open." The woman gave a blank look, and Arandras suppressed a sigh and shook his head. "No shop open. No."

"But, letters!" Old Jess pointed to the pile on Arandras's desk. "Read, write," she said in Kharjik, and then again in heavily accented Jervian. "Read, write."

"No," Arandras said. "Read, but no write."

"Read, write!" Old Jess glared. "You gone months! Double-months!"

"Gone, yes. Not coming back." Arandras pointed to himself. "No scribe now. Understand? No scribe." A fresh scowl began to form on Old Jess's face, and Arandras raised a hand to forestall her. "Read, yes. And no charge. Read yes, silver no. But to write, find someone else. Other scribe. Not me."

"Yes you. Write daughter-niece. Tell of winter. Ask of cows. Tell of potatoes. You write."

"No, I..." Something snagged in his mind and he trailed off, unsure what he'd just noticed. "What did you say?"

"Potatoes! Dig from ground, put in pot. You write!"

Arandras sighed. "All right, fine. I'll write to your grand-niece about your potatoes. But this is the last time, understand? After this, you need to find another scribe."

"Ah." Old Jess's scowl lifted, and she gave a satisfied nod. "Now?"

"No! Not now. Come back tomorrow. Actually, make it the day after." The confused look returned, and Arandras held up a couple of fingers. "Two days. Come back in two days. Then we write about potatoes."

Old Jess nodded her understanding. "Two days. So." With a final glare — perhaps a warning against Arandras changing his mind — she turned and left.

Weeper help me. Arandras closed the door and leaned his head against it. *This I did not miss at all.*

Several of the letters slipped off the desk, falling to the floor with a gentle flutter. There were dozens of the things, enough to keep him busy for a week if he was to read every one. Perhaps he could just hand them over with some coin, enough for the recipient to hire someone else to read them. He'd been doing that a lot lately, he realised — using money to make amends for his failings — but it was better than making no amends at all.

Still, perhaps it was worth making the effort to read them himself. Some of them, anyway. These people had supported him for years, and if the finances of many had given them little choice in the matter, some at least had become... well, not friends, exactly, but something. Something that deserved more acknowledgement than a handful of coins and a fare-thee-well.

He'd only arrived in Spyridon a few hours ago. There was no

pressing demand to be elsewhere. No great rush to move on. If it took a few days for him to put things in order, so what? Mara would still be waiting for him in Neysa whenever he arrived.

Perhaps, if he took his time, he might even figure out what to say to her when they next met.

CHAPTER 8

Beware the man who discovers a truth and imagines his search to be over.

— Jeresani the Lesser

CLADE STOOD HALFWAY ALONG THE bridge near Onsoth's house, eyes closed, the afternoon sun warming his face. His hands hovered just above the worn timber rail, the one whole and healthy, the other shrunken and deformed. The posture was not strictly necessary while constructing sorcery, but Clade had often found it helpful when assembling a particularly delicate binding. Even now, despite the ruin of his right hand, he found his thoughts settling once more as he allowed his awareness to sink into the hard, fibrous weave of the wooden beam.

This was his third construction of the same spell: a finely poised binding to weaken the bridge's stability. He'd spent the better part of an hour setting the other two in place, one in each of the main load-bearing horizontals on which the bridge had been laid. Though not as complex as the grand binding with which he'd freed himself from Azador, in their own way these spells were just as demanding. Too much and the structure would collapse beneath him; too little and he'd have no chance of bringing it down when he needed to. And in either case, he wouldn't know until it was too late.

He'd been delayed in his preparations by the Kefiran road preachers, who had returned to the bridge the day following his foray into

Onsoth's home and again for several days thereafter. Today marked their first absence, and Clade had seized the opportunity to work without their company. Patience was a virtue in undertakings such as this, but delays also invited change that might upend the most carefully laid plan. And the time Hesca had given him to accede to her demands or leave the city was almost gone.

He pressed his thoughts downward, past the rail to the upright that extended all the way to the bottom of the narrow, rock-choked crevice. This upright was different to the other two beams: older, thicker, and already carrying a binding of its own. Frowning, Clade felt his way along the insubstantial lines of the spell, tracing out its contours and piecing together its function. Here was the ground of the sorcery, embedded in the timber's core; there, laced throughout its length, a repeated pattern warding against rot and woodworms. The spellcraft was simple and clean — a Quill job, perhaps, or one of the more reputable smaller practitioners. Clade continued his survey, checking for any hidden turns, but the binding was indeed no more than it appeared: a basic protective spell of the sort that could no doubt be found a hundred times over between the Library and the shore.

And one that precluded the timber from being invested with any additional sorcery.

Clade exhaled sharply. Sometimes a binding was concentrated in a particular section of an object, such as the blade of a sword, leaving the hilt untouched and capable of grounding some other spell. But the upright offered no such purchase for further sorcery. Short of taking an axe to the damn thing, there was little Clade could do — except, perhaps, to try to remove the existing spell.

An unbinding. It was years since he'd last attempted one. Removing a binding was a notoriously dicey proposition. The bound object almost always suffered damage, but the precise nature and degree of that damage was impossible to predict. Ridding the beam of its sorcery might bring the entire bridge down, or it might have no more effect than a stray knife.

But there were ways to stack the odds. Pull out the sorcery more roughly and the likelihood of serious damage increased. Certain parts of the binding would be more delicately balanced than others, with a greater potential for harm if he pushed in just the right way. And with the other two beams already weakened, even a simple break in the upright would likely send the bridge tumbling into the crevice.

Clade straightened reluctantly. *Likely* was far too unreliable for comfort. But what choice did he have? To increase certainty — by killing Onsoth in his home, perhaps — was to reduce deniability. Every option carried risk, and doing nothing would be worst of all.

He turned from the rail, stepping softly as he made his way off the bridge even though he'd been standing there all afternoon as people crossed behind him. There was nothing more he could do to prepare the site. All he needed now was his victim.

~

There was a place at the edge of the crevice just downhill from the bridge, a space between buildings too narrow to be called an alley but wide enough, barely, for one person who wished to avoid being noticed. Clade stood in the shadowy opening, his greatcoat wrapped close to prevent it becoming snagged on either of the enclosing walls. An unpaved track followed the slope past his hiding place, running parallel to the cleft until it terminated a short distance away at a set of stairs that led down into the rocky fissure. The air was cool but thick with moisture, the usual late afternoon breeze all but absent.

He'd scouted the area, hoping to find a better place from which to work his unbinding, but in the end there had been little alternative. A line of sight to the bridge was essential, and proximity to the stairs was almost as important. The last thing he needed was for someone to enter the crevice ahead of him and prevent him from searching Onsoth's corpse. He would have stationed himself down among the rocks for the entire operation, except that the crevice was too deep to offer any view of the approach to the bridge. His present vantage point was only slightly better, but the difference was crucial. Clade would see Onsoth several paces before he stepped onto the bridge — time enough to perform a crude but targeted unbinding and bring the bridge down.

A drunk labourer reeled into view, the man shedding slurred obscenities as he crossed to the other side. Clade shifted uncomfortably,

his shoulders wedged between the walls. The tension of the anticipated kill was beginning to fade, sucked away by the simple tedium
of waiting. Danger lurked here, he knew: a moment's inattention
might allow Onsoth to slip past unnoticed. He gritted his teeth,
forcing himself to focus on the short stretch of road before the
bridge. The hour was right. Onsoth might appear at any moment.

Laughter sounded and a trio of young women appeared, each
carrying a sheathed knife at her belt. Clade watched them pass, the
breathy giggle of the one in middle just reaching his ears above the
steady wash of the waves below. A gull screeched somewhere overhead and one of the women jumped, prompting renewed laughter
from her companions. They stopped halfway across the bridge, one
leaning against the rail and pointing at something in the sky — the
gulls, presumably — while her friends began poking at each other's
ribs, hits and misses alike prompting increasingly helpless peals of
merriment.

Oh, by all the hells, Clade thought in disgust. *Move on, damn
you.* But the women showed no sign of budging. One launched a renewed assault, prompting a shriek of mock terror from her intended
victim. She leapt sideways, striking the rail with her hip such that
her upper body tilted out above the rocky plunge before dropping
back to the safety of the bridge. There was a moment of shocked silence; then the laughter redoubled, the women collapsing in hilarity
at the near miss.

And there, right on cue, came Onsoth, his stride slowing as
he noticed the women blocking his path. Clade muttered a vicious
curse and began assembling the spell that would bring down the
bridge. If those hells-damned chits would just *move on* —

Onsoth stepped onto the bridge. Cursing in frustration, Clade
emerged from his hiding place, clutching tightly to his half-finished
unbinding. "Onsoth," he called. "Hold up."

Onsoth whirled. "Clade? What are you doing here?"

Clade moved closer, his hands open. "I bring news."

Visibly tense, Onsoth peered back. "What news?"

What, indeed? Clade could think of nothing even remotely plau-
sible. Now that he thought of it, he'd much rather be asking Onsoth
questions than feeding him lies. "It concerns the woman we spoke

of," he said, improvising wildly. "Have you heard of a group that call themselves Oculus?"

Onsoth went still. "Who?"

"Do you know them?" Behind Onsoth, two of the women had recovered themselves and were hauling the third to the far side. "I've heard some disturbing things."

"What things?"

The women passed from the bridge to the street on the other side. Clade exhaled and moved the next-to-last pieces of the unbinding into place. "They're recruiting, I hear. Looking for allies among the city's leaders. Have they approached you?"

Onsoth scowled in disdain. "What is this? If you're fishing for something new to threaten me with, you can save your breath."

"It's not that," Clade began; but Onsoth was already turning to resume his course over the bridge. One pace, two paces, three. Four, five. Six.

Clade triggered the spell.

The middle of the bridge burst apart, splinters flying through the air. Onsoth's boot plunged through the boards. He fell to his hands and knees with a shriek, his ankle caught in the jagged hole. The bridge groaned and tilted sideways, its weakened upright bending but unbroken. Onsoth scrabbled for purchase as the slope increased, his body sliding in an arc around the anchor of his trapped foot.

"What have you done?" he screeched as his head slipped under the rail to dangle above the crevice. "I'll feed your bones to the Gatherer myself, you bloody bastard. You're a dead man."

"No," Clade said, a fresh spell already forming in his thoughts. "You are."

Timber exploded. Onsoth fell screaming into the crevice. There was a thump and the screams abruptly cut off. Satisfaction bloomed in Clade's chest. *Got you.*

There was another groan, following by a harsh tearing sound as the abused upright broke at last. The centre section of the bridge collapsed, timbers crashing onto the rocks below. Clade stared, triumph souring as he imagined Onsoth's body entombed in debris. *Hells, the book.*

He hurried to the staircase and down into the crevice. Onsoth lay a short distance away on a large rock, buried to the waist in broken timbers. The shadows were beginning to deepen, and he picked his way cautiously over the rocks, keeping a tight rein on his desire for haste. The young women had reappeared on the other side of the divide and gazed at the ruined bridge in horror, but Clade spared them only a glance. He felt his way forward, testing each step, holding himself steady with his good hand. Onsoth was ten paces away. He was seven paces away. He was four.

He was here.

Clade dug into the man's jacket. "Is he alive?" someone called from above, and Clade shook his head before realising that the questioner had assumed his intent was to save. He leaned over Onsoth's lifeless body, trying to obscure his purpose from the observers above as his questing fingers closed over soft leather and drew out their prize.

Pulse racing, Clade opened the cover and squinted at the writing beneath. Large letters on the first page proclaimed the book's unwieldy title: *An Investigation and Compilation of Matters and Events Pertaining to the Most Fearsome Monstrosities Ever to have Walked the Dreamer's Earth: to Wit, the Famed Golem Servants of the Valdori.* The next sentence began to set out the author's method and intentions, but everything beyond the opening words was obscured by a dark stain: Onsoth's blood, still sticky to the touch. Clade turned the page, but the lower corner clung to its neighbour, the bloody parchment slowly pulling free to reveal an identical stain on the page below.

Ah, hells.

Clade snapped the book shut and began picking his way back down the cleft to the stairs, leaving a string of curses behind him in the evening air.

~

Rhothe's Bar hadn't changed.

Arandras pushed open the door to the back room, halting abruptly as a server hurried past with a tray of empty mugs. Though the early evening rush had passed, the tables and booths were as well populated as ever by patrons who had finished their meals and moved onto drinks, games, or both. Dirty strips of cloth hung from the iron chandeliers, a tradition of the bar that predated Arandras's arrival in Spyridon. Shortly after midwinter, wide ribbons of green and yellow and pink would be hung to brighten the space, the colours slowly disappearing over the following weeks beneath layers of candle soot. Eventually, when the different colours could no longer be distinguished, the arrival of spring would be declared and celebrated with drinking, hired musicians, and in some years an informal *dilarj* tournament. The fact that this typically occurred a month or more after the actual equinox was regarded by most who cared to think of it as an unfortunate shortcoming of the solar calendar.

Arandras scanned the room, looking for Druce's thin frame or a cluster of empty mugs that might mark his position. After considering the acrimonious nature of their parting, Arandras had decided against turning up unannounced at Druce's home like he had for Jensine. The superstitious thief rarely spent much time at home in any case, and Rhothe's had always been his favoured haunt. But tonight, it seemed, Druce was elsewhere. Relief sparked in Arandras, followed closely by disappointment and frustration. He exhaled sharply. He could still try several other establishments before calling it a night. The Dead Magpie, perhaps, or Dragoneyes —

The rear door banged open and Druce ambled in, wobbling slightly as he fumbled with the laces of his trousers. His gaze locked on Arandras and he froze, points dangling from his fingers. Arandras raised a hand in greeting. Frowning, Druce deliberately re-tied his laces, then forged an unsteady path across the room to where Arandras stood. Ale and cider warred with each other on his breath, but the glower in his eyes was clear.

"You have some gods-damned nerve showing your face here," Druce said.

Arandras nodded. "I realise that."

Druce's grunt might have signified disdain, curiosity, or something else entirely. "What do you want?"

"To apologise," Arandras said. Druce's expression hardened, and Arandras hurried on. "And to make amends."

"What kind of amends?"

"The kind I should have made at the time."

"Ho, Druce! All good over there?" The call came from a table near the side wall, where a thickset man with no visible neck studied Arandras suspiciously. He raised a curved knife in response to Arandras's glance and waggled it meaningfully.

"It's fine, Mock," Druce said, his attention fixed on Arandras. "Reckon I'll want to stick this one myself if he needs sticking."

Mock gave a windy sigh. "Whatever you say."

A group of students made a noisy exit, and Arandras nodded at the vacant booth. "Mind if we sit down?"

Druce shrugged. "If we must."

"First, let me say this," Arandras began as he slid into the booth. "I'm sorry. I had no right to keep the urn. We were friends, and I treated you badly." A waiter appeared to clear the table and Arandras paused, looking for some response from Druce, but the man's expression was unreadable.

"Hmm." Druce glanced disinterestedly at Arandras as though waiting for some requisite formality to be over. "Is that all?"

"Not quite. Here's what I owe you."

Arandras placed a pouch on the table and Druce picked it up, opening the mouth and peering inside. His brows rose. "You owe me all that, do you?"

"I do," Arandras said. "For the urn, and for our friendship."

"No," Druce said. "For the urn, and for your lies."

I never lied. The thought was a reflex, there almost before Druce had finished his sentence. But in truth, Arandras could no longer remember what words he had and hadn't said. And it didn't matter anyway. His intention had been to hide, if not exactly to deceive — if, in fact, there was any difference. He swallowed and nodded. "As you say."

"Huh." Druce gave Arandras a long look. "Well. Just so long as we're clear."

Arandras leaned back in his seat. "So," he said, trying for a more casual tone and not entirely succeeding. "How are things in Spyridon? Steal anything interesting lately?"

"Not hardly," Druce said. "What, is that really what you think? 'Druce was always good with the locks and the sneaking around, so he must be filching things for a living?'"

"Um... no?"

"Our various expeditions aside, I don't think I lifted so much as a scudi in all the time you knew me."

"What about that stash in the house near the sewer entrance?"

"Salvage." Druce folded his arms. "Can't steal something if it doesn't have a recognised owner."

"Or the time you let those pigs loose in front of Urjo's chamberlain's carriage and swiped the chest off the back while he shooed them away?"

"Oh, shut up. Point is, all that running around is a young man's game."

Arandras raised an eyebrow. "You're not even thirty."

"So," Druce continued over the top of Arandras's objection, "I decided to, you know, diversify. Establish a more secure source of income."

Arandras's second brow joined the first. "You're working now?"

"What, for someone else? Don't be ridiculous." Druce gestured expansively. "If you really want to know, I took a leaf from your book. Realised it's much easier to get your hands on people's money if they give it to you willingly. All you need to do is offer the right service."

Arandras shook his head, thoroughly baffled. "What service?"

"Making connections." Druce gave a self-satisfied grin, and Arandras felt himself relax slightly. This bickering was almost like old times. "One fellow would very much like to get his letters back from a spurned paramour but has no way to retrieve them. Another young lady has a particular talent for climbing walls and discovering unlocked windows but no good purpose to which she can apply her gifts. I bring them together."

"For a reasonable fee, no doubt."

"Of course," Druce said. "And before you get any ideas, it's not all shadows and knifeplay. Just the other day a Gislean fellow came in. Barely able to stand, he was, and all but coughing his lungs out. Couldn't find a street healer with any idea what to do, couldn't afford a fleshbinder, and the hospice wouldn't help because he wasn't a citizen. I sent him off to a physician I know who works at the hospice but doesn't mind earning a little extra coin on the side. Probably saved the poor bastard's life."

"Very commendable," Arandras said.

"Damn straight. Mock over there watches my back and impresses upon people the importance of prompt payment. Honestly, I don't know why I didn't do this years ago."

"Well. Sounds like things are working out for you."

"Yeah." Druce pulled himself straight from the slouch he'd fallen into and peered into the pouch once again. "You really get all this from selling the urn?"

"Not quite," Arandras said.

"So this comes from where, exactly?"

Arandras hesitated. He'd barely thought twice before telling Jensine the entire story — the Quill, the golems, everything — yet here in the crowded bar with Druce's hired muscle shooting suspicious glares from across the room, he felt reluctant to even mention the golems, let alone spend the better part of an hour reciting the tale of the past year. "It's a long story," he said at last. "Let's just say that the urn led to something else. And this," he glanced at the pouch, "comes from what we found there."

Druce made a non-committal sound. "And what about that grand quest of yours? Find whoever it was that killed your wife?"

Arandras nodded slowly. "I found him."

"You kill him?"

"No."

"You wish you had?"

Arandras shook his head. "No."

"Because I know a guy who's pretty good at solving that sort of problem, if you know what I mean. I could make an introduction. For a reasonable fee, of course."

It was a peace offering, Arandras knew, and part of him was grateful for it; but another part heard only the invitation to death and flinched in recoil. "I'll keep that in mind," he managed.

"Suit yourself." Druce flapped his thin hands in the direction of the door. "Now get out of here. I got customers to talk to."

They stood, Arandras searching for words that might solidify their nascent reconciliation but coming up empty as usual. Druce was already glancing back toward Mock, his brows raised in silent communication. The moment dragged, and at last Arandras raised a hand in farewell. "Be well," he said, and turned for the door.

"Hey, Arandras," Druce called from behind him. "One last thing."

Arandras glanced back. "What's that?"

Druce nodded sideways in the direction of the taproom. "Buy me a drink on your way out, would you?"

~

Wil appeared at Arandras's shop early the next morning, peeking around the door as Arandras upended a drawer filled with old pens, orphaned inkwell lids, and other assorted objects onto the desk. The ditch-digger's son was a head taller than the last time Arandras had seen him, but his quiet bearing and the wax tablet clasped in his hand were just as Arandras remembered.

"Are you back, then?" Wil said, his gaze drifting around the shop and landing hopefully on Arandras.

"Only for a couple of days," Arandras said, and the boy's face fell. "Do you want to show me how you're going with your letters?"

Wil gave an unhappy shrug. "I'd rather you stay," he mumbled.

"Hey." Arandras dropped the empty drawer beside the desk and crouched before the boy. "What's all this? You miss me that much?"

Wil shrugged again, his eyes fixed on the floor.

At a loss, Arandras sat back on his heels. Wil had often accompanied his father on visits to the shop and stayed behind afterwards, sitting in the corner with his tablet and stylus to watch as Arandras wrote whatever needed writing and to practise his letters under Arandras's somewhat haphazard guidance. Arandras had grown accustomed to the boy's presence and even to enjoy his earnest, soft-spoken questions, but that had been all. He'd never really thought about how their relationship might have seemed to Wil.

The boy shuffled his feet. "Did you find out what the vase said?"

"The urn. Yes, I did."

"You said you'd tell me when you found out."

"So I did." Arandras sat awkwardly on the floor. "I guess you could say it was a kind of memorial. Do you know what that is?"

Wil gave a serious nod.

"Right. But this one was about an army from a long time ago. That's why it had such strange letters, do you remember? They were strange because no-one uses them any more."

"What did it say?"

"It said, may their spirits lie undisturbed until the end of time."

"Oh." Wil considered. "Was something bothering them?"

"What, the spirits? No, no. That's just something people say."

Wil nodded absently. Arandras laced his hands around his knees and studied the boy standing quietly in the middle of the shop, his gaze turned inward to some vista only he could see. There was something refreshing in the simplicity of his questions — a reminder of the strangeness of life in the eyes of a newcomer. *Is this what it would have been like if Tereisa and I had had a child?* The thought brought pain, but not as much as it might have even a year ago. Or perhaps the pain was the same, but the anger that used to accompany it was gone. Funny how he hadn't noticed the anger at the time.

With a grimace, Arandras pushed himself to his feet. "You're welcome to stay a while if you want," he said, gesturing to the corner table. "I'm not writing anything today, but I'd be glad for the company."

But Wil looked unhappily away, scuffing the floor with his worn shoes. "It's not the same."

Arandras gave a soft sigh. "Go on, then," he said. "And Wil." The boy paused in the doorway. "You've got a talent for it, you know that? Letters, I mean. Never let anyone tell you different."

Arandras spent the rest of the morning sorting through his possessions. There'd been little opportunity to prepare for an extended absence and his supplies had suffered for it. Ink-cups had dried out, paper had spoiled, and some of his clothing in the small living area upstairs had apparently served as a snack for moths. His books, at least, seemed to have weathered his year away, though in some cases that was to be expected: several of the volumes he'd brought with him from Chogon bore the Quill's own sorcery to enhance their hardiness.

It was near midday when Old Jess trundled through the door, a covered basket clutched tightly in one hand. In all the years

Arandras had known her, he'd never seen her in possession of so much as a duri; instead, she paid Arandras and others with an apparently inexhaustible supply of jams, conserves, pickles, and other comestibles. Some of her letters to a particular nephew had hinted at arrangement with local farmers to keep her supplied with vegetables and fruit, but even Arandras had no idea where she obtained so many jars.

"Write letter now," Old Jess said without preamble, apparently unconcerned by the piled rubbish occupying the better part of Arandras's writing desk. She set the basket down and lowered herself into a vacant chair. "We begin."

"A moment." Arandras cleared a space and located a piece of the heavy-stock paper intended for formal documents which had survived his absence unharmed. "All right," he said, breaking open a fresh bottle of ink and filling a cup. "To your grand-niece, wasn't it?"

The letter consisted of Old Jess's usual mixture of the mundane and the uncomfortably personal, dictated in her witch's-brew of languages. Her potatoes, she said, had tasted unusually bitter lately, which she suspected was to blame for her disturbed bowel movements of recent days. She hoped that her grand-niece's cattle had come through the winter without loss, and the same for the girl's husband, although the latter seemed to be of less concern. She observed that it would soon be two years since she had last seen either of them, and requested that they visit her in Spyridon soon.

"Hold on," Arandras said as Old Jess completed a brief diversion about her neighbour's shortcomings as a parent. "Say that last bit again, would you?"

Old Jess frowned. "Friend-of-daughter," she said in thick Jervian, then switched to even thicker Valdori. "Girl-child is rude. Require spank."

"Friend-of-daughter," Arandras murmured. Old Jess had said something similar the other day, something that had tugged briefly on his thoughts but had slipped away before he could catch it. *Daughter-niece, that was it.* A daughter earlier, and another one now. But then, when she switched to Valdori, she'd changed the word...

Valdori. Of course.

Arandras set down the pen. "Could I ask you something? These words in Valdori — what do they mean?" And he recited to her the words Tiy had said as it stood on the beach in the hour before sunrise. *A relic. A girl, dancing.*

Old Jess glared suspiciously. "This is all?"

"Yes," Arandras said. "In Yaran, if you could. Or Kharjik. Whatever's easiest."

The old woman grunted. "Is simple. A... how you say? Ah, yes. A memory."

Arandras blinked. "A what?"

"A memory," Old Jess repeated. "My daughter dances."

"A... memory? But how could Tiy...?"

She frowned. "What is Tiy?"

But Arandras was no longer listening. *A memory?* The golems were constructs. They didn't have memories, and they certainly didn't have daughters. They were creations of the Valdori, crafted from stone and sorcery. They'd never actually *lived.*

Except there was the urn. *Here lies the Emperor's First Legion. May its spirits rest undisturbed until the end of time.* And the tale he'd come across in the schoolhouse in Anstice, the one claiming that each golem housed the spirit of an actual Valdori man or woman. Fas, too, had commented on the supposed connection between the lost Valdori art of spiritbinding and the golems. Even Senisha had said it, before they'd so much as translated the inscription.

Weeper's tears. That's it, isn't it? The golems were more than just constructs. Once they had been people. More than that: on some level, *they still were.* Tiy's words could mean nothing else. *And I've been herding them about the countryside like so many cattle. Like my own personal troupe of slaves.*

Nausea twisted Arandras's gut. *Weeper forgive me.* He bent over, barely able to keep from retching. *Dreamer, Weeper, and Gatherer, forgive me this crime.*

I had no idea.

PART 2:
TO COHERE
AND TO OBEY

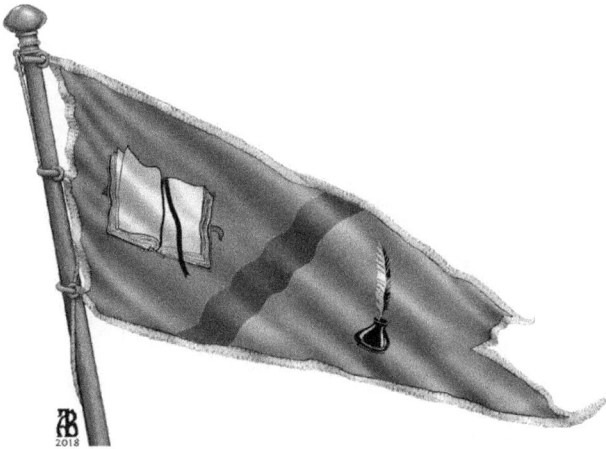

CHAPTER 9

Let us accept that the All-God is, as the Tabernacle teaches, supremely powerful. Now let us consider the world around us and ponder this question: to what purpose does he bend this power?

Not the relief of suffering; that much is plain. Not the overthrow of tyrants; nor the honour of those who do good; nor even the instruction of his creatures as to his own nature, despite what the Tabernacle may say.

What, then, is left?

— Barais neb-Ohel, *A Theodicy*

THE FOUR HANDS OF THE All-God was no less busy in the late morning than it had been the other day at mid-afternoon. Clade scanned the entry hall, stepping around a delivery woman with a handcart of wrapped bundles that smelled of dried patchouli; but before he could complete his survey, a touch at his elbow alerted him to a rangy attendant whose pale robe appeared to have been made for someone half a head shorter.

"Clade, is it?" the attendant murmured, head bobbing as though in answer to his own question. "You're expected."

Clade folded his arms. "Is that so?" He'd come early so as to catch Hesca as she arrived for her massage, but also to establish whether anyone else had installed an observer to watch the subcommander's comings and goings. "By whom, may I ask?"

The attendant gave him a peculiar look, and Clade resisted the urge to check his hands and clothing for blood from the previous night. "Um," the attendant said, swallowing, and something in the man's discomfort made Clade relax. "By one who instructs me to tell you that she is fully clothed this morning."

"Ah." An image of Hesca rising almost naked from the massage table flitted through Clade's thoughts. "Lead on."

The attendant led Clade through the same door as before and up several flights of stairs, bypassing the massage chambers to emerge in a wide hallway with an angled ceiling. Two soldiers stood on either side of an open door, and Clade recognised the pair that had marched him through the building on his previous visit. Cas gave him a searching stare, her expression flat, while her companion, Zann, grinned and mouthed the word *mouse* as Clade passed between them.

Hesca stood within, clothed as promised, a large window at her back overlooking the road to Port Gallin. The room was furnished with a rectangular table in its centre and a tall sideboard on one wall, though the table was strewn not with plates or cutlery but with an assortment of papers. The occasional brassy note of a Sarean horn could be heard from a nearby chamber, its long tones putting Clade in mind of an inquisitive, overly-friendly cow.

The door closed and Hesca looked up, scowling. "Why did you come back?"

Clade stopped short. "I was told you were expecting me."

"That's not an answer. Why are you here?"

"Your Onsoth problem has been solved. I'd have thought some gratitude might be in order."

"*Solved?*" Hesca shook her head, but Clade thought he saw a glint of confirmation in her regard. "No. You'll not get a single duri out of me for that."

"I recall being offered ten luri —"

"As part of a deal with specific terms."

"Arrest and a trial? That's practically an invitation to creativity."

"I told you I wanted Onsoth alive!"

"Actually, you didn't. You said you wanted to avoid killing him if you could help it." Clade shrugged. "Onsoth's death was an unfortunate accident, but some accidents can't be helped. A military commander should know that better than most."

Hesca's lips thinned. "And if I had told you to leave him alive?"

"Then alive he would be. Probably."

"*Prob*ably..." Hesca's expression hardened. "You have no idea how precarious this makes my position."

"Then perhaps you should have made yourself clearer," Clade snapped. "You approached me, *Subcommander.* I told you I didn't want to play, but you insisted. Well, here we are."

"You think you're playing now?" Hesca snorted derisively. "You're a tool, nothing more. Get out."

"My payment —"

"I said get out."

Clade swallowed his retort. Hesca turned to face the window, putting her back to Clade with the same brazen contempt as she had at their first meeting, as though he posed so little danger as to not merit even a sliver of her attention. Or was it something else? Not brazen, perhaps, so much as brittle: a refusal to engage with yet another threat out of spite, or stubbornness, or simple fatigue. And if that were so...

He took a breath. "This is about more than just the Library, isn't it? You've got a whole army at your disposal, but you thought your best way to Onsoth was through me? And why are you here at the Four Hands?" Clade gestured at the table. "Those papers didn't arrive this morning. You've been here for a while. Doesn't the army give its subcommander an office? And those guards are the same two you had the other day. Is that chance, or are they the only two you can trust?"

Hesca continued to gaze out the window, her arms folded. "Are you done?"

"Seems to me you're at odds with your own people," Clade said. "Or perhaps just your commander. Maybe you're an honest soldier who saw something she wasn't supposed to. Maybe you want Piator's job and you don't mind how you get it. Whatever it is, you've realised that Cas and Smiley out there aren't enough. You need someone to do the things they can't. Someone like me."

"Is that right?" Hesca turned, brows raised in challenge. "I thought you didn't want to play."

"I don't," Clade said. "But as it happens, I find myself in a similar position to you."

"Oh?" Hesca's tone was sharp with amusement. "How so?"

"I have a project of my own. Still in the early stages, but something that might eventually benefit from, shall we say, an influential friend. Someone who could arrange things that require connections."

"A project." Hesca snorted. "Let's hear it, then. Smuggling? Pimping? Some personal vendetta?"

"Nothing like that," Clade said. "Nothing criminal at all, unlikely as it may sound. But one that attracts enemies all the same. That woman who attacked me in the street was just the first."

"And you don't care whether I am, in your words, an honest soldier or just out for my commander's job?"

"I'm not in a position to be choosy."

"Mmm." Hesca gave him a long look. Exhaling abruptly, she slid one of the papers across the table. "What do you make of that?" she said as she turned back to the window.

Clade examined the document. It seemed to describe a summary of payments, not dissimilar to the accounts he had kept back in Anstice as Overseer. The total at the foot of the page had been circled in a darker ink, and a different number written beside it.

He looked up. "Someone's stealing from you?"

"Perhaps," Hesca said. "Could be that somebody's siphoning off the army's gold and sending it elsewhere. Or it could just be an accounting error."

"But you don't think so."

"No."

Clade glanced at the papers covering the table. "You must have more to go on than one set of totals."

"You can take that pile at the end. Nothing else."

Grimacing inwardly, Clade set the piece of paper atop the indicated pile. He didn't know what task he'd hoped to be set, but sitting at a desk trying to reconcile accounts was not it. Still, it was an opening.

A pouch clunked on top of the pile. Clade looked up in surprise. "What's that?"

"Payment for Onsoth," Hesca said. "Half a luri, on account of your creativity."

Clade tipped the coins into his own purse, unsure whether his creativity had earned him the half luri or cost him the nine and a half. *Probably both.*

A rumble sounded somewhere outside. "Come here," Hesca said, and Clade rounded the table to join her at the window.

A heavy wagon lumbered north, four oxen at its head. Another followed it, and another, and another. Their loads were covered, the objects beneath forming strange, cylindrical lumps in the heavy canvas. It wasn't until the fifth wagon passed below that Clade realised what they carried.

"Tahisi cannons," Hesca said. "Arrived in Port Gallin this morning. The second shipment of four. Most of these are going to the north wall, the rest east. Enough to give us minimal coverage all the way around."

Clade watched as the weapons rolled past. "Impressive."

"Not really," Hesca said. "It's no more than Spyridon deserves." She turned. "Perhaps you don't care who I am. But you should. I *am* an honest soldier, Clade. If you, or Piator Pronn, or anyone else does anything to threaten my city, I will find out about it, and I will hunt that person down, and no prior arrangement will make any difference to what I'll do to that person when I find them."

Clade blinked, and Hesca offered her hand.

"Do we have an understanding?"

～

Arandras followed the lumbering wagons as they made their laborious way east through the congested Spyridon streets. Cannons, someone exclaimed, though Arandras barely listened. He plodded in their wake, thoughts whirling as impatient carters and pedestrians shouted at the lead driver to hurry up and get out of their way.

The golems were alive. Somehow the Valdori had twisted living spirits into subservience, imprisoning them in hulking shells of earth and sorcery. And he, Arandras, had grasped their chains with barely a moment's thought, insouciant as a Kharjik slavemaster, as if they were truly the unthinking puppets that the Valdori had laboured so hard to make them.

The wagons turned at last, moving ponderously down a narrow

lane as the knot of frustrated traffic behind them burst forward into a suddenly clear street. Arandras allowed the crowd to carry him past the barracks, through the empty gates and out onto the Acantha road where the mix of riders, walkers, and drivers soon separated into a series of groups, each proceeding more slowly than the one before it.

The stretch of coastline where he'd left the golems lay several hours walk from the city. A twisted, white-barked tree beside a small track marked Arandras's departure point from the main road, but the track soon petered out, leaving him to clamber across a sandy incline thick with thorny, wind-sculpted bushes. Gulls patrolled the shore, sifting through the shells and seaweed washed up by the tide and squabbling over finds. Most signs of the golems' presence had been scoured clean by wind and sand; only a torn branch from a scrappy, loose-barked tree betrayed their passage several days before.

Arandras halted at the waterline. The golems' presence brushed the edge of his thoughts, that whisper-thin touch that had always felt so alien but which now seemed charged with vast, unspoken pain. Just his imagination, probably. Or perhaps it had been there all along but he'd never thought to listen for it.

Tiy, Arandras thought, reaching mentally toward that golem's individual spark. *Has any creature disturbed you since I left?*

Tiy's rough drone sounded in his thoughts. *Fishes. Crabs. Diving birds. No others.*

Good. Arandras glanced up and down the beach. There were still several hours before sunset, but the sands appeared deserted. He took a breath. *Come here.*

He felt Tiy's approach before he saw it: a slow, steady pounding beneath his feet, faint at first but gradually growing stronger as the golem emerged from the sea, water streaming from its head and shoulders. Always before, the sight of even a single golem marching from sea to land had filled Arandras with awe; but this time he found himself studying Tiy's bearing, its gait, looking for anything that might suggest the existence of a living being within its earthen shell.

The golem came to a halt an arm's length from Arandras, its feet sinking into the mushy sand at the water's edge. Its pinprick orange-yellow eyes stared unblinking at a point just above Arandras's head.

Tiy. What do you recall of the time before I bound you?

He'd asked the question before, of course. In the early days he'd spent hours interrogating the golems about their history and their memories. Most of his questions had met with silence, and the rare answers he'd received had been uniformly vague and frustrating.

Stone, Tiy replied, just as it had the first time. *Darkness.*

Arandras nodded. *And before that?*

Tiy said nothing.

Where were you made?

No answer.

How old are you?

Nothing.

Arandras studied the golem. It stood perfectly motionless, hands at its sides, water still dripping from its fingertips. Something in Tiy had broken through the night they'd raised the ship, and again below the bleaching fields; but neither utterance had been in response to a question. They'd come spontaneously, prompted by some sight or sound that had chanced to catch Tiy in just the right way.

He pursed his lips. There had to be something he could say to reach whatever lay buried beneath the Valdori sorcery. Some way in...

A thought occurred to him. *Golem. What was your name?*

Something flickered at the edge of Arandras's thoughts. The presence that was Tiy seemed to shift slightly, like a spider's thread caught by a breath of wind. *My name,* Tiy said, and for just a moment it hesitated. Dimly, Arandras sensed a swirl of fragmented thoughts, not images so much as ideas: a red-panelled door with a gilt handle; a clear blue sky reflected in a bowl of water; a feeling of pride and loss and purpose and regret. Then, in the space of a heartbeat, the disturbance passed. *My name is Tiy,* the golem said, its words firm once more.

No, Arandras said. *Before that. What was your name before it was Tiy?*

A gull fluttered down to perch on Tiy's shoulder. The golem stared ahead, oblivious or uncaring, and said nothing.

Listen to me. You don't need to follow my orders, do you understand? You can simply be free. Go where you like. Do what you will. Do you understand me?

The golem said nothing.

Why do you not answer me?

I answer you now.

"Damn it!" Arandras said, and the gull launched into startled flight. Something had almost made it through, but it had faded too quickly for Tiy to put it into words. But it was there. Old Jess was right. These were memories, suppressed somehow by the complex weave of sorcery and now almost impossible for the golems to recall.

But only almost.

Golems, Arandras said, reaching out to the others still beneath the waves. *Come here.*

He would find out what the Valdori had done to bind these people into servitude. He would find a way to free them, if not from their new bodies then at least from the inhibition that had been placed upon their wills, their compulsion to obey. To reduce a person to something lower than a beast — to make them nothing more than a tool — was an abomination, pure and simple.

No price could be too high to reverse such an atrocity.

~

"There she is," Mara said, and Eilwen looked up.

The city of Spyridon stood in the distance, the hill a hazy mosaic of red and brown before the deep blue of the Sea of Storms. Eilwen stood in her saddle to survey the surrounding fields, gritting her teeth against the ache in her knee, but to her relief there was nothing to see beyond the usual patchwork of crops and pastures. She sagged down and let out a long breath. *We're in time.*

They'd travelled together from Neysa after all. Eilwen had roused Orval while it was still dark, and they'd bid a hasty farewell to Den and Irilli before hurrying through the pre-dawn streets to a hostler at the edge of town whose discretion she knew she could rely on. Mara had been coming out with a dark-maned bay just as they arrived. She'd given them an enigmatic glance and trotted off; but a short distance outside the city they'd found her waiting beside the road, rubbing oil into her blades as the eastern horizon began to lighten. After witnessing Mara's ruthless expertise the night before, Eilwen had welcomed the prospect of travelling to Spyridon together, but Orval had been taken aback by the sudden addition of a cutlass-wielding Kharjik woman to their party. He'd withdrawn even further, if such a thing were possible, resisting Mara's attempts at conversation and shooting suspicious glances at her when he thought she wasn't watching.

For the first time in a long while, the nausea that had once followed Eilwen's every kill returned. It was barely a ripple compared to what she'd once endured — some agitation in her stomach leading to a slightly reduced appetite, and several unpleasant dreams involving the disembodied head of the man she'd killed — but in a strange way, Eilwen found herself encouraged by her discomfort. It seemed to mark a recovery of sorts from her disastrous expedition to the golem cavern in the wake of Havilah's death; a further sign that she was truly beginning to master the beast.

Mara stirred beside her. "Probably best if we're not seen arriving together," she said, and Eilwen nodded. The Kharjik woman raised a hand in farewell. "Don't stay too long, eh?"

Eilwen returned the gesture, and Mara cantered away toward the city. *No chance of that.* Once Clade heard that an Oculus army was heading this way, he'd be out of Spyridon as soon as he could find his boots.

Orval rode up alongside, peering suspiciously at Mara's departing back. "Why'd she say that?"

"Nothing you need to worry about," Eilwen said. The words came out more abruptly than she'd intended, and she drew a breath and gentled her tone. "I'll explain later." By unspoken agreement, she and Mara had kept their association vague, omitting any mention of their midnight raid or what they'd discovered until late at night while Orval slept. It hadn't been difficult — Orval had kept to himself, barely uttering a dozen sentences between getting up each morning and lying down at night, most of them directed to his horse, a blue roan he'd dubbed Cinder and insisted on seeing to himself. The boy's experience hadn't matched his zeal for the task — Eilwen had had to show him how to brush the horse down without irritating her and the correct order in which to fit and remove her gear, among other things — but he'd learnt quickly and seemed to have a knack for calming the animal when she startled at an unfamiliar sound.

"If we're not going to stay here, why did we come?"

"Because my employer is expecting me." Orval's withdrawal had allowed Eilwen to avoid any mention of Clade in Mara's company, but in the wake of her departure he seemed to be rediscovering his voice. *And that's nothing to the questions Clade will have when he learns I've got my nephew in tow.* She nudged her horse to a walk. "Come on."

The press of traffic entering Spyridon was no more or less than usual, and the chatter held no edge of panic or even anxiety. Yet as Eilwen emerged from the tunnel beneath the wall she saw a crew of labourers manoeuvring a thick cannon barrel up some stairs to the top of the fortification, their activity barely noted by the people passing below. Perhaps someone in the city already knew what she and Mara had discovered? The possibility was at once comforting and disturbing. *Gods, how I wish Havilah were here.*

The Neysan hostler's partner in Spyridon was located a short distance west of the gate. Eilwen and Orval deposited their hired horses, Eilwen using her old Woodtraders' letters of reference to persuade the stable master to hold them until the day after tomorrow. Orval gave Cinder a parting pat, the horse flicking her ear in response as the stable master led her away.

The northwestern part of the city was among Spyridon's poorer districts. The streets were narrower here, many of the smaller laneways unpaved and home to dusty merchants calling their wares from shop doors, harried parents driving herds of children, and the occasional dog seeking its fortune amid the haphazardly piled rubbish. The main road in these parts followed the path of Spyridon's landward sewer, an underground channel that carried waste from the northern side of the hill to a swamp an hour's walk from the city. Despite the occasional unsavoury whiff, the buildings atop its route formed a thread of relative affluence through the district, winding like well-fertilised trees through a barren plain all the way to the squat guardhouse where the sewer passed beneath the wall and left the city.

Ebek's Boarding House stood at the last crossroad before the wall. Eilwen had stayed here on her first visit to Spyridon as a lowly assistant buyer for the Woodtraders, and she'd returned from time to time when she wanted her visit to go unnoticed by rival merchant houses. The tall brick-and-timber structure had been added to numerous times over the years, sometimes by means of a planned extension, at other times simply by knocking a doorway through to an adjoining building. Rooms at the rear of the establishment offered the best of both worlds: convenient proximity to plumbing without the smell of slow-moving shit.

The clerk at the front desk was an unfamiliar youth with the first wisps of hair about his upper lip and chin. He looked up from a slender volume as they approached, and Eilwen caught a glance of the cover as he flipped it shut: a printed account of the life of Giarvanno do Salin I, first king of Coridon. She carefully suppressed her smile. *Only in Spyridon.*

"I'd like a room on the south side, please," she said as she dropped her bags beside the desk. "Two beds."

The youth surveyed a large board affixed to the wall beside his desk. "That's fine, so long as you don't mind a room on an upper level," he said. "If you want a ground suite, it'll have to be in the main building."

"First floor up, then," Eilwen said, and the clerk unlocked a drawer and retrieved a key. Ground floor would have been better for her knee, but the improved aroma in the rear building would be worth a few steps. She placed some coppers on the desk and picked up the key. "No need to show me the way."

Grimacing, she reached for her bags and hefted them once more. *Find the room, get Orval settled, then report to Clade.* Tomorrow, no doubt, they'd be on the road again — heading for Damara, perhaps, or Rondossa. Somewhere far away from the increasingly long arm of the Oculus. And perhaps then there'd be a chance to take a breath and make some sort of plan, both for Orval and for whatever in the hells she still hoped to achieve with Clade.

But all that could wait. Tonight, at least, she could look forward to sleeping in an actual bed.

All she had to do first was figure out how to break the news of the Oculus advance to Clade.

~

Clade pushed Hesca's papers away with a sigh. The accounts were a warren of payments, transfers, assets, fees, and expenses, only a fraction of which seemed to be covered by the documents he'd been given. If Eilwen had been there, he'd have handed the whole lot over to her and judged it an even bet as to whether she'd be able to wring anything useful from the endless lines of crabbed numbers. How Hesca had imagined that a sorcerer would be capable of finding the missing money was beyond him. Then again, perhaps she hadn't given it much thought. Perhaps her straits truly were as desperate as he'd painted them, and she simply had nobody else to ask.

Once again, it seemed, choosing a side had done little more than win him new enemies. As if opposing Azador wasn't enough, he now found himself allied with Hesca against the bulk of Spyridon's military, let alone the Library and the gods knew who else. So much for trying to make friends. He should have known he'd be better off on his own.

Stretching, Clade glanced around the room. His rented suite was like a miniature version of the space he'd had as Overseer in Anstice. The front room was less than a third as large as his old study, sparsely furnished with a small cupboard, even smaller chest, and the narrow table at which he sat. The adjoining bedroom consisted of more bed than room, and not because of any generosity in the size of the cot. An impressive variety of stains and blemishes marked the plaster walls, some spread around small dents which marked the impact of something full and heavy. The larger building was no more inviting — several of the other suites had lost the glass from their windows, and the doors lining the dark entry hall had long since lost most of their numbers, forcing Clade to count his way to the sixth door on the left to avoid accidentally disturbing one of his neighbours. But the view to the southeast was impressive, and the price was as low as one was likely to find in Spyridon this side of the hill.

And that was still what it came down to. Welcome as the coin from Hesca was, it didn't particularly change his position. Unfortunately, he'd not thought to take Onsoth's silver the other night; though all things considered, that may have been for the best. It would take an unlikely amount of imagination for anyone investigating the death to theorise that Onsoth had been robbed while his pouch still hung on his belt.

Clade turned in his seat. The book he'd taken from Onsoth's body stood on the sill of the closed window, its first few pages fanned out to dry. The bloodstain was not as bad as he'd feared — though the lower corners of the opening pages were unreadable, the blemish eased thereafter, leaving most pages unmarked. The scribes at the Library would no doubt have been horrified by the condition of the slender tome, but to Clade it was just another frustration.

He picked up the book and began flipping through it, pausing to read more closely when something caught his eye. Yevin had characterised the book as a Yanisinian tale of battle against the invading Valdori golems, but none of the pages Clade saw appeared to fit with such a narrative. Here was a description of the sorcery used in some aspect of the golems' creation, with particular emphasis on the peculiar earthen substance from which they were formed. Here was a verbose speculation on the golems' mortality, its style in sharp contrast to the military report of Yevin's extract. Here was a page with a break midway through the text, at which point a training chronology shifted to a discussion of how some enterprising landholder devised an unlikely set of accoutrements to enable a trio of golems to plough, plant, and harvest his fields.

A series of short pieces, then. Clade sat back, trying to contain his disappointment. He'd come across several collections like this while preparing to leave the Oculus, each more preposterous than the last. Supposition and embellishment may have served to titillate the masses, but they were of no value to Clade.

He turned to another page, idly scanning the first few lines, and froze.

I look onto a great cavern. The Magnified enter in single file, line upon rumbling line, their count vastly greater than the bare handful of ministers to whom this task has been entrusted. Our paucity is the greatest weapon that remains to us, greater even than those we seek to entomb. The One who Watches has spies everywhere, yet I am assured that Ahazedorai has no knowledge of this place or what we do here. Neither does Erushalakai suspect our plans. Madness, this would seem to both; a wilful weakening of our hand. Long may our course of action elude even their dreams.

About my location I will say nothing, save to observe that the secret of its existence had been kept even from me. Korozel and the others have spent long hours modifying the ministers' dais, transforming it from mere convenience into a further measure against misfortune. Even if someone should discover this site by chance, the Magnified will not heed their words, save by measures that I shall not describe here.

I am told that the Magnified elsewhere are being hidden in like manner, but I suspect it to be false. More likely they have already been taken in hand by one side or the other. If war can no longer be avoided, may it at least be curtailed. May the Magnified in this place be spared the horror of turning upon their kin. And may the gods look in favour upon what we do today and preserve us from the slaughter which, I fear, lies just beyond the rise.

The text ended at the foot of the page. Clade turned eagerly to the next, but the passage did not continue. A new section commenced in its place, describing the different shackles that might be used to hold the golems at various stages of their construction. He turned back, rereading the brief account as thoughts cascaded through his mind.

What fools. To voluntarily relinquish the golems just as war drew near was beyond absurd. Yet it must have been a daunting task all the same. *Ahazedorai, the One who Watches. And Erushalakai.* Was that the other of the pair mentioned by Niele in her treatise: Azador's coequal from beyond the veil? Its rival, perhaps — or maybe that was reading more into the text than was there. But the cavern was unmistakable, and the text held just the right amount of desperation to feel authentic. *If even a fraction of the accounts in here are as revealing as this one...*

A knock at the door jolted Clade from his thoughts. He started from his chair, slapping the book shut and dropping it into the small chest by the wall. "Who's there?"

"Clade? Thank the gods. Open up, will you?"

He frowned. "Eilwen? You're back already?"

"Yes, it's me," Eilwen said. Her voice was strained. "Can you please just let me in?"

Clade reached for his eating knife. "Are you alone?"

"What? Yes, Clade, I'm alone. Gods."

He sidled to the door, reaching for the levered handle with his withered hand; then, knife raised before him, he flung it open.

Eilwen stood in the hallway, her stance favouring her bad leg, shoulders drooping with exhaustion. She looked from the knife to Clade, and something flickered in her eyes. "You already know, do you?"

"Know what?"

"Not out here," she said, and something in her tone filled Clade with dread. She pushed past him and sat heavily in the chair he'd just vacated. "Close it."

He did. "What's going on?"

She took a breath. "You're not going to like it."

"I can see that. Just tell me."

"It's the Oculus," Eilwen replied, and the moment before she said it, Clade knew. "They're coming here."

CHAPTER 10

Contradict me, and you may yet become my dearest enemy or fiercest friend; but deny the import of our dispute, and you remain a stranger.

— Attributed to the ancient Valdori sorcerer Korozel

ARANDRAS LOWERED HIMSELF ONTO THE stone bench and gazed south from his vantage point halfway up Spyridon hill, the harbour and breakwater of Port Gallin spread before him. New walls reached into the sea like enclosing arms, each ending in a squat, round tower, from which an oversized red and grey flag flapped in the stiff sea breeze. Ships queued within and without to pass between the towers and either enter the bustling harbour or make sail for some new destination. A dark slash just visible at the far tower's waterline marked the place where heavy chains of sorcery-hardened metal could be winched tight at need to close the harbour mouth.

He'd spoken to the golems on the beach until stars filled the sky, peppering them with questions, entreating them to reach out and grasp the freedom he offered. Yet apart from that brief swirl of thoughts when he asked Tiy its real name, they'd made less response than the gulls squabbling at their feet. Eventually, exhausted, he'd returned them to the sea and trudged back to Spyridon, falling into bed some time after midnight. He'd awoken unrefreshed, his legs sore from clambering across the soft sand, his rumbling belly reminding him of his neglect the previous day. Eventually he'd come here, seeking calm, solitude, and the chance to put his scattered thoughts in order.

He'd been foolish to imagine that a few well-chosen questions could defeat whatever measures the Valdori had taken to bind the golems. In truth, he'd barely taken a moment to think it through, buoyed by the zealous rush that had carried him from the city. *The golems are alive,* he'd thought, over and over. But was that really a fair conclusion? Only Tiy had ever said anything strange to him, and that only twice. Even yesterday, only Tiy had so much as acknowledged his incessant questions, and the golem's confused response had lasted only a moment. Perhaps Tiy's behaviour was nothing more than a defect, a unique flaw in its construction with no greater meaning for the other golems. Perhaps all this was nothing more than Arandras latching on to some new, impossible quest to fill the void left in the wake of his confrontation with Clade.

Grimacing, Arandras forced himself to consider the possibility. It was true that he'd felt at something of a loose end lately. But so what? Old Jess's translation had filled him not with excitement but with dread. Tiy's strange statements had really happened, and if none of the other golems had said anything similar, perhaps that was to be expected. Arandras had spoken to Tiy more than any of the others, and even Tiy had only begun to say such things a few weeks ago. Perhaps the act of communicating had shaken something loose, allowing some corner of Tiy's true self to emerge from whatever constraints had been placed upon it.

Perhaps, the more Arandras spoke to it, the more Tiy would find ways to reveal itself.

Perhaps, perhaps. Everywhere I turn, I find another perhaps. He needed knowledge, not more conjecture. Well, this was Spyridon. The Library ought to have something worth reading, assuming he could get in. He grimaced as he recalled Onsoth barging into a reading booth and ejecting him, the man's expression filled with smug satisfaction. Onsoth had taken a particular dislike to Arandras in his last year in Spyridon, visiting his shop and harassing him in an attempt to persuade him to take up Library membership, then retreating to petty antagonism when his efforts failed. But with luck,

Onsoth's ban on Arandras entering the Library would be forgotten by now. And if not, he might even consider asking Narvi and the Quill...

A boot scraped on the stone behind him. "You're a hard man to find," Mara said, stepping over the bench and sitting beside Arandras.

"Mara," Arandras said in surprise. A dozen different greetings raced for his lips, but the one that came out was, "Aren't you supposed to be in Neysa?"

"Been and returned. Pleased to see you too, by the way."

"What happened? You get kicked out for talking back to the archon?"

"Hardly." Mara stretched out her legs. "Found a job, but not in Neysa. There's a huge payday waiting for us right here in Spyridon."

"Oh, yes?" Arandras said cautiously. "What's that?"

"The Oculus are coming."

Arandras blinked. "And when you say 'the Oculus', you mean what exactly?"

"I mean everything that landed on Neysa's doorstep six months ago. Cannons. Sorcerers. Mercenaries. All of it."

"Weeper's breath. Are you serious?"

Mara turned to him, her eyes bright. "Haven't you wondered what the golems could do in battle? This is what they were made for! We just have to wait for the Oculus to arrive, then go to the city circle and offer our assistance. We'll make more in a week than we'd earn in years."

Arandras frowned. "No."

"I've been in sieges before. It's nothing we can't handle if we drive them off quickly. Which we will. Gods, think of it. They won't know what hit them —"

"I said no."

Mara closed her mouth slowly, her brows drawing together. "Why?"

"The golems..." Arandras trailed off. "I learnt some things while you were gone. They aren't what we thought. Or they're not what I thought, anyway. This may be hard to accept, but they're... well, they used to be people. And I think they still are."

"People," Mara repeated flatly.

"Tiy remembers things, Mara. Things from before it, or he, or she, became a golem. That night when we raised the ship, Tiy had a memory of a daughter. *A daughter.* That parent is still in there, somewhere!"

Mara stared, her face immobile. "You don't have to shout it."

Arandras swallowed. "I'm sorry," he said. "But they're not slaves. And there is no gods-damned way I'm going to send them off to get blasted apart by sorcery and cannon fire."

He gazed down at the ships and docks of Port Gallin, waiting for Mara's reply. But after a moment he sensed her turning away, cutlass sheaths scraping against the stone bench as she settled beside him. A heavy carrack edged into port, sailors in yellow vests clambering across its bare masts. Three toy-sized wagons waited on the dock, the driver of the last gesturing dismissively at a gaudily-dressed woman. *A god's-eye view, this.* The thought came unbidden, and something in Arandras twisted painfully.

"Gods," he muttered. If this was what they bore, the weight of lives they held in their hands, then they were welcome to it. "I wish I'd never bound the damn things."

Mara shifted beside him. "Yeah," she said distantly. "Because if the Quill had ended up with them, everything would have been so much better."

"You know what I mean."

There was a pause. "You're going to try to release them, aren't you? Restore them. Whatever."

"Yes," Arandras said. "I am."

"Figures." Mara heaved a sigh. "I suppose you've considered the fact that setting thousands of walking statues loose to do whatever they like might not endear you to the people living nearby?"

"Doesn't change what I have to do."

"Right. Of course not."

Arandras glanced sideways. "I need to visit the Library," he said. "See what I can find that might help me figure out how to do this. Once I'm done, we should probably leave the city. Get clear before all those cannons arrive."

"I'm staying," Mara said.

"Maybe we'll make for Rondossa…" Arandras trailed off. "What?"

"I'm staying," Mara repeated. "Why not? There'll be plenty of work going. And it seems my former source of income just dried up."

"Mara —"

"This is my city, Arandras. I abandoned my home once before. I'm not doing it again. If you have to go, then go. I'm staying."

Arandras stared. "It's not safe."

"No. It probably isn't. But guess what?" Mara stood. "That doesn't change what I have to do."

She turned on her heel and stalked off, Arandras gaping after her as she slipped into a twisting alley and out of sight.

～

"We have to leave," Eilwen said. Clade stood before the window, his back to the room, giving her no way to guess his thoughts. "Are you listening to me? We have to get out of Spyridon before the Oculus get here."

Clade rubbed his chin. "How far away are they?"

"I have no idea. I wasn't even sure I'd get here before they did."

"Days, then? Maybe weeks?"

"I just told you I have no idea —"

"And you want to just leave and hand them another city?"

"What? They have an *army*, Clade —"

"And we have a city!" Clade spun, and the expression on his face quelled Eilwen's protests as effectively as a blade to the throat. "Neysa was bad enough. But to step back and let them take Spyridon too? No. This ends here. We're going to defend this city. Whatever they send against us, we'll beat it back. We are going to serve Azador its arse on a fucking plate."

Eilwen coughed. "Just the two of us, then?"

A ghost of a smile crossed Clade's face. "I made some friends while you were away. Speaking of which…" He pushed a stack of papers across the table. "What can you tell me about these accounts?"

The topmost page showed some sort of payment ledger. Eilwen ignored it. "What friends?"

"I'll tell you about it later —"

"No, tell me about it now." Eilwen folded her arms. "Do you

know how long it took the Oculus to get into Neysa? Two days. They had people inside, Clade. Someone opened the gates, in marched the soldiers, and that was that. Unless your friends can prevent that and then drive off a gods-damned army, we need to get out of here."

Clade gave her a long look. "What else did you learn?"

"About the Oculus?" Eilwen shrugged. "A lot of their soldiers are Mellespene mercenaries, or so I was told. Good ones, too. Whoever they are, they're more disciplined than you'd expect. Sounds like they went after the people in charge and left the city more or less alone. Except they've adopted a rather unsociable recruitment strategy — the kind that involves bursting into your house in the middle of the night and carting off anyone who might be a sorcerer." She paused. "Or a fighter."

Clade frowned. "They're recruiting fighters now?"

"Apparently. I suppose it makes sense. Imagine how much those mercenaries must cost."

"So why didn't they start pulling in fighters years ago as preparation for Neysa?"

Eilwen opened her mouth, then closed it again. "I don't know."

Clade grunted distractedly. "Anything else?"

I stole about a dozen sculundi from the Oculus, but I'm keeping that for myself. Oh, and my nephew came back from Neysa with me, and I promised his parents I'd keep him safe, so I'm really not keen to hang around and wait for a hostile army to get here. Eilwen took a breath. "I've got family here, Clade. I've got to get them out."

"Nonsense," Clade said. "You said it yourself. Even if the Oculus win, they'll just do what they did in Neysa. Go after the leaders and leave the city alone."

"We don't know that."

"I'll tell you what we know," Clade said. "Unlike Neysa, we know that the Oculus are coming. Unlike Neysa, we know their methods. We know how to tell when someone is working for them. *We know how to beat them back.*"

"And by 'we', you mean...?"

"You. Me. And Hesca Matharan, subcommander of the Spyridon army."

Eilwen narrowed her eyes. "Subcommander Matharan...

already knows?"

"She will when I tell her." Clade stepped closer. "By all means, send your family away. But you know what we face. You told me you wanted to fight it. Well, here we are, and here it comes. If Spyridon falls, do you think that will be the end of it? How are we going to stop them anywhere else if we can't stop them here?"

The beast within her stretched lazily, and Eilwen reached beneath the back of her shirt for the goatskin belt. Yes, she'd wanted to fight. But that had been the beast talking as much as her, and it had been well before Den and Irilli entrusted Orval to her care. Yet Clade's words held a certain irresistible logic. If he really had gained the trust of the subcommander, here was an opportunity unlikely to be repeated. A chance to truly strike back at the one who had sunk the *Orenda* and turned Eilwen against her own people.

"What does it want, Clade?" she said softly. "Neysa. Spyridon." *The* Orenda. *Me.* "What's it all for?"

Clade looked away. "I don't know," he said. "But whatever Azador's goal, this city is part of it. Keep the Oculus out of Spyridon, and maybe we start to turn the tide."

Eilwen nodded slowly. "All right."

"Good," Clade said. "I'll talk to Hesca. But before I do..." He gestured at the stack of papers. "Someone's redirecting money from the army's coffers. I told Hesca I'd help her trace it, but this is beyond me. Have a look, would you?"

And if I said no, what would you do? But Clade had already turned away, distracted by his own thoughts. She blew out a breath and pushed the rebellious notion away. They were, after all, on the same side.

Eilwen bent over the table and glanced at the first few pages. The accounts had been summarised into totals: daily for expenditures and weekly for income, the dates marked at the corner of each page in red ink. She licked her finger and began leafing through the pages, looking for the detailed ledgers. "Is this everything?"

"It's what I was given," Clade said absently. "What's 'everything'?"

A correction at the foot of one page caught her eye and she pulled it out of the stack. "I don't know yet," she said, settling into the chair. "Give me a few hours and I'll tell you."

~

Arandras slogged up the hill, still not quite able to wrap his mind around the conversation he'd just had.

Mara was staying.

A grocer hauling a basket of cabbages bumped against him. The basket escaped her grasp and fell to the paved street, a single cabbage jolting free and rolling away downhill. Arandras muttered an apology and trudged on, squeezing between a pair of Library students who had stopped to laugh at the grocer's misfortune. A playful bark and a shouted curse in Kefiran sounded somewhere further down the hill, prompting a fresh wave of laughter from the students and from a passing printer's apprentice.

It wasn't that he felt let down. Actually, if he was being honest, perhaps he did. But the Weeper knew she didn't owe him anything, and if he'd allowed himself to think otherwise then a little disappointment was exactly what he deserved. No, what baffled him was why she would choose to stay. Mara had always been the pragmatist, never afraid to cut her losses or change plans to steer around whatever misfortune the gods served up. So why stay now? Did she really think one fighter more or less would make a difference? Or did she just want to be present when the city was attacked as some strange expression of solidarity?

Did she truly care about Spyridon so much?

He emerged onto the Arcade still wrapped in his thoughts. The breeze had cooled in the last hour, the chill air blowing in from the sea in irregular gusts and leaving the Arcade more sparsely populated than usual. Arandras climbed the steps to the Great Square, which also seemed oddly vacant given the hour. Only a small group of onlookers stood waiting for the puppet show to begin, and neither Prince Urjo nor his coterie were anywhere to be seen.

Puzzled, Arandras made his way across the Square. Between the fountain, the patches of lawn, and the spreading maples, nothing seemed out of place — there were simply fewer people. The Library, too, looked just as it always had, dominant in fiery sandstone, flags flapping in the wind.

Except that its doors were shut.

Arandras drew up before the high, steel-banded doors and gave them an experimental push. The doors barely moved, a dull clank revealing the presence of a heavy chain or bar on the other side. The Library was closed.

In all Arandras's time in Spyridon, he'd never heard of the Library closing while it was still day. Did they know about the Oculus? It seemed like a strange measure to take against the chance of a siege, but Arandras had long since given up being surprised by the decisions of others. At a loss, he wandered back into the Square, his steps taking him toward the small knot of people crowded around the puppet show, which had now begun. Someone bumped against his arm and he paused, treating the culprit to a half-hearted glare.

A short-necked man in a Jervian-style woollen cap met Arandras's gaze, his features vaguely familiar beneath his hat. "Druce didn't stick you, then?" the man said, and Arandras recognised Druce's associate, Mock.

"Evidently not." Arandras eyed Mock uncertainly. "Here for the puppets, are you?"

Mock shrugged, the gesture bringing his shoulders up to the level of his ears. "I am now."

"Right." The stage was too far away to comfortably hear what was going on, but several of the puppets were clearly wearing robes of Library grey. Arandras caught a mention of Port Gallin, at which one of the puppets puffed out its chest and began strutting back and forth, prompting laughter from the crowd.

"They closed the Library," Mock said conversationally.

Arandras nodded, his attention still on the puppets. "So it seems."

"Yep." Mock shifted his stance. "Guess you were headed there. A long climb for no reason. That must be annoying."

Arandras shot Mock an irritated glance. "Yes."

But Mock seemed to have decided that Arandras was, if not a friend, then at least a friend of his employer, and apparently such a relationship could only be affirmed by means of idle chatter. "Same for me. But —"

"Onsoth!" shrieked one of the puppets, and Arandras looked up. A grey-robed puppet lay prone, a knife sticking from its back, while several others ran around in comical hysteria. "You're dead!" the first puppet declared, and Arandras felt a thrill of surprise and something else.

He turned back to Mock. "Is that true?"

"About Onsoth?" The man shrugged again. "Sure. An accident, they say, except now the Library's closed, so everyone reckons someone must have killed him."

"Do they really?" A rush of memories flitted through Arandras mind. Onsoth leaning over Arandras's desk, his mocking smirk a finger's breadth from Arandras's face. The contempt in Onsoth's voice as he denounced Arandras as Lord Swine. And then, Arandras standing across from Yevin in unwitting echo of the hated Library official.

His pleasure at the news vanished, replaced by an odd feeling of shame. "What happened?"

Mock fingered the curved knife at his side. "Nobody's saying. But word is that the book's gone, too."

"What book?"

"Ah," Mock said, unable to hide his satisfaction at being asked. "Conservator Skaratass's pet project. I hear she spent upwards of fifty lurundi just to get hold of it. Onsoth was overseeing its reproduction."

"And what was this book about?"

"That's the question, my friend. That's the question." Mock glanced back at the stage. "According to the satirists, the book was Conservator Skaratass's personal journal, a notion which at least has the virtue of being entertaining."

"Hardly the sort of thing the Conservator would want copied," Arandras observed.

"Just so," Mock said. "Then there are all the other rumours you'd expect to hear. Buried treasure. Secret plans. The usual." He paused significantly.

Somehow, Arandras managed to resist rolling his eyes. He took a breath and summoned the words Mock wanted to hear. "And you?"

"Ah." Mock leaned closer. "Not sure I'd blame you if you didn't believe me. But the way I hear it, that book was about something entirely different." His voice dropped to a whisper. "Golems."

≈

Clade stared at Hesca in surprise. "You knew," he said.

"I suspected." Hesca perched on the edge of the table in her makeshift office at the Four Hands, her auburn hair loose around her shoulders. "We've had odd reports from towns to the northeast. A steady stream of armed strangers passing through in groups of ten or twelve. One lot leaves in the morning, a fresh batch trundles in with a wagon that night or the next day. Some say they're going to Fanon, others to Vorsa or Acantha. The one place none of them will admit heading toward is here."

"Wagons?"

"Yeah." Hesca exhaled heavily. "Piator will want to talk to this associate of yours himself. Will that be a problem?"

"No."

"Can you tell me anything else?"

Clade considered. *About the Oculus? No.* Best not to reveal that particular connection if he could help it. What else had Eilwen said? "Apparently they had an agent inside Neysa who opened the gates."

Hesca gave a dismissive wave. "That won't be a problem. Once the new gates are in and shut, there'll be no opening them without a suitably talented sorcerer and a squad of soldiers. The sewer entrances are guarded too."

"I see," Clade said. "It seems you have the matter in hand."

Hesca snorted. "Not even close. Tactically, yes, we're better prepared than Neysa was. But there's still a thousand things that need doing before the Oculus arrive, and I know for a fact that three-quarters of them aren't going to get done. As for strategy..." She shook her head. "Hells, Clade, we don't have a gods-damned clue. This is the most arse-about-face way to fight a war I ever heard of. What do the bastards *want?*"

And there it was: the question he couldn't answer. Clade had been turning it over ever since Eilwen's return, trying and failing to make the pieces add up. Not even Councillor Estelle had offered a reason for Azador's bloodlust — although now that he thought about it, she'd hinted that Neysa wouldn't be the end of their ambitions. But why? And why not take the time to consolidate their gains around Neysa before striking out at some new target? Splitting their forces left them vulnerable to counterattack as soon as

Anstice roused itself to action.

Perhaps the decision to take fighters into the Oculus was a recognition of their weakness — but if so, it only made their current
haste more baffling. It took years to make a sorcerer ready for the
binding, and even among the best-prepared classes, one or two of
every ten would fail to withstand the god. Clade supposed the Oculus could hasten the training if they didn't mind a higher rate of
failure, but why wait so long to begin? Was Azador truly so impul-
sive that the Council had been caught wrong-footed by the god's
play for Neysa? Or was there some other factor involved, some piece
to the puzzle that he couldn't see?

And then there was Onsoth. Had the Oculus intended him to
play some part in their assault on Neysa? Had they been keeping
him in hand as a reserve, something for them to fall back on if
their military foray failed? Or had he already fulfilled whatever role
they'd given him — perhaps by delaying construction of the city's
defensive wall? If only Eilwen had arrived a few days earlier, Clade
might have found a way to interrogate Onsoth instead of simply
killing him.

"I don't know," Clade said. He thought briefly of revealing Onsoth's connection to the Oculus, but let the notion pass. The risk
of implicating himself was too great. "I wish I could say otherwise."

"You and me both." Hesca pinched the bridge of her nose.
"Meanwhile, our walls have barely half the cannons they should, the
circle's in a flap over the idiot Conservator closing the Library, and
the army's leaking gold like an incontinent sailor." She looked up.
"Speaking of which, where are you at with the accounts?"

"The Library's closed?" Clade said cautiously.

"You haven't heard? You must be the only one." She caught the
question in his eyes and gave a weary sigh. "Yes, it's about Onsoth,
but not in the way you think. This, my dear Clade, is as close to
a witless panic as you're likely to see. It seems Onsoth was heavily involved in some secret project of the Conservator's — copying
some rare book or other. Now the precious book has gone missing,
and with Onsoth dead they're all pointing fingers at each other. If
it wasn't for the small matter of an army heading this way, I'd be
sitting back with some candied nuts and enjoying the show."

"This from the woman who didn't want Onsoth killed because it would leave her in a — what was the phrase? A *precarious position*."

Hesca pursed her lips in mock-disappointment. "And here I thought you were the practical type."

"Excuse me?"

"I'm a soldier, Clade. When someone screws up, I deal with it and move on. Standing around moaning about things you can't change is the kind of behaviour that gets you killed." She shrugged. "Or did you expect me to cling to my thwarted preferences more tightly than you do to your scruples?"

As Clade stared, Hesca resumed her seat and began sorting through a bundle of outgoing messages. For all that they were working together now, he still found himself confounded by her uncomfortably often. At times she seemed to adopt and discard opinions almost at whim. Was it just a way to keep herself amused? Deliberate provocation to see what she might shake loose in response? Or maybe it was all misdirection — an attempt to keep him distracted from something she didn't want him to see. *Some other goal? A betrayal? Something else?*

Well. Two could play at that game. Maybe she was up to more than she'd let on, maybe she wasn't, but Clade was damned if he'd indulge her needling without returning the favour.

He ambled to the table, affecting a tone of idle curiosity. "How did you get that scar?"

Hesca looked up. "What scar?"

"You know." Clade traced a line across his front. "That scar."

Her eyes narrowed. "Why do you ask?"

"No reason. Only it seemed you went out of your way to show it to me the other day." He shot her a deliberately appraising look. "It was the scar you were showing me, right?"

Hesca's expression folded into a cryptic smile. "What do you think?"

"I don't know. Maybe you're even harder pressed for cash than the accounts would suggest."

It was a barbed reply, calculated to give offence; yet Hesca merely inclined her head, neither accepting nor denying the intimation. "And what progress have you made with said accounts?"

Clade shrugged. "My associate requires more documents to trace the missing gold."

Hesca's smile vanished. "Your associate?"

"The same one who brought news of the Oculus army, yes."

"She'd better not say anything of this to Piator —"

"Relax. She knows how to keep her mouth shut." He dug in his pocket for the list of missing documents Eilwen had given him and pushed it across the table. "Well?"

"Tell me her name."

Clade paused. "Eilwen Nasareen. Formerly of the Woodtraders Guild. Lived most of her life in Anstice. No connection to Piator or the Conservator or anyone else in your little city circle."

"Are you sure about that?" Hesca said.

"Are you sure about me?"

She treated him to a glare — the first he'd seen from her, he realised — then grudgingly picked up the scrap of parchment and scanned the list. "I'll send what I can," she said. "No promises."

Clade gave an easy shrug. "It's your investigation."

Hesca continued as if he hadn't spoken. "In the meantime, I have another task for you." She selected one of the sealed messages and passed it across the table. "Take this to Taroqul, the construction boss in charge of the walls. Tell him the circle has agreed to pay for the binding on the gates. Tell him the sorcerers need to finish their work and see the gates hung by the day after tomorrow or he gets nothing. Is that clear?"

Clade nodded. "And in return?"

"Hmm, let's see," Hesca said. "How about, in return Spyridon will have its gates shut when the Oculus get here?"

"Very good," Clade said. "By all means, let's make sure that happens. But a man has to eat."

"You can't possibly have spent everything I gave you for Onsoth already."

"Look, I want to defend this city as much as you," Clade said. "But I don't sleep in your barracks, I don't eat at your mess, and I have no desire to start doing either. If you want me running errands, I'm going to have to insist on a retainer." He looked her over, smiling slightly as he met her eyes. "Coin only."

Her grin returned, hard and vulpine. "Believe it." She fished at her belt and flipped him a scudi, making him grab after it with his good hand. "Shall we say, one of those every day? If you want a raise, find me that gold."

Clade made a sweeping gesture. "A pleasure doing business with you." He turned to leave, then paused as a thought struck him. "Those gates. Has the circle really agreed to pay for them?"

"You worry about your job," Hesca said, her face revealing nothing. "I'll worry about mine."

His last image of her before he left the room was of her hair falling about her face as she bent her head to her messages once more.

SECOND INTERLUDE

With wide eyes and outstretched hands speak anger, and envy, and sorrow, and joy.

— *Wisdom of the Pekratan Sages,* translated by Hila Sen

O N THE THIRTY-FIRST DAY AFTER he stopped eating, Nezhar made the first test of his heightened abilities.

He stood in the place he'd selected for the purpose, a flat patch of bare earth with a clear view of the fields all the way to Spyridon. The task he'd set himself for the morning was a simple one: to determine how far his reach had grown in the month since he'd stopped taking food.

Nezhar took a deep, centring breath. His sense of smell wasn't what it had been in the days before his childhood transgression and punishment, but the rich scents of spring could hardly be missed. Many of the trees around his campsite had blossomed in recent days, adding their aroma to that of the smaller bushes studded with pink, scarlet, and yellow flowers. The air was calm today, the leaves overhead barely moving, their stillness bestowing the kind of blissful silence that couldn't be found anywhere but here, away from the endless jabber and scramble of city life.

He'd begun to notice the improvement in his visual acuity several days ago, just as expected. But his ability to shift focus always lagged behind his enhanced vision, so today he gradually ran his gaze down the slope, glancing from one tree to another a little more distant, from thick shrub to fallen branch like a climber picking his way down a treacherous incline.

There. Near the base of the hill, maybe a quarter of a league away, a pale boulder lay half-obscured by wildflowers, its flattish top dotted with orange lichen. Nezhar extended his arm and pointed at the boulder. The campsite, the firepit, and the trees overhead all faded from his awareness, leaving only the lichen-spotted boulder and the earth beneath his bare feet. Unmoving save to breathe, Nezhar opened himself to the slow, inexorable energies at the roots of the world. He pushed his feet below the soil; he drew the earth into his legs. Strength coursed through him, and he channelled it into his outstretched arm.

Move, he mouthed, and stabbed his finger at the stone.

A chip flew off the boulder and spun away behind a tree.

Nezhar shifted his arm ever so slightly. Again he drove his feet down, drew the strength of the hill into his body, and thrust it at his target. *Move.*

The boulder wobbled, tilting away for a heartbeat before settling back in place.

Nezhar drew a hissing breath between his teeth. His body felt locked into position, a frozen shell that had once been flesh but was now no different to the stone he sought to displace. His arm ached, begging to relax, but he would not permit it to fall.

Move.

The boulder stood firm, his feeble prod not even raising a tremor.

Nezhar sank to the ground, exhausted. *Hardly an auspicious first attempt,* he thought dimly, cradling his arm against his belly. But such things were never precise. Perhaps the boulder was more deeply rooted than it looked. Perhaps he'd tried to cover too great a distance too early. More important was that he'd been able to strike his target. His strength and control would continue to grow with each day of his fast, so long as he continued to practice.

Nine more days. It would be a fine-run thing, but that was nothing new. All he could do was remain disciplined and hope that no more surprises awaited him.

He raised himself to a sitting position and perched on a thin tuft of grass. A pair of lorikeets darted by, their chirps flatter and shorter than the sounds he was used to, and he glanced after them, amused by the difference. Even birds had accents, it seemed. He wondered whether the birds back home would consider their cousins here vulgar or uncouth, or perhaps exotic, more attractive as a potential mate. Or perhaps they would regard such unfamiliar inflections as simply wrong, a sad deviation from their own plainly correct style of speech.

A third lorikeet flew past, chirping wildly after its companions, and Nezhar loosed a chuckle. Everyone liked to imagine themselves untainted by the peculiarities of accent, but only for people like Nezhar himself was it actually true.

With a sigh, Nezhar brushed his feet clean and reached for his socks and boots. The place where he had stood showed no sign of his sorcery, not even an indentation where his feet had drawn power from the earth. Behind him, the firepit had burned low before the surviving walls of the lean-to, the loose dirt around it unmarked by prints. The stripe-backed wolf had returned several times in the days following his initial encounter, and on each occasion he'd stood with his back to the fire, axe in hand, watching closely until it loped away. Four nights ago he'd noticed it turn to avoid his privy hole, and more in hope than expectation he'd spent the next day pissing a crude circle around his campsite. Surprisingly, it seemed to have worked, although Nezhar wondered if the creature had taken his gesture less as a claim over his own camp than a surrender of all the territory beyond.

He'd glimpsed it twice since, once while refilling his skin at the creek, the second time when he glanced up to see it slink across the hill just below the rocky outcrop at its peak. Something in the animal's bearing as it slipped into the dusk had made him wonder if he'd ever seen it so high on the hill before. Its movements had seemed furtive, as though it were hoping to escape the eye of some other creature in whose domain it knew it was intruding.

Or perhaps he'd simply imagined it. The outcrop was steep and bare. He could think of no creature that would make its home in such a place and could in any way intimidate a stripe-backed wolf. Perhaps the beast simply found the rocky ground uncomfortable and chose to avoid it more often than not.

Hells, I hope so. The last thing Nezhar needed was yet another wild creature in the neighbourhood. From now on he could ill-afford even a minor disruption. The hours remaining were strictly numbered. One afternoon spent honing his control could mean the difference between success and failure.

And on an assignment like this, the only payment for failure would be his death.

CHAPTER 11

The contempt visited by the wealthy upon the impoverished is rivalled only by the contempt visited by the impoverished upon the wealthy; but one of these came first.

— Vissbronaumi, *On the Tragedies*

ARANDRAS CROUCHED BESIDE THE BROKEN bridge, peering into the rocky crevice where, according to Mock, Onsoth's body had been found. Shattered timbers littered the gorge about the jagged remnant of the central upright. Curiously, the ends of the bridge had escaped all but the most superficial damage. Arandras pressed cautiously against the near rail, giving it as much of his weight as he dared, but it held firm with barely a creak. The structure, or what was left of it, seemed sound. Yet most of the debris in the crevice had been smashed nearly to splinters.

Arandras knew little about engineering, but he found it hard to imagine how such selective misfortune could have come about through age or wear — or, for that matter, as a result of some honest accident. Add to that the timing that gave every appearance of targeting a particular victim, and it seemed reasonable to conclude that the bridge had been brought down with sorcery.

He straightened. If Onsoth had treated others with the same contempt he'd shown toward Arandras, then he'd doubtless had no shortage of enemies. Perhaps one such victim had reached the limit of their patience and decided to do away with their tormentor for good.

Or perhaps not. Sorcery was expensive, and even more so in Spyridon where distrust of sorcerers ran deep. It was one thing to kill using sorcery, but it was quite another to advertise the fact. If Arandras could read the signs, so could others. Surely no sorcerer would draw that sort of attention to themselves if they hoped to go on practising their craft beneath the Library's watchful gaze.

Yet it seemed somebody had. Someone from out of town, perhaps, who didn't plan to stay. Or someone who had decided that the cost of so public a killing was worth the reward.

Conservator Skaratass's pet project, Mock had called it. The book that Onsoth had supposedly had custody of, and had perhaps even been carrying the night of his death. A book about golems, or so Mock had claimed. And if the rest of Mock's story checked out, as it seemed to, then perhaps that part was also true.

"Are you Arandras?" An unshaven man stood a few paces from the edge of the gorge, his bearing that of an ex-soldier or a ship's mate. Three others stood behind him with matching expressions of dour intent. He grunted at something in Arandras's response and gave a minute nod. "We need to talk."

Arandras scratched his beard. "About what?"

"Not here." The man gestured in the direction of an alley a short distance away. "Follow me, please."

"No, I don't think I will." Turning deliberately, Arandras wandered to the side of the street. "We can talk here," he said, putting his back to a windowless brick wall and folding his arms. "Out in the open, like the respectable people I'm sure you all are. Or you can tell your friends to leave and we can go find a bar."

The man frowned. "This isn't a negotiation —"

"Good," Arandras said, and waited.

One of the man's companions, a burly woman with a blade tattooed on her cheek, glared at Arandras and muttered something in her leader's ear. The man gave Arandras a long look, evidently considering the woman's suggestion, then slowly shook his head and stepped closer to Arandras.

"Very well," he said softly, his breath warm on Arandras's face. His companions crowded behind him, the tattooed woman staring openly at Arandras over the leader's shoulder while the others scanned the street. "Mistress Agli of the city circle has a business proposition for you."

"And is Mistress Agli in the habit of conducting her business through such obliging intermediaries as yourselves?" Arandras asked, forcing himself to hold the man's gaze. "Or have I somehow merited special attention?"

The man smiled coolly. "You can ask her yourself. We have a carriage waiting just around the corner."

"You'll forgive me if I require a little more information before I agree to go anywhere with you and your friends."

"Come, now," the man said, his voice barely more than a whisper. "You have at your disposal a unique service. Mistress Agli wishes to buy it. She also wishes to ensure your safety while you are her guest —"

"No," Arandras snapped. "No deal."

"Mistress Agli wishes to discuss it with you in person —"

"Too bad. You can tell Mistress Agli that the service she seeks is no longer available. Not to her, and not to anyone else."

The man grabbed Arandras's forearm, the strength of his grip causing Arandras to gasp involuntarily. Before he could recover, the tattooed woman stepped forward and seized his other arm. "We'll see," she said, smirking at his expression as they dragged him around and began marching him down the street.

"Going somewhere?" someone said, and Arandras looked up to see Mara standing a few paces away, one hand resting on a cutlass hilt. *Thank the Weeper.*

"This is city circle business," the tattooed woman barked. "Be smart and piss off."

"Funny," Mara said, half-drawing the cutlass. "That's just what I was going to say to you."

The leader glared, his grip flexing around Arandras's arm. "Pretty sure you can't take all of us at once," he said.

"Ah. And how sure is that, exactly?"

The man fell silent. Several passers-by had halted near the bridge and now watched the stand-off with a combination of wariness and curiosity. Scowling, the man shoved Arandras forward and released his arm. "You've made a bad mistake."

"Well, that makes —" Mara broke off to conduct a quick count. "Five of us. Is that right? Yes."

Glowering, the man and his companions stalked off, leaving Arandras alone before Mara and the knots of gawking passers-by. "Thank you," he said. She caught his arm and herded him in the opposite direction as the reality of what had just happened began to sink in. "Weeper's tears. That was not good."

"Agli's people, were they?"

"So they said." Arandras drew a shaky breath. "You can guess what they wanted. How in the hells did they find out?"

"It was bound to happen sooner or later, wasn't it?" Mara said. "You're lucky it was the merchants. If Piator Pronn decides he wants a chat, his pickup detail won't be nearly so easy to deter."

"Gods. Thank you for that cheerful thought." The street widened and they drew to a halt, Arandras trying to gather his thoughts. "Look, I'm sorry about yesterday. Spyridon's your home. I understand that. I just... can't do what you want me to do."

"Are you sure you know what I want you to do?"

"What? Of course I do. You want me to use the golems to defend the city." He paused. "Don't you?"

Mara gave him a look of mock-forbearance.

Arandras's brows rose. "What, then?"

"Tell me again why you have to leave Spyridon."

"You mean apart from the bit about possibly getting my head stoved in by a stray cannonball?"

"Yes. Apart from that."

"Well, I —" Understanding dawned. *You just want me to stay.*

"I've taken a contract to guard an estate up on the hill," Mara said. "It seems the owner was seized with a sudden and urgent need to take his family, his household, and as many valuables as they could all carry off to Rondossa." She glanced at him sidelong. "And I gather there's a book hiding somewhere in the city which might be of some small interest to you."

"You heard about that, huh?"

"You don't think I came past by chance, do you?" Mara gestured with her chin back toward the broken bridge. "Might be I can find someone who saw what happened."

"Is that right?"

A smile played about her lips. "Might be I already have."

Arandras considered her. "Well, when you put it like that," he said. "This estate of yours. How's the view?"

~

By the time Clade reached the construction office near the east gate-house, the sun was high overhead and his belly was reminding him of the hours that had passed since he last supplied it with food. The office consisted of a large, almost military-style tent, the canvas stained brown and marked with a pale blob that vaguely recalled a bricklayer's trowel. A remarkable array of tools and materials filled the surrounding yard: bricks, stones, and lengths of timber; barrels of ash and lime for mortar; racks of hammers, saws, and chisels, several bearing some form of enchantment; a smith's furnace in the corner; two smaller tents, within which Clade could sense more sorcery-bound items; and there, propped beside a ladder against the city's new wall, two massive gates of thick metal, each more than twice Clade's height.

Most of the workers seemed occupied with some task or other — either carrying something or else hitting one object with another, as far as Clade could tell — but near the middle of the yard he spotted a table of four labourers eating pastries around a game of tiles. A Sarean woman looked up at his approach, brows raised beneath a mop of unruly hair. "Help you?"

"I'm looking for Taroqul," Clade said, his withered fingers brushing the sealed missive in his greatcoat pocket.

"He's up on the wall," the Sarean said. "Leave your message with Burr in the office."

"Actually, I need to speak with him directly."

The Sarean rolled her eyes. "Hey! Burr!" she bellowed, startling both Clade and a gull that had just alighted on one of the gates. With a last glance at Clade, she turned back to her lunch.

A short, bespectacled man emerged from the tent, both hands raised to shade his eyes against the sun. He peered around the yard, a bemused scowl on his face. "Who called?"

"Master Burr, is it?" Clade said, striding forward. "My name is Clade. I have a message for Taroqul."

"Oh, is that all?" Burr stuck out a hand. "I'll pass it on."

"You misunderstand," Clade said. "I must deliver this message to Taroqul myself."

"All right." Burr pointed up to a tower along the wall where two people could just be seen behind the battlements. "That's Taroqul there. How good are your lungs?"

Clade frowned. "When will he return?"

"Whenever he chooses to." Burr gestured to the street, where a woman with a half-eaten apple peered curiously toward them. "If you're going to wait, do it outside. I won't have you getting in the way."

"I'll go to him, then," Clade said.

"No, my friend, you won't. No-one's allowed up there without leave of a duly authorised representative of the Spyridon army."

"Ah." Clade drew out Hesca's message. "Would that be the same army whose seal you see here?"

Burr peered at the paper. "Fine," he said abruptly. "Whatever. Ladder's over there."

"Wait." Clade slid the message back into his pocket. "Surely there must be stairs somewhere."

"Indeed there are," Burr said. "Take that seal of yours to the gatehouse and maybe the soldiers will let you use them. Here, it's the ladder or wait."

Clade scowled. There was no telling what reception he might find at the gatehouse. But to climb the ladder with just one good hand… He looked at it across the yard, following it past the top of the unmounted gates and up to the edge of the wall. Suddenly it seemed like a very long way.

A murmured question and chuckle drew his attention to the Sarean woman and her companions. Two seemed to be concluding some sort of wager as the others watched on with lazy amusement. His scowl deepening, Clade turned back to Burr.

"Right," he said. "Ladder it is."

He stalked across the yard, doing his best to ignore the eyes on his back and focus on corralling his nerves. The ladder seemed

sturdy enough, the uprights smooth beneath his hand and reassuringly thick, the rungs grimed with dirt but not unduly worn. Clade
stepped experimentally onto the first rung, bouncing slightly to test
its stability. The ladder didn't move.

He climbed.

The first dozen or so rungs felt just as solid as the first, but as
Clade climbed higher the ladder began to creak and shift beneath
him. He slowed his movements, trying to make them as smooth as
possible: reach for the next hold with his good hand, step with one
foot, then the other, reach, step, step, all the while holding his coat
to his body with his withered hand.

An insect flitted across his vision and alighted on his cheek.
Clade blew at it from the corner of his mouth and it darted away,
leaving a faint tingle on his skin. He climbed higher, coattails flapping about his knees, his every move now setting off some corre-
sponding motion in the ladder. Reach, step, step; reach, step, step;
and then he was up, clambering past the hooks that held the ladder
in place and onto the walkway atop the wall.

Wobbly with relief, Clade looked back down at the yard. Money
was changing hands among the tile players — as he watched, the
Sarean woman glanced up and extended a raised thumb. Burr was
nowhere to be seen; elsewhere, most of the labourers were returning
to their tasks or had never left them in the first place. Clade closed
his eyes and drew a long, centring breath. *Perhaps I'll try the stairs
on the way down.*

Viewed from the top of the wall, the towers could be seen for
what they were: little more than roofed platforms positioned at out-
thrust points where the range of fire was presumably greatest. Clade
started toward the nearby redoubt where the men Burr had pointed
to now crouched beside a set of gleaming cannons. The battlements
on the wall's outer side reached nearly to Clade's head, and he found
himself hurrying down the broad walkway with almost as much
ease as if he'd been at ground level. The men straightened as he drew
near, a soldier with a major's epaulettes frowning thoughtfully at the
cannons while the other man, darker of skin and wearing civilian
clothes, looked at Clade inquiringly.

"Taroqul?" Clade said, and the civilian nodded slightly. "I have a message for you."

Taroqul's broad face folded into an expression of wry amusement. "You might have left it with Burr and saved yourself a climb."

"I'm afraid it couldn't wait." Clade reached for Hesca's letter, then glanced at the major and hesitated. "Could we speak privately?"

The major glanced distractedly at Taroqul. "Find me in the gatehouse when you're done." He wandered away, lost in thought.

"So," Taroqul said when the major was out of earshot. "A message both secret and urgent. Why do I find myself bracing for bad news?"

Clade withdrew the sealed paper and passed it over. "Subcommander Matharan bids you bind and install the gates as soon as you can."

"Does she indeed?" Taroqul broke the seal and opened the papers. "A moment, if you please."

As Taroqul read the message, Clade glanced idly about the tower. No fewer than half a dozen cannon-sized embrasures had been built into the outer wall, though only two guns had as yet been installed. Between the merlons, Clade could see all the way from the coast to the northeastern hills. A company of perhaps fifty soldiers in Spyridon livery were nearing the city on the eastern road, the lack of interest from the gatehouse suggesting that their arrival was expected.

"You sweeten her words," Taroqul said, folding the message in his hands. "The subcommander threatens to withhold payment unless the sorcery is completed and the gates hung three days from now."

"Will that be a problem?"

"Were I confident of her capacity to pay, no." Taroqul studied Clade, the mildness of his expression almost enough to conceal the shrewd gleam in his eyes. "Tell me, nameless messenger. Should I be confident?"

"You should."

"It was the city circle that ordered me to delay the sorcery on account of — how did they put it? Ah, yes. 'Immoderate and unwarranted costs.' Yet the instructions you bring me come not from the circle, not even from Commander Pronn, but from his subcommander. Why, precisely, should I now feel confident of receiving payment?"

Clade met his gaze. "Because a city with gates has a much greater capacity to settle its debts than a city without them."

"Ah. I see." Taroqul gave a wry smile. "How far away are they, then?"

"I don't know," Clade said. "Not far."

"It does rather depress the craftsman in me, I fear," Taroqul said. "To build something for the express purpose of watching someone else try to tear it down. How long will our work stand unmolested, do you think? Weeks? Days?" He shrugged. "But my purse scoffs at such considerations. Ensure that it is filled, and the rest of me will fall grudgingly into line."

"Subcommander Matharan will be delighted to hear it."

"Perhaps not," Taroqul said. "Tell her I will see to it that the gates are finished by evening three days hence. And tell her that my fee to expedite this work will consist of an additional forty-five luri."

For a moment, Clade wasn't sure he'd heard correctly. *"Forty-five luri?"*

"Yes," Taroqul said mildly. "Will that be a problem? Or do you need to run back to the subcommander to check?"

Clade swallowed. To find Hesca, gain approval for the payment, and return to Taroqul might take half a day. "No," he forced out. "An additional forty-five luri if the gates are hung in three days' time."

"Splendid. And just so there is no confusion later about who said what to whom: tell me, my good messenger, what is your name?"

There was no evading the question. Not if he wanted to be sure the work would be done. An undefended city, or the prospect of an unhappy creditor? Really, it was no choice at all.

"My name is Clade."

~

Eilwen perched on the low, roughly made stool, her chin in her hands, and stared at the papers spread across her bed. A man wearing a dark cloak had appeared at her door before sunrise, waking her and Orval both with his insistent knocking, but when she roused herself and opened the door he'd simply dumped a string-bound bundle of documents in her arms and left without a word. She'd more than half expected Subcommander Matharan to refuse her relayed request for more detailed accounts, or at least to supply only a selection of the documents she'd asked for. But her request seemed to have been met in full, at least so far as the past several months were concerned, suggesting that Hesca was either woefully indiscreet or even more desperate than Clade had indicated.

Neither option was particularly encouraging.

Yet so far, none of the additional accounts had revealed anything untoward. Money came in as it was supposed to. Money was spent, each transaction of itself seemingly unremarkable. But when the reserves were assessed at the end of each week, the total was never as much as it should be.

In other circumstances, Eilwen would have judged it to be a simple matter of repeated theft. But the amounts that had gone missing would have required a handcart to shift, and surely no-one could have moved cartloads of coin out of the army's vaults week after week without raising some rather pointed questions.

Loud barks from outside pulled Eilwen's attention from the papers to the room's lone window. She crossed the room and swung the window open, peering into the dusty lane one floor below. A plump, pale-skinned woman laden with an improbable array of bags and sacks seemed to have dropped one of her smaller bags and carried on for half a dozen paces before realising it. A short-haired dog now stood across the bag, snarling at the woman and barking whenever she tried to approach. And behind the animal sat Orval, his back to the neighbouring building's wall, watching the encounter but making no move to intervene.

Scowling, Eilwen thrust her head through the window. "Hey! Orval! You going to help her get her bag back?"

Orval glanced up, then pointedly looked away. The woman edged hopefully toward her bag, prompting a fresh volley of angry barks. "Orval!" Eilwen shouted as the woman extended a tentative hand. The dog's barking grew increasingly frenzied until at last it lunged forward, snapping at the woman's outstretched fingers. Shrieking, she jerked her hand away and scurried back to a safe distance, cursing the dog, Orval, and Eilwen herself in an unfamiliar, northern-accented tongue.

Damn it! Eilwen pulled the window shut and hurried from the room, sparing just enough thought to lock the door behind her and pocket the key. She strode down the stairs and out to the rear of Ebek's Boarding House, where she found Orval still sitting on the ground, the dog with its nose buried in its prize and the plump woman nowhere to be seen.

"She's gone," Orval said, his bland tone belied by a spark of challenge in his expression.

Frowning, Eilwen crossed the lane. "You didn't help her."

Orval shrugged. "She shouldn't have dropped it in the first place."

"Maybe not. But she did."

"Yes. And now Jak gets to eat."

The dog had retrieved a haunch of meat from the bag and was now tearing the flesh from the bone and gulping it down. From here Eilwen could see what she hadn't noticed before: the dog was gaunt, its ribs clearly visible beneath its short, reddish fur. It caught her gaze and tensed, a low growl sounding in its throat.

Reluctantly, Eilwen looked away. "Who told you its name?"

Orval shrugged again. "He looks like a Jak."

Eilwen leaned wearily against the wall. She'd promised Den that she'd look after his son, and at the time it had seemed straightforward enough. Truth be told, in her mind it had more or less come down to feeding the boy and maintaining a sensible distance from Neysa. The notion of acting as a substitute parent hadn't even occurred to her. *How would Den deal with whatever the hells this is? Would he push back? Ignore it? Sit down and try to reason with the boy? Gods, where do I start?*

"It's a stray, Orval," she said.

"So?"

"So there's no sense in getting attached —"

"Why?" Orval gave her a sullen glare. "Because we're not staying?"

Eilwen hesitated. She'd extended their room booking the previous day but hadn't yet mentioned it to Orval. Perhaps he'd found out somehow and that was the reason for his recalcitrance. "There's been a change of plans," she said. "My employer needs me to stay for a while."

Something flickered in Orval's eyes. "How long?"

Until the Oculus come and put the city to siege. Eilwen looked away. She and Orval should be on the road right now, for Den's sake if no-one else's. But Clade was right. Here was an opportunity to strike back at the thrice-damned Oculus. And even if they failed and the Oculus won, there'd be nothing to stop the two of them from simply walking away as they had from Neysa.

She'd promised Den that she'd keep the boy safe, and so she would. And perhaps she could do something else for him as well.

She lowered herself to a crouch, the twinge in her knee warning her that she had only a few moments in this position before it began to ache in earnest. "I need to tell you something, Orval," she said. "Just between us. No word of this back to your parents. Understand?"

Orval nodded warily.

"I said before that I'm working as a trader. Truth is, there's more to it than that. My employer isn't really a merchant. I don't know what word would fit, exactly. But he's working very hard to fight the people who attacked your city and took your sister. I've been helping him, even before I heard about Vess." She paused. "There might be a way that you could help, too. If you want to."

"Are you saying you're a spy?" Orval asked.

"Gods, no," Eilwen said, then thought of her raid with Mara on the city hall in Neysa. "Not exactly. It's complicated." Her knee was beginning to throb, and she set the question aside and pressed on. "You can think about it, if you like. There's no rush. But if you decide you're interested, tell me."

Orval nodded slightly, his eyes meeting hers for only a moment before shifting back to the dog, who had finished its meal and was now gnawing on the bone. Somewhat nettled by Orval's muted response, Eilwen pushed herself upright. *You'd think I'd just suggested there's a good chance the sun's going to rise tomorrow. Gods help me.*

Perhaps, she thought as she made her way back to their room, she'd been overly hasty when she agreed to Den's request. But what else could she have done? Den was family, and so was Orval. Of course she'd agreed. Yet she couldn't help wondering if they'd still have asked for her help if she had told them what she'd just told their son.

The documents lay on the bed where she had left them, unmoved save for the slight riffling of the breeze. Sighing, Eilwen resumed her perch on the stool and surveyed the spread of numbers. As obvious an explanation as it seemed, straightforward theft was unlikely to pose so deep a conundrum as to prompt the army to seek outside assistance. Something else must be going on, something hidden in the accounts before her. If the money wasn't being physically removed from the premises, how else might it be leaving?

The obvious answer was spending. Eilwen discarded it. No doubt the subcommander had already run a fine comb over the recorded expenses. In any case, the problem was precisely that more was being spent than appeared in the accounts. The carefully-noted transactions of purchase had revealed the dimensions of the problem, but there was no chance of them holding the solution.

Income, then. Most of the army's coin arrived weekly, as consignments of tax revenue from vaults beneath one of the few hilltop buildings that belonged neither to Prince Urjo's palace nor the Library but the city itself. On occasion, these consignments were replaced by deliveries of gold and silver directly from the mint. Aside from those two sources, the army enjoyed remuneration from a range of lesser entities. Numerous receipts were notated "for assorted services", a suitably vague phrase that might hide any number of activities not strictly within the army's mandate. But the totals involved were comparatively small — certainly not large enough to cover the missing funds.

She set aside the smaller receipts and considered again the two main sources of income. The amount received each week from the mint and tax revenue combined was consistent, but the split between them varied widely. Some weeks the army received all of its funds from the city; on others, the mint might supply a quarter, a half, or even more. But the unexplained losses, too, were irregular: a small amount one week, more the next, and nothing at all on the third. And the most recent sizeable loss had occurred the week before last — a week which coincided with a larger than average delivery from the mint.

Eilwen flipped back through the accounts, matching up losses with income to see if the pattern held.

It did.

That's it. A laugh escaped her as she sat back on her stool, the documents' secret laid bare. Of course it wasn't straightforward theft. Why go to the trouble of stealing something that had already been locked away?

Far easier to lift the gold before it ever reached the army's vault.

~

The estate Mara had contracted to guard belonged to a merchant named Charle Trattasi and was set into the eastern side of the hill above the artisan district, with views of the fields north of the Acantha road. Arandras followed as Mara gave him a tour of the three-storey, Coridon-style sandstone house, the modest garden at the back, and the slant-roofed stable attached to the side. The family bedrooms and living areas had been stripped of valuables — anything decorative or with personal significance was gone, though most of the furniture remained, as did the more mundane items such as cutlery and earthenware. The servants' rooms were similarly bare, although the character of the furnishings suggested that such had been the case prior to the household's departure. But it was the gallery one floor up that caught Arandras's attention: a spacious, high-ceilinged hallway stretching the entire length of the building and supported by a series of thick pillars, its stone floor littered with empty stands and plinths of all sizes, each marked with a small sign.

White bear, Arandras read. *Spiked anteater. Three-horned lizard.* He glanced at Mara. "Some sort of game hunter?"

"More like a natural historian, I think," Mara said. "Though strictly of the amateur variety, judging by the far end."

Arandras followed Mara's gesture, smiling as the labels on the empty displays shifted from the exotic to the outright fanciful. *Phoenix. Dragon. Giraffe.* "Shame they're not here, even so. Must have been quite a sight."

"There's one left." Mara pointed to the corner where a stocky, cat-sized creature stood on its hind legs above the label *Smiling pouch-rat.* The grey-brown hide was either real or the most artful fake

Arandras had seen — no joins were evident, and the smiling face was disarmingly cute despite the glass eyes. "There's another stand with the same name a little further down. Maybe they only had enough space to take one of them."

"Huh." Arandras straightened, imagining the gallery filled with the whole strange collection. "Once this is over and Trattasi brings everything back, we should see if we can't convince him to let us spend an afternoon here."

Mara's brows rose. "Spoken like someone who's decided to stick around after all."

Something in her tone made Arandras give her a second look; but there was nothing in her expression except her familiar, teasing grin. "You know how it is," he said. "Books to find. Golems to free. Hard to do all that on the road." He surveyed the room once more. "Speaking of which, do you think Trattasi would mind if we moved those stands?"

Although the house was deserted, a pair of oxen had been left behind in the stable, as had a large covered wagon adorned with what appeared to be a crest representing either Trattasi's family or his business interests, or both. As the sun sank in the west, Arandras drove the wagon down the hill and out of the city to where the golems had been hidden beneath the waves.

His run-in with Mistress Agli's men had made several things clear. For one, the golems were no longer the secret he'd assumed they were. If one member of the city circle knew about them, others probably did too or would soon. For another, if he was going to remain in Spyridon, he needed to start taking his own safety a little more seriously. He was fortunate Mara had come by when she had. He couldn't count on that happening again.

It was time, then, to move the golems into the city. Mistress Agli aside, the approaching Oculus army was reason enough to keep the golems close to hand. Trattasi's estate provided the final pieces: a place in which to keep them and the means by which he might retrieve them with at least a modicum of discretion.

The wagon turned out to be large and sturdy enough to carry three golems laid flat, two on the bottom and one lying atop the others. Arandras directed the remaining golems to follow the wagon on its return journey, leaving them in a patch of forest just beyond the city as he drove in with his first load. Given the late hour, he'd expected the guards to challenge him at the gate and had resigned himself to Piator hearing about the golems by morning; but to his surprise, the guards stood aside and waved him through as soon as they saw the wagon's crest. It seemed Trattasi had reached some sort of arrangement with the army to overlook any nocturnal comings and goings, no doubt for a suitable fee. Not wishing to question his good fortune, Arandras nodded and waved as he drove through, repeating the gesture with each successive batch until the final group of three joined the others in the gallery which had been cleared of the empty displays.

Thank the Weeper, Arandras thought as he surveyed the filled gallery by the light of a raised lantern. When was the last time he'd done something that proved easier than expected? He couldn't remember. *Perhaps the tide is turning at last. From here on, nothing but fair winds and plain sailing. Ha.*

Trattasi had apparently instructed Mara that the family bedrooms were to be left unoccupied during his absence; she, and by extension Arandras, were to sleep in the servants' beds. Exhausted by the night's activities, Arandras stumbled downstairs and through the discreetly-placed door to the servants' rooms, feeling his way in the dark for the communal bedroom and collapsing onto a bed several along from the sound of Mara's soft breathing. Within moments he was asleep.

He was woken by a shaft of light pouring onto his face. Blinking blearily, Arandras sat up and glanced around. Early sunlight streamed through a series of narrow windows to announce the arrival of day as irresistibly and unpleasantly as the most obnoxious rooster. Arandras glared at the windows through slitted eyes. If this arrangement was going to have any future, they'd need to see about hanging some curtains.

Mara's bed was already empty, but Arandras could hear movement elsewhere in the house — a great deal of movement, in fact, some of it directly outside the bedroom door. Smoothing his rumpled clothes, he ventured out to find a porter lugging a crate down the servants' hallway toward the kitchen. Mara stood at the end of the hallway, overseeing the delivery with evident satisfaction. "Ah, Arandras, there you are. If it's food you want, you'll have to wait just a few moments."

Arandras squeezed past the crate, earning a black look from the porter. "What's all this?"

"Supplies, of course. Dry food. Watered wine. Enough to keep us going for a good while, should the need arise."

Her subtle emphasis on the last words cut through Arandras's sleep-fogged thoughts. *If the siege drags on, you mean.* He nodded fractionally, unwilling to attempt a more vigorous motion until he'd woken up a little. "Right. Good."

"I was just about to rouse you," Mara continued, lowering her voice. "There's been news."

Arandras rubbed his forehead. "Uh-huh."

"That's the last one," called the porter, and Arandras leaned tiredly against the wall as Mara counted out some coins and passed them over.

"For the prompt delivery," she said, placing the final coin in the man's palm. Arandras trailed behind as she escorted the porter to the grand front door. "You have Master Trattasi's gratitude."

The door closed, and Arandras gave a long sigh. "Please tell me we can eat before we talk."

"In a moment," Mara said, steering him toward a dark green divan. "You need to hear this."

Arandras sat heavily. "What is it?"

"You remember Corron? My friend in the city guard?" Mara paused. "You know, the one I bribed to get Druce off that time he misheard the address and broke into a city grain store by mistake?"

"Not really."

"Well, it doesn't matter. Point is, I went and saw him when I arrived. Asked him what was new in Spyridon. Most of what he told me was the usual rubbish, but then he mentioned Onsoth. Wouldn't tell me much about what happened, so I offered to trade information. Told him that an army was coming this way and he should do whatever he needed to do to prepare. He laughed at me and walked off."

Arandras stifled a yawn. "That's fascinating, Mara, but do you think —"

"Just listen. After we spoke, it seems Corron overheard a similar tale elsewhere, or at least enough to decide I wasn't blowing smoke. Enough to pack up his family and leave the city, in fact. He found me last night on his way out, told me what he knew about Onsoth. They haven't found anyone yet who saw the collapse, but they've got a couple of witnesses who arrived just after, with Onsoth at the bottom of the crevice and the other man already halfway down."

"Other man?"

"Yeah. Apparently one of the witnesses thought he was trying to help, but the other's not so sure. Could be that this supposed rescuer was what he seemed. Or it could be that he was more interested in searching Onsoth. Could even be that he found something on the body and took it with him."

The thought clicked into place. "Something like a book."

"Exactly."

Arandras muttered a curse. "By now the damned thing could be anywhere —"

"Not quite," Mara said. "Between the two of them, our witnesses did manage to get a partial description of the man who may or may not have taken said book from Onsoth's corpse."

"Well?"

"Tall," Mara said. "Lean. Hair swept back to his shoulders. Seemed to favour one arm while he was climbing."

Arandras frowned. "Favoured his arm?"

Mara made a dismissive gesture. "Forget that part. Who do we know who fits the rest of that description? Someone who'd be interested in a book about golems. Someone who would almost certainly be able to bring down a bridge at just the right moment to get his hands on it?"

The last of Arandras's tiredness blew away. "Clade," he breathed.

"Yeah. Eilwen never told me if she was still working for him, but a couple of things she said made it sound like he survived that sorcery of his. Could be that Clade's right here, and with an Oculus army due to arrive at any moment. Strange coincidence, wouldn't you say?"

"You think they're coming all this way just for him?"

"Maybe. Or maybe he's been working for them all along and he just fed you a line back at the caverns so he could get out with his skin. Hells, even Eilwen might not know the truth." Mara shrugged. "Or maybe it was someone else with Onsoth, and Clade's a thousand leagues away. Who knows?"

"If Clade's in Spyridon, and he's trying to learn more about the golems…" Arandras broke off, scenarios multiplying in his mind. "Weeper's tears, Mara. We need to find out what's going on. Why he's here, if he's here at all. What he's been doing. What he's going to do next. We need to know."

"Yes." Mara met his gaze, and her usual air of amusement was nowhere to be found. "We really do."

CHAPTER 12

Like all men, I am accustomed by long habit to consider the wishes of others inferior to my own. Why would the gods be any different?

— Kassa of Menefir, *Solitude*

THE CITY HALL IN SPYRIDON was a narrow, oddly-shaped building wedged between the back of the Library on one side and what remained of the once-grand palace grounds on the other. There was, no doubt, some historical explanation for the building's presence on a piece of land belonging to neither the prince nor the Conservator, but as Eilwen climbed the not-quite-circular staircase and followed Clade down the close, twisting corridor, she found herself wondering whether the negotiators of that deal had quite understood the architectural compromises their arrangement would entail.

Piator Pronn, commander of the Spyridon army, had requested her presence — or so Clade had told her, though he'd been unable to explain why they were to meet here rather than at the barracks or wherever Pronn kept his office. On one point, however, Clade had been adamant: she was to say nothing of the discovery she'd made in the army's accounts, or indeed of her examination of the accounts at all, let alone Hesca's role in providing the documents. All Pronn needed to hear about was the Oculus army heading toward the city, and on that matter she was to answer his questions as completely as she could.

The suggestion that Pronn could be trusted with the defence of the city but not the funds provided for that purpose was odd, to say the least. She'd pressed Clade on that point — did Hesca believe Pronn to have stolen the missing gold himself? — but Clade had claimed ignorance. Eilwen sensed that despite his easy projection of authority, Clade too was struggling to disentangle the threads of influence and mistrust that wound between and within Spyridon's numerous factions. Perhaps, she thought as Clade opened a door and ushered her through, today's summons was more opportune than she'd realised. It was past time that she begin to meet the players for herself, and with an army headed their way there was no better person to start with than Piator Pronn.

"Ah. There they are." A jowly man with greying hair turned from admiring a painting of some battle or other to greet her, his face creased in an avuncular smile. White braids and epaulettes of rank adorned a uniform slightly too small to accommodate the man's bulk, most of which seemed to consist of neglected muscle gone to fat. Beside him stood a sinewy woman in a less decorated uniform who studied Eilwen appraisingly. "Commander Pronn," the man said. "And my deputy, Subcommander Matharan. You must be Eilwen."

"I am," Eilwen said, glancing from Pronn to Hesca and back again. There was no obvious sign of distrust between the two, though Hesca's assessment of Eilwen seemed to hold an edge of caution.

"Commander." Clade nodded to Pronn and introduced himself with a faint stiffness that made Eilwen smile. *Seems he's not used to being overlooked.*

"Clade, yes, of course. Hesca mentioned you to me." Pronn gestured to some armchairs gathered around a small chocol table sadly empty of refreshments. "Shall we sit?"

Eilwen sat gratefully, stretching out her bad leg to rest her knee after the climb through Spyridon. Pronn chose the seat directly across from her, lowering himself into it with care. The commander's days in the field were clearly well behind him, a circumstance Eilwen suspected he found more pleasing than not. No doubt a soldier's life became far more comfortable when they no longer had to worry about actual fighting.

"Now," Pronn said when they were all seated. "Hesca tells me you have some rather disturbing news."

Eilwen folded her hands. "I hope she's already delivered that news to you, Commander."

"Well, yes, she has." Pronn's expression shifted to one of empathetic concern. "I'm told the Oculus have tired of Neysa and are headed our way. What can you tell me about them?"

"The Oculus?" Eilwen glanced sidelong at Clade, who frowned without meeting her eyes and shook his head ever so slightly. "Only what we all know. They're sorcerers, they're based somewhere on Pazia, and six months ago they appeared out of nowhere to claim Neysa. Since then, they've more or less kept to themselves."

"Until now."

"Just so."

"You were in Neysa recently, I believe," Pronn said.

"That's right."

"What's your assessment of the Oculus position there?"

"Secure enough," Eilwen said. "There are patches of discontent, but not enough to threaten their control. Not that I heard of, anyway." She shrugged. "If you're thinking of trying to protect Spyridon with a strike against Neysa, I'd say you're about five months too late. Neysa's not the battleground any more. Spyridon is."

"I see." Pronn gave an easy smile. "Thank you for bringing this to our attention. You can rest assured that we'll take care of things from here."

That's it? Eilwen stared at Pronn in surprise and dismay. Havilah would have skinned the hide off anyone asking such a pathetic set of questions.

"If I may." Hesca leaned forward, her gaze locked on Eilwen. "What do you do for coin, Eilwen?"

"I'm a trader," Eilwen said automatically, then hesitated. "Freelance at the moment. Or rather, in partnership with Clade here."

"And before that?"

"I worked for the Woodtraders Guild."

"What did you do for the Guild?"

Eilwen narrowed her eyes. "I traded," she said. "I bought goods. I sold them. You understand the concept, yes?"

"I do indeed," Hesca said. "Tell me, does the Guild have many regular customers here in Spyridon?"

Realisation dawned. *You want to know who among your tangle of enemies and allies I might have had dealings with.* Eilwen almost laughed. Years of experience had left her so accustomed to the subtle back and forth of trade negotiations that the military woman's blunt enquiries had momentarily taken her aback. "It certainly does," she said. "Primarily among the craft guilds and the merchantry. I don't believe I ever sat down with anyone from the Library. Or the army, for that matter."

Hesca gave a slight nod and seemed to relax. After the shock of Pronn's complacency, Eilwen found herself oddly encouraged by the exchange. At least Hesca had brains enough to ask a sensible question. Pronn seemed to think he was here to comfort an apprehensive grandchild.

"Commander," Clade broke in with an edge of impatience he couldn't quite smooth away. "This is not some idle fancy. The Oculus are coming. Any day now you're going to wake up with an army camped outside your city, just as Neysa did. You need to be ready."

"You think we're not," Pronn said genially.

"Last I checked, there was a great big hole in the wall where the gates were supposed to be."

"And you believe I'm responsible for that."

Clade raised his brows. "Aren't you?"

Pronn studied Clade, and for the first time Eilwen thought she saw a glint of intelligence in the man's eyes. "You're not from Spyridon, are you?"

"What's your point?"

"My point is this. Why do you care?" Pronn folded his hands. "From what Hesca's told me, you have no ties to this city. Most people in your position would simply pack their bags and leave. Why haven't you?"

Clade hesitated. "Let's just say that I've had dealings with the Oculus before."

"What sort of dealings might those be?"

"The sort you don't forget," Clade said. "The sort that begrudges them a single copper duri, let alone a city."

"Ah. Of course." Pronn smiled. "The righteous warrior, filled with the passion of his cause."

Clade blinked. "If you like."

He knows. The thought came to her unbidden and she sat forward, studying Pronn afresh. Nothing she'd told him was news. No, more than that: nothing she *could* tell him would be news, or so he believed, but he'd indulged Hesca and held the meeting anyway for reasons of his own. And now he had turned his attention to Clade, assessing the depth of his opposition to the Oculus, perhaps to judge his suitability as an ally — or perhaps, if Pronn no longer served the city, the threat he might pose as an enemy.

Abruptly, Pronn stood. Hesca jumped to her feet beside him, Eilwen and Clade following more slowly. "Eilwen, my thanks again for bringing this matter to us. I trust you can see yourself out." He turned to Clade. "You may leave with her, if you wish. Or you can come with me right now and make your views known to the city circle."

Eilwen and Clade exchanged a surprised glance. "I believe I'll come with you," Clade said.

"Splendid."

Pronn marched from the room, Hesca and Clade trailing in his wake, and abruptly Eilwen found herself alone. She sank back into her chair and tried to make sense of the exchange she'd just witnessed. Perhaps the commander simply wanted Clade's testimony to bolster the argument against the Oculus. Such an approach might make sense if Pronn felt himself to be politically weak and unlikely to be heard. But there was another explanation too, one in which Pronn hoped to allay fears of the Oculus by presenting Clade and then discrediting him before the circle. One in which Pronn was already an Oculus agent.

She shifted uneasily, reviewing everything Pronn had said, every gesture he'd made. The man's expression had revealed nothing, save for that one moment in which she'd glimpsed a hint of some unspoken thought.

Maybe this was why Hesca had come to them. Maybe she'd

sensed the same thing Eilwen had, and hoped that solving the puzzle of the missing funds would in turn uncover Pronn's secret.

There was, Eilwen supposed, only one way to find out.

~

Clade followed Pronn and Hesca down the stairs, his surprise carefully corralled and shut away. By chance, he'd been looking at Hesca when Pronn made his sudden invitation. Her expression had betrayed nothing: not surprise, not approval, not displeasure, not even amusement. Perhaps Pronn had discussed it with her ahead of time and she'd known to expect it. Or perhaps her command over her own responses was greater than Clade had credited — which made him wonder what else she might have said solely to gauge its effect on him.

Everyone lied, of course. Clade would have thought less of her if she hadn't at least tried to turn him to her will. But if she'd actually succeeded... He stared at the back of her head as they descended, wondering what was going through her mind. He'd been surprised by her lack of reaction to Taroqul's demand for more coin — the missing army funds would more than cover it, she'd said — but the ugly thought now occurred to him that perhaps she was simply content to have him carrying the can for this particular debt. Had she claimed to be an honest soldier simply to position herself as Clade's ally against the Oculus? But no, he'd never even hinted at his own connection to the Oculus before now. *If you've been playing me false — if you've been playing this city false — I swear I'll find a way to make you pay.*

On reaching the ground floor, Pronn led them through a guarded doorway into a narrow, downward-sloping corridor. Tapestries along the walls depicted a variety of cities and towns, none bearing any resemblance to any part of Spyridon that Clade had seen. It wasn't until they'd walked past half a dozen hangings that Clade recognised one of the images: Acantha, with the sea on one side and slag on the other. He glanced back at the earlier tapestries, their significance now clear. *These must be Spyridon's client cities. Each of the major ones, anyway. Hells, there are a lot of them.*

The end of the corridor opened onto a round, brightly-lit

chamber filled with the low murmur of voices. More tapestries adorned the walls, each depicting some feature of Spyridon — the Library, the high market, Port Gallin, and so on — and in the gaps between hangings Clade could see patterns carved into the stone, pieces of an abstract design unfamiliar to him but not bearing any sorcery that he could sense. The chamber was dominated by a large, seven-sided table, around which close to a dozen people already sat, and as Pronn led him and Hesca to a vacant side Clade scanned the room and tried to put names to those present.

To their right sat Conservator Feren Skaratass of the Library, clad in the same simple grey as the two assistants flanking her. Beside her lounged Prince Urjo, his scarlet sash slightly askew, unattended save for the bottle dangling from his hand. Next along was a man little older than Clade himself, wearing robes that marked him as a priest of the Dreamer. *Dathreos,* Clade thought, summoning the name from the puppet show he'd witnessed the other day. The satirists' depiction of him had been inconsistent: at times a bumbling innocent, at others acting in venial self-interest, and at yet others motivated by base cowardice. Clade wondered which was closest to the truth.

Mistress Agli of the merchants had brought no fewer than three offsiders and sat in the centre of the group like a mother magpie, all beady eyes and sharp glances, the slender bracelets on her wrists jangling every time she moved. Next to Agli's group sat a man who could only be Ernst of the craft guilds, his burly frame offering a stark contrast with his lone assistant, a fine-fingered woman whose plaited hair reached to her waist. A smith, the other puppets had called him. *Looks like they had that much right.*

The final space, presumably designated for the governor of Port Gallin, was empty.

"Who's the newcomer, Piator?" Agli's voice sounded like someone scratching a stick across a window. "He's not going to do much damage with a hand like that, is he? Looks more like a singer than a soldier." Laughter sounded from among her entourage as all eyes turned to Clade. He affected a polite smile, unsure whether word of his activities in the city — and more importantly, his description — had reached the ears of the other circle members; but if anyone recognised him, they gave no sign.

"Clade has been assisting us with our preparations," Piator said, and Clade could hear the chuckle in his tone.

"Ah, of course," Urjo said. "We'll need someone to serenade our new overlords as they march their army through that convenient hole we've left in our walls."

"The gates will be hung by sunset tomorrow. Small thanks to some." Hesca shot a look in the direction of Urjo or Feren, or both. "We'll hold off on closing them a while longer. No point creating a panic before the enemy shows their face."

Feren gave a disdainful snort. "Spyridon's strength lies its alliances. Do you have any notion how many archons, governors, and generals across the Free Cities were educated here at the Library? Anybody who picks a fight with us will have the whole region coming after them. No-one's that stupid."

"You sure about that?" Dathreos said. "Nobody blinked an eyelid when Neysa fell."

"Oh, I strongly suspect there was some blinking," Urjo said. "In Anstice, especially. But half their traders were already in bed with these Oculus, and that's what it comes down to in Anstice. The almighty luri. If they figured the best way to fill their coffers was to sit on their arses, that's exactly what they'd do, Neysa be damned." He raised the bottle in a mock-toast. "And where Anstice leads, so go the Free Cities."

Ernst drummed his thick fingers on the table. "Are you saying Anstice probably will help us, or they probably won't?"

"This is insane!" Feren sat back in disgust. "Who in their right mind would carry on a campaign like this? Seize Neysa, fine. That much makes sense, so long as you spend the next year or two consolidating your territory. But instead you want me to believe that barely six months later they've marched the better part of their forces out of Neysa to strike at us *fifty leagues away?* Gods, Piator. You of all people should know better than to spin a line like that."

"Oh, I agree," Pronn said. "It's entirely ludicrous. But it seems to be happening anyway."

A clash of bracelets drew everyone's attention to Mistress Agli. "Perhaps they can be bought. If not the leaders, then those beneath them."

"No." Heads turned in surprise or disapproval at the new speaker. Clade stared back at them all, filling his words with as much conviction as he could muster. "The Oculus cannot be purchased. If all you wanted was to delay them, perhaps you might find a few squads who were willing to turn. But that's all. Once the Oculus have fixed their sights on something, there's no way to dissuade them."

Feren glared. "And you know this how?"

"I've dealt with the Oculus before," Clade said. "I know them."

"Dealt with them how?" Feren demanded.

"What do these Oculus want?" Dathreos said at the same moment.

Clade turned to the latter. *What does Azador want? Hells, how I wish I knew.* The answers he'd been given when he joined — restoration of the Valdori Empire, healing of the world's ills — had long since been revealed as lies, at least as far as Azador was concerned. "They believe they serve a god. Not the Tri-God, and not the All-God, either. Something else."

"And what does their service entail?"

"Does it matter? Right now they're coming for your city. You can let them take it or you can fight back. That means contributing whatever resources you have to the city's defence. Gold, food, men, women — all of it."

"Gods, here we go," Feren said.

Hesca leaned forward. "Neysa didn't know the Oculus were coming. We do. We've recalled as many squads as we can spare from the nearer towns. Messages are going out to more distant garrisons with instructions to assemble a force capable of breaking a siege."

"How big a force is that?" Dathreos said. "Do we know the size of the army ranged against us?"

"Not yet," Hesca said. "Which is all the more reason to gather as much strength as we can —"

"Perhaps." Mistress Agli folded her hands, bracelets clattering against the table. "Or perhaps what you need is already here. All you need do is take it."

"Ah!" Urjo took a swig from his bottle. "How very poetic. I generally expect to hear such cryptic banalities from the priest, but he seems to have lost his taste for them today. But may I say, my dear, you make an admirable replacement."

"Pffft." Agli turned, pointedly addressing everyone in the room except Prince Urjo. "There is a man in this city who has at his disposal no fewer than ten soldiers of the Valdori First Legion. Perhaps more."

Clade started. *Arandras, here? Surely not.*

"First Legion?" Ernst asked.

"She means golems." Dathreos shook his head. "They're a myth, Agli. Or if they ever did exist, they were lost when the Valdori fell."

"Were they?" Agli's gaze flicked to Feren. "Not everyone thinks so."

"Not everyone believes a thing just because someone claims it," Feren returned, cool scepticism in her voice. "What makes you think there are golems here?"

"One of my traders had it from an eyewitness in Acantha. Said to look for a man named Arandras." Agli paused. "A scribe by that name used to do business with several antiquities dealers here."

"Used to?"

"His shop is closed. There's talk he once frequented a bar west of the hill, but nobody can say which one."

"Sounds to me like he's probably not in Spyridon at all."

Prince Urjo burst out laughing. "Ah, Agli, Agli. Surely you can do better than this? Distract us all from your appealingly confiscatable riches by spinning a tale about an imaginary scribe in possession of even more imaginary golems? If such a person truly existed, the last thing Mistress Agli, merchant extraordinaire, would do is spill the beans to the city circle. Give up a fortune in Valdori sorcery for so petty a concern as the good of the city? Gods forfend!"

Scowling, Agli began shouting at Urjo just as Ernst started to pound the table and loudly demand an explanation. Pronn and Hesca inclined their heads to confer softly, leaving Clade to his thoughts. Arandras, here in the city. If it was true, then maybe, just maybe they could do more than merely defend Spyridon. *Send those golems through whatever force the Oculus have assembled and they'd be crippled for years. Maybe longer. Hells, we could stop Azador in its tracks right here.*

The shouting grew louder, but Clade was no longer paying attention. All he could see was the Oculus fleeing before the implacable fury of hundreds of rampaging golems.

～

The prospect of Clade's presence in the city hung over Arandras like lingering haze on a still day: unexpected, unpleasant, and inescapable. Arandras had given the man little thought since their parting at the cavern beside Tienette Lake. When he'd gone back in to retrieve the golems, he'd found Clade lying motionless on the floor, his sorcery complete but its outcome not yet clear. The woman, Eilwen, had been content to watch him lead the golems out, and Arandras had left the cavern with no expectation of ever seeing Clade again, or even an indication of whether the man had survived his audacious bid to free himself.

Perhaps he really is dead. It would be foolish to discount the possibility, particularly after so complex and invasive a binding. *His body still lying in that cavern, just bones now, undone by his own sorcery at the last.*

Or perhaps he wasn't. Perhaps he was in Spyridon right now. Perhaps he'd killed Onsoth, stolen the Conservator's prized book, and was now awaiting the Oculus army in order to... what?

I'm not here on behalf of the Oculus. I'm here to escape them. So Clade had told him in the cavern. If he'd succeeded, might he now be plotting some form of revenge on his former masters? It was possible to fit some of the pieces together that way. If he and Eilwen were indeed still working together, then perhaps her curiosity about the Oculus in Neysa had derived from his. Maybe she'd been seeking something he needed — something that would allow him to mount some sort of strike against them when they arrived.

But if that were the extent of Clade's plans, why his ongoing preoccupation with golems? Either he'd managed to learn of another lost cache — something Arandras judged unlikely in the extreme — or else he still harboured a desire for the golems bound to Arandras, and his denials in the cavern had been nothing more than a last, desperate attempt to save his life.

And if that were the case, then perhaps the rest of what he'd said was similarly false. Perhaps he'd been working for the Oculus the whole time, in which case the reason for his presence in Spyridon with an Oculus army on its way required no explanation at all.

He arrived at Rhothe's Bar as the sun was setting, slipping in through the side door and ordering a large serve of the day's tagine of lamb, apricot, and drizzled honey. Druce, it seemed, had not yet made an appearance, but Mock could be seen in the corner booth tucking into a plate of his own. Arandras wondered if there was any protocol for people wishing to engage Druce's services. Was he expected to make himself known to Mock first? Probably not. There hadn't exactly been a queue of prospective customers the other night.

The sight of Mock turned Arandras's thoughts back to their conversation outside the Library. Mock had been unable to say anything more about the missing book beyond its supposed subject matter, and although Mara seemed to have heard the same rumours, there was still the possibility that both were mistaken. He wondered where the tale had started, and what the source had thought about it. Everyone had heard of golems, of course — they were a *dilarj* playing piece, for the Weeper's sake — though on the other hand, so were dragons, and Arandras knew of nobody who had ever seen one of those. Yet the way Mock had spoken of golems suggested that he, at least, took the subject seriously. Did others feel the same way? If he were to march his golems down the main street in broad daylight, how would the city react?

A whole lot of screaming and running around, most likely, with a few offers of coin and the chance of a knife in the back.

As if summoned by Arandras's thought of coin, Druce appeared in the doorway. He surveyed the room, frowning when he spotted Arandras. For a moment he seemed inclined to ignore him; then he exhaled and strolled over.

"You going to be coming here often?" Druce asked as he reached Arandras's table. "Because this is kind of my place of business now."

"That's why I'm here." Arandras nudged his empty plate aside. "I'd like to engage your services."

"Oh." He studied Arandras, thoughtful. "I don't do special rates," he warned. "You'll pay the same amounts on the same terms as everyone else."

"Fair enough."

"Right, then." Druce pulled out a chair and sat. "What have you got?"

"I'm looking for someone," Arandras said. "Someone here in Spyridon."

"Doesn't sound too hard. Got a description?"

"His name is Clade, though he might be going by something else. Tall, lean, hair to about here. He's a sorcerer, so watch yourself." Arandras paused, remembering Mara's description. "Might be favouring one arm."

"Where's he likely to be?"

"I have no idea," Arandras said. "To be honest, I'm not completely sure he's here. But if he is, I need to find him."

Druce gave a slight smirk. "And?"

"And what?"

"Come on, Arandras, give me some credit. You need to find this Clade, *and...?*"

"And talk to him," Arandras said.

Druce gave him a look.

"All right, fine. *If* he's here, and *if* he's been doing what I think he has, then I may need someone to... uh..."

"Yes?"

Arandras hesitated. Now that it came to it, he found himself reluctant to order the book's theft. Mara would have laughed at his qualms, told him he was being foolish. If Clade was trying to wrest control of Arandras's golems... But suppositions were all he had, and that wasn't enough to condemn a man, not even Clade.

Before he did this, he needed confirmation.

"Nothing," Arandras said. "Not yet. We'll cross that bridge when we come to it."

Druce shrugged. "Suit yourself," he said. "But if I were you, I'd be crossing as many bridges as I could right now. You might not get the chance later on."

Arandras frowned. "What does that mean?"

"Something's coming." Druce leaned closer. "Merchants are packing their families off west. The Quill have closed their schoolhouse and pulled all their people back to Anstice. The Library is shut for the first time in years. And there are some wild rumours about. Talk of armies on the march. Talk of invasion. That part hasn't spread among the general populace yet, but it can't be long before it does. When that happens…"

"The Quill are gone?" Arandras said. "Huh. Good, I guess." He hadn't thought much about the Quill since leaving Narvi and Halli in Lissil, injured but alive and with every chance of making a full recovery. Narvi was probably back at work by now. Perhaps he'd even returned to Spyridon. If so, at least the Quill's decision to evacuate meant he wouldn't be caught in the middle of a siege.

"Why?" Druce's gaze latched onto him like a hawk's. "What do you know?"

Arandras glanced around the room. "That army on the march? It's real," he murmured. "Apparently the Oculus have decided that Neysa isn't enough for them. Might be you want to leave the city yourself if you don't want to find out what a siege looks like from the inside."

"Oh, I'm not going anywhere. Change is opportunity, as they say."

"Well, keep your head down —"

A figure caught Arandras's eye. He broke off, looking across the room — and there was Clade, just as Arandras remembered him, standing in the doorway and scanning the tables with one hand tucked awkwardly into a greatcoat pocket. Astonished, Arandras stood. Their eyes met, and Arandras thought he saw something flicker in Clade's eyes, something more than just recognition.

An end to a search.

Suspicion flared, hard and undeniable. *The bastard's been looking for me.*

"Never mind," Arandras growled. "Looks like I just found my man."

❧

By good fortune, Clade found Arandras in the second bar he visited. Half of Spyridon lay west of the hill, and no doubt half its bars as well, but Rhothe's straddled the narrow middle zone between the poor districts and the estates, artisans, and other civilised features of the city's east. Even the bar's layout reflected its dual nature: the raucous taproom at the front separated from a quieter back room for dining and conversation, the chandeliers of the latter inexplicably hung with strips of dirty cloth.

They spotted each other at almost the same moment, Arandras rising to his feet with an expression of something close to shock. His beard was a little rougher than it had been at the cavern, its salting of grey perhaps a little deeper. His tunic and trousers were stained from travel, and his face was tanned from long days in the sun. But his movements seemed indefinably sharper than Clade remembered, as though some internal encumbrance was no longer present, or some new potency had been discovered.

It wasn't hard to guess what lay behind such a change.

A wave of envy swept over Clade. He clenched his jaw and batted the feeling away. This was hardly the time for such indulgences. Right now, his desire for Arandras's golems could only be an impediment to his purposes. He had a city to think about.

Arandras approached slowly, his eyes bright with distrust. "What in the Weeper's name are you doing here?"

"Not so loud," Clade muttered. An empty booth halfway along the wall beckoned. "Follow me." Without waiting to see if Arandras would obey, he struck out across the room and slipped into the booth.

Several moments later, Arandras joined him. "This had better be good."

"There's an Oculus army heading this way," Clade said in a harsh whisper. "Neysa was just the first. Spyridon's next. That good enough for you?"

"That's your news?" Arandras said. "Tell me something I don't already know."

Clade suppressed a curse. He'd prepared an entire argument to convince Arandras of the necessity of opposing the Oculus, but somehow Arandras had learnt of their approach already. Clade sensed that there was little to be gained by belabouring the topic. "Fine," he said. "I'm going to stop them."

"Is that right?" Arandras studied Clade suspiciously, but his voice held surprise. "Good for you."

"But I need your help."

"No."

Clade leaned forward. "Listen to me, Arandras. This is the Oculus we're talking about. This is Azador. All the wrongs I ever did you were done as their instrument. You can't possibly want them to succeed."

Arandras scowled.

"We can defeat them. Save Spyridon and the gods know how many other cities. All we need are your golems —"

Arandras's gaze hardened. "No," he said again.

"Damn it, Arandras, will you just listen? We might never get another chance to halt their advance —"

"You want me to listen? Then say something worth listening to." Arandras fixed Clade with a stare and leaned back in the booth's padded seat. "Why did you kill Onsoth?"

With a supreme effort of will, Clade managed to avoid gaping like a fool. How in the hells had Arandras heard about that? For a moment Clade considered denying the charge. But if Arandras wasn't guessing, if he knew about the event but only suspected Clade's reasons...

"It's complex," Clade said at last.

"Is that right?" Arandras said again; but this time the words held not surprise but vicious satisfaction. "Then let me make it simpler for you. I know about Onsoth's book. I've got a pretty fair idea of what's inside. And try as I might, I can only think of one reason why you, of all people, would have a killing interest in such a tome. I would have to be the king of all idiots to agree to anything you suggest that involves *my golems*."

I don't want your golems. It was the right and necessary response, to be made with as much passion and conviction as Clade could muster. But he'd said that to Arandras once before, and in that moment his words had held the full measure of his sincerity. No lie he told now could measure up to that statement; and if he tried to mislead Arandras but failed, he would lose whatever remained of the man's willingness to listen.

"I didn't come here to cheat you," he said, matching Arandras's gaze and inviting him to see the truth of his words. "That's not why

I'm here."

But Arandras smiled as if he knew exactly what Clade's statement extended to and what it left out. "I think we're done."

"Wait." What could he say, *what could he say* that might convince Arandras to set aside their differences? "If you're not prepared to fight, then you should leave. Now. Take the golems and go." He held Arandras's eyes, imploring him to listen. "The Oculus *must not* gain possession of them. Do you understand? Not even the city is more important than that."

Arandras stood. "Don't worry about it," he said. "In fact, don't think about them at all. The sooner you forget they exist, the happier we'll all be."

He stalked away, returning to the table he'd been sitting at earlier and commencing a vigorous exchange of whispers with his young, faintly anxious-looking companion. Cursing, Clade leaned back in the booth and tried to ignore the young man's furtive glances in his direction.

Damned fool. What were the golems for if not to fight battles like these? Perhaps another member of the circle would have better luck persuading Arandras to the city's defence when they inevitably tracked him down, but Clade doubted it. The man was as stubborn as a mule.

But the Oculus were coming, whether Arandras wanted to hear it or not. And if Clade was going to save the city, it seemed he would have to do it on his own.

CHAPTER 13

On an island far to the southwest live a people short in stature and pale of skin, but with a remarkable capacity for memory. The stars have revealed to these people, or so they claim, that there exist but ninety-one phoenixes in all the world — no more, no less — and these have become the basis of a most peculiar form of exchange. When food is purchased or labour is sold, it is traded not for beads or coins but for a share of ownership in one of these wondrous birds. At any moment, any of the island's two dozen elders can recite who among the people is deemed to possess each part of every phoenix. A single bird is enough to elevate one to the ranks of the wealthy, whereas a poor family may own little more than a handful of feathers.

The fact that no islander in generations has so much as glimpsed a phoenix disturbs them not at all.

— Eneas the Fabulist, *One Hundred Truths and Ninety-Nine Lies*

THE SPYRIDON MINT WAS IMPOSSIBLE to miss. The walled compound loomed amid the workshops and studios of Spyridon's artisans like a military encampment in a wheat field. Behind the nails and spikes embedded in the top of the wall, Eilwen could see the roof of the mint itself: an almost flat expanse of tiles with a series of thick chimneys on one side and a walkway on which a pale-skinned archer made slow circuits of the perimeter. Both the studded timber gate and the door beside it were closed, though an open shutter in the door offered a glimpse of a scowling, grizzled man dressed in the same earth-toned colours as the rooftop guard.

She'd considered asking Clade to arrange an escort for this visit, but in the end she'd decided against it. A lone woman visiting the city's moneyer might go unnoticed. Add a squad of soldiers and tongues would inevitably wag. Yet the visit held risks. It was possible, even likely, that someone within the mint was involved in the thefts. Success depended on Eilwen revealing her true purpose only to the moneyer herself, Sandrine Velle, a widow who had assumed control of the mint some years ago on the death of her husband. Sandrine was said to be as precise as she was scrupulous — in all her time with the Woodtraders, Eilwen had heard nothing about the moneyer to suggest anything other than the strictest propriety.

While she was pondering the matter at breakfast, Orval had surprised her with an offer to come along. "If there's something you think I can do," he'd muttered, as if embarrassed to suggest he might be of use. "Me and Jak." She'd found herself unexpectedly moved by the earnestness she'd sensed beneath his words and had longed to say yes, but unfortunately, it had been impossible. Gaining the moneyer's trust would be difficult enough without a moody teenage boy in tow. "Next time," she'd said, touching his arm to soften the rejection. "And Orval. Thank you."

A carriage for hire rattled past and the archer atop the building glanced down at its wake, his gaze pausing for a moment on Eilwen before moving on. Gripping her satchel tightly, Eilwen crossed the street and hailed the man through the open shutter. "Hello, inside? I am Eilwen Nasareen of the Woodtraders Guild. I need to speak with Moneyer Velle as a matter of urgency."

The guard stomped to the door and studied Eilwen through narrow eyes, his jaw working methodically on something tucked inside his cheek. "Woodtraders, eh?"

"That's right," Eilwen said. She drew the Guild's letter of reference from the satchel and passed it through the window. "See for yourself."

It was a calculated risk, using her old papers to gain admission. News of her undignified departure from the Guild may well have reached as far as the Spyridon mint. But Eilwen guessed not. Ria's description of the division within the Guild suggested she was unlikely to have been cast as scapegoat as far afield as Spyridon. And in any case, that news was almost a year old — even if it had travelled this far, there was an excellent chance that by now it had simply been forgotten.

The guard frowned at the letter for several moments, then shrugged and made to return it. "We don't have any dealings with the Woodtraders."

"Perhaps you have more than you know," Eilwen returned, refusing to take the letter back. "I'm here to discuss matters that bear directly on the security of your operations. Moneyer Velle will not want to hear that you turned me away."

The guard scowled, but a moment later the letter was withdrawn and the shutter slammed to, leaving Eilwen to wait outside as the man stomped away. After a few minutes his heavy footsteps returned, the door jerked open, and the man beckoned her ungraciously inside. She endured a brief but efficient search of her bag and person, and when no weapons were found she was escorted across a wide courtyard to an unobtrusive side door in the mint's main building.

A strange collection of machines filled the mint's cavernous interior. Eilwen gazed about in fascination, trying to guess the purpose of each instrument. Something like a gigantic screw stood only a few paces away, its weighted horizontal arms wrapped around with string, presumably to improve the grip of those required to turn it. Additional mechanisms lay scattered about the space, some partially obscured by columns or handcarts: an overlarge roller; a table supporting a wheeled apparatus above a narrow channel; and other, stranger devices. All lay idle at present, save for one of the furnaces on the far wall where a cluster of workers wearing heavy aprons and gloves watched the oven for some predetermined signal.

"You coming?" the guard said.

Eilwen tore her attention away from the machines and followed the man around a partition to an area that evidently served as a small office. A woman wearing a floral headscarf sat behind a battered desk, a pair of lenses at the end of a stick raised to her eyes, Eilwen's letter of reference open before her. She looked up at Eilwen's approach and gestured with the lenses to a vacant chair.

"Thank you," she said to the guard. "Wait by the door, would you? I doubt this will take long." She turned to Eilwen and subjected her to a long stare through the lenses. "You are Eilwen Nasareen."

"That's correct," Eilwen said.

"Of the Woodtraders Guild."

"Yes." Some instinct made Eilwen pause. "Until about a year ago."

"Ah." To Eilwen's surprise, the woman gave a slight smile and set the lenses down. "Quite so." She folded Eilwen's letter and pushed it across the desk. "I am Sandrine Velle," the woman continued. "And as it happens, Eilwen Nasareen, I know your name."

"You do?" Eilwen said cautiously.

"You are no longer a Woodtrader," Sandrine said with the confidence of one reciting well-known facts. "Your break with the Guild was difficult. I've heard several conflicting accounts of your departure. I won't ask for yours. What I will ask is the name of your current employer and the true purpose of your visit." Sandrine folded her hands. "Might I encourage you to be as open and forthright in your response as you possibly can."

Eilwen swallowed. Clearly, the moneyer's information was better than she'd imagined. Perhaps it wasn't surprising — the mint would have more reason than most to guard against swindlers and cheats. "I'm here on behalf of the army," she said. "Subcommander Hesca Matharan, to be specific. The subcommander is investigating the theft of some funds from the army vaults. We — that is, she and I — have reason to believe that the stolen money consists of newly-minted coins that, in fact, never made it to the vaults but were taken en route from the mint to the barracks." She bobbed her head in apology. "I regret the deception, but I needed to speak with you directly without alerting anyone else to my investigation."

Again Sandrine studied Eilwen for a long moment. "You'll understand that I need more than your word to support your claims."

"Of course." Eilwen opened her satchel and produced the documents Hesca had given her: the original consignment notices for the last two deliveries. "I received these from the subcommander herself."

A harsh clanging began somewhere in the building. Unperturbed, Sandrine studied the notices with the help of her lenses. "These amounts seem correct to me."

"Just so," Eilwen said. "The paperwork is correct. The delivery, I fear, is not."

"Are you certain of this?"

Eilwen hesitated. "No," she said at last. "But I strongly suspect —"

"No need to explain," Sandrine interrupted. "I merely seek precision." She set the notices down. "Understand me, Eilwen. Security is of paramount importance to my operation. I interview every new worker personally. I enforce strict protocols to remove any opportunity for momentary temptation, let alone systematic theft. I am at least as certain of every one of my people as you are of your suspicions. Not a single coin leaves this building unless it has been duly authorised by me or my second."

"I see." Eilwen thought a moment. "And after it leaves this building?"

"Delivery is the responsibility of the recipient. The army engages a merchant by the name of Ral Garvan to transport its coin. Garvan has held this contract for several years without any irregularities."

The name seemed vaguely familiar, but Eilwen couldn't place it. She made a mental note to consider it later and moved on. "Are there documents that verify this? The consignment notice originates with you and comes to us, but you must also keep records of your own."

"Of course." Sandrine reached for a large book. "Garvan's people arrive in the hour before noon. Two names are recorded: the individual responsible for the delivery and the carriage driver. The money is counted, both parties sign, and the carriage leaves on the stroke of midday."

The moneyer opened the book and turned it to face Eilwen. In small, precise notation, the delivery of fortunes was laid out: dates and amounts, names and signatures. Eilwen tapped the page. "The last few signatures are different."

"That's correct," Sandrine said. "Garvan rotates these duties between several trusted employees every six months. I believe he sees it as a way of reducing temptation."

Eilwen studied the page. The last change of signature had occurred four months ago — just before the army's funds began to go missing. "Whose signatures are these?"

Sandrine glanced at the book through her lenses. "Most recently, the deliveries have been driven by Morrus Tresener and overseen by Ral Garvan himself."

"I see." So the merchant had begun taking custody of the coins in person just as they started to disappear. "I believe I have only one more question. Where can I find this Ral Garvan?"

~

The night after his encounter with Clade, Arandras returned to Rhothe's Bar to await Druce's arrival — and with him, Arandras hoped, the book Clade had been willing to kill for.

It was the man's evasions that had resolved Arandras's uncertainty. *I know about Onsoth's book,* Arandras had said, and Clade had made no effort to deny it, hadn't so much as moved a muscle, but had sat there trying to concoct a plausibly misleading explanation before giving up the effort and resorting to platitude. *I didn't come here to cheat you.* As if Arandras were so simple that he couldn't hear everything Clade left unsaid.

Druce was reluctant to take on a job at such short notice, but Arandras had named a sum several times what he considered a reasonable amount and Druce had acquiesced. Perhaps Druce's hesitation had been genuine, or perhaps it was merely a bargaining tactic. Arandras didn't care. He wanted that book, and the gold he'd earned over the past months was enough to cover the expense. And so, a few moments after Clade left the bar, Druce had followed; and now Arandras waited to find out if his opportunistic scheme had borne fruit.

He signalled a passing barmaid and ordered a cider, but when it arrived he found he was less thirsty than he'd thought. He'd never had much taste for drinking alone — Rhothe's had been a place he visited solely for the company of their group. But Jensine no longer lived in Spyridon, and if Mara had come by to see Druce since her arrival, she'd done so while Arandras was elsewhere. Bereft of companions, Arandras felt strangely out of place, as though he were trespassing in someone else's space.

With nothing to do but sip his cider, Arandras found his thoughts returning to the previous night's exchange with Clade.

Golems aside, the man had seemed genuinely concerned about the impending siege. Even if he assumed Clade's argument to have been aimed at prising Arandras from his golems, the man's words still carried force. *This is the Oculus we're talking about. All the wrongs I ever did you were done as their instrument. You can't possibly want them to succeed.*

It was true, as far as it went. There was a part of him that wanted nothing more than to fight, to send the golems against those who had orchestrated Tereisa's death and make them pay. And there was another part, one he found himself reluctant to acknowledge, which thrilled at the notion of ordering the golems into combat and wielding them as the weapons they had been made into by the Valdori. But the larger part of him shied away, sickened by the thought. This was how the Quill perceived the world, and the Valdori before them: as a place for the exercise of power, where people existed simply to be used and expended in the service of some larger goal. Arandras hated it; yet it seemed that he carried the same canker deep in his heart.

Well, if that were so then he would smother it, burn it, find a way to cut it out. He hadn't snatched the golems from the Quill only to fall victim to the same corruption himself. As for vengeance, he'd learnt to his sorrow that such pursuits led down precisely the same path. Yes, the Oculus had wronged him; but if he could not yet forgive them, he could at least deny them the power to direct his steps.

A presence beside the table caused Arandras to look up. Druce stood there, his forehead marred by an angry cut that descended from his hairline to his brow; and in his hands, not one but two slender tomes, the topmost cover stained with what looked like blood.

Excitement filled him. "You got it?"

"Of course I got it," Druce said, grimacing as he slipped into a chair. "And I'm fine, thanks for asking. Mostly."

"What happened?"

"What do you think? I told you it was a bad idea to try something like this without surveying the place in daylight."

Arandras frowned. "I thought you had people to, uh, perform these tasks," he said in a low tone. "What did you say about not wanting to run around any more?"

"Yeah. Well." Druce reached up to rub his forehead, but aborted the motion with a grimace. "Truth is, that's what you might describe as an aspirational statement. I mean, I'm starting to find some good people, don't get me wrong. But for a job like this, with no notice at all…"

"Oh." The revelation was oddly unsurprising. Arandras wondered why he hadn't guessed it earlier. "Well, thank you for making the effort —"

"Yeah, yeah. Your coin is thanks enough." Druce considered. "Although if you could fetch me a Quill so I could spend said coin to fix my face, that would be handy, too."

"Is it painful?"

Druce waved dismissively. "It'll be fine. Eventually." His eyes fell on Arandras's half-finished cider. "If you really want to thank me, how about getting me one of those?"

Arandras summoned the bar staff and ordered the drink. "Anything I should know?"

"Not particularly. I'm pretty sure I got in and out without being heard. Your man snores like a consumptive ox. This," Druce indicated his brow, "happened at the end. Window wasn't as wide as I thought." He tapped the topmost cover thoughtfully. "The books were in a chest with a few other odds and ends. Wasn't sure in the dark which one you wanted, so I grabbed them both. If he hasn't missed them yet, he probably will soon."

Arandras nodded. Druce's hand still lay atop the books, and Arandras had the sense that he wasn't quite done. "Something else?"

Druce exhaled heavily. "This is the book the Library is in such a tizz about, isn't it? Do you know what Feren gods-damned Skaratass would give to have this back?"

Arandras went still. "Honestly, I have no idea."

"Yeah. That's what I thought." Druce eyed Arandras speculatively. "Once you get the bit between your teeth, you pretty much stop thinking about anything or anyone else."

Arandras moistened his lips. "We had a deal."

"Yeah," Druce said. "We did."

"And?" Arandras searched Druce's face, trying to read his

intention. Druce was both lightly built and injured. If it came to it, Arandras could probably take the books by force...

Druce sighed again. "Unlike you, I keep my word." He pushed the books across the table. "We had a deal. Now it's done."

Arandras placed his hand over the thin tomes, the tension slowly draining out of him. "Thank you."

"Don't." Druce's expression hardened. "Don't ever think that this deserves thanks. Just remember it the next time someone's foolish enough to trust you."

~

Clade was finishing his breakfast of fruit rolled in flatbread when a summons from Hesca arrived in the person of Zann. "Subcommander wants to see you, mouse," the soldier said with a grin, propping a booted foot beside Clade on the street bench. "Best you don't keep her waiting."

"Tell her I'll be there soon," Clade said around a mouthful of food, waving to send the man on his way.

Zann's grin widened. "Subcommander's not at the Four Hands. You're to come with me."

"Oh?" Clade swallowed a little too hastily and winced as the unchewed lump went down. "And where might we be going?"

"You'll see when we get there," Zann said, evidently savouring each word. "Mouse."

Clade sighed in resignation and stood, wiping his hands clean on his trousers. "Fine. Lead on."

In the wake of his failed attempt to persuade Arandras to his cause, Clade had spent the afternoon and evening by the city wall, watching as Taroqul's people finally hung the gates. The process had required the temporary closure of the street as each gate was driven out on an oversized cart and manoeuvred into position with a bewildering array of ropes, hooks, and pulleys. When the rigging was finally removed and the gates pushed open to the cheers of onlookers, Clade had found himself breathing a sigh of relief. At least on this one matter he'd been able to aid the city against the Oculus.

But it wasn't enough. Arandras's distrust had forced him to re-evaluate his own priorities: the safety of the city versus the acquisition of his own cadre of golems. Beyond question, the city came first. If the Oculus continued to make inroads into the Free Cities, his own plans to free individual sorcerers from Azador's grasp would quickly become irrelevant. Necessity required that he set those ambitions aside and focus solely on repelling the Oculus advance. Once the present crisis was over, he could return his attention to the problem of destroying Azador's hold over its people.

As a result, Onsoth's book remained locked in his suite's single chest with the lexicon he'd acquired earlier, while Clade pondered the defence of the city and wondered when the advancing army would finally arrive.

Zann led him south and east in the direction of the Acantha road, the newly-hung gates, and the barracks, but just as Clade was beginning to relax, the soldier turned into a narrow but well-kept street lined with modest houses. At the sixth or seventh house he stopped and knocked on the door in a rapid, oddly-patterned rhythm. There was a pause; then a voice that might have been Hesca's called softly from behind the door. "Come in."

Gripping Clade by the arm, Zann shoved the door open and they stepped into a narrow hallway. Hesca stood poised for combat half a dozen paces from the door, her bare sword pointed at Clade's heart like the finger of the Gatherer's avenging angel. When she saw they were alone, she exhaled slowly and lowered her blade.

"Thank you, Zann," she said. "I won't need you for the next few hours. Feel free to entertain yourself until midday."

"Subcommander." Zann's eyes flicked to Clade, his expression conveying his doubts at the wisdom of leaving Hesca alone with the sorcerer. But Hesca was clearly accustomed to being obeyed, and Zann hesitated only a moment before giving a tight nod and departing.

"So," Clade said once Zann's footsteps could no longer be heard. "What's going on?"

"There's been news." Hesca sheathed her sword with more force than was necessary and beckoned Clade into a side room. "Dathreos is gone."

"Dathreos?" Clade recalled the priest from the meeting of the city circle. The man had asked plenty of questions but hadn't offered enough of his own views for Clade to get a sense of where he stood in Spyridon's tangled politics. "What do you mean, gone?"

"Just that." The room was scarcely wider than the hallway and equally bare of decoration. Several hard chairs and stools filled what little space was available. Hesca settled herself on one with a scowl that might have hidden anger or fear or something else entirely. "Disappeared. Vanished. Whereabouts unknown." She paused. "And rumour has it that Mistress Agli hasn't been seen since the last meeting either."

"Dathreos *and* Agli?" Bewildered, Clade shook his head. "You think someone's had them killed?"

"It's possible." Hesca exhaled heavily. "But probably not. Agli has half a dozen bolt-holes scattered across the city. Bunkering down now means she can keep her options open until it's clear which way the wind blows. As for Dathreos, smart money says that he's fled the city. His manservant is missing too, as is a horse that Dathreos was known to favour. They're probably halfway to Jorth by now."

Clade considered. Hesca's analysis seemed reasonable, assuming her facts were correct. "So why all this business with swords and secret knocks?"

"Because *probably* is still a guess. And even if that's all, it's bad enough." She gave a disgusted sigh. "The gods-damned Oculus haven't even shown their noses and the city is already falling apart."

"Well," Clade said. "The circle, perhaps, though I can't say I ever expected much from them." They'd barely managed to shut up long enough for Clade to complete a sentence before resuming their bickering. "At least Piator Pronn seemed willing to listen."

Hesca snorted. "Willing to listen, indeed. Piator should have been banging heads together, demanding every duri of support the circle could dredge up. Instead he smiles and mouths genial banalities, and the circle carries on its petty squabbles as if he's not there. The man is useless." She looked at Clade. "He asked me about you. Where you're from, how I found you. The sort of questions that made me think he wanted to handle you himself."

Clade bridled. "*Handle* me?"

"You know what I mean," Hesca said. "I told him you wouldn't work with anyone but me. That any attempt to interfere would just drive you away."

"Why are you telling me this?"

Something shifted in Hesca's tone. "Because I need to know if it's true."

Clade gave her a long look. Was she expecting him to pledge his loyalty? The idea almost made him laugh out loud. Yet the moment seemed somehow unsuited for a straight rejection.

"You're right," he said after a moment. "Piator should have been banging heads. If we leave the defence to him, Spyridon is lost."

Hesca eyed him, her expression once more inscrutable. "Yes," she said. "It is." Her gaze narrowed. "What do you make of Agli's claim that there are golems in the city?"

"It'd be nice, wouldn't it?" Clade said neutrally. "A Valdori army turning up just when we need it? It'd make our task a damn sight easier."

Hesca cocked an eyebrow. "You don't think they're real?"

"Maybe. Who knows? But I wouldn't count on them showing up to save the day." He chuckled. "Though if they did, I'd say even Piator would be hard-pressed to screw things up."

She didn't buy it. He saw it at once. And at his mention of Piator, her expression tightened ever so slightly. Fear — perhaps for Spyridon, perhaps for her own ambition. From the outside, it all looked alike.

"Well," she said. "Perhaps you're right. But if you hear anything, let me know. I'll make it worth your while."

She'd scored a hit, managed to lift the corner of Clade's dissimulation for just a moment; but Clade sensed that she was off-balance too, struggling to maintain her own facade of calm control. He affected an amused smile, pressing for advantage. "I hope you remember what I told you. Coin only."

"So you did." A new expression crept over her face, sly and inviting; yet the calculating glint in her eyes remained. Slowly, she stood and sauntered across the room. "Are you sure you wouldn't like to reconsider?"

Clade's eyebrow rose. *Really? You'd go this far?* But he could see in her face that she knew he wasn't fooled, knew that they both understood exactly what game they were playing. And perhaps because of that, he found that he did, in fact, want to play.

"You never did tell me how you got that scar," he murmured.

"Neither I did," she said. "Maybe if you see it again, you'll be able to guess."

She took his hand, and he allowed her to lead him to the next room where a straw pallet barely large enough for two filled the floor. As they shed their clothes, she grasped his withered hand and pressed it against her scar, and Clade found himself holding back an unexpected surge of emotion. "There, you see?" she said, half to herself, and Clade was dimly aware that her voice was thick with some unnamed passion of her own. "It's just flesh. That's all it ever was."

In the end, when at last she cried her release, Clade couldn't tell if she was faking or not.

～

The sun shone down from a clear midday sky as Eilwen rode up the hill toward the Great Square. Her last climb — to meet with Piator Pronn — had left her leg aching for the rest of the day, so today she'd opted to hire a carriage with some of the money she'd obtained in Neysa. Reasonable though the decision was, the expense sat uncomfortably with her. Surely there were better uses for her coin than to spoil herself in such a fashion. She stared half-heartedly out the window, watching the buildings scroll by and resisting the irrational urge to close the shutters so nobody might spy her within and think less of her for her indulgence.

Beside her sat Orval, gazing out on his own side with rapt concentration. Eilwen glanced sidelong at him as often as she dared, fascinated by the delight in his gaze. At moments like this he seemed younger than his fourteen years, still open to wonder despite the pain and anger from losing his sister to the Oculus. Eilwen felt a sudden rush of sympathy for Den and Irilli who, after having one child stolen from them, had somehow found the strength to surrender the other to Eilwen's care. She doubted she could have done the same in their place. *Gods, may I never have to find out.*

It occurred to her that she and Orval had never discussed his parents' decision to send him away with her. At first, Mara's presence had made it hard for the two of them to talk freely. By the time they arrived at Spyridon, the pattern of their exchanges had been set, and soon after she had become distracted by Clade's demands and the approaching Oculus army. She looked away, ashamed by her neglect. How must he feel to be uprooted from his home and entrusted to the care of an aunt he hadn't seen in years, only to be left to linger at the boarding house while she spent her time working?

Well. When they returned to their room, she would put aside her work and they would talk. Perhaps, if it helped, she might even make an effort to befriend the dog.

This morning, however, Jak had been left behind. No carriage would have admitted so unsightly a stray, and in any case a dog on the Great Square would have attracted too much attention. Eilwen had explained to Orval the importance of keeping a low profile. The direct approach she'd employed with Moneyer Velle would not help her with Ral Garvan — Eilwen had been fairly confident that the moneyer was innocent, but she could make no such presumption about Garvan. Sandrine hadn't offered much insight into the man, but she had made passing mention of certain political inclinations. It seemed Garvan was a frequent participant in public disputations, typically arguing in favour of whatever proposition might reduce the taxes and levies for which he was liable. By good fortune, one such disputation was scheduled for tomorrow — today, now — giving Eilwen an opportunity to assess the man and consider her next step.

The carriage deposited them just below the Arcade on the edge of a wide circle filled with vehicles: private conveyances for the most part, their drivers waiting for the return of their masters, though several other carriages for hire could be seen dropping off passengers or circling for custom. Picking their way through horse dung, Eilwen and Orval climbed to the top of the road and up the broad staircase that led to the Arcade and the Library beyond.

The Square had been busy enough the other morning, but midday was busier still. Students swarmed the food vendors and congregated on the small patches of lawn around the fountain, their numbers undiminished by the Library's closure to the public. Across the Square, a debate was already underway on the raised platform: a red-faced man with curled moustaches stood haranguing his opponent, a gnome-like woman who seemed to shake her head at every other word.

A shiver of recognition passed through Eilwen at the sight of the man. *Ral Garvan.* The Woodtraders' dealings with him had been few, but she'd crossed paths with him once as a junior trader working on behalf of a more senior colleague. She could no longer recall the specifics of whatever proposal the Woodtraders had put forward. All she remembered was that Garvan had refused to discuss the matter with her, insisting that her colleague deal with him directly rather than through a wide-eyed flunky.

The beast stirred in her belly at the thought, raising its head in question. *A hunt?*

No, Eilwen returned. *No hunt.* All she sought today was information. Perhaps she couldn't assume Garvan's innocence, but neither could she presume his guilt. And even if the man were guilty, that would merely give her one more link in the chain, one more step toward the missing gold and whoever had orchestrated its theft.

"What is it?" Orval said, and Eilwen realised she'd stopped still. "Do you see him?"

Eilwen resumed her course, moving slowly toward the platform. "Up there, with the moustache."

"Piator Pronn is a relic of a bygone age," Garvan shouted as they drew near. The man was dressed in maroon trousers and a charcoal shirt, with a pair of pins on the points of his collar in the shape of a stylised G. "If he cannot or will not perform the job we all pay him to do, then I say the standing army should be abolished and a general militia formed in its place. What need have we of men and women who sit around all day, polishing their swords" — he stressed the phrase, eliciting a round of coarse laughter — "and growing fat on food purchased with our taxes? The time has come to release these people, and the cost of their upkeep, to the city that supports them. Who knows better than we how to defend our own city?"

"Ah, such a noble proposition," said the gnome-like woman with the sorrowful air of one forced to correct an embarrassing relative. "Such concern for the city's wellbeing. Yet my interlocutor is the most prominent dealer of weapons and what he inventively terms 'defensive services' in all of Spyridon. Who, I ask you, would stand to profit if his proposals became policy? Why, none other than Ral

Garvan himself!"

A murmur rose and then died down on the other side of the Square. Eilwen ignored it. Garvan's denunciation of Piator Pronn sat awkwardly with the notion that Pronn was also involved in the theft. Then again, perhaps Garvan's diatribe was merely a ploy to present a facade of conflict over their clandestine cooperation. The latter explanation might also account for the proposal's odd timing. Surely Garvan was sufficiently well connected to have heard the rumours of an approaching army. Why suggest something like this now, when in a matter of days the entire city would be looking to Pronn to deliver it?

"Self-interest?" Garvan retorted. "Precisely the reverse! Release our soldiers from the city's teat and I will instantly face an array of competitors all seeking to provide the same services that I do. Disband the army and my biggest purchaser of weapons will vanish overnight." The murmur behind Eilwen rose again, louder this time, forcing Garvan to raise his voice yet further. "But I am in a unique position, my friends. I see the problems confronting our city. I see the solutions. How can I not speak out?" People around Eilwen began to jostle her, turning around and craning their necks. "Oh, for the Weeper's sake, what is going on?"

Eilwen turned. The centre of the commotion seemed to be on the other side of the fountain. She and Orval exchanged glances, then pushed into the crowd, Orval pressing ahead and clearing a path for Eilwen to follow. As they approached the edge of the Square, Eilwen felt a growing tension in the air: a charged uncertainty edging toward outright fear. "Who *are* they?" someone said just ahead of her; and in that moment she knew.

Oh, Orval. I'm sorry.

The boy froze. Somehow Eilwen managed to slip beside him. They stared past the Arcade, past the city, where the fields and pastures now crawled with movement.

"It can't be," he said in a quavering voice unlike anything she'd heard from him before. "Not again."

An army marched toward the city. Squads and companies, guns and cavalry, and everywhere the glitter of sun on killing steel.

The Oculus had arrived at last.

CHAPTER 14

Your hand betrays you with every clenched fist.
Your eye betrays you with every wanton stare.
Your mouth betrays you with every whispered falsehood.
The worm coils ever tighter, and you are undone.

— Traditional Sarean chant

Tiy. Arandras stood before the golem at the edge of the crowded first-floor gallery, searching its pinprick orange eyes for any reaction. *Tell me of your making.*

Silence answered him, hard and impenetrable. Tiy stared sightlessly past Arandras, the other golems arrayed haphazardly behind it as though frozen in mid-conversation at some unlikely social gathering.

Arandras tried again. *Tiy. You spoke of this before. You said you saw streams of light. Describe them for me.*

Tiy made no response. From somewhere upstairs came the sound of muffled footsteps: Mara moving from one room to another.

Arandras exhaled. *Tiy, can you hear me?*

I hear you.

Then why do you not answer me?

I answer you now.

No elaboration was forthcoming. None ever was. Whenever Arandras accused Tiy of ignoring his questions, its response was always the same. *I answer you now.* As though whatever had happened leading up to this moment was no longer worthy of discussion.

Frustrated, Arandras left the gallery and traipsed downstairs, past the smiling pouch-rat that now stood watch at the foot of the stairs to the entertaining room he'd chosen as his makeshift study. The large windows looked onto a green, shade-filled garden, and although the room's shelves had been stripped bare, the comfort of its oversized suede armchairs more than made up for any lack of ornamentation. Arandras sank into a chair with a sigh and considered what he knew.

He'd spent half the night looking through the books Druce had given him. One, heavy with old scents, was a lexicon offering translations between Yaran and Old Valdori. When he realised what it was, Arandras had felt a surge of savage vindication. Old Valdori was the language of the golems, the only language they understood. Why else would Clade study it if not to prepare for some attempt at communication?

But the other book, the one that Onsoth had presumably been killed for, was the real prize. Arandras had never before seen so diverse a collection of texts recounting so many aspects of the golems' existence at first hand: their crafting, their training, the tactical advantages offered by particular deployments, even what looked like a description of their concealment in the cavern Arandras had found. No doubt some of the pieces had been embellished — the paranoia evident in the final pages seemed excessive, to say the least — but in his first hasty skim he'd found nothing that contradicted his own experiences since binding the golems almost a year ago.

There was even a breakdown of sorts listing the sorcery required to create a golem. Much of the terminology meant nothing to Arandras, but one section in particular caught his eye.

The final infusion of life into the Magnified body occurs in a chamber built singly for this purpose. At the appointed hour, when the sun strikes the apparatus just so, its rays begin to gather about the ceiling; slowly at first, then ever more rapidly, filling the chamber with an effulgence so great that we must bind our eyes with cloth. When the sun itself grows dim beside our own incandescent light, the creators of this miracle begin their final, most complex working: the Seed, the Strand, and the Chain. The three must be constructed together and resolved in unison, else the Magnified will assuredly fail in some manner: either to cohere or to obey, to enter the moment or to remain in it.

Arandras read and re-read the passage with growing excitement. Here at last was the answer, or at least the outline of one. Other sections scattered throughout the book spoke in more detail of Seed, Strand, and Chain, each of which appeared to serve a different purpose in the golem's complex weave of sorcery. Removing just one of those bindings — the Chain, if Arandras had to guess — might be enough to free the golems.

He picked up the book and reviewed the passage once more. *The three must be constructed together and resolved in unison, else the Magnified will assuredly fail in some manner: either to cohere or to obey, to enter the moment or to remain in it.* The structure suggested an equivalence between the two pairs, as though "cohering" and "entering the moment" were two descriptions of the same thing. Maybe the analogy carried a meaning that was now lost, informed by reference to some cultural touchstone of the time. All the same, it was an odd likeness. *A failure to enter the moment, or to remain in it...*

I answer you now. The words were Tiy's standard reply whenever Arandras questioned its lack of response. Beyond question, Tiy and the others existed in the moment. Arandras had observed more than once that the golems seemed incapable of discussing anything that strayed into the past or the future. Yet Tiy had spoken of "relics", which could only be memories of past experiences. How could that be if they knew nothing beyond the present?

Or did the golems no longer understand what memory was?

Maybe that was why his questioning had failed. Tiy's flashes of memory had occurred as present experiences, triggered by sunlight on the hill and some feature of the beach at night. The "relic" had, in a sense, appeared before Tiy; then it had vanished, and none of Arandras's questions had been able to bring it back.

But what if it were to be triggered again?

Arandras jumped from his seat and hurried up the stairs. Between the top of the staircase and the end of the crowded gallery was a large door leading to an uncovered balcony. Arandras pushed the door open and summoned the golem.

Tiy. Step onto the balcony and look at the sky. The golem jolted into grinding motion. Arandras waited until it was in position. *Can you see the sun?*

Yes.

Position yourself so that you look directly into it.

Tiy obeyed.

What do you see?

I see the sun.

What else?

There was an uncharacteristic pause. As the silence stretched, Tiy tilted its head, the movement barely perceptible save for the faint scrape that accompanied it. Then, slowly, Tiy began to speak.

A relic. Streams of light. The makers gather. I am planted and woven. I am tied. I am complete.

A surge of triumph filled Arandras. There it was: confirmation not only of his own guesses but also of what he'd read in the book. Planted, woven, tied. On some level, Tiy was aware of the sorcery that had given it form.

Come inside, Arandras commanded. Asking Tiy to remember the details of its binding would be futile — but in the cavern Arandras had once asked a golem what it saw and it had told him of Clade's sorcery. *Look at the golem standing nearest to us. What do you see?*

My sister.

Do you see her Seed?

No.

The answer caught Arandras by surprise. For a moment, everything had seemed so clear. *Is that because she doesn't have one?*

No, Tiy returned without hesitation. *The Seed cannot be seen.*

Arandras frowned. *What about the Strand? Or the Chain?*

The words rolled in Arandras's thoughts like boulders. *My sister's Strand. Slender and everlasting. It loops and dives and fills. My sister's Chain. Held and holding. Order. Orders. My sister inclines.*

Tell me of the Chain. Tell me how its sorcery is composed.

Sorcery. My sister's Chain. One foundation. Thirty-three stream-conduit-vincula. Eleven ligament-stream-contractors. Five ligament-stream-expanders. Seventeen first-level compound components. Among them, two modules of direction-determination, each consisting of: One foundation, subordinate. Fourteen flow-passage-vincula —

Stop. A wide grin formed on Arandras's face. *This* was how the binding could be broken. Tiy's description could give a suitably talented sorcerer the insight they required to understand and remove the binding. It was possible. By all the gods, *it was possible.*

"Hey, Mara!" Arandras shouted in delight. Was she still upstairs? He wasn't sure. "Guess what?"

There was a rattle of a window latch from somewhere above. "I see them too," Mara called back. "Ugly, aren't they?"

"I know how to — what?" Arandras broke off. "What are you talking about?"

"Look east."

Confused, Arandras stepped onto the balcony. The sun was high overhead, and for a moment he wasn't sure which way to turn. Then his gaze fell upon the horizon and his question was answered.

Soldiers filled the fields like ants. A line of wagons snaked down the road, the sun flashing off the polished cannons they conveyed. Mounted figures trotted here and there, directing the movements of guns and squads and companies.

No banners flew above the army. None were needed.

"Shit," Arandras said.

"Yeah." Mara stood at an open window just above and behind him, and although her tone was dry, Arandras could hear the dread underneath. "Tell me about it."

～

"In battle," Clade said, his fingers running lightly along Hesca's scar and brushing her breast. "Saving some wet-behind-the-ears recruit from tripping over his own sword."

Hesca gave a languorous smile. "No."

"No?" Clade's fingers reached the end of the scar and reversed direction. "Don't tell me you were the recruit who tripped over her sword."

"Shame on you," Hesca said. "And no."

"I don't know. Attacked by a wildcat while scaling a peak in the Kemenese."

"Wrong again." Hesca yawned and stretched, and the sheet that had been struggling to cover her stomach slipped further to pool at her waist. "And with that, boys and girls, the game is over. Better luck next time."

Next time? The bait was plain enough, but Clade didn't bite. "Where to now in the busy life of a Spyridoni subcommander?"

"Where else?" Hesca rolled to a sitting position and began collecting her clothes. "Back to the barracks. See what crises have sprung up in my absence. Then to the Four Hands." She picked up Clade's trousers and tossed them onto his chest. "You should put those on if you don't want Zann admiring those shapely legs of yours."

Clade wasn't sure how he felt about having his legs described as shapely. "Zann's coming here?"

"If I don't get to the barracks first." Hesca dressed unhurriedly but efficiently. "Are you getting up, or what?"

"Hmm? Oh." Clade swung his feet reluctantly to the floor. "Of course."

His back to Hesca, Clade began to pull on his clothes. Dressing was awkward these days — his withered hand made tying points difficult, and merely getting his arm through the sleeve of his shirt was often a challenge. Taking a breath, he thrust his feet into his trousers and hauled them up as best he could.

"So, how long did you work for the Oculus, anyway?"

The knot he was trying to form fell away in his fingers. "I never said I worked for the Oculus."

"No. But you did, didn't you? The way you steered the discussion away from yourself in front of the circle." Fully clothed but not yet armed, Hesca strolled around to his side of the pallet. "Tell me I'm wrong."

Clade glared, but she met his gaze without flinching. After a moment he looked away. "You're not wrong."

"How long, then?"

Clade returned his attention to the points of his trousers. "Long enough."

"They give you that?" Hesca gestured at his hand.

"After a fashion."

Hesca sighed. "Listen, I'm not unsympathetic. But if you know something you haven't told me yet, something about why the

Oculus are here, what they want, how they fight — anything — now's the time."

"I told Pronn what I know," Clade said. "I would have told the circle the same if they'd let me. There's nothing else worth discussing."

"I hope that's true," Hesca returned. "I really do."

His points tied at last, Clade looked up. "I assure you, I have no desire to see Oculus mercenaries marching through these streets."

They stared at each other for a long moment. Slowly, Hesca nodded. "Good."

Clade grabbed his shirt and forced his withered hand into a sleeve. Suddenly he couldn't clothe himself quickly enough. "Good," he muttered.

Relaxed once more, Hesca picked up her sword belt and began strapping it on. "How's Eilwen progressing? Found anything that points to Piator?"

"She'll be done when she's done," Clade said. "If Pronn's the guilty party, we'll know soon enough."

"'If?' You said it yourself. With Piator in charge, Spyridon is lost."

Clade shrugged into his greatcoat. "I agreed to find out where your gold went," he said roughly. "Not to arrange events to your liking. If the evidence points elsewhere but you want to stitch Pronn up anyway, that'll be your problem, not mine." He held out his good hand, palm up. "Now, if you're quite done?"

Hesca glanced down. "What's that for?"

"My retainer, of course. Today's. Yesterday's. Don't think I collected the day before, either."

Her mouth settled into a hard line. "Fine." Digging in her purse, she pulled out some coins and slapped them into his palm. "Satisfied?"

"Thank you." His composure restored, at least in part, Clade inclined his head and gave a faint smile. "Until next time."

He left her then, striding from the house with his boots still unlaced. Only when he heard the door swing shut behind him did he permit himself the luxury of a long, steadying breath.

Hells, but that woman was dangerous. Up until this morning he'd felt confident that he had the subcommander's measure, but now he found himself wondering. She wasn't as polished a player as some — in retrospect, her attempt to use both carrot and stick to induce Clade to her cause was painfully obvious. But her willingness to go to such lengths suggested a level of desperation with which Clade was all too familiar. Clade had felt it himself while planning his escape from the Oculus. It had made him unpredictable, given him an edge — a double-edge, truth be told, as likely to cut himself as his enemies, though in the end he had prevailed.

But here and now, the edge was hers. Did she truly seek the good of the city above all, as she continuously insisted? Did she welcome the looming crisis as an opportunity to revive baulked ambitions and move against Piator Pronn? Had her intentions changed now that Spyridon was host to Arandras's golems? All Clade knew for certain was that Hesca perceived him as important to her plans, whatever they might be.

And yet there had been that moment between them, scar pressed to withered hand, in which it had seemed she wanted nothing more from him than simple human connection. In that moment, Clade could almost have imagined that he wanted nothing more than that himself.

Probably it had just been one more ploy to keep him off-balance.

He was halfway back to his suite before the growing tension caught his notice. People scurried past, most heading deeper into the city, several glancing over their shoulders as though they feared pursuit. Distant cries carried above the ordinary noise of the city, followed by the unmistakable sound of horns from somewhere near the gates. Filled with sudden foreboding, Clade quickened his pace, feet slipping in their unlaced boots. He could think of only one event that might trigger such a reaction. The sooner he got back to his suite and off the streets, the better.

"Clade?" someone called from the other side of the street. "Clade, is that you?"

Clade looked up. A stoop-shouldered man holding a large earthenware bowl stared back, his face strangely familiar. "Do I know you?"

The man smiled and nodded, and heaved the earthenware bowl at Clade.

Time slowed. As the bowl tumbled through the air, three distinct thoughts struck Clade in rapid succession.

Rathzange.

Oculus.

Claybinder.

Spinning, Clade covered his head and dived for the ground. The bowl shattered in mid-air, flinging wicked shards at his arms and back. Panicked screams filled the air as pain struck Clade in half a dozen places: neck, back, ear. Groaning, he rolled over just in time to see Rathzange launch himself at Clade with a knife in his hand.

"Traitor!" he hissed, swinging wildly at Clade's face. "Fucking traitor! How dare you?"

Clade grabbed for Rathzange's knife hand, missed, ducked his head as the blade rushed past and grabbed again. Snarling, Rathzange slashed back and forth, slicing into Clade's forearm. Clade shoved back, desperate to shift his attacker's weight and find some leverage. The man swung again, and this time Clade barely avoided the blow. His good hand scrabbled for a rock, a pottery shard, anything that might serve as a weapon —

Rathzange jerked upright. A sword point sprouted from his chest like a message from the gods, then withdrew. With a gurgling whimper, Rathzange fell sideways to reveal Zann standing behind him, his blade dripping scarlet.

"Well, well. If it isn't the mouse himself." Zann's grin looked positively delighted. "It's like I always thought. Squeaks like a rusty wheel, but no teeth."

Clade stared at Zann, blood pounding in his ears. "You followed me."

"You're welcome, mouse." Stooping, Zane grabbed Clade by the shirt and hauled him to his feet. "Best you run along home now. The big boys and girls have work to do, and I have a feeling it's not going to be pretty."

~

Eilwen shouldered her way through the crowd, Orval at her heels. The beast uncoiled within her, aroused by the growing commotion. She tried to return it to its cage, tugging half-heartedly on her goatskin belt, but to no avail. Fear filled the air, and the beast drank deep.

"Where are we going?" Orval said, his voice almost lost in the clamour. "Did you know they were coming here?"

Eilwen dismissed his questions with a shake of her head. There would be time to talk later. Right now an opportunity presented itself, one that might not arise again. Shouts filled the Square: threats and imprecations, prayers and cries for help. Students milled uselessly about, adding to the press of bodies. With luck, it might take Ral Garvan the better part of half an hour to reach his waiting carriage. Time enough for Eilwen to make some enquiries of her own.

They squeezed down the first set of stairs to the Arcade. Eilwen kept to the inner side where the view was poorer and the crush not so bad, but even so the flow of traffic was against her. More people were arriving, streaming up from the lower districts to see the approaching army. Teeth bared, Eilwen forced her way forward, glaring at anyone who crossed her path until they reached the stairs and emerged at the top of the road.

With a quick glance to check that Orval was still with her, Eilwen hurried down the side road that led to the carriage circle. "We need to find Garvan's carriage," she said, slowing slightly to allow Orval to come alongside. "It's probably marked with the same G symbol you saw on his collar. Tell me if you see it."

"Why?" Orval demanded. "What does it matter? The Oculus are *here* —"

"I'll explain later," Eilwen snapped. "But we need to do this *now*. Can I count on you?"

Orval gaped at her. "But... the Oculus..."

"I know." Eilwen took a breath, forcing herself to soften her tone. "I know. But they're not going to get in. Not here. What I'm doing will help, all right?" She nodded as if in agreement, willing him to believe her. "Are you with me?"

Fear filled Orval's voice. "Promise me they won't get in."

Nobody could make such a promise. Eilwen did anyway. "I promise."

"All right." He drew a shaky breath and pointed past her. "Is that the carriage you mean?"

It was parked a third of the way around the circle, large and black, with the same stylised G painted on the door. The trim and the hubs of its wheels were of polished brass: decorative enough to draw attention but not so much as to be deemed garish. Like everyone else, the driver stared down the hill, ignoring the nervous whickers of his horses.

"That's the one." Eilwen gave Orval a swift smile. "Good job. What I need you to do now is wait here and watch for Garvan. If you see him, shout. Can you do that?"

"I think so."

"Good." Eilwen lifted his chin so that his gaze met hers. "I'm relying on you."

Orval nodded uncomfortably and Eilwen let him go. As she turned to consider her route, the beast rose within her. *Now we hunt,* it thought, sniffing the air as it considered the scene before her. *Approach on the near side, then climb up behind him. Dagger through the back or across the neck.*

No. Eilwen yanked the goatskin belt hard. *We do not kill today. We seek information, nothing more.*

The beast subsided, and Eilwen set off: past a pair of unhitched carriages bearing the colours of the Library, around a particularly large pile of horse dung, and giving a wide berth to a knot of children at the mouth of a narrow path that dropped steeply to another street below. Garvan's driver seemed mesmerised by the view beyond the wall, staring and mouthing something that might have been a ritual prayer. Eilwen set her foot in the carriage's step, grimacing at the pain in her leg as she pulled herself onto the bench; but the driver was so transfixed by what he saw that he made no response to her presence until she pressed the point of her dagger against his back.

"Steady," she said as he flinched, grasping his shoulder with her other hand to prevent him from turning. "I'm not here to hurt you. I just want to ask you a few questions."

"No," the man said, his throat bobbing as he swallowed. "Piss off."

Eilwen leaned closer. "You haven't heard my questions yet," she murmured in his ear. "They're really not worth your life."

But the man seemed to possess more courage than his reaction to the Oculus army suggested. "My name is Morrus Tresener," he said thickly. "I work for Ral Garvan, who will skin you alive when he hears of this. I have nothing more to say."

"Thank you, Morrus," Eilwen replied. "Your name was my first question. See how easy this can be?"

The man cursed, but otherwise remained silent.

"Do you want to know my next question, Morrus? Here it comes." She tightened her grip on his shoulder. "Where do you take the coin that's supposed to go to the barracks?"

The man twisted savagely, tearing himself free from Eilwen's grasp, and the beast surged within her. Ducking beneath his flailing arm, Eilwen darted in, whipping her blade around so that it pressed against the man's throat.

"*Where?*" she demanded, channelling all of the beast's rage and menace into a single word. "Answer or die."

"I can't tell you." Morrus made an abortive attempt to swallow, his throat rising and falling beneath Eilwen's dagger. "Ral will kill me."

"Ral's not here," the beast and Eilwen snarled together. "I am."

"All right!" Morrus cried, blinking fearfully as Eilwen increased the blade's pressure. "It's true. We take some to the barracks. The rest goes to the Lasavis." Eilwen narrowed her eyes. "The Lasavi twins! The stained-glass makers. Their workshop is just north of the mint." He closed his eyes. "It's practically on the way. No detour, no reason to suspect..."

There. The beast swelled in satisfaction. *Now we feast.*

Eilwen hesitated. It would be easy enough to do. Press a little harder, open the man's throat and slip away. She could be gone before anyone noticed.

"Please." The man's nerve was gone. Only fear and supplication remained. "I've told you everything."

He is one of them, the beast insisted. *Now he is ours.*

"No," Eilwen whispered. The man was just a merchant's employee. Yet he had aided the Oculus, however indirectly. Perhaps he did deserve to die.

A distant voice reached her ears. "Eilwen!" The voice sounded familiar, but just at the moment she couldn't place it. "Eilwen! He's here!"

Growling, she looked up.

For a moment she didn't know what she was looking for. Then she saw him. A man in a dark shirt stared at her from across the crowd, his face red behind his curled moustaches, his eyes filled with murder.

Garvan.

The sight was like a slap of cold water. Eilwen flinched, eliciting a yelp from Morrus as her dagger drew blood. "Don't kill me," he begged, then cringed as he spotted Garvan. "Oh, gods. He's here."

Shaking off the beast's hold, Eilwen lowered her dagger. "I won't tell him if you don't," she murmured in the man's ear.

She turned and slid from the bench, grunting at the jolt in her leg as she landed. The beast howled, mourning its lost prey, and she yanked the goatskin belt tight. Slipping between carriages, she crept around the circle, hurrying past the knot of children and away down the path to the street below.

~

Over the course of the afternoon, Arandras and Mara watched the Oculus army deploy around the city. Two large companies positioned themselves just out of cannon range to the north and east, cutting off the roads to Anstice and Acantha respectively. Their numbers were not yet great enough to encircle the city's star-shaped wall, but Arandras suspected that this was merely the vanguard. The army's peculiar mode of travel — moving in small squads so as to maintain secrecy for as long as possible — meant that the arrival of soldiers would be staggered over several days.

A bold commander might have seized the moment and ordered an immediate strike, but for whatever reason, Piator Pronn made no such move. The Oculus were permitted to establish their position without disruption, digging trenches and laying spikes, pitching tents and building rudimentary emplacements. In a matter of hours, the fields around the two main roads were transformed into twin camps bristling with defensive weaponry.

Five hours after the army's arrival, the east gate opened and a single rider trotted out under a flag of parley. The rider made it halfway to the camp before a flurry of arrows launched from his destination, the missiles striking the ground just ahead of the horse's path. After a lengthy pause, the emissary decided to heed the warning and returned to the city.

"Gods." Mara shivered despite the mild afternoon. "It's like watching thugs line up in the street to burn down your house."

They sat on a claw-footed settee in an upper room, turned around so that it faced the window. Even though they'd been talking about the impending siege for days, the reality of seeing it unfold before him gave Arandras an unexpected sense of heaviness. Mara seemed to feel it more — her normal sly humour was gone, replaced with a strange morbidity that appeared to derive perverse satisfaction from every fresh movement they observed.

"It's just posturing so far," Arandras said. "Nobody's burning anything."

Mara exhaled. "Not yet, maybe. But there'll be fire aplenty before this is done, mark my words."

As if to confirm Mara's prediction, campfires began springing up within the encampments. Arandras leaned back and stretched his arm across Mara's shoulders, unsure if the gesture would be welcomed. "As long as it stays out there, I'd say we're fine."

"Yeah," Mara said, her voice barely above a whisper. "As long as it stays out there."

The last of the day's light ebbed away. Arandras resisted the urge to shift position, reluctant to break the fragile moment. The streets outside sounded no different to normal, though that didn't mean much. Any unrest was unlikely to find its way to the wealthier part of the city, or at least not yet. But with the fall of night it was almost possible to imagine themselves somewhere else, away from Spyridon and all that it entailed — just the two of them, alone somewhere, sitting together in the dark.

"Arandras," Mara said softly, and he felt her turn toward him. The faint scent of the spiced Kharjik solution she used to wash her hair tickled his nose.

Arandras took a breath. "Yeah?"

"I really need to pee."

For a moment there was silence; then Arandras gave an

involuntary laugh. "Best go do that, then."

Mara shifted on the settee, and Arandras found himself pulled into a swift, fierce hug. "Thank you," she whispered in his ear. She released him before he could form a response, standing and heading downstairs.

"You're welcome," Arandras murmured. He stared out at the array of tiny lights: stars above, campfires below. It had been a long time since he'd had occasion to offer comfort. He'd never been particularly good at it, not even with Tereisa. Perhaps it helped that Mara hadn't seemed to want anything more than his presence. That, at least, he could give.

Sighing, he pushed himself to his feet and followed Mara downstairs. He'd intended to return to Rhothe's while it was still light, but if he hurried he should still be in time.

He found Mara in the kitchen digging through one of the crates that had been delivered the other day. "You had the same thought, huh? Unfortunately our supper options are rather limited."

"I have to go out."

"To see Druce. Right." Mara looked up. "Are you sure that's a good idea after a day like today?"

"Perhaps not. But I have to go anyway." Arandras had told her about his discoveries and what they meant earlier. "You could come too."

"And leave the estate unattended?" Mara shook her head. "One of us has a contract to satisfy, remember?"

"We're not at the looting stage just yet," Arandras said. "Maybe it's different down in Port Gallin, but things seem calm enough up here."

"If the streets are as quiet as all that, you won't need me anyway."

Arandras gave a faint smile. "Fair point."

"Arandras," Mara said as he turned to go. "Be careful, all right?"

"I'll be sure to give a wide berth to any angry mobs that cross my path."

The streets around the estate were practically deserted, but the amount of traffic increased as Arandras approached the bottom of the hill. The people he passed seemed evenly split between the sombre and the agitated, though the balance shifted significantly toward the latter whenever he neared a bar or drinking house. Rhothe's Bar turned out to be no exception: numerous drinkers had spilt out into the street, forming a belligerent throng that seemed torn between blaming the army's arrival on each other and taking it up with the city circle forthwith.

Arandras slipped past as quietly as he could manage and made his way to the crowded back room. Subtle tension charged the air, though the voices expressing it were neither as loud nor as slurred as those outside. Here, a group of labourers huddled together, apparently debating whether to show up at their construction site tomorrow; there, a young loudmouth bragged that she'd be out of the city before sunrise; and in the corner, a trio of old men drank ciders around a *dilarj* table as though nothing were any different. Druce sat at his usual table, speaking intently with a flustered young woman wearing a Library student's robe; but when Arandras moved to approach, he found his way blocked by Mock.

"There's a whole line ahead of you," Mock said, his expression apologetic but firm. "You'll have to wait."

"Oh?" Arandras thrust his hands into his pockets. "How long?"

"Long." Mock's gaze travelled the room. "Quite a day, eh?"

"That's the truth," Arandras said, reluctantly allowing himself to be drawn into the inconsequential chatter Mock so clearly enjoyed. "Our new friends have barely arrived and the roads are cut already."

"Port's still open," Mock said. "I hear it's a madhouse down there."

"That's unlikely to last, surely."

"Yep. Figure that's how the rest of the army's getting here. Put 'em to shore somewhere close, then the ships can establish a blockade."

"Maybe." More likely the transports and the blockade would each consist of a different set of ships, but the general idea seemed right. "It's got to be an expensive business, though. Where do you think they found the money?"

Mock gave an amiable shrug. "A year ago nobody had even heard of the Oculus. A week ago they were just another reason to feel superior to Neysa. Who knows how long the bastards have been planning this?"

Who, indeed? Clade had told him nothing of the Oculus's history save that they'd been behind Tereisa's murder. The documents Mara had found were similarly light on detail, although they seemed to suggest a flow of resources onto the mainland from the eastern island of Pazia. For all Arandras knew, they might have been lurking out there for centuries.

A laugh sounded from Druce, apparently at something Druce himself had said. The Library student forced a smile in response. "You might as well settle in," Mock said. "Half the people in this room are already waiting their turn."

"That many?" Not a single booth or table was free, and some were clearly being shared by multiple groups. "We'll still be here at dawn."

"Could be." The student rose from Druce's table leaving behind a small pile of silver, and Mock pointed at the group of labourers. "You're up," he called.

Arandras muttered a curse. "What if I leave a message, and you pass it along when you get a chance?"

Mock shook his head. "Druce doesn't like messages. Prefers to know who he's dealing with."

"He already knows me. Come on, I'm not some panicked drunk who's going to vanish without paying. I've got no intention of leaving Spyridon. I just need Druce to find someone who can help me with a project."

Mock eyed Arandras dubiously. "What kind of project?"

"An unbinding," Arandras said. "I need a sorcerer, Mock. A good one. No Quill — strictly independent. I'll want to interview them myself, and I'll negotiate their rates directly if I decide to hire them, but I'll pay Druce a finder's fee of... what, two scudi? Is that sufficient?"

"Mmm." Mock drummed his fingers against the table. "Make it three," he said. "Plus a fourth right now on account of the message. Delivery charge."

Arandras frowned. "Say again?"

"You heard me." Mock met Arandras's gaze without shame. "A man's got to eat."

"Fine," Arandras said resignedly. "Send word when you have someone." He gave Mock the estate's address and placed a silver bit on the table. "Have the runner slip the note under the door if there's no answer."

"As you say." Mock looked past Arandras and pointed a finger. "You're next."

Arandras glanced around to see a balding, furtive-looking man replace the labourers at Druce's table. He spoke in a rapid whisper and Druce responded in kind, eyes gleaming with pleasure, as though the army beyond the wall represented nothing more than a welcome boost to patronage.

"He really is loving this, isn't he?" Arandras said.

"Why not? Tonight, business is good." Mock scooped up the coin. "Can't begrudge a man enjoying his work."

"I suppose," Arandras said. But as he turned to go, he felt an odd sense of relief that Mara wasn't there to see Druce ply his trade.

CHAPTER 15

Our passions are at once too large and too small for this world.

— Herev Gis, *First Sermons,* Chapter 11, Verse 8
(as ordered by the Gislean Provin)

CLADE PACED THE LENGTH OF his suite, one step after the next in an endless loop as his thoughts followed a similar circuit in his head. Bandages covered the gash on his withered forearm, applied by a physician at whose shop Clade had stopped on the way back. His other injuries, though painful, were relatively minor: some shallow cuts about his neck and ears from the shattered bowl, bruises on his hip and elbow, and some sore muscles in his back that were just as likely to have been caused by his morning encounter with Hesca as Rathzange's attack. Every step hurt, and he'd lost count of the number of times he'd forced himself to sit down. Yet for some reason he couldn't keep still.

The ferocity of Rathzange's assault still shocked him. Clade had known Rathzange as an unassuming, softly-spoken man with a faint Gislean accent and a moderate talent for claybinding. He'd rarely volunteered his thoughts on anything, and his stoop-shouldered posture had given the appearance of one content to take each day as it came. Clade couldn't recall the man so much as raising his voice, let alone threatening violence.

Yet the passion with which he had called Clade traitor had been unmistakable. For Rathzange, Clade's renunciation of Azador had been personal.

Rathzange still believed, Clade reminded himself. Restoration and renewal — Azador's grand purpose for the Oculus. Clade had been a believer himself before he'd seen through the lies. Or no, that wasn't quite right. He'd never stopped believing in the cause. The only faith he'd lost was the portion he'd devoted to his faithless god.

It occurred to Clade, as he completed another circuit, that he'd managed to escape the Oculus without truly facing the reactions of those he left behind. Kalie and Meline, Sinon and Garrett — all had died ignorant of Clade's true intentions. To Estelle he had revealed himself only at the point of her death; she had been more concerned with saving herself than with the weight of what he intended. Only Sera had glimpsed the truth, and her respect for him as a teacher had acted as a counterweight to her distress at his betrayal. Rathzange's murderous hatred was the first honest response he'd seen, and it depressed and frightened him in equal measure.

How easily he had imagined that other Oculus sorcerers would flock to him once he could guarantee the means of their unbinding. How quick he had been to dismiss the forces opposed to him as blind lackeys of Azador and the Council. He'd become so caught up in his own struggles that the possibility — indeed, the likelihood — of rejection from ordinary members of the Oculus had scarcely crossed his mind.

Better to face the truth now than be brought undone by it later on. However much he might wish it were otherwise, he had made himself anathema to the vast majority of Oculus. Even those who might harbour similar feelings would be forced to deny their doubts and publicly condemn him. There would be no wave of dissension, no secret communities of malcontents plotting to follow in his footsteps. If his example did inspire anyone else to flee, there was a good chance they'd be caught and killed before they reached him, and he would never even know that they had tried.

And besides all that, the Oculus clearly had no intention of letting Clade himself escape their grasp. Rathzange had been the second to come after him. More would follow. If he were to stay in one place for any length of time — essential if he wanted to be found by anyone seeking to join his cause — he would draw the attention of yet more assassins until, one day, his luck would run out and the Oculus would finally reclaim its own.

Gritting his teeth against his sore hip and back, Clade forced himself to sit once more. Night had fallen some time ago; a lamp in each of the two main rooms provided the suite's only light. If Zann's comment meant what Clade thought it did, the Oculus army had finally arrived. No doubt Hesca and Piator Pronn were holed up somewhere in the barracks right now discussing the city's defence.

Hesca. The day's events had left him scrambling to catch up. Images spun through his thoughts like leaves on the wind: Hesca asking about Arandras's golems; Hesca moving above him on the straw pallet; then Zann pulling his sword from Rathzange's body with a grin as wide as the sea. Surely there was no way Hesca could have anticipated the attack — so why in the hells had she sent Zann to follow him? Did she still trust him so little?

Perhaps she did. And maybe that wasn't unreasonable. Clade had himself been pondering Hesca's intentions just before Rathzange's assault. He could hardly blame her for harbouring the same doubts.

Yet Zann's presence did little to illuminate the subcommander's motives. Perhaps, unlikely as it seemed, she was truly concerned for his safety. Or perhaps she had simply wanted to track his movements, find out where he might go and who he might speak to. Whether such an interest was motivated by suspicion, malice, or some deeper scheme was impossible to guess.

All the same, Clade resented it. After everything he'd gone through to rid himself of Azador's prying eyes, the thought of someone else taking it upon themselves to spy on him left a foul taste in his mouth. It was small comfort to think that Hesca wanted to keep him alive. So had Azador.

With a grimace, Clade pushed himself to his feet and began pacing the room once more. The problem of Hesca and the problem of Azador were the same. When it came down to it, he was just not strong enough. Azador had no end of willing bodies it could send against him. Hesca had the Spyridon army at her disposal. Aside from Eilwen, Clade had nobody but himself.

And that thought brought him back to the reason he'd come to Spyridon in the first place, a reason he'd only just decided to put aside in order to focus on the Oculus invasion.

There'd be no need to fear assassins if he had a squad of golems serving as his bodyguard. No need to meddle in local politics with such power at his disposal. Even the Oculus army would not be able to withstand the might of the Valdori. If he could only find a way to claim Arandras's golems for himself, all of Clade's problems would vanish at a stroke and he would be free to pursue his true goal: the liberation of the Oculus from Azador, whether they wanted it or not.

He'd been foolish to set aside his original plans as if they were less important than the fate of the city. He saw that now. The truth was that there was nothing he could do just now to help Hesca or anyone else. But there was most definitely something he could do to help himself.

Clade turned in mid-circuit and knelt before the suite's chest. Fumbling at the catch with his good hand, he opened the lid and reached for the book he'd taken from Onsoth's corpse.

But the book was nowhere to be seen.

No, that's not possible. He dug into the chest, shoving and then flinging its remaining contents aside. Onsoth's book was not the only thing missing — the lexicon had disappeared too. Fear and anger surged through him as realisation sunk in. *Subcommander wants to see you, mouse.* Hesca had quizzed him about the golems, she'd fucked him on the pallet, and then she'd quizzed him some more — all to keep him from leaving too soon.

Clade stared sightlessly out the window, his fist clenched in rage. *You gods-damned bitch. I'll see you burn for this. I swear it.*

∼

"You knew." Orval glared accusingly at Eilwen from across the table. The morning sun was yet to rise above the roof of the neighbouring building, leaving their room and the lane below the window in shadow. "You knew the Oculus were on their way, but you brought us here anyway."

"It's not that simple," Eilwen began.

"Bullshit!" Orval turned as though trying to put more distance between them, but the room was too small and too bare. "You said talking to that carriage driver would help keep them out. How could you know that if you didn't already know they were coming?"

Half a dozen evasions flitted through Eilwen's mind. *I wasn't sure Spyridon was their destination. I thought we still had time to get out. I just meant I was trying to help the city.* She let them pass. Perhaps she had misled Orval by omission, but nothing she'd said to him since leaving Neysa had been false. She didn't want to change that now.

"Yes," she said. "I knew they were coming."

"Then *why did you bring me here?*"

"I told you." Eilwen said softly, offering the words as a gentle reminder rather than a rebuke. "I needed to see my employer. Part of that was warning him about the Oculus."

"Oh, so you told him, just not me."

Eilwen took a breath. "I thought we'd only be here a day. Maybe two. Then we'd be gone, and it wouldn't matter."

"You thought," Orval repeated, his attempted sneer betraying him with its brittleness. "Then what? Your *employer* told you to stay?"

"Told? No. Clade asked me, and I agreed." Eilwen resisted the urge to reach out in entreaty. "This is our chance, Orval. Don't you see? Spyridon hasn't fallen. If we can beat the Oculus here, maybe we can weaken them so much that they'll leave Neysa, too. Send them back to wherever they... what's wrong?"

Orval's face had drained of colour. "No," he whispered, sinking to the floor and turning his face against the wall. "No, this isn't happening."

"Orval?" Mystified, Eilwen crouched beside him. "It's all right. You don't have to help if you don't want to. You can just stay here and look after Jak."

"You don't understand."

"Then explain it to me."

Orval buried his head in his arms. "I can't."

Gods have mercy. Eilwen drew a breath, torn between concern for the boy and her own frustration. Her leg was still suffering the effects of yesterday's exertions, and her crouch just now wasn't helping. "Nobody's going to hurt you," she said. "You're safe here. I won't let anything happen to you."

Orval huddled against the wall and said nothing.

Eilwen straightened with a grimace. Something she'd said had set him off, but she had no idea what it was or how to get him to talk. "I need to go out soon," she said at last. "Is there anything else you want to tell me? Any other questions you want to ask?"

Orval shook his head.

"All right. We'll talk more when I get back." Eilwen paused. "And Orval? Maybe think about staying inside while I'm gone."

She left, her thoughts filled with the image of Orval curled against the wall. The boy's distress was plain, but there was something else there too, some fear that he seemed reluctant to put into words. Perhaps the prospect of fighting the Oculus had stirred up some painful memory of the assault on Neysa. Was he ashamed of something he'd done — or failed to do — while Neysa was besieged? Did he doubt his courage if a similar situation were to arise? Maybe Den and Irilli had glimpsed whatever this was and had hoped to grant him some distance from it by entrusting him to her care. Her face grew hot at the thought. *Ah, gods, let me not have failed him that badly.*

The area north of the mint was a maze of streets and lanes. Carts and wagons trundled past, transporting tools, raw materials, and finished goods to and from the countless artisans inhabiting the district. Eilwen was forced to ask directions several times before she located the workshop operated by the Lasavi twins: a modestly-sized studio with tall, clear windows. A small piece above the door showed off the stained-glass-makers' craft: a rising phoenix, every feather a different colour, the nest beneath it wreathed in orange and red.

Eilwen entered the shop cautiously and glanced around. In the centre of the room stood a large worktable, upon which lay a partially-filled moulding surrounded by fragments of glass and odd tools. A fat kiln lurked in one of the rear corners; in the other, large panels of coloured glass rested endwise in a frame. A peculiar scent tickled Eilwen's nostrils, metallic and caustic at the same time, and she fought the urge to sneeze.

"Hello?" A rangy woman in a heavy apron — one of the Lasavis, presumably — rose from behind the glass panels and eyed Eilwen doubtfully. "You buying, or just gawking?"

Eilwen gestured to a pair of completed pieces propped against the wall: portraits of what appeared to be a wealthy merchant couple. "These are good," she said. "How long does it take to complete something like this?"

"How long does it take to wind a ball of string?" the woman returned, then paused and drew a breath. "Forgive me. My brother —" She shook her head. "It's been a trying morning."

"It's quite all right." Eilwen glanced around the shop in what she hoped was a suitably impressed fashion. Nobody else seemed present at the moment, but the doors at the side and back of the workshop were both closed. "You and your brother are very talented."

The frown in the woman's forehead eased slightly. "Would you like to commission a piece?"

"Very much," Eilwen said. "As soon as funds allow." If there was anything here to confirm what Garvan's driver had told her, it would be in the rear of the shop, not out in plain sight. "Are there other sample pieces I could look at?"

"Not just now," the woman said, tucking a rag into her apron pocket and moving to the front of the shop. "What did you say your name was?"

"A pity," Eilwen said as though she hadn't heard the question. "I'm more interested in landscapes than portraiture —"

"No name? Perhaps we have a mutual friend." The woman now stood before the front door, a growing tension in her posture belying her casual tone. "Do you happen to know a merchant by the name of Ral Garvan?"

Eilwen forced herself to meet the woman's eyes. "I don't think so."

The woman stared at her, and Eilwen knew her lie had been detected. A door opened and closed behind her, but she didn't dare break the woman's gaze to look.

"Is that her?" asked a male voice.

"Could be," the woman replied.

"Turn around," said the voice, and Eilwen did so to find a lanky man bearing a clear resemblance to the woman she'd been speaking to. He gave her a hawkish look that reminded her uncomfortably of Caralange, the Woodtraders sorcerer back in Anstice. "What's your name?"

"What's yours?" Eilwen shot back.

The man affected surprise. "You don't know me? I am Osco Lasavi. This is my sister, Yasa. And you are?"

"Leaving." The beast growled warily, and Eilwen eased her hand to her belt. "If you'll excuse me."

"Not so fast." Yasa's hand closed over Eilwen's arm. "Let's talk —"

Eilwen grabbed her dagger and whirled around. Yasa fell back with a cry, clutching her forearm, and Eilwen leapt to the doorway. "Let's not," she said, raising the dagger and glaring at Osco as he stepped forward. "Don't try to follow me."

The rear door swung open and a pair of scowling, heavily-built men burst into the room. With a final wave of her dagger Eilwen turned and ran into the busy street, swerving to dodge a pale wom-an eating an apple, then darting forward to avoid being trampled by a draught horse pulling a high-sided wagon. Ignoring the driver's curses, she ducked behind the wagon and swung herself up onto its side.

Something boomed in the distance, and from somewhere near the shop came a shout of frustration. Eilwen flattened herself against the wagon as best she could, biting her lip against the fresh pain in her leg as she was carried down the street. Another boom sounded, then a third. Confused, Eilwen looked up. Patches of high cloud drifted across the sky: too thin for rain, let alone a storm.

Only when the wagon carried her around the corner and out of sight did she realise what the booms signified.

Cannon fire.

Gods help us.

～

The bombardment began at mid-morning near the north gate, at the edge of the view afforded to Arandras by the estate house window. The Oculus hauled a group of cannons into range and let off half a dozen volleys before the Spyridon army managed to bring their defensive guns to bear and return fire. As soon as the defending gunners began to find their range, the Oculus pulled those guns back and advanced another group on the east side, whereupon the cycle began again. Gnat-bites, Mara called them: more annoying than anything else, designed to keep the defending army occupied and off-balance. Most of the cannonballs simply slammed into the city's thick wall, but a few sailed over the top to land in the streets or crash into some unfortunate building. In one case, a chance ball sparked a fire at the edge of the artisan's district, the thin plume of smoke raising a cheer from the onlooking army.

Around lunchtime Mara declared herself weary of the spectacle and commenced an inspection of the wrought-iron fence that enclosed the estate's modest lawn. Arandras descended to the gallery and directed Tiy's attention to the invaders, curious to hear how it would identify the cannons. *Fire-barrels,* Tiy said in its familiar, inflexionless tone, leaving Arandras to wonder if the Valdori had possessed such devices themselves or if the golem was simply describing what it saw using the best term it could find.

It was now early afternoon and the gnats showed no sign of growing tired. Clouds of acrid white smoke swirled above the city in the slight breeze. The besiegers' numbers had swelled overnight and seemed to be still growing: an unbroken line of soldiers now linked the two large camps to the north and east, leaving only the west side of the city open. Arandras could see Mara below, moving from one ornamentally-spiked bar to the next, pausing occasionally to frown at some defect too small for him to see, or perhaps at a neighbouring tree that might offer a way over the barrier. One of the front gates, Arandras knew, was already a source of concern: the cleats intended to secure the crossbar had come loose, rendering the bar useless. They'd left the gate unsecured for now to leave the way clear for messengers and deliveries. If the situation deteriorated, Arandras supposed he could block the gate by sending a golem to stand behind it.

As if prompted by his thought, a loud knock sounded at the front of the building. Mara looked up from the fence, and as she did a familiar voice called out. "Ho, Arandras! You in there?"

Druce? Surprised, Arandras hurried down the stairs to the front door. He hadn't expected to hear from Druce for several days, and he certainly hadn't anticipated Druce paying a visit in person. *Something's happened,* he thought, and felt a chill run through him.

Something bad. Mock's been hurt. But then why come here?

He swung the door open. Druce stood on the threshold, his thin hands lodged on his hips; and behind him stood Jensine, a travel bag slung over her shoulder, taking in the house with a speculative air.

"Hello, Arandras," Jensine said, and her words were amiable if not exactly warm. "Looks like I'm taking you up on your offer after all."

"Your sorcerer," Druce said with a half-smile. He glanced past Arandras into the house and raised a hand in greeting. "Mara."

"Mara!" Jensine rushed past Arandras and pulled the other woman into an embrace. "Dreamer, but it's good to see you."

Druce watched as the women disappeared into house. "Well. I'll leave you to it, then."

"Wait," Arandras said. Something about the moment — having the four of them back together — demanded acknowledgement. "Why don't you come in?"

For a moment it seemed Druce might accept. Then he shook his head. "You know how it is. Places to be. Cider to drink."

Arandras yielded reluctantly. "A moment, then," he said, fishing in his purse for some coins. "Your fee."

Druce considered the silver. "And if Jensine can't do what you want?"

"Then I'll come and hassle Mock again." Arandras exhaled. "There's an army outside the city, Druce. The Weeper only knows how all this will play out. I'll sleep easier knowing you and I are square."

"Yeah," Druce said as he accepted the coins. "These are exciting times, that's for sure." He gave a slow nod, then turned and made his way back up the path.

"I'm pretty sure I passed a couple of squads on the way in," Jensine was saying as Arandras re-entered the house. "If I'd known they were coming here I'd have turned around and gone home."

"They'll have to do a lot better than this," Mara said, and Arandras wondered if Jensine could hear the pain beneath Mara's scorn. "You could probably slip out westward tonight and they wouldn't even notice."

"Maybe if it was just me," Jensine said. "But with the port closed there'll be hundreds of people with the same idea."

"Port Gallin is closed?" Arandras said.

"Since this morning. Guess the rest of the ships arrived." She eyed him curiously. "But enough of that. I believe you owe me an introduction."

"So I do." He nodded sideways, and she followed him past the smiling pouch-rat, up the stairs, and around the corner to the gallery. "Jensine, may I present the golems of the Valdori. Golems, this is Jensine."

"Don't all bow at once," Mara added as she came in behind.

Jensine gazed around the crowded gallery, her eyes wide. "Do they really do that?"

"What, bow?" Mara chuckled. "They knelt when Arandras bound them. That was a sight to see. Though if I'm honest, watching the Quill realise what was happening was even better."

Arandras singled out a golem armed with a flange-headed mace. *Golem, bow to Jensine.*

The golem bent forward with a low rumble, its head inclining slightly in a rough semblance of a courtier's bow.

"Gods." Jensine stared from the golem to Arandras. "You didn't even speak to it."

"Yeah." Arandras glanced away. "I, uh, communicate with them by thought."

Jensine goggled, prompting a wry laugh from Mara. "Welcome to my life," Mara said. "I suppose we should be grateful Arandras doesn't wish people dead very often."

"It doesn't work like that," Arandras muttered.

"Make it walk down the stairs," Jensine said. "How many can you move at once? Can you march them around the house like a palace guard?"

"They're not puppets," Arandras snapped. "They're not here for you to play with."

Jensine gave Arandras a startled look. "Whatever you say."

Arandras exhaled. "I'm sorry. I only found out myself a few days ago." He drew a breath. "Every one of these golems was a person, once. Beneath all that sorcery, I think they still are."

He'd expected her to protest, to shake her head or laugh at such an outlandish idea. Instead she stared at him, the colour draining from her face. "Dreamer's daughters," she breathed. "That's how they made them, isn't it? Stripped them of their flesh and shut them up in shells of clay and stone. Immortality, I suppose. But what a price to pay."

"They're still in there," Arandras said. "They remember things, sometimes. But they're trapped. Forced to obey whatever command I give them." He held her gaze. "Druce told you I needed a sorcerer. This is why. I want to free them."

Jensine hesitated. "Is that a good idea? Would it be… safe?"

"What's safe?" Arandras demanded. "Is it safe for you or me to decide what we want to do today? Is it safe for Mara to carry those scimitars around? What's to stop any one of us from laying into the next person we pass on the street? Weeper's tears, we've got cannons pounding at our walls as we speak. How could freeing the golems be any worse than that?"

"They're bigger than we are," Mara said drily.

Arandras turned. "And if that was you trapped in there, compelled to obey your master's every whim, what would you want?" He looked from Mara to Jensine. "It's the right thing to do. You know it is."

Jensine put a hand to her brow. "I don't know if you're the Weeper's own paragon or stark raving mad. Probably both. But even if you're right… gods, Arandras. These things were made by the Valdori. I'm just a dabbler. I wouldn't have the first idea where to start."

"You're an experimenter," Arandras said. "You're an inventor. And you're a healer."

Jensine shook her head.

"And I'll pay you," Arandras added.

She burst into laughter. "Well, that's settled, then. Everything about this is impossible, but what does that matter if there's hard coin on offer?"

"Then you'll do it?"

"I don't know. Even if I could…" She studied the golem before her, still frozen in mid-bow. "I need to think about it, all right? I need to understand what you're asking me to do."

Arandras sent a command. The golem straightened, pivoted, and marched back to its place among its companions.

"Tell me what you want to know," he said.

～

The streets were chaos. Eilwen battled her way westward, at times barely able to move against the press of opposing traffic, at others all but swept off her feet as the crowds carried her closer to her goal. In the rare moments of sanity between the two extremes, she marvelled at how thoroughly the city resembled an anthill kicked by an almighty, powder-charged boot.

The wagon upon which she'd escaped the Lasavis had carried her dangerously close to the wall. Scarcely a minute after she'd hopped down and started back into the city, a chance cannonball had crashed into a tinsmith's shop, punched a hole through the wall and ploughed on into the street, narrowly missing Eilwen herself. A passing grocer's cart hadn't been so lucky. The cannonball had bounced off the street and struck it clear amidships, sending onions, potatoes, and lettuces flying, the cast iron sphere finally coming to rest among the scattered produce like a shrivelled, unseasonal melon.

For a few moments, Eilwen had simply stared; then, as the shock of her near miss began to pass, she'd felt a frisson of excitement slither down her spine. A mad urge seized her: to turn around, to climb the wall, to feel the missiles whistle past her head and laugh at every one that flew wide. Then the panicked lows of the grocer's ox reached her ears, and the deep, throbbing ache returned to her knee, and the crazed moment passed. Shuddering, she put her back to the wall and set off, making it almost as far as the end of the street before the crowd began to boil and mercifully remove any chance to consider what had just happened.

She jostled and elbowed her way through the throng, and was jostled and elbowed in return. Somewhere within, the beast observed that daggers would be even sharper than elbows; but somehow the suggestion carried an edge of humour, as if the beast were deliberately teasing her, and Eilwen found it easy enough to ignore. Time ceased to have meaning: there was only the next corner, the next step, the next person in her way. Cannons fired from the wall behind her, then from some other, more distant point, adding their sonorous booms to the disorienting cacophony.

At last the crush began to ease. Eilwen limped past an arriving hospice wagon to the edge of the street and gathered her bearings. Before her rose the hill, its large houses and well-appointed shops as yet unscathed by enemy fire. She'd emerged from the artisans' district further north than she'd intended, though under the circumstances she was fortunate to have come as close to her goal as she had. Grimacing, she set off once more, following a series of side streets that led around the base of the hill to Clade's suite.

The door was bolted shut when she arrived, and her initial knock drew no response. Eilwen drummed her fingers against her leg, resisting the urge to hammer on the door until Clade responded. *Don't you know there's a war on?* she wanted to shout. *Don't you know where I've been?*

Footsteps sounded at last, and the door opened to reveal a scowling Clade. "Oh, it's you," he said in a tone that suggested either relief or disappointment. "Come in."

"I've figured it out," Eilwen said as soon as the door closed behind her. "I know where the gold's been going." Speaking rapidly, she related her progression from the mint to Ral Garvan to the Lasavis. Clade stood at the window as she spoke, offering no reaction and asking no questions, not even when she described her narrow escape from the Lasavis. "Ral Garvan must have given them my description. They're clearly up to their eyeballs in something — them, and whoever's covering for them within the army. But I'll need help to learn more."

Clade gazed out of the window at something Eilwen couldn't see. "Is that all?"

"All?" Eilwen glared. "You want to hear about the cannonball that almost knocked my head off on the way here?" *Or how part of me wanted to climb the wall and do it again?* "Yes, that's all, damn you."

"All right." Still Clade stared outside, his tone and posture a study in disinterest. "Thank you."

"'Thank you?'" Furious, Eilwen strode across the room and grabbed Clade by the shoulders. "You've had me going at this for days. I almost *died* on the way here, and all you have to say is *thank you?*"

Clade met her gaze at last. His face was stony, but his eyes burned with a rage Eilwen had never seen before. "Remove your hands."

She did. "What happened?"

He turned back to the window. "It's no concern of yours."

"The hells it isn't. Tell me what's going on."

Her only answer was the soft sound of Clade's breaths.

Eilwen tried again. "What are we going to do about the Lasavis?"

"Nothing right now," Clade said thickly. "First I must talk to the subcommander. Come back tomorrow."

"What?" Eilwen stepped closer. "Have you heard a word I've said? For the gods' sake, the Oculus are right outside. Stand on your toes and you can probably see them. You told me that finding this gold would help defend the city. Is that true, or have you just been leading me by the nose?"

"That's not important right now —"

"It's pretty damn important to me!"

"*Go!*" The word burst from Clade in a ragged cry, laden with inexplicable fury. They stared at each other in mutual shock; then, with a palpable effort of will, Clade drew his rage back inside. "Go," he said again, his voice tight with control. "We can do nothing more for now. Be assured that I will inform you as soon as that changes."

Inform me. Eilwen felt her own anger rise. "You do that," she said. "In the meantime, I'll just go and amuse myself, shall I? While the city falls down around us."

She stormed out, slamming the door with as much force as she could muster. *Damn you, Clade,* she thought as she limped through the hall and back out to the street. *Damn your arrogant, insufferable arse to the hundred hells.*

Gunfire boomed in the distance, low and weighty, as if in witness to her curse. Then another boom sounded, closer this time, and that one was just a cannon.

CHAPTER 16

The finite, the limited, the unexpected and the absurd: only here can humour be found. Perhaps this is why the All-God created the world. Perhaps he simply wished to laugh.

— Barais neb-Ohel, *A Theodicy*

ARANDRAS REACHED UP WITH HIS thoughts to where the golem stood just out of sight at the entrance to the gallery. *Tiy. Descend the stairs.*

With its now-familiar rumble, Tiy obeyed, pausing slightly before each heavy footfall. Jensine followed a few steps behind, her fingers trailing the banister, her gaze fixed on wonders Arandras could never see.

"Fascinating," she breathed, staring enraptured at some piece of sorcery beneath the golem's shoulders and back. "Now tell it to stop."

Tiy, cease your descent.

The golem ground to a halt three steps from the bottom of the staircase. Jensine stared at it for several heartbeats before pulling herself free with obvious reluctance. "Dreamer, I could watch it do that all day. It's like... gods, I don't know. Imagine a vast mechanism of Rondossan clockwork, as big as a house, which tracked, say, the movements of every man and woman in the city, or the progress of the stars. Then imagine someone found a way to shrink the mechanism to something the size of a bread loaf — *but it all still worked.* It shouldn't be possible. The gods only know how the

Valdori did it."

Arandras merely nodded. A marvellous prison was still a prison. "Can you see what's holding them?"

"Sort of." Jensine squeezed past Tiy to join Arandras in the hall-way. "There's a sequence of bindings that activate every time you give them a command. Perhaps that's the part your book calls the Chain."

"You don't sound convinced."

"It's not that. Even if I agreed to this…" Jensine sighed. "Gods, Arandras. You've read the account. As near as I can figure, the Valdori sorcerers used some form of lightbinding to complete their work. They built a chamber specifically for that purpose. Do you know what that means? The sorcery, or at least the final part of it, was *grounded* in light. Or it drew on the light, somehow. I'm not even close to understanding it."

Arandras grimaced in understanding. "But we have no such chamber."

"Right. And even if we did, I'm no lightbinder."

"Perhaps not," Arandras said. "But you're pretty damn good with air. I saw you make that fisherman's bandage. That looked pretty much the same as what you're talking about, only with air instead of light."

"That was completely different. Well, maybe not completely." She frowned. "But if it was that simple, why didn't the Valdori do it the same way? If you believe that book, it sounds like ordinary light wasn't enough. They used mirrors and lenses to brighten it so much they had to cover their eyes. I don't even know what an equivalent to that would be. How do you make air more dense?"

"Maybe you wouldn't have to," Arandras said. "You're not giving life to them. You'd just be modifying one little piece of their sorcery."

Jensine gave a short laugh. "You make it sound so easy. Every piece of sorcery in there is connected to everything else."

"Even so —"

"Arandras. This isn't a debate." She crouched, her gaze fixed on something around the level of the golem's knee. "If I have more questions, I'll find you."

Arandras bit back a reply. "Of course." He turned to leave, then turned back as a thought occurred to him. "We've got plenty of space here. You're welcome to stay as long as you like."

"I know. I've already arranged it with Mara," Jensine replied. "But thank you."

"Oh. Good."

With a sigh, Arandras pushed the discussion aside. The afternoon was fading, and the booms of cannon fire had settled into a semi-consistent rhythm. Leaving Jensine to her study of Tiy, Arandras climbed the stairs to find Mara returned from her review of the estate's perimeter and observing the bombardment below.

"They're calculating our positions," Mara said distractedly as Arandras sat beside her on the settee. "I should have seen it before. Why bother advancing for half a dozen shots? You'd barely finish calibrating your gun before you have to pull it back."

"What are you talking about?"

"Look there." Mara pointed at a cluster of Oculus guns on a slight rise to the northeast. "There's another squad just like them behind that line of trees a little further down. Each time one of them withdraws, the other comes out. They've worked out that we only have a couple of cannons capable of covering that area."

Arandras frowned. "Couldn't we send some archers up on the wall to pick them off?"

"At this range?" Mara shook her head. "Not even the sea breeze is going to carry an arrow that far."

"What, then?"

Mara shrugged. "Simple. Send out a raiding party and destroy some of their armament. Or set a trap — pretend our guns are spread more thinly than they really are, then hammer the Oculus when they come into range." Mara shrugged. "That's assuming Piator Pronn has the brains for one or the guts for the other. Right now I'm not too sure about either. But even if he did..."

Arandras turned. There was a note in Mara's voice that he'd never heard before. Not despair, exactly, but a deep despondency that seemed to rise from her bones. "What is it?"

Mara exhaled. "What's the one thing we know for sure about the Oculus?"

"Weeper, I don't know." Arandras racked his memory for

anything Clade might have told him. "They're interested in Valdori artefacts?"

"And why is that? *Because they're sorcerers.* Clade is, anyway. Others must be as well if that story about Azador is true." Mara gestured at the army below. "So where's their sorcery?"

"All we've done so far is shoot rocks at each other," Arandras said. "What sorcery do you expect to see?"

"I don't know. Maybe nothing, yet. But that's my point." Mara gave an unhappy sigh. "When the battle gets closer, we can expect the Oculus to have sorcerers ready to jump in. Who does Piator have?"

Arandras felt a heaviness settle over him. Spyridon's distaste for sorcery was hardly a secret. The Library liked to claim that its network of connections among the elite of the Free Cities outweighed any tactical disadvantage arising from its lack of sorcerers. Narvi had tried to build some bridges, but his Quill were already gone, and even if they'd stayed they'd probably have declined to get involved. No doubt the army had a store of anamnil set aside for such contingencies. But anamnil was passive and easily detected, and all but useless against any kind of sorcery that could be cast from a distance.

"Nobody," Arandras said slowly, and the taste in his mouth seemed to serve as confirmation of the bitter assessment. "We've got nobody."

～

As the afternoon turned to evening, the bombardment eased and Clade ventured forth, assessing the mood of the street like a fox sniffing the air outside its burrow. In the hours since Eilwen's visit, he'd laboured to regain his composure, drawing on his old practice of control and self-discipline. Eventually he'd managed to isolate his rage and wall it off from the rest of him. It seethed within its cage, twisting and kicking, but he had its measure now and allowed it its tantrum, knowing that before long it would fade away like any other unwelcome emotion.

To an extent, Clade had to admit, the loss of the book was his own fault. He'd neglected to secure the suite when he first arrived, partly because he hadn't possessed anything of particular value at the time, and partly because of the obstacles the suite had presented. The door still held the remnants of an old, ineffective binding, leaving little space for a sorcerous lock. The chest, though mostly timber, had been edged with iron, its metal lip inaccessible to his sorcery. He'd deemed the mechanical locks sufficient for his needs, and he'd not thought to revisit that assessment when he gained possession of Onsoth's book. In short, he'd been careless, and Hesca had taken advantage of his lapse with a readiness that in other circumstances he might almost have admired.

Contrary to what Eilwen had told him, the streets were largely empty. Probably the panic she'd described had only lasted a couple of hours. At some point, even the city's more stupid inhabitants must have realised that the best thing they could do for themselves was go home and sit tight. Whatever the reason, the lull was welcome, and Clade hurried through the city to the barracks where he guessed Hesca would most likely be found.

As it turned out, his guess was wrong. "The subcommander is with Commander Pronn at the northern command post," the spotty-faced desk attendant said when he asked after Hesca's whereabouts. Directions were forthcoming, and Clade set off in search of the described redoubt.

The streets of the artisans' district were no more crowded than those near Clade's suite, but the emptiness here felt more wilful than it had elsewhere. People scurried past in ones and twos, their heads low and hands tucked into their pockets. Broken windows, smashed crates, and other signs of destruction could be seen on most blocks, although nothing on a scale to suggest wholesale rioting or looting. Nevertheless, Clade found himself increasing his pace through the gathering dusk. None of the street lamps he passed had been lit, and tonight probably none would be. On his return journey, Clade decided, he would take a carriage.

The command post proved easy enough to find. The low stone redoubt had been built on a small rise about halfway between the wall and the base of Spyridon's hill, with a slender tower sprouting from one end to offer a view of the terrain from the southeastern shore right around to the Anstice road and beyond. Two soldiers guarded the narrow doorway, one of them a woman Clade recognised from his visit to the city chambers with Hesca and Piator Pronn. He angled toward her, nodding as though the street held just the two of them.

"Where can I find Subcommander Matharan, please?" Clade said, ignoring the other guard's movement to bar the way.

"You can't go in there, sir." The second guard seemed barely old enough to carry a sword. He stared at Clade with the wide-eyed intensity of one determined not to reveal the depth of his fear.

"Yes, good lad. Very diligent." Clade patted the youth's shoulder, then turned back to the woman. "You saw me with Piator and Hesca at the last meeting of the city circle. My news can't wait. Where are they?"

The woman studied Clade's face and made a swift judgement. "Downstairs, I believe," she said, stepping aside and gesturing for her companion to do likewise. "Last I heard, they were heading down to review the armoury."

Clade swept past with a nod, ducking his head as he passed beneath the thick outer wall and through the iron-banded door. A brightly-lit hall extended a short distance before rounding a corner, while to the side a spiral staircase extended both above and below. Clade followed the stairs down, emerging in a hallway almost identical to the one above. From somewhere nearby came the sound of muffled voices raised in argument; then a door swung open and Hesca strode out, her lips pursed in frustration. At the sight of Clade her scowl deepened and she closed the door behind her.

"What in the hells are you doing here?" she hissed. "Get out. We'll talk later."

"We'll talk right now," Clade retorted, then cursed and twisted away as Hesca reached to cover his mouth.

"Piator Pronn is in the next room," she mouthed, glaring at Clade as if she'd caught him running a blade through one of her soldiers. "Whatever it is, it can wait."

"No." Clade pitched the word at a volume low enough to go unheard beyond the hallway but high enough to constitute a threat. "It can't."

"Gods." Rolling her eyes, Hesca yanked open a door on the other side of the hall and waved Clade inside. She fumbled in the shadows and a lamp flared to life, revealing a storeroom crammed with barrels and crates. A metallic tang hung in the air beneath the usual packed-crate scent of wood shavings. Hesca pulled the door closed. "Make it quick."

Clade folded his arms. "What are you playing at?" The words came out low and flat, devoid of emotion or adornment.

"Aside from the defence of the city?"

"Yes. Aside from that."

"Is this about Zann?" Hesca said. "Because the way I heard it, he's the only reason you're still with us."

That was likely true, though Clade was hardly in the mood to concede it. "Zann overestimates his own significance," he said. "And that's not an answer."

"What do you want me to say? Yes, I ordered him to keep an eye on you. Yes, I trust you, but no, I don't trust you that much." She fixed him with a hard stare. "Please don't insult us both by claiming surprise."

"And if I hadn't been attacked, what then? Would Zann have come up with some other way to keep me from getting home too soon?"

Hesca shook her head. "Too soon for what?"

"If you wanted the damn book, why didn't you say so in the first place?"

"What in the hells are you talking about?"

"You know exactly what I'm talking about," Clade began, but trailed off at Hesca's blank expression. "Don't you?"

"Are you accusing me of something?" Anger suffused her tone. "Do you really think I have time to pursue little side-schemes against you with the *gods-damned Oculus sitting on our front door?*"

The answer, of course, was yes — but the growing outrage on Hesca's face seemed entirely unfeigned. *Who, then?* Nobody else knew he had the book or even knew of his connection to Onsoth's death. But no, that wasn't true. Arandras knew. He'd flung the accusation in Clade's face, and in that moment Clade had lacked the wit to deny it. Hells, Arandras had said it in as many words. *I know about Onsoth's book.* An odd thing to say if the man was planning to steal it; but then, Arandras seemed to delight in defying expectations.

"Well?" Hesca demanded. "Nothing to say, all of a sudden?"

"Never mind." Fresh anger sparked within him, this time at Arandras's impudence; but this was the familiar indignation at being momentarily outplayed, not the pain of betrayal, and was easier to corral and contain. "It was a misunderstanding. Forgive me."

Hesca scowled. "A misunderstanding."

Squashing his impulse to apologise, Clade moved toward the door. "I won't bother you any further."

"Not so fast." Hesca folded her arms. "Since you're here, why don't you tell me about your progress with the missing gold?"

The fate of the army's gold seemed trivial beside Arandras's theft of his books, but Clade took a deep breath and checked his impatience as best he could. "The gold was lifted in transit from the mint to the barracks. We've established the involvement of the merchant Ral Garvan and a particular stained-glass workshop. There's nothing yet to suggest Pronn was a part of it."

"There will be. Gods, there has to be." Hesca's voice dropped to a bitter whisper. "That man will be the death of us. The only thing he was ever good for was riding in with his cavalry and slaughtering would-be insurrectionists. Pitchforks and garden trowels he can just about handle. He's got no idea how to defend a city." She leaned closer. "Find me a way to get rid of the commander. Or else bring me those golems, if they really exist. I don't care which. Just do it quickly."

"Forget the golems," Clade said roughly. "You're never going to pry them loose —"

He snapped his mouth shut, but it was too late.

"So they are here," Hesca breathed. "Is that what you've been chasing this whole time?"

Shit! Furious with himself, Clade made to grab Hesca by the shoulders, but his withered hand failed to find a grip. "I mean it," he growled. "Golems won't win this for you. We're on our own."

"So you say."

A door swung open somewhere nearby, followed by the sound of footsteps. "Subcommander?" someone called. "Subcommander

Matharan?" Clade and Hesca stared at each other in silence as the footsteps paused, shuffled in apparent confusion, and at last moved off.

"Yes," Clade whispered fiercely. "So I say."

Hesca held his gaze without flinching. "Then find me enough evidence to get rid of Piator Pronn."

～

Eilwen sat on the bench beside the narrow, sloping lane, her knee throbbing beneath her clasped hands, and watched the campfires outside the city spring to life.

Days of hard use had caught up with her at last. By the time her wanderings brought her to Raelen's Salves and Remedies, an apothecary's shop just down from Goldsmiths Row, she'd no longer been able to deny the severity of her limp. Raelen had been unable to supply the liniment Eilwen sometimes turned to on such occasions — not that it typically did much good anyway — but had suggested in its stead a yellow-green unguent which supposedly contained several of the same ingredients. As the apothecary closed up her store for the night, Eilwen had settled herself on the bench outside the shop, rolling up her trouser leg and rubbing the thick, herb-scented salve into her old scars.

She'd been startled to find that the day was almost over. The sun had been high in the sky when she'd left Clade's suite. Had she really meandered away the better part of the afternoon? Dark memories of her departure from the Woodtraders Guild stirred within her, and she shifted uneasily. But that had been different, of course. Nobody had died at her hand today, and the beast lay quiescent, at least for now.

Evidently, Clade's peculiar manner had touched some nerve within her. Something had happened to him, some setback or disappointment, and he'd been too preoccupied to listen to her news. If she hadn't been so frayed from her own brush with death a few hours earlier, she might have found a more productive response than the one she'd given. *Gods, I just blew up at him. As if that would persuade someone like Clade to confide in me. Havilah would be so proud.*

A rustle sounded from the direction in which she'd come,

downhill and to the right: a dog, probably, though the shadows made it impossible to tell. Once again, she found herself missing the old Guild spymaster. Havilah had always been calm, always treated her with respect, always known what to do. He'd had his secrets, to be sure, but Eilwen had never felt threatened by them the way she did with Clade. Beneath everything else, Havilah had wanted only one thing: to defend and advance the interests of the Woodtraders Guild.

Clade, too, wanted one thing, but defence and advancement had nothing to do with it. Oh, he might have been helping the city prepare its defences these past few days, but Eilwen knew enough to understand he had no real concern for Spyridon as such. To Clade, this was an opportunity to oppose Azador, nothing more. When the battle came to an end, win or lose, he would move on to the next one, and the one after that, until either he or Azador were finally, utterly defeated.

It wasn't as though she'd been under any illusions when she'd signed on. There in the caverns, her blood high with the beast's rage and with her own pain at failing to save Havilah, a war against Azador had seemed like everything she wanted. Except she'd come to realise that it wasn't true. Hatred was no longer a good enough reason to fight. Her time working with Havilah had changed her — or perhaps it had simply brought to the surface what had always lain beneath, even while she hunted Oculus agents at the prompting of the beast.

A lone cannon boomed somewhere to the north, prompting another rustle from the dog, or whatever it was. Eilwen closed her eyes, hearing again the crack of the cannonball as it bounced off the street half a step in front of her and crunched into the grocer's cart, and a thrill of remembered excitement passed through her. In that moment she'd felt *alive,* just like she once had during her hunts with the beast, where every step carried the weight of life or death. To stand on the wall and stare down at the erupting gunfire would give her that once more, filling every heartbeat with vast, terrifying meaning...

Realisation struck her and she trailed off, aghast. They were the same, the beast and this new insanity. Both sought to fill the same void within her. Only once had she found a foothold firm enough to resist the beast's call: those few precious weeks spent working with Havilah, when the void had been filled not by contrived hazard or the promise of death but by something real. The good of the Woodtraders.

Hot tears stung her eyes. The Woodtraders had been her home, her family. Havilah had given her a chance to serve and she'd failed him, failed the Guild, and in doing so she'd ripped out a part of herself — a second, to go alongside the piece she'd lost at the *Orenda*. Perhaps climbing the wall and braving the Oculus barrage was not so foolish a notion after all. Better that than to yield to the beast once more and slake her thirst in the blood of others. Because sooner or later, the void would insist on being filled, and what did she have to offer it except death?

There was nothing. Allied to Clade, she had no greater good to defend. No home. No family.

Except Orval.

Eilwen blotted her tears with her sleeve. Here, too, she had failed. But her failure was not yet permanent. Orval still lived, and though the arrival of the Oculus had wounded him in ways Eilwen should have foreseen, their defeat might go a long way toward healing whatever damage had been done.

Orval's wellbeing. Den and Irilli's trust. Perhaps they would serve to fill the void, at least until the present crisis was past.

She drew a long, shaky breath. The best thing she could do for Orval now was to ensure that the defence of Spyridon prevailed. At this moment, the most effective way she could do that was by remaining in Clade's employ. But as soon as the Oculus were defeated, she and Clade would part ways. She'd had enough of his presumption, enough of his endless hostility toward Azador and everything it touched. Perhaps she would do in truth what she'd claimed back in Neysa: strike out on her own, use her contacts from the old days to find some likely market and establish her own trading concern. It might even give her something to look forward to while they waited for the Oculus to be driven off.

Until then, however, she would endure. For Orval's sake.

Grimacing, Eilwen rolled down her trouser leg and pushed

herself upright, then began to retrace her steps downhill. As she rounded the corner, a huddled shape beside the wall shifted abruptly. Startled, she looked down to see a woman crouching beside the wall, her pale face staring up at Eilwen, one hand frozen in the act of lifting an apple to her mouth.

"You," Eilwen breathed.

The woman surged to her feet and sprinted away downhill. Eilwen moved to pursue, then gasped in pain at the jolt in her knee. As the woman vanished around a corner, Eilwen reached for the black amber egg in her pocket and dug her fingers beneath the wrappings. It thrummed against her hand, the rhythm fading rapidly but unmistakable all the same: the thin pulse of an Oculus token-bearer.

~

Tiy, Arandras thought. *Within your sister's Chain, tell me of the compound component positioned between the third ligament-stream-contractor and the fifth stream-conduit-vinculum.*

"It's called a volition-proportion-attenuator," he reported, and Jensine dipped her pen and made a note on one of the dozen pieces of paper spread across the floor. "Something like that, anyway. I recognise the roots of the words, but I've never heard them in quite this form before."

Jensine nodded without looking up. "And are there any other instances of the same component anywhere in the binding?"

Arandras put the question. "No. Tiy says that's the only one."

"All right." Jensine put down the pen and rubbed her eyes. "Let's take a break."

They'd been at it for most of the morning, and already the scope of the problem was clear enough to be daunting. The golems' sorcery was patterned like veins on a leaf, each branch possessing a series of smaller branches that held smaller branches again, and so on until they were too fine to see. So far they'd avoided going too deeply into any one component. Jensine thought that creating a kind of architect's schematic of the larger components would provide enough reference for her to orient herself within the sorcery. Arandras could only hope she was right. The prospect of mapping the complete binding in all its detail was too dizzying to contemplate.

"It's remarkable," Jensine said, sitting back on her heels and surveying their progress. She'd used that word repeatedly over the past few hours, her tone shifting between astonishment, awe, and the wondering laugh of someone who couldn't quite believe that fate had made her witness to the wonders before her. "You can see the elegance of the binding, can't you? The way it maximises efficiency without once sacrificing beauty. It's like the gods' own handiwork."

"If you say so." All Arandras could see was a series of indecipherable scrawls. "Do you think it can be changed?"

"Maybe. I have some ideas. But I still don't know…" She sobered. "If you're right about what the golems are, well, I can see why you'd want to release them. But if not, if the memories you heard are just an echo…" Jensine shook her head. "Destroying that kind of sorcery would be like, I don't know, defacing some priceless text, or desecrating the remains of Herev Gis, or Daro of Talsoor."

"Is that what you think?" Arandras said. "That the golems are things?"

"I don't know, Arandras. Really. But I'm asking you. What if the people you want to free aren't there any more? Have you thought about it?"

He hadn't. If he was honest, perhaps he hadn't wanted to. Or perhaps he'd sensed that such reflection would get him nowhere.

"What are we really asking?" Arandras said. "We know what the Valdori did to create them. We know they can't communicate it now. Is it because the sorcery prevents them, or because there's nothing left of the people they once were?" He shrugged. "It's impossible to tell, isn't it? The only ones who might know are the golems themselves."

"Can you ask them?"

"I've tried." Oh, how he had tried. "Maybe there's a crack in the binding somewhere, some question I could ask that would let them tell me what I want to know. But if the Valdori did their job right, that sorcery will be impenetrable. There'll be nothing to tell us which explanation is right."

"So you admit it's possible that they're already gone."

Arandras blew out a breath. "Yes, it's possible. But think, Jensine. What if they *are* still there? What if Tiy and the others are listening to us debate their existence right now, locked inside those shells, unable to move so much as a finger without my express order? Weeper's tears, can you think of a greater crime?"

Jensine lowered her eyes.

"If there's nothing left and we break the binding, then what? Maybe these golems become nothing more than impressive statues. That's fine. There are plenty of others under that lake, believe me. But if there really is someone still inside and we give up on them..." Arandras shook his head. "We have to try, Jensine. We have to."

A hard knock sounded on the front door, and Arandras looked up in surprise. Mara had ventured out earlier in search of some fresh food, reasoning that they might as well make the most of it before the last deliveries from the farms were exhausted, but he hadn't expected her back for another hour.

"Stay here," Arandras murmured, and sent a command to the nearest golem. *Tiy, come with me.* He padded to the end of the hallway, instructing Tiy to stand alongside the door and out of sight. "Who's there?" he called.

"Feren Skaratass," came the brusque reply.

It took Arandras a moment to place the name. "*Conservator* Skaratass? From the Library?"

"If you open the door you can see for yourself," the woman said tartly.

Arandras did so.

A fair-skinned woman in her mid-fifties stood outside with two men at her back, one short and wiry, the other larger and sporting a shaved head, all clad in the same robes of Library grey. The men studied Arandras with similar expressions of suspicion and contempt, but the implied threat in their gaze paled beside the iron assurance in the woman's regard. She looked him up and down like a farmer confronted with the unwelcome gift of a half-starved cow. "You are Arandras, I take it?"

Arandras folded his arms. Despite his occasional run-ins with self-important lackeys like Onsoth, he'd always held the Conservator in a certain amount of respect. Even from afar, the force of her intelligence and competence had been clear. But recognising such qualities from a distance and opening the front door to find them focused directly on Arandras himself were two distinctly different experiences. "What's this about?"

"You didn't answer my question."

"Nor did you answer mine," Arandras retorted. But Feren peered at him with her hawk's eyes as if he hadn't spoken, and Arandras relented. "Yes, I'm Arandras."

"Huh." Feren gave him a sceptical look, then shrugged. "Let's speak inside."

The Conservator started forward and Arandras found himself already several steps back before he could recover. "Just a moment," he began; but it was too late. Feren turned toward Tiy, a hint of astonishment slipping through her tightly controlled exterior.

"So it's true," she murmured, reaching out to brush her fingertips against Tiy's arm.

"Yes," Arandras said. "It's true." And he gave the golem a command.

Tiy's hand shot out and grabbed Conservator Skaratass by the shoulder.

The two men leapt forward, the shorter one twisting Arandras's arm behind his back as his bald-headed companion produced a blade from somewhere beneath his robe and laid the flat of it against Arandras's cheek. "Let her go," he said, his sour breath filling Arandras's nostrils. "I'll count to three. Then I start cutting."

"Kill me now and your Conservator will have a golem hanging off her shoulder for the rest of her life."

"Ease up, boys," Feren said, shifting position beneath Tiy's heavy grip. "Nobody's hurt anyone yet. Let's keep it that way."

"You want to talk?" Arandras said. "Send your muscle outside."

Feren snorted. "Perhaps I should demand the same." But she glanced at her men and nodded to the door, and reluctantly they complied.

Arandras allowed Tiy to ease its grip. "So," he said as the bald-headed man took up position just beyond the door and glared venomously inside. "I'd ask again what you're doing here, but as it happens I think I can guess."

"I'm relieved," Feren said acerbically. "For a moment I thought the large army camped outside the gates had escaped your notice."

"I'll save you time, then. The answer is no."

"You haven't heard my offer yet."

"My answer won't change."

"Two thousand lurundi," Feren said. "In exchange, you will direct your golems to join the defence of the city."

Arandras blinked in surprise. Two *thousand?* The amount was so large that he found himself struggling to comprehend it. Would such a sum buy an estate like this? Several estates? He had no idea.

And it didn't matter, anyway. "No deal," he said.

"Five thousand," Feren said.

Arandras swallowed. "No."

A pause. "Ten."

Arandras shook his head.

Feren scowled. "You drive a hard bargain."

"I make no bargain at all. The answer is simply no."

"You would rather see this city fall?"

"This city, Conservator, is not my problem," Arandras snapped. "It's yours, and Piator Pronn's, and the rest of the circle's. If your collective incompetence has left you with no better recourse than to beg for my help, then perhaps you should simply surrender and save us all a great deal of inconvenience."

Anger darkened Feren's expression. "I'm not trying to purchase the damn things, just hire them. Isn't that what you do? Rent out their services to whoever's willing to pay? You're never going to see a better offer than this."

"Yes, you're very generous. But you're not the first to come sniffing after my help. A few days ago Mistress Agli thought it would be fun to try bundling me off to the Weeper only knows where to make a proposition of her own. Sadly, I never got to find out whether there was anything more to her offer than threats."

"That was nothing to do with me —"

"Force from the merchants, now gold from the Library," Arandras mused. "I suppose tomorrow I'll have the priest turn up on my door offering knowledge, or the army offering revelation of the divine mysteries."

Feren stared. "Are you telling me you won't help the city because you're holding a *grudge?*"

"No," Arandras said. "I'm telling you that the golems are no longer for hire. To anyone. Ever." He sent Tiy a command. "So stop bloody asking."

Tiy lurched into motion, turning the Conservator around and marching her unceremoniously out the door. As Feren stumbled to a halt in the unwilling embrace of her bald-headed companion, the golem stepped ponderously to one side, allowing Arandras to slam the door shut behind her.

A muffled curse sounded from the other side of the door, followed presently by the scrape of retreating footsteps. Arandras sagged against the door and gave a long, slow exhalation.

"Are you all right?" Jensine stepped gingerly from the other room, her pen still clutched in one hand. "Do you think she'll be back?"

"Yes," Arandras said. "Her, or someone else. To people like her, the golems are just…" He waved his hand. "Slaves. Power. A means to an end."

"I know. I do. But —"

"This is why I have to free them, Jensine. It's the only way to make people stop asking. Or worse." He took a breath. "Will you help me?"

Jensine nodded slowly. "Yes," she said. "I'll help."

THIRD INTERLUDE

What a sorry pass we come to when we imagine that we understand ourselves.

— *Wisdom of the Pekratan Sages,* translated by Hila Sen

O N THE THIRTY-SEVENTH DAY AFTER he stopped eating, Nezhar stood at the edge of his camp and watched a man several leagues away cheat at cards.

Though the day was largely clear, the distance and slight haze combined to give the man a blurry, washed-out appearance as he drew the card from his sleeve and added it to his hand. Beneath Nezhar's augmented vision, the man scratched his cheek, then selected a different card and placed it face-up on the worn table before him: a small rank, perhaps a three or a four, though Nezhar couldn't quite make out the suit. He peered closer, trying to identify the blob in the card's corner...

A dark shape cut across his vision and Nezhar jumped back, stumbling against a tussock and falling to his arse. Blinking wildly, he waved his hands in mad swipes to ward off whatever creature had caught him off-guard.

The blows found nothing but air. No sound met his ears save that of his own scrambling. Cautiously, Nezhar lowered his arms and peered around the camp. All was as he had left it. Before him, the besieged city of Spyridon lay at its usual distance once more, the tower in which he'd spied the card cheat now small enough to cover with his thumb. And there, wheeling above and around the wall, a scattered flock of gulls.

Feeling foolish, Nezhar reached for his boots. *Damn seagulls. Try getting in my way three days from now.* A dull throbbing commenced behind his temples in reaction to the sudden shift in his vision. It had taken him the better part of an hour to focus in on the card game, and he'd planned to take at least half that long on the return journey — time he'd now spend willing the headache away. But such was the cost of the power he sought. His sorcery was improving as expected. In a few days he'd be ready to put an end to the siege unfolding before him.

He'd watched his client's army arrive, watched them arrange themselves around the city and fire their first exploratory volleys. With little else to distract him between exercises, he'd whiled away the hours analysing each side's strategy. It was clear enough that the defenders had fewer cannons than they needed to cover so long a wall, perhaps as few as half, though their tactic of repositioning guns in response to particular attacks made it hard to put a number on it. The Oculus commanders had evidently realised the defenders' weakness and had launched a series of precisely positioned attacks intended to glean as much as they could about specific vulnerabilities along the wall. Hostilities had so far been confined to gunfire — the Oculus had not yet made any assault on the gates, while Spyridon was yet to send out a sortie against the attackers. The former was unsurprising, but Nezhar found himself unsure of the reason for the latter. Perhaps the defenders were deliberately presenting themselves as vulnerable to prime the Oculus for their inevitable raid. Or perhaps Spyridon had cracked the secret behind small guns that could be fired by individual soldiers — presently known only to the Tahisi, so far as Nezhar was aware — and wished to lure the Oculus into the range of their new weapons.

Nezhar picked his way across the camp to the grassy patch where he had left his waterskin. Only a mouthful remained and he drained it, wiping his sleeve across his lips before setting off down the hill at a gentle walk. Several times in the last few days he'd made the mistake of stepping too swiftly and been brought to his knees by a wave of dizziness. The potential for ruin was all too clear: a moment of carelessness, a fall, a broken leg. If he were to suffer such an injury in his current condition, leagues away from help, it would almost certainly mean his death.

At the swift-flowing creek he crouched cautiously and lowered the skin into the icy water. The bones and ligaments of his wrist jutted in sharp relief beneath his thinning flesh. Nezhar glanced hurriedly away, pushing aside the memories that clamoured for attention: of himself as a boy before the Hungry Men had taken him in, starving on the streets of Yenene, and the crime that had brought him undone. This was no place for such thoughts. *Focus on the present. One breath, one heartbeat.*

The skin was full once more. Nezhar capped it and straightened. The muddy patches on the other side of the creek showed no new prints. Wherever the stripe-backed wolf was, it hadn't been here for at least a day. But he'd glimpsed it the evening before last, and as he watched it skulking across the hill with its ears flat against its head, an unlikely theory had begun to form.

As far as he could tell, the creature was alone. That was already unusual. Perhaps it had fallen out with its pack, or perhaps the others had died. More interesting, however, was the fact that it had chosen this place for its home — a place claimed by no other pack. A place that it seemed simultaneously frightened of yet unwilling to leave.

Perhaps, like Nezhar, it was already committed. Maybe it had young hidden in a den somewhere on the other side of the creek, forcing it to stay until they could all move together. Or maybe it had chosen this site for the same reason that frightened it: the presence of some other creature, which would discourage a pack from following it here.

Yet Nezhar had seen no such creature. Anything powerful enough to scare a stripe-backed wolf would surely have betrayed its presence by now.

With one exception.

A phoenix. The outcrop above his campsite consisted of sheer stone on all sides. No ground animal could possibly make its home in such a place. And Nezhar knew of no bird that might intimidate a wolf yet go unseen for so long, save only a phoenix.

As a rule, Nezhar put little stock in omens. But a phoenix... well, that was different. One of his earliest memories was of his Pekratan grandmother crooning over him in her strange tongue. *Phoenix at dawn, the Weeper smiles; phoenix at dusk, the Gatherer rides.* The rhyme didn't translate well, but the words had lodged deep. Somewhere within him a three-year-old boy still lived, convinced that the success or doom of his project might be assured by a single glimpse of the auspicious bird.

Bah. Nezhar shook his head. The rhyme represented an old woman's superstition, nothing more. Success would be his regardless of whether or when he might chance to spy his bashful neighbour, assuming it even existed. Effort and will would make it so.

Yet as he climbed back to his camp, filled waterskin in hand, he found himself unable to resist glancing at the sky.

CHAPTER 17

Valdori this, Valdori that. It seems one cannot leave one's house and not be assailed with another paean to the Valdori. But what do we really know of an Empire now two thousand years dead? Did they truly devise the wonders we praise them for, or did they merely ride the shoulders of those who came before them: the Yanisinians, and others of their age? Perhaps the Valdori were nothing more than glorified grave robbers who destroyed themselves when the potency of their finds at last outran their wit.

— Zelig the Goad, *Against Reason*

CLADE LISTENED TO THE BOOMS of the Oculus cannons from the relative safety of his rented suite and contemplated the peculiar conjunction of divinity and madness.

When stripped of their pretensions and taken at the word of their followers, it was remarkable how foolish the gods appeared. The Tri-God, for instance, seemed several mummers short of a show: Dreamer, Weeper, and Gatherer, each riding the heels of the one before as if together they represented the sum of human experience. If that was life, as the Tri-God priests claimed to believe, then life was a thin gruel indeed. The All-God, on the other hand, seemed less interested in the world than in its own inscrutability, although its disciples insisted that it nevertheless clung to some core obsession: law for the Kefirans, indifference for the Sareans, or a bizarre notion of perfection for the Gisleans.

Yet in truth, a god's sanity could be judged only if one trusted its self-appointed representatives. The All-God or the Tri-God, if either being truly existed, might be nothing like the views espoused by its worshippers. For such gods, perhaps the foolishness belonged solely to those who chose to speak on their behalf. Without some independently verifiable communication between deity and human, who could know for sure?

Only those who followed Azador had any real insight into the nature of their god.

Other gods could be misinterpreted. Other disciples might convince themselves that their god said one thing when in fact it meant another. Azador left no room for such confusion. The Oculus were its hands and feet, its eyes and ears. Azador spoke and the Oculus obeyed. If that obedience involved going to war, then one could be sure that war was Azador's will.

But war was a tool, not an end in itself. Its soundness as a strategy depended entirely on one's ultimate goals. And Clade had no more idea of Azador's purpose now than he had when he arrived in Spyridon.

He'd gone over and over those last few days in Anstice, trying to recall everything Estelle had told him about the Council's plans. *We need to expand our influence,* she'd said. *We're going to take Neysa.* And then... Clade wasn't sure. A vague reference to *next time* hovered in his thoughts, but he could remember nothing beyond those words.

With nowhere else to turn, he'd shifted his analysis to Azador's actions. The Oculus had conquered Neysa almost bloodlessly, and followed it up with measures designed to embed themselves atop the city's existing power structures. But there'd been no effort to secure Neysa's wider territories. Instead, they'd launched a surprise assault against Spyridon with the coming of spring. If they prevailed here, what then?

In persuading Eilwen to stay, Clade had argued that this battle might be their last opportunity to halt the Oculus march and prevent an even wider conquest. Beyond doubt, the risk was real. Yet the Oculus, too, risked much. If Anstice were to rouse itself from its slumber and attack Neysa, it would likely encounter little resistance. The Gisleans, too, could easily take advantage of the situation by pushing their border south of the Nerin River into Neysan land. If Azador's goal was to establish new territories for itself, its hasty assault on Spyridon seemed foolish in the extreme.

All of which left three possibilities that Clade could think of. Perhaps Azador's true goals lay elsewhere. Perhaps it had some as yet unrevealed strength that made its current position more secure than it seemed. Or perhaps it was indeed mad.

He was still pondering the conundrum when Eilwen pushed the door open and limped to the nearest chair.

"Where in the hells have you been?" Clade said.

Eilwen gave him a flat look. "Resting."

"You really think this is the time to take a break?"

"My leg does," she said, grimacing as she stretched it out.

"Perhaps we should ask the Oculus to suspend their bombardment on account of your leg." Clade took a breath and smoothed out the edge that had crept into his tone. "I don't suppose you have any insights you haven't shared?"

"About the Oculus?" Eilwen shrugged. "Have you considered that they might be here for you? Maybe saving the city is as simple as walking through the gate and handing yourself over."

Clade gave her a narrow look. There was something new and disturbing in her tone, something he'd seen far too often in his time with the Oculus: a studied disinterest that stopped just short of defiance. *Disrespect.* The beginning of the end, just as it had been for Garrett and for others before him.

He pursed his lips in frustration. Why was it that everyone he worked with shared the same failing? Sooner or later they all fell away, leaving him to battle on alone once more. There was only one of him, for the gods' sake. He couldn't do everything himself, least of all in the present crisis.

"I don't think so," he said neutrally, determined not to give her the satisfaction of a response in kind. "If they'd wanted anything instead of the city, they'd have told us by now."

"Yeah, probably," Eilwen said, grimacing as she massaged her knee. "Just a thought." She opened her mouth as if to say more, then closed it and glanced away.

Clade exhaled. He'd been planning to send Eilwen back to the stained-glass-makers' shop, her protests be damned, but he suspect-ed now that such an order would only serve to deepen her disillu-sionment. Better to give her his other task instead. Perhaps, in truth, she would be better suited to it than him.

"I need you to do something," he said. "You remember Arandras?"

She looked up with a frown. "What about him?"

"He's here in Spyridon. And he's stolen something from me." He watched the play of expressions over her face as she connected his statement with their conversations over the past few days. *Yes, go ahead and believe that this is what I didn't want to tell you. It's half the truth, anyway.* "I need you to get it back for me."

"What?"

"A book. Two books, in fact." The Valdori lexicon was no less important to his plans than anything he might learn about the go-lems. He recited the address he'd gleaned from some local fixer's assistant on a return visit to Rhothe's Bar the previous night. "It's a merchant's house, apparently. Shouldn't be hard to find."

Eilwen folded her arms. "And how exactly will this help Spy-ridon?"

He'd wanted to keep the golems' presence to himself. Old habits died hard, and all the more so when they were simply good sense. But Eilwen was no fool. Sooner or later she'd put it together herself. Better to tell her and give her reason to think that she still held his trust.

"Two ways," Clade said. "First, Arandras isn't here alone. Some of the golems are here too. Get me those books, and I may be able to find a way to bring them into the battle on our side."

Eilwen absorbed this with a faint smile that didn't reach her eyes. "And the second reason?"

"It'll free me up to do the other thing that needs doing."

"Which is?"

Clade matched her expression with his own, smile for insincere smile. "I'm going to pay those glassmaker friends of yours a visit."

～

Arandras and Mara sat on the settee before the window nibbling on candied walnuts, a jar of which Mara had found tucked behind one of the unused beds in the servants' chamber. Beyond the city, the Oculus cannons had fallen silent, though Arandras had little doubt that this was merely a temporary pause. From their vantage point in the upper room they could see pockets of vigorous activity along the enemy line — guns being loaded onto carts, driven partway around the city, then unloaded again — though exactly what the effort was meant to achieve remained unclear.

"Look at that," Mara said, pointing at a hollow not far from the northern road where a cart had lost one of its front wheels. "Why in the hells isn't Piator sending his cavalry out there? They could ride out, lop off some heads, drop a few pots of burning pitch and be back before the Oculus knows what hit them."

Arandras shrugged. "Maybe he doesn't have the men."

"Or maybe he wouldn't know a bright idea if it smacked him in the face," Mara returned, glaring at the struggling cart.

Arandras studied the vista with a frown. His familiarity with games like *dilarj* had as yet yielded little insight into the operation of real war. Far from move and countermove, the siege so far had been largely static — just two armies on opposite sides of a wall shooting rocks at each other. The tactical plays going on within the larger equilibrium and the openings that Piator Pronn was failing to capitalise on would have largely passed him by had Mara not been there to point them out.

Mara heaved a sigh. "Gods, this is depressing. It'd be bad enough if we were just outgunned. But losing by inches through sheer cluelessness…"

"Maybe Piator has some strategy we don't know about," Arandras said, reaching for another candied walnut.

"Yeah, right. And maybe my arse will grow wings and fly me to the moon." Mara gave him a sidelong glance. "You don't really think Piator is going to win this for us, do you?"

Arandras chewed on his walnut. He knew too little to form his own opinion of Piator's expertise, but if Mara considered him incompetent then Arandras was inclined to trust her judgement. And if that were so, then the city was very likely doomed. The inclination of every organisation was to turn its people into extensions of its leaders' will — Arandras had seen it for himself among the

Quill — and surely that tendency would only be magnified for a body of armed soldiers. Barring some violent shift, Piator's subcommanders would simply follow the orders they were given and the army's discipline would become its downfall.

"Yeah," Mara said. "Me either." She drew a breath. "Perhaps we should start thinking about other alternatives —"

"Hey, Arandras!" Jensine called, the excitement in her voice matched by her rapid footfalls on the stairs. "I've had an idea. You were right, believe it or not. We *can* root the sorcery in air. In fact, we almost have to. But the trick is..." She trailed off as she rounded the settee, glancing from Arandras to Mara. "Am I interrupting something?"

"No, it's fine," Mara said, and if Arandras hadn't been right beside her he'd almost certainly have missed the tightness in her smile.

"Right." Jensine beamed at Arandras. "Here's how we do it. We get at the golems' sorcery through you."

Arandras blinked. "Um... what?"

"Think about it! You bound the golems, right? You're connected to each of them. So, where in the golem's sorcery is the part that makes them obey orders? Logically, it must be whatever's at the other end of that connection."

"All right." Arandras supposed it made sense. "So that tells you where to disrupt its binding."

"More than that." Jensine gestured as if willing him to understand. "*It gives me a way in.* Think of the golems' binding like, I don't know, a woollen jacket. We're trying to unravel the collar, say, without destroying the rest of the weave. Without knowing where the thread ends, I'd have to just start cutting and hope for the best. Even if it worked, the result would be ugly. But that contact point — it's like a loose end in just the place we need."

Mara raised an eyebrow. "So you give it a tug and that's it? No more collar?"

"A very carefully measured tug. But essentially, yes. I can focus on the little piece of sorcery that matters and ignore the rest of it. And do you know what the best bit is?" Jensine grinned. "I only have to create one binding to free every golem in the house."

"By channelling the spell through me," Arandras said cautiously.

Jensine gave a gleeful nod.

"What about the rest of them?" Mara said.

"Where did you say they were, back at Tienette Lake?" Jensine shook her head. "Elsewhere in the house, sure. Elsewhere in the city, maybe. But no spell I cast here will reach that far. You'd need to travel there and create the binding again."

"Well," Arandras said. "That sounds very... creative. Are you sure it's safe?"

"What, for you?" Jensine affected a contemplative pose. "Hmmm. I didn't think of that." Arandras scowled, and Jensine burst into laughter. "It's fine. Really. I mean, yes, if the entire spell goes to shit then all bets are off, but that's no less a danger for me than for you." Her smile faded. "And in all honesty, that's a genuine risk. This is not the sort of binding you learn from the Quill. There's a small but real chance that the whole thing might blow up in our faces, and I mean that in a literal, goodbye-to-the-back-of-the-house way. I'm going to want several days to prepare the binding. And we'll need to take other precautions."

"Such as?"

"Your idea of using air as the binding's foundation was a good one. But it complicates things, too. The Valdori used lenses and mirrors to intensify the light, but I'm betting they did something to purify it as well. That's how sorcery works. Your foundation needs both density — or at least size — and purity if it's to support a complex binding. If either is insufficient, the spell won't work. Now, we won't need anything like what the Valdori needed to create the golems, but we'll still need better than that." She gestured at the window.

Arandras frowned. "Yet here we are."

"Yeah." Jensine sighed. "If I could choose anywhere to attempt something like this, I'd pick a bare mountainside on a still day, or maybe a big stone cavern. The one place I wouldn't choose is a city surrounded by cannon smoke."

"What if we shut the house up?" Mara said. "Board up the gallery, keep the doors closed, that sort of thing."

Jensine nodded. "I think that's our best bet. We'll have to open it up when the sea breeze comes through in the evening so the air doesn't get stale. That should give us maybe an hour afterwards where we have the right balance of freshness and stillness. And all this only matters when the binding is activated — I should be able to construct the sorcery beforehand without too much trouble."

Arandras gave her a narrow look. "'Should?'"

"That's right." Jensine reached between Arandras and Mara and plucked a candied walnut from the jar. "These are uncharted waters. I'd be lying if I said success was guaranteed. But I'll tell you one thing. If I can't make it work, no-one can."

"Because we'll all be dead, and the house will be in ruins, and nobody will ever have reason to attempt something like this again?" Arandras asked.

Jensine smiled and popped the walnut into her mouth. "Pretty much, yeah."

~

Eilwen limped northward through the city, pushing her pace as far as her knee would allow. Though the cannons had been silent for several hours and the air was almost clear, the resulting stillness felt charged with tension, like a breath before the deep, icy plunge. Almost everyone she passed shared the same posture: head down, shoulders hunched, hands tucked into clothing or hovering near a blade. Nobody met her gaze.

She glanced from face to face, but none belonged to the woman she'd seen near the apothecary, and before that outside the Lasavis'. *The Oculus agent.* In a city the size of Spyridon, encountering the same person twice within a day seemed unlikely at best. Was the woman following Eilwen? If so, why? Had Eilwen piqued the woman's interest with her hasty exit from the stained-glass-makers' shop, or had she already come to her attention before that?

She'd almost told Clade about it, but something had held her back. *Well, several somethings, really.* His secrets, his arrogance, his disregard for anyone beside himself — she was weary of it all, and she no longer trusted what he might do if he knew an Oculus bearer was following her around. *Set a trap, like as not, with me as the bait. What could possibly go wrong?*

Eilwen rounded the corner, traversing the dusty lane and

pausing at the rear door to fumble for her key. Despite its proximity to the northern wall, Ebek's Boarding House had as yet escaped the bombardment unscathed. She twisted the lock open, then started as something moved near the lane's opposite wall — but it was only Jak the dog, head cocked in an inquisitive pose as its tail brushed the ground noncommittally. With a wary nod to the dog, Eilwen stepped inside and made the painful climb to the first floor.

For some reason the door to their suite was unlocked. Eilwen pushed it open, glancing around the small living space. "Orval? Are you here?"

A groan answered her from the next room. She followed the sound and found Orval stretched out on his bed, his face turned to the wall and one arm wrapped around his head. The smell of stale booze filled the air.

Anger spiked in her breast. She marched across the room, grabbing Orval by the shoulder and rolling him onto his back. "By all the gods, what's the meaning of this?"

Orval groaned again, covering his eyes with his forearm. "Eilwennn…?" he slurred.

"You're damn right it is." She pulled Orval's arm away, and the boy blinked up at her. He was pale and clammy, and his hair was a mess, but his face and shirt were both clean. If he'd thrown up, at least he'd had the sense to do it before coming inside. "Gods, what would your parents think if they could see you now?"

Orval closed his eyes. "Don' feel good."

"Really? Because you look *wonderful*."

"'M ssorree. I jus' —" His hand waved limply. "You know."

Eilwen heaved a sigh. "All right." Evening, and therefore dinner, wasn't too far away. Perhaps she could find something in the kitchen to aid the boy's recovery. "Sit up. Drink some water. I'll be back soon."

Remind me never to become a parent, she thought with a grimace as she descended the stairs she'd just climbed. But as she approached the boarding house's common dining area, she found herself softening. Half of Spyridon was probably in its cups by now, and never mind the hour. Anything to forget about the threat on their doorstep for a while. Orval was scared, stuck in an unfamiliar city, and left alone for the better part of most days. Perhaps the only surprise was that it had taken this long.

She should have spent more time with him, tried harder to break through his sullen reserve, especially once the Oculus army arrived. *What would your parents say if they could see you now?* she'd asked; but in truth she had a pretty good idea. *They'd say, why in the hells didn't you both leave when you could?*

The clash of pans and utensils greeted her at the kitchen door. Inside, the cook — a red-faced woman bedecked in a floral apron large enough to serve as a curtain — barked orders from behind a chopping board at a trio of young assistants. A row of jars beside the door filled the air with the scent of spices: cumin, sumac, cinnamon, and others; and beneath them, the smell of woodsmoke and cut vegetables. Eilwen hovered in the doorway, waiting for a break in the stream of instructions to introduce herself. But the cook barely paused for breath between directions, and at length Eilwen cleared her throat and stepped forward.

"Dinner's in an hour!" the cook snapped, shooting Eilwen a glance as she reached for a fresh carrot. "Come back then."

"I know, I just need something plain. Boiled cabbage, maybe, or —"

"Lunch leftovers are in the corner." The cook jerked her head in the direction of a large pot. "Half price."

Eilwen entered cautiously, giving the cook and her harried assistants a wide berth. The lunch pot was almost empty. Only a half-portion of limp, colourless vegetables remained in the partly separated sauce: carrots, tomatoes, and yes, a few torn leaves of cabbage. She scooped the mixture onto a plate and slapped a coin down on the bench. Then, plate and cutlery in hand, she retraced her steps yet again, climbing the stairs one by one and re-entering the suite.

Orval was sitting at the table with his back to the window, a cup in his hand and the pitcher holding the afternoon's water upright on the floor beside him. He looked up at her entrance, blinking blearily as she placed the sad-looking meal on the table.

"Here." Eilwen passed him the cutlery. "Eat. You'll feel better."

He peered dubiously at the plate, but nevertheless lowered the fork and began to eat. Sighing, Eilwen folded into the chair opposite.

Gods, how had it come to this? Between the army outside, Orval's brooding restlessness, and Clade's latest task for her, she felt caught, hemmed in by her own foolish commitments. Everything that had brought her here seemed to have been decided by someone else. Clade's absurd campaign against the Oculus. Den and Irilli's pleas for their son. Clade's insistence that she stay and fight for Spyridon. What was the last thing she had decided for herself, unswayed by someone else's demands?

But she knew the answer to that question. *Death.* Death to Clade's sorcerers at the golem caverns. Death to Trademaster Laris. Death to all the others that had come before, all those she and the beast had found and killed together. Even now she felt it stir within her, whispering to her, urging her to dig out the black amber egg from the bottom of her bag and go hunting once more.

That was why she'd taken up with Clade in the first place. Havilah had died, the tragedy of her own choices had been laid bare before her, and she'd latched on to the first person she'd found who — well, why not state it plainly? The first person who could relieve her of the burden of making her own decisions.

And now, here she was.

It was futile, all of it. Every path led to failure. Perhaps Orval had the right idea after all. A bottle to forget, and another the next day, and the day after that. At least she wouldn't harm anyone beside herself —

"I miss them." Orval stared at his half-empty plate, the words barely a murmur. He drew a breath, then released it in a gusty sigh, his lips moving soundlessly. *I miss them.*

Eilwen stared, her thoughts grinding to a halt. Orval scooped another forkful, lifted it slowly to his mouth. Chewed. Swallowed. To her surprise, Eilwen found her hand creeping across the table, reaching out to cover his. "Yeah," she said, her voice thick with something she couldn't name. "I miss them too."

Slowly, so slowly, Orval raised his head. Tears glistened in his eyes. "I'm scared," he whispered.

Her fingers dug beneath his, clasping his hand tight. "So am I."

"They took Vess." A tear broke free, slipping past his nose to drop on the table. "They took her away."

"I know." Eilwen held his gaze, ignoring the sudden stinging in her own eyes. "But you listen to me. They're not going to take you. Do you hear me? If the Oculus win, we'll leave, just like we left Neysa."

"But what if —"

"No. No what-ifs." She stood and rounded the table, lifting him to his feet. "You're safe with me."

Eyes brimming, Orval shook his head; but Eilwen pulled him to her, hugging him against her shoulder as the sobs escaped him at last. *There, now,* she thought, and in her mind it was Havilah's voice which spoke. *There, now. I'm here.*

~

Clade edged past the piles of refuse strewn across the narrow alley, his breath shallow against the noisome air. Strange undertones lurked beneath the dominant smell of rotting produce: paints, glues, solvents, and a dozen other by-products of the various crafts to which the workshops that lined the alley were dedicated.

He'd found the Lasavis easily enough. Surely no other shop in Spyridon boasted a stained-glass phoenix above the door. Despite the mid-morning hour, only a small number of people could be seen on the streets: locals for the most part, or so Clade guessed, each conspicuously intent on their own errands. The browsers and casual shoppers were almost entirely absent, and the few Clade passed stood out like parrots among crows. He'd lasted barely a minute studying the shopfront from across the road before the desire to avoid notice had driven him into a nearby side street.

A short way along, he'd discovered the alley in which he now stood: little more than a pathway, really, but one that ran parallel to the main street, providing access to the rear of each shop. A succession of fences and back walls enclosed the alley on both sides: high and low, windowed and plain, stone and plaster and wood. He peered over a blackened timber fence into a coffin-maker's yard, the small space stacked high with kite-shaped boxes. How far down had the Lasavis been from this shop? Three doors? Two?

"Hold up, there," someone said behind him, and Clade turned. But the alley was empty, save for the side street at its end where a pair of harnessed black horses were just drawing to a halt. There was a bang from somewhere out of sight — a carriage door hitting the wall? — followed closely by a sheepish apology.

"Really, Arnol?" said a new voice — wry, impatient, and oddly familiar. "You couldn't have given me a little more space?"

Clade spun about and scurried down the alley. An upturned barrel beckoned, and he crouched behind it. He knew where he'd heard that voice before: in the chamber below the city hall, at the meeting of the circle.

There was a short discussion between the two voices, and an elongated grunt. Then a man strode into view brushing fussily at his trousers, a scarlet sash draped over his shoulder. Clade huddled behind the barrel, watching as the man picked his way down the alley. *Prince Urjo.*

Coughing, the prince fished a handkerchief from his sleeve and pressed it over his face. Clade eased himself lower, not trusting the shadows to conceal his face. He listened as Urjo scraped to a halt and rapped a short, evidently coded sequence of knocks against a door. There was a pause; then the door jerked open and Urjo went inside.

Clade emerged from behind the barrel just in time to see the door slam shut in the dirty limed wall. The workshop was three down from the coffin-maker's — the Lasavis, surely, unless Urjo just happened to be visiting their immediate neighbours in the mother of all coincidences. *And Hesca was so sure it was Piator Pronn.*

He tiptoed to the door and pressed his ear against the boards. Muffled voices rose and fell within, but the wood was too thick for him to make out the words. The handle yielded to his touch, but no amount of cautious pushing could persuade the door to move. A small head-high window in the wall provided the only other opening, but it was glazed and curtained and offered no improvement on the door.

Clade let out a frustrated sigh. His quarry was almost in touching distance, save for the architecture barring his way. Perhaps he could circle around, enter the shop like a normal customer and make his way to the back...

Or perhaps he'd done enough. Hesca had made it clear that she no longer sought the true conspiracy behind the theft of the army's gold. She simply wanted evidence with which to condemn her commander. If that evidence didn't exist, then nothing else Clade did here would interest her. And aside from Hesca's interest, Clade had no reason to pursue the matter any further.

Except... If the gold was still around, he'd be a fool to let it slip through his grasp. For one thing, that foreman Taroqul still expected to get paid, and if the city didn't settle his account then he just might come after Clade. For another — hells, it was gold! Clade had no shortage of good purposes to which he might put it, his ongoing food and shelter foremost among them. And if Hesca no longer cared about the missing funds, she'd hardly mind if he helped himself to whatever he found.

With a last glance at the door, Clade crept back up the alley. Urjo's black and scarlet carriage stood in the street, the royal insignia emblazoned on it a dozen times over — even the horses' blinkers bore the design of crown, wreath, and horned beast. Apparently Urjo's concept of stealth extended little further than entering at the building's rear rather than its front. A short, greasy-haired man in matching black and scarlet livery — Arnol, presumably — stood with his back to the alley, muttering to himself and rubbing at the carriage door with a rag. Clade turned the other way, slipping past the horses and onto the side street where he began strolling back and forth beside the carriage in the idle manner of one waiting for a friend.

He was in luck. The carriage's brake lever was positioned on the side of the driver's bench, almost in arm's reach. Slowing, Clade extended his awareness and began to construct a simple binding.

Destruction would not serve this time. Instead, he began to build a lock, a variation on the spell he'd used to secure the door to his suite back in Anstice. First came the ground, then the scaffold. After that, a series of resistors, each packed tight against the next within the dense timber, concentrated in the brake block and at other points where the dark lacquer had worn off and wood pressed hard against wood. Unlike ordinary locks, this would have no trigger. Such a piece would require too much time. Its focus was strength, pure and simple. The long brake lever would multiply the force exerted by the driver several times over, and the lock would need to resist it long enough to win Clade the moment he sought.

Working as quickly as he dared, Clade strung chains of resistors together, filling the brake mechanism with his sorcery. A single resistor would be fortunate to hold against a decent gust of wind, but several dozen in combination could support a child's full weight, and more again would defy even a carnival strongman. All he needed was time —

"Arnol!" Prince Urjo emerged from the mouth of the alley. "Stop fussing about and drive me home. You can worry about the door when we get back."

Shit. Hurriedly, Clade began closing off the binding's loose strands and prepared to activate the spell. On the other side, Urjo clambered into the carriage and pulled the door closed, the mundane lock shooting home with an audible *snick*. No time now to review the spell's structure. When he closed the last line, the binding would either hold or it would fail. Arnol swung up to the driver's bench, his greasy hair falling around his face; and as he settled himself and reached for the brake lever, Clade sucked in a breath and activated the binding.

The spell flared to life, invisible to everyone but Clade. Arnol pulled on the lever and the resistors engaged, clasping hold of whatever pieces of carriage they found beside them. Frowning, the driver pulled a second time, then a third, but the lever remained stuck fast.

"Now would be good, Arnol," Prince Urjo called from within the carriage.

"Yes, sir. Right away." His frown deepening to a scowl, Arnol hopped to his feet and planted himself above the lever. He stooped and grasped the lever in both hands; then, with a grunt like a pained sow, he drove his feet against the bench and heaved.

The binding flexed beneath Clade's outstretched thoughts, straining against the opposing force. A resistor slipped partway along the shaft, then another. Then an entire chain broke loose, the load slamming against the section of the spell that filled the brake block. A few more moments and it would fall apart...

"Hey!" Clade strode to the driver's bench and waved his arms. "Hey, I think I see your problem."

Glowering, Arnol released the lever. "What do you mean?"

"Something's jammed against your brake block." Clade pointed beneath the carriage, stepping back and around as Arnol jumped lightly to the ground. "There, do you see?"

"Where?" Arnol dropped to a crouch. "I don't see anything wrong —"

Clade grabbed the man by the neck and drove him as hard as he could against the side of the carriage.

Head struck wood with a crack that echoed across the street. Arnol fell to his arse and emitted a long, mournful groan. Wheeling about, Clade wiped his hands on his trousers and climbed to the driver's bench where he reached for the brake lever, grasping it with his good hand and wedging his other underneath.

Teeth clenched, Clade pulled with all of his strength. His bad hand slid ineffectually along the lever, and Clade cursed it beneath his breath. For a moment he feared he'd made the binding too strong — then the lever flew upward, narrowly missing his face and sending him sprawling across the bench. He pushed himself up, edging sideways to sit behind the horses, which had begun to whicker nervously.

"I say!" A series of sharp raps sounded within the carriage. "What's going on? Explain this delay at once!"

"Get out!" Arnol cried groggily from the street; but his voice was too soft for the warning to reach its intended target. "Kidnap... Prince..."

Clade retrieved the reins from the hook around which they'd been looped and felt a pang of doubt. Before today, he'd only ever driven a carriage in Zeanes. If the training given to horses here was much different to what he was used to, this might be a very short journey.

He wedged the whip between the fingers of his unresponsive hand and used it to tap the animals lightly on the rear. "Walk," he said firmly.

The horses sprung into motion, the one on the left snorting as if relieved to finally be underway. A low wail rose from the street. "No. Nooo, come back..."

Clade tapped the horses again. "Trot."

The wail receded behind him. Reins in one hand, whip in the other, Clade bounced uncomfortably on the bench as he drove through Spyridon's streets, its prince in tow behind him.

CHAPTER 18

Many years ago I wintered at a monastery high in the Sorenese Mountains. The daily life of those who lived there was governed by an array of rules and traditions, but a single decree stood above them all: that each monk must disobey one rule every day. Such a practice, they believed, would equip them to more boldly oppose cruelty and injustice, and they enjoined me to take up this custom myself.

Naturally, I declined.

— Eneas the Fabulist, *One Hundred Truths and Ninety-Nine Lies*

THE BLAST SOUNDED WITHOUT WARNING — a deep, many-voiced boom that shook the windows in their frames. Arandras looked up from his crouch at the edge of the gallery, the plank of wood almost slipping from his grasp. "What in the hells was *that?*"

Above him, Mara paused, the nail she'd been hammering still protruding a finger's breadth from the board. "Guns starting up again?"

"Well, yeah, but..." Shaking his head, Arandras straightened the plank and Mara resumed her hammering. *A dozen firing all at once, maybe. Weeper, but that was loud.*

A second boom reverberated around the gallery, louder than the first. This time he did lose his grip on the board and it sagged sideways, swinging from its single nail. "Damn it!" Mara exclaimed, grabbing after the dangling board. "Just hold it straight, will you?

It's not that hard —"

"Um." Jensine's voice floated in from the balcony. "You two should probably come see this."

Exhaling in frustration, Mara set down the hammer and stalked to the balcony. Arandras straightened, brushed the knees of his trousers clean and followed.

A glittering array of cannons spread across the front of the Oculus line, more than twice as many as yesterday. Clusters of guns alternated with empty stretches of land, the arrangement evidently designed to minimise the effectiveness of Spyridon's defensive battery. As Arandras watched, a series of flashes sparked raggedly across the line, followed a moment later by a third thunderous boom. But as the missiles leapt skyward they burst into sorcerous flame, transforming into a rain of fire that plunged toward Spyridon. Most crashed into the outer wall, but several flew over the top and fell like comets into the city below. One smashed through a tower at a point of the wall's star, sending a gun and half a dozen soldiers tumbling to the ground.

"Weeper have mercy," Arandras breathed.

"I can't watch this." Mara shouldered past Arandras, her face a mask. "Are we putting these boards up or what?"

Swallowing, Arandras pulled himself away from the bombardment. "Piator Pronn will order some raids. He'll have to —"

"Just hold the damn board," Mara said. Stooping, she positioned a fresh nail and began pounding it into the plank.

The following hours passed in a thumping, headache-inducing crawl. Every barrage without was answered by Mara with ever more ferocious hammering within. When she struck a nail askew, flattening it lengthways into the board or sending it flying across the room, she simply reached for another and resumed her murderous pounding. Slowly they extended the makeshift barrier down the length of the gallery, walling it off from the outside world. As the daylight was gradually shut out, Jensine brought in some lamps and positioned them at points along the inner wall. The flickering lights struck multiple shadows from each golem, the effect giving Arandras the strange feeling of crouching at the edge of an indoor forest, every stone tree looking on in silent disapproval as he and Mara completed their slow imprisonment.

"Better," Jensine said as the last hammer blows faded beneath yet another burst from the cannons. She closed her eyes, face raised to some imperceptible breeze, her hands outstretched on either side. "Mmm. Yes, this I can work with."

Stifling a groan, Arandras pushed himself to his feet, stretching to relieve the ache in his lower back. Beside him, Mara grabbed the bucket of nails and strode off without a word. He thought about following, but Jensine appeared at his elbow and he turned to her with a voiceless sigh. "What's next?"

"I'll need to try some things," Jensine said. "Just to confirm I can construct a binding the way I need to. That shouldn't take any longer than this afternoon."

"So... tomorrow?"

"Tomorrow. I'll start at sunrise. If all goes well, I'll be ready for you around mid-afternoon." She paused. "That doesn't mean the spell will be ready to cast, mind. For one thing, we'll have to wait for the sea breeze to come and go. For another, it'll take several hours to, uh, lace you in. So make sure you go to the privy first."

"All right." Arandras took a breath. "Tomorrow. Good." He should have been excited, but whatever he might normally have felt had been battered into retreat by the Oculus assault. "I'll be here."

He shuffled from the gallery, reaching awkwardly to rub the sore spot in his back. At the top of the stairs he found Mara glaring through the balcony door with folded arms.

Arandras drew to a halt, unsure what to say. *Are you all right?* seemed hopelessly inadequate, but he could think of nothing that offered any real improvement. He looked away, wondering if it would be kindest to simply slip past and leave her to her thoughts.

Unexpectedly, she stirred. "Tomorrow, then," she said, still staring outside.

Arandras nodded. "Tomorrow."

"Then the golems will be free."

He nodded again. "That's the plan."

Mara took a slow breath. "Before that happens, I want to ask you something —"

A series of bangs filled the air, and between the cannons and the hammering it took Arandras several moments to identify the sound as a knock on the door.

Mara exhaled. "For the gods' sake, what now?"

She stepped aside, giving him space to pass; but as he did so, her expression slipped. Anguished eyes met his, pulling him to a halt mid-stride. "Mara..."

"Go," she said. "See who it is."

"All right," he said; but for a moment he couldn't move. "I'll be right back."

"I know. Go."

Arandras tore himself away, stumbling down the staircase and past the pouch-rat. At the foot of the stairs he took a breath to compose himself, then reached out and yanked the door open. "What is it?"

A woman wearing the uniform of the Spyridon army stared back — tallish, though not as tall as Mara, and with entirely different colouring: auburn hair, pale skin, and even paler eyes. She studied him with the narrow expression of one accustomed to assessing people in terms of the threat they posed. "Are you Arandras?"

"Who's asking?"

Her lips twisted in a tight smile. "My name is Hesca Matharan. Subcommander of the Spyridon Army."

"I thought you army types all had pressing business down at the wall."

The smile twisted further. "You'd think so, wouldn't you?" She started forward, and he shot an arm out sideways to bar her passage. "Let me in, Arandras."

"And why would I do that?"

"Because I promise not to bother you again, if you'll just hear me out."

Arandras's gaze flicked to the sword at her belt. *And if I refuse?* But Tiy and the other golems were upstairs — too far away to be useful to him at the front door. Scowling, he dropped his arm and turned inside.

"Thank you," Hesca said, and he heard the clunk of the door being pulled shut. "Where can we talk?"

"The answer's no," Arandras said as he started up the stairs. "I'm not interested in gold, power, threats, or any of the rest of it. You're on your own."

"That's good. I have no gold or power to offer you. And threats, I realise, are of strictly limited utility. But I need your golems all the same."

"Did you not hear me? The answer's no. And I guarantee that you'll get tired of asking before I get tired of refusing."

"This is my city, Arandras. You have no idea the lengths I'll go to in its defence..."

Hesca trailed off, eyes widening as the golems came into view at the top of the stairs. Cautiously, she approached the gallery, angling across the space like a predator sizing up some new competitor. She slowed to a halt just out of reach of the nearest golem, her head shifting this way and that as she studied the motionless constructs.

"I see we have a guest," Mara said from the other side of the stairs, and Hesca whirled. Mara sauntered forward with a lazy smile, one hand resting on a cutlass hilt. "Care to introduce yourself?"

"Hesca Matharan," she replied, her own hand drifting to her sword. "Subcommander of the Spyridon Army —"

Arandras sent a command and the golem rumbled in response. Hesca whirled again, but too late: the golem lunged forward and closed its massive hand around her upper arm, arresting her turn and lifting her hand just before it could grasp the hilt of her blade.

"There," Arandras said as a fresh volley of cannon fire split the air. "Now we can talk."

∽

Orval was still in bed when Eilwen left the boarding house. She'd considered trying to rouse him, worried that he might be sick, but his colour and temperature seemed normal and in the end she'd let him be. Perhaps it was simply an aftereffect of the previous evening. The gods knew how exhausting the release of pent-up fears could be, physically as much as emotionally.

Even so, Eilwen thought as she ventured out of the building and onto the sparsely populated street, surely only a teenage boy could sleep through the din of the renewed bombardment.

Her resentment at the task assigned to her by Clade had grown steadily since their meeting the previous day. Clade had tried to dress it up as part of the city's defence, but the edge in his voice when he mentioned Arandras's name told her otherwise. In any case, she had matters of her own to attend to. Somewhere in the city was a woman carrying a token of the Oculus, and Eilwen meant to find her.

A rough wooden fence barricaded the road a short way ahead. Behind it lay the square adjoining the north gate, the space now transformed into a series of defensive rows bristling with spikes, torches, and soldiery. Eilwen cut inward, making for the avenue in which carriages for hire customarily gathered to seek the business of new arrivals. The broad lane was all but empty — just two dubious conveyances waited, the first a battered green vehicle sporting a gouge in its door that might have been made by an axe, the second more a cart than a carriage. Eilwen climbed inside the first, sighing with relief as she lowered herself onto the padded seat and took the weight off her knee.

"To the hill," she called through the space in the front of the compartment, and the driver gave a small nod beneath his folded cap. "East side. I'll give you more directions when we get closer."

They set off, the driver selecting a route that took them through the north part of the city before commencing their climb. Eilwen gripped the black amber egg, her senses straining for any hint of the dark, alien presence. A faint thumping rose at the edge of her perception, heavy but distant, like a giant's footfalls on the other side of a hill. *The army.* Too far away to sense individually, the collective mass of sorcerers and tokens provided just enough of a presence for Eilwen to make out.

She stared out of the small, grubby window, watching as the buildings became gradually larger and richer, and the streets wider and more busy. When a squat rainwater well came into view, she leaned forward and tapped on the front panel. "Turn here," she called, and the carriage hewed right into the lane that led to the apothecary's shop.

It was all she could think of to do: drive around the places the woman had been and hope to pick up a trace of her presence with the black amber egg. But as the minutes turned to hours, and the carriage made its way down to the artisans' district and then back up the hill, Eilwen felt her enthusiasm for the hunt begin to wane. Around mid-morning the carriage driver stopped and insisted Eilwen pay what she owed so far. Only when she counted the silver into his hand did he scratch his chin and consent to another circuit.

On their third climb toward the apothecary's shop, Eilwen at last felt the egg quiver. Closing her eyes, Eilwen strained toward the source of the disturbance, but the jolting carriage made it impossible to get a fix on the direction. She rapped the front panel. "Stop!"

The carriage slowed and swung to the side of the road, then lurched to a halt. Eilwen took a slow breath and allowed the faint pulse of the egg to fill her awareness. The beast opened a slitted eye, drawn by memories of the hunt; but it seemed content to simply watch, and Eilwen let it be. The pulse grew stronger, and Eilwen turned sideways on the carriage seat, searching for the right direction. A token-bearer, yes, just like before, coming from... behind her?

She pushed the door open and stuck out her head. Porters and pedestrians laboured up the hill in their wake, though none resembled the woman Eilwen had seen. Further back, another carriage turned into view: a light gig with open sides, drawn by a large piebald. The throbbing of the egg intensified, and Eilwen slid back inside. The piebald clopped past, then the gig, and Eilwen glimpsed a stout driver smoking a pipe — and beside him, a small, pale-skinned woman.

Eilwen yanked the carriage door shut and thumped her fist against the front panel. "Follow that gig!" The carriage jerked into motion, and Eilwen cursed. "Don't be obvious about it! Give them some space, but don't lose them."

They trundled up the hill, Eilwen glancing out the windows on either side as the buildings rolled past and wishing she could see what was happening ahead. At the rainwater well they turned left, away from the apothecary's shop and onto a street with a more gentle slope. The beast stretched within her, drawn to wakefulness by the throbbing egg. *We hunt,* it said, its lips pulled wide in a hungry smile, and Eilwen did not correct it.

They turned several more times, but the slope of the streets remained slight for the most part, indicating a route that skirted the east side of the hill. Eilwen fidgeted in her seat as wealthy residences began to replace the shops outside, and tried to work out where the woman could be going. Not to the Library, obviously, nor to the artisans' district below them. Perhaps she was headed to Port Gallin, though with the harbour closed it seemed an odd destination. Or perhaps it made sense — of course an Oculus agent would want to know the state of the city's defences, and look for any gap or weakness that the army outside might exploit.

But as Eilwen settled in for the ride to the harbour, the carriage turned once more and drew to a halt. Her hand tightened around the egg — but its pounding continued. *She's stopped.* Eilwen opened the door to find the driver just outside, his hand raised to knock. "Well?"

"They stopped just around there," the driver said, indicating the corner they'd just turned. As Eilwen turned to look, the gig rolled past, the pipe-smoker alone on its bench.

"Good." She dug hastily in her purse and slapped some coins into the driver's outstretched hand. "Don't bother waiting for me."

She hurried to the junction, egg throbbing against her fingers. The cannons sounded different here: more of an echoing boom, like thunder rolling in over the hills. Large houses of fiery Spyridon sandstone stood at wide intervals — and there, leaning against an ivy-covered stone wall, stood the woman Eilwen sought, her attention apparently fixed on the house across the street as she munched on an apple.

Eilwen glanced around. Something about the location seemed familiar. The sandstone, the multi-storey houses, the fences of wrought iron... Realisation came, and she exhaled sharply. This was the street Clade had instructed her to visit, the one where Arandras was reportedly holed up. The house itself was owned by a merchant, Clade had said. Tratta-something. Three levels, a stable on the low side — just like the one that the woman was staring at right now.

Or had been staring at a moment ago, before she saw Eilwen standing like an idiot in the middle of the street.

They locked eyes, and a look of startled recognition passed fleetingly across the woman's face. The beast snarled its satisfaction and

Eilwen strode forward, the egg singing in her whitened fist. "You," she breathed, and the woman paled. "Oculus."

The woman backed away — but there was nowhere to go, just the wall marking the boundary of the house behind her. "I don't know what you're talking about."

"Bullshit." The beast's lips split into a grin. "Tell me why they're here."

"I don't know —"

The egg cracked against the woman's head and she slumped to the ground, Eilwen staring down as the sudden pain in her hand penetrated the beast's haze. *Gods, no. Not again.* The beast hissed its displeasure, and Eilwen fumbled beneath her clothes for the goat-skin belt and yanked it tight. *I said no!*

Groaning, the woman pushed herself up to a seated position. "Gatherer spare me. You're crazy."

"Maybe I am." Eilwen dropped to a crouch and leaned close. "But I know who you're working for, and I can just imagine what the people in this city would do if I told them."

The woman touched her head gingerly and grimaced when her fingers came back smeared with blood. "I'm not working for anyone."

"No?" Eilwen brandished the egg still clenched in her fist. "Look familiar? Want to show me yours, or are you going to make me search you?"

The woman's eyes widened. "Then... you're Oculus too?"

"Hardly." Eilwen straightened. "How long have you been taking their coin?"

"What does it matter?" The woman glared up at her. "You want to kill me, is that it? Add another of those to your collection?"

Yes! The beast roared its approval. Eilwen sucked in a breath and shook her head. "No," she said thickly. "Nobody dies today. Not if you answer my questions."

The woman eyed her uncertainly. "Fine. I first met the Oculus almost a year ago. I didn't know who they were back then, nobody did, but —"

"Never mind that," Eilwen said. "Why are they here?"

"Isn't it obvious? They want Spyridon."

"To what end?"

"You think they'd tell me?" The woman gave a mirthless laugh. "I know they want the Library and the palace intact and undamaged, for whatever it's worth. If you're looking for more than that, you'd be better off finding a general to interrogate."

Eilwen exhaled through her teeth. "What's your job, then? You followed me after you saw me at the Lasavis', didn't you? Why?"

"I thought you might have been part of whatever scheme they've been cooking up with Urjo. But you're not, are you? You're... what? Trying to figure it out, same as me?"

"And what does the Oculus care for the Lasavis or Prince Urjo?"

The woman shrugged. "Spyridon will be theirs soon. Of course they care what the city circle is doing."

"You sound very sure about that."

"Oh, I am. Spyridon will fall. All the cannons in Tan Tahis couldn't save you now."

"Why?"

The woman clamped her mouth shut and looked away.

The beast growled at the non-answer, but Eilwen shoved it down. "Don't like that question? Let's try another. What brings you here, to this street, across from that house? Well? Could it be that the circle isn't the only thing you're checking up on? Could it be that there's still something — or should I say 'some things?' — in the city that could turn the fight against you?"

The woman's shrug was almost genuine. "What things?"

"You tell me." Eilwen paused. "Nothing to say? Perhaps you'll be more forthcoming to my employer. But I should warn you, he's not as easygoing as I am —"

The woman surged to her feet and drove her shoulder into Eilwen's midriff. Eilwen fell backward and hit the road in an ungainly sprawl, the dagger at her waist jolting free and skittering away. "No more questions," the woman hissed, her clawed fingers reaching for Eilwen's face.

Eilwen twisted aside and scrambled to her feet. The woman strode toward her, and the beast howled in response, the rage in their eyes one and the same. "No," Eilwen whispered. She stumbled back, her feet struggling for traction against the slope; but the woman and the beast kept coming, and she knew she could never outrun them both.

"You should have kept your nose to yourself," the woman said as she stepped toward Eilwen's lost dagger. Her second blade called to her from its hiding place in her boot, the beast begging her to draw it, but Eilwen shook her head. *Find another way.* Thwarted, the beast snarled in displeasure; then its gaze locked onto the woman, and Eilwen saw.

The woman stepped sideways once more, and as she glanced down to where the blade lay, Eilwen burst into a run. In the last moment before impact, the woman straightened and tensed; then Eilwen was wrapping her arms around the woman and driving her back toward the ivy-covered wall. *Nobody dies.* But as the woman staggered backward beneath Eilwen's charge, her foot slipped and she lost balance, falling from Eilwen's grasp and tumbling head-first against the wall.

The crack of skull striking stone reverberated around the street like a cannon shot. The woman sagged to the ground, her head smearing the ivy red where it passed. Shocked, Eilwen dropped to her knees, her gaze falling on the cause of the woman's stumble: the crushed remains of a half-eaten apple.

~

Clade brought Urjo's carriage to a jolting stop in an alley several blocks west of the army command post. The horses snorted disdainfully, stomping their hoofs in apparent protest at Clade's clumsy driving. Ignoring them, Clade slid from the driver's bench to the ground and strode to the carriage, where he rapped twice on the emblazoned door. "We're here."

"And where's that?" came Urjo's peeved reply. "For that matter, who are you, and where's Arnol?"

"Arnol's right here," Clade lied. "Open the door and see for yourself."

"Arnol? Say something. What's going on?"

"All right, Arnol's not here. But I'm sure he's fine, wherever he is."

"Bastard! What do you want?"

Clade permitted himself a brief smile. "To talk to you, Prince

Urjo. What else?"

"So talk."

"No, no. This discussion really needs to be held face to face."

"I don't think so." Despite having been kidnapped by a stranger and driven to an unknown part of the city, Urjo sounded more defiant than scared. "Talk if you want, or go fondle the horses, but this carriage stays shut."

"You think they'd like that?"

"They couldn't find it any less pleasant than your driving."

Clade laughed despite himself. He felt strangely light-headed after the success of his improvised abduction. "All right," he said, leaning against the dirty brick wall. The alley terminated in a dead end a few strides past the horses, and its mouth was distant enough that the shadows would conceal the carriage's insignias from anyone who happened to glance in their direction. "We'll try it your way. Let's talk about gold."

Urjo made a disgusted noise. "I should have guessed. Another good-for-nothing who thinks no further than his own coin-purse. Was robbing me really the best plan you could come up with?"

Clade chuckled. "Does this happen to you often?"

"Every day. Only usually not quite so literally. Feren gods-damned Skaratass and her underlings tend to favour more sophisti-cated ways of separating a man from his money."

"So you decided to steal some back, did you?"

There was a long pause. "That's quite an accusation."

"Oh, I'm just getting started."

"And who, exactly, are you here on behalf of?"

"I thought you'd have recognised my voice by now."

Urjo paused again. "The last meeting of the city circle," he said. "You were there, with Piator Pronn. Cale, or something."

Clade began to correct him, then changed his mind. "Close enough."

"Did Hesca put you up to this? Or is this your idea of showing initiative?"

"Hesca?" Clade said. "Don't you mean Pronn?"

Silence stretched. From somewhere within the carriage came a soft scraping — Urjo shifting on his seat, perhaps. Another round of cannon fire sounded from outside the city, and still the prince said nothing.

Realisation dawned. "Of course you don't mean Pronn," Clade breathed. "He's in on this too."

"Is *that* what this is about?" With the carriage wall between them, Urjo's disdain almost sounded genuine. "You think Piator and I are conspiring to... what? Rob the *city?*"

But Clade was not to be deterred. "Not the city. Just the army."

"This is outrageous. I demand you return Arnol to me. Piator Pronn will hear of this —"

"Shut up, Urjo," Clade said pleasantly. "And open that door."

"Never!" Urjo retorted. "Where am I? Help! Can anyone hear me? I need help!"

Clade stepped back from the carriage and worked a swift binding. As a fresh bombardment split the air, Clade triggered the half-formed spell. The carriage door burst apart, its pieces clattering against the alley wall to reveal the prince huddled in a corner, an expression of pure astonishment on his face. An empty bottle rolled across the floor, coming to rest against the prince's finely worked leather shoe.

"Now," Clade said. "About that gold."

Urjo's face twisted in anger. "You fool," he snarled. "Just what is it you think you know?"

"I know the army's missing a small fortune. And I know you've been diverting shipments from the mint and funnelling the gold through the Lasavis."

"It's the army's gold! Piator is the army's commander! He has every right to dispose of it as he sees fit!"

"While keeping it off the books?"

"Is that really your entire complaint? Piator spent some of the army's own gold and he *didn't write it down?*"

"Of course not! He..." Clade trailed off. What *was* his complaint? "If it's all legitimate, why so much secrecy?"

"Oh, and I suppose you announce your every purchase from the middle of the Great Square?"

"You're evading the question —"

"And you haven't asked a single one worth answering!" Urjo

shook his head in disgust. "You *are* here for Hesca. That slippery minx somehow convinced you to do her dirty work, didn't she? I don't suppose you ever stopped to wonder about her interest in all this?"

Clade folded his arms. "Forget about Hesca," he said. "Tell me about you and Piator Pronn."

Urjo shifted uncomfortably. "Answer me something first, Cale. In your discerning opinion" — the sneer could almost have gone unnoticed if Clade hadn't been listening for it — "how fine a job would you say the city circle is doing?"

Another volley boomed out. "Can't say I'm especially impressed with them just now."

"Huh." Urjo eyed him appraisingly. "Perhaps you're not a complete moron after all."

"Says one of the members of that very circle."

Urjo barked a laugh. "Feren Skaratass owns the circle, Cale, or enough of it to make no difference. The Conservator owns half the gods-damned city. The only reason I'm still permitted in that room is because she hasn't worked out how to get rid of me without hurting herself in the process."

"I've heard this before," Clade said. "The Library on one side, the army on the other. You'd prefer to see Piator Pronn in charge, would you?"

Urjo snorted. "Hardly. The man's an idiot. But a useful one, for now."

Clade glanced pointedly in the direction of the city wall. "You sure about that last bit?"

"This wasn't supposed to happen. Not yet, anyway. I mean, it was obvious that the Oculus weren't going to stop at Neysa, but nobody thought they'd come this way so quickly."

"What, then? This whole scheme is your way of fighting the Oculus?"

Urjo flushed. "You're not from around here, are you, Cale? If you were, maybe you'd know what a shambles this city is. Year after year, the circle flaps about, unable to decide what to do or how to do it, and Feren Skaratass takes advantage of their idiocy to grab a little more power. Do you know what it took to convince them to build that wall? Gods and demons, you'd think you were persuading cats to take a bath."

"Sounds to me like you and Hesca would get along just fine."

"Ah, Hesca." A peculiar smile twisted Urjo's lips. "I'll tell you a secret, Cale, if you haven't already figured it out. Hesca is an idealist. She believes in Spyridon. Few have done more on the city's behalf. But alas, she also believes in the circle."

Clade frowned. "And you don't."

"All Hesca sees is Piator Pronn's incompetence. Well and good, as far as it goes. But that's the least of Spyridon's problems." Urjo exhaled. "The city is ungovernable, Cale. *The circle* is ungovernable. Spyridon is a lordless city. Feren can barely see the nose on her face, but even she sees that much. She thinks she can solve the problem by making herself queen."

"Whereas your solution... is to make yourself king?"

"I have the blood." Urjo lifted his head, a strange pride filling his voice. "I have the name. And I'm not foolish enough to think you can cram the whole world into ink on parchment. Feren would be a disaster. If she'd had her way, that wall would never have been built. Spyridon would already have fallen."

"So... what? You enlisted Pronn's support, promised to look after him under your benevolent future regime, and persuaded him to send you as much gold as he could spare? Which you were then going to use to tear Feren down and reestablish your family's position?"

Urjo sagged back into his seat. "Something like that."

"You really thought that could work?"

"What do you know about it?" Urjo snapped. "I've been working toward this for years. Neysa's fall made it clear that it was time to act. If the Oculus had waited just a year, even six months..."

"But they didn't," Clade said. The faint sound of voices rose from somewhere to the east, a distant commotion of some sort, but he ignored it. "They're here. And that useful idiot of yours is charged with the city's defence."

"All right, you don't have to spell it out." Urjo made a weary gesture. "You want me come with you, confess Piator's financial sins, and force him to stand aside so Hesca can take charge and save us all. Is that about the shape of it?"

"And you'll return the missing gold, as well."

"Ah." Urjo gave a faint smile. "That gold, my dear Cale, is no longer within the city. I couldn't give it back even if I wanted to."

Clade subjected the prince to a dubious stare. "Is that true?"

"If you want my assistance, you'll be well advised to believe that it is." Urjo slid gingerly across the seat and climbed to the ground. With a resigned sigh, he straightened his scarlet sash and set off toward the mouth of the alley. "Let's get this over with."

~

Hesca's face contorted in rage. "Let me go, damn it," she snarled, pulling uselessly against the golem's rock-hard grip.

"I don't think so," Arandras said. Behind the subcommander, Jensine emerged at last from the forest of golems, one hand raised in a manner that suggested sorcery and a questioning look in her eye. Arandras made a negating gesture, and Jensine reluctantly lowered her hand. "You want the golems. My answer is no. What else would you like to discuss?"

Hesca bared her teeth. "Look at you. You think all you have to do is put up a wall and the world outside will go away?" She gestured furiously at the makeshift barrier and everything that lay beyond. "If you don't want to listen to me asking for help, take down the boards and listen to *them!*"

Guns boomed; and from somewhere closer came a thunderous crash, like a wave of stone breaking upon the shore. Arandras resisted the urge to stride to the balcony and see what had been hit. Faint cries filled the air: screams of pain, calls for others to respond, and the wild barking of half a dozen dogs.

"Hear that?" Hesca said. "What do you think those people would say to you if they were here in this room right now?"

Thank the gods I wasn't at home when that cannonball hit, some part of Arandras thought; but the fury in Hesca's eyes squashed any thought of humour. "It's not that simple."

"This is just the start," Hesca said. "If the Oculus commanders have even half a brain between them — and at this point I think we can safely say they do — they'll have a team of sappers digging toward the city right now. They'll bring down a section of the wall, open up the city to the rest of their army. And what happens next will make this seem like a Sarean massage in comparison."

"Damn it, Hesca, I can't save the gods-damned world!"

"Nobody's asking you to! Just help us!" The anger in Hesca's voice fell away, replaced with naked entreaty. "We need to mount a sortie against the Oculus positions. Piator Pronn won't authorise it, and even if he did we can't spare the soldiers to hit them hard enough. If we just sit here inside our walls, sooner or later they'll find a way in." She held his gaze, imploring him. "People are going to die. Only you can save them."

"*No*," Arandras said. How many times did he have to explain this? "Everyone dies, Hesca. None of us can prevent a single death. All we can ever do is delay them. But you want me to use living beings as if they were nothing more than convenient murder weapons. Maybe you don't have a problem with that. But *I do not use people*."

Jensine gave a loud sigh. "Just toss her out the door, already. We've got work to do."

"Wait," Mara said. Turning her back on Hesca, she leaned close to murmur in Arandras's ear. "Can we talk?"

"About what?"

"This. All of it." She gripped his arm and nodded toward the balcony. "Please."

Reluctantly, Arandras followed Mara outside. The cries from the direction of the fallen building were diminishing, but someone nearby had begun a long, keening wail that seemed to slice into Arandras's skull. "What is it?"

Mara met his glare without flinching. "She's right, you know."

Arandras folded his arms. "Right about what?"

"The battle. The city." Her words were soft, edged with both determination and distaste. "If we let the Oculus pound away and do nothing to counter them, we'll lose. That's just a fact."

"And the golems?" Arandras demanded. "Is she right about them, too?"

"Of course she is." Mara shrugged. "You don't need me to tell you that."

Anger flared; and beneath it, something else, something he didn't want to acknowledge. "But apparently you think I do need to be told something."

"Told? No." Mara turned and leaned on the balcony rail. "Hesca might be right about the battle, but I doubt that's all she cares about. She's a player, just like Feren and everyone else. Power is the only thing any of them understand. Toss her out the door like Jensine said, and good riddance."

"All right." His anger wavered, undercut by confusion. "So why are we out here?"

"They don't understand why you're doing this," Mara said. "But I do." She gazed out at the city, not meeting his eyes. "This isn't just a, I don't know, a *decision* you've made. Like it was some kind of choice. If you don't free the golems — if you don't at least try — you feel like some part of you will shrivel and die. I get it."

"I, uh…" Arandras groped for words but found none. Was that truly what she saw? "It's not about me," he managed. "It's about them."

"I know. But there's something I need to do, too. Something I have to ask you. And if I don't…" Her voice quavered, but still she kept her gaze locked on the scene before them, sparing him the burden and pressure of her emotion as best she could. "Before you do this, before Jensine casts her spell… would you help my city?"

Arandras's throat tightened. "Mara…"

"Maybe you only take them out once." Her voice was soft, like a child's. "Just one sortie. Enough to give the city a fighting chance. Hells, Jensine could probably make a start on her binding while they're gone. You wouldn't have to delay anything. But that might be all we need."

"You're asking me to kill," Arandras whispered. "More than that. You're asking me to make killers of them. Send them out like the Gatherer's angels to cut down whoever crosses their path, unable to resist, unable even to look away —"

"They're killers already, Arandras. You must know that."

"Are they? How can we be sure?"

"Then destroy the guns and leave the soldiers be. Just do *something*." At last Mara raised her head, and the pain in her eyes was like a hammer blow to Arandras's heart. "Please."

He swallowed, unable to deny her, unable to accede. The silence stretched, and he hung suspended in the moment as though he were the construct and his master had deserted him at last. Then, as though watching the actions of someone else, he found himself turning and walking back into the gallery where Hesca still stood in the golem's grip.

"If I were to help you," he heard himself say, "I'd need to make a few things clear."

"What?" Jensine stared, her shock unmistakable yet strangely distant. "You can't be serious."

"Anything you want, it's yours," Hesca said. "We can show you the enemy's positions, point out where we think they're vulnerable. We'll support you with as many soldiers as we can spare, or you can go alone if you prefer. Timing, positioning, anything — you get final say over it all."

"No, this is madness," Jensine protested. "I've got a binding to prepare, for the gods' sake —"

"You said you were getting to the golems' sorcery through me," Arandras said. "So you don't require them to be physically present, do you?"

"I —" Jensine sputtered in disbelief. "One of them, yes. I can't just build a spell without some reference to its ultimate target."

"Fine. I'll leave Tiy." Arandras turned to Hesca. "I'm not going to fight this war for you, understand? This is one strike, nothing more."

Hesca nodded sharply. "Absolutely. Whatever you say."

"Good." Arandras sent an instruction and the golem holding Hesca released its grip. "Where do we start?"

Hesca rolled her shoulder with a grimace. "There's a command post north of here. That's where Piator Pronn is running things," she said, placing a faintly sarcastic emphasis on the last two words. "More importantly, that's where we'll find the intelligence you'll need."

Arandras hesitated. "Do you speak for the commander? Or has this conversation been just between us?"

"Piator won't be a problem," Hesca said. "One way or another, I'll keep him out of your path."

"Fine." It was too late to quibble about such details. Somewhere in the past few moments he seemed to have reached a decision. All he could do now was see it through.

Golems, attend. As one, the golems turned in their places to face him, the sound of their movement for a moment obscuring even the bombardment outside.

Hesca's eyes widened. "Gods," she muttered. Then her face filled with savage glee.

Arandras's arm moved, and he found that he had gestured toward the stairs. When he spoke, his words came not from within but from somewhere else; yet it was his own lips that moved and his own tongue that gave them voice.

"Follow me," he said.

PART 3:
THE TYRANNY
OF THE REAL

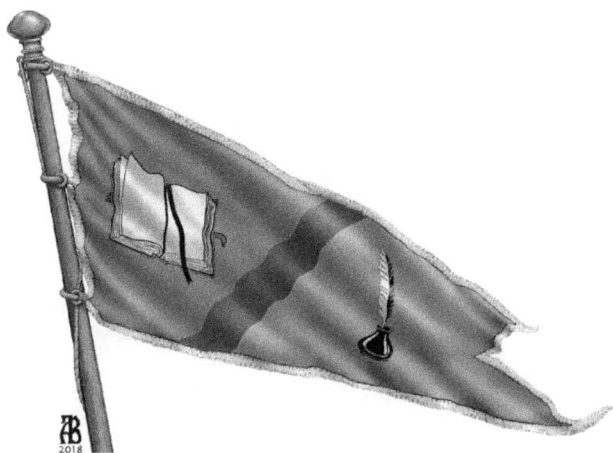

CHAPTER 19

Thanks are like children. Singly they are often a delight; in pairs they may still be enjoyed; but in crowds they can only ever be endured.

— Vissbronaumi, *On the Tragedies*

DULL THUDS AND THE CHATTER of approaching voices sounded from the house across the road. Eilwen stood hastily and strode up the street, away from the woman's lifeless body. Inside, the beast capered in celebration. *I tried not to kill her. Gods, but I tried.* Yet the beast had had its way after all.

The front door opened and a figure stepped outside — Arandras, Eilwen thought, though the wrought-iron fence obscured her view. With an effort, she pushed aside her dismay. The woman's death was an accident, nothing more. The beast had won no victory; it had merely been favoured by chance. Eilwen had given it nothing.

A second figure appeared beside Arandras: a woman in military attire, her posture vaguely familiar. The woman glanced up, revealing her face, and Eilwen started in surprise. *Hesca Matharan, here?* The subcommander had won Clade an appearance before the city circle. Hells, as far as the missing gold was concerned she was practically their employer. What in the name of all the gods was she doing in the company of Arandras?

Then another figure emerged from the door, and her question was answered.

In the cavern by the lake, the golems had appeared almost otherworldly, creatures of some nether realm divorced from the virtues
and passions of humanity. Here they seemed paradoxically both less
terrifying and more. Daylight provided perspective. They were large,
yes, but not too large to fit through an estate house front door. Their
glowing eyes, though uncanny, held little of the malevolence they
had possessed below ground. Yet the sight of the ancient Valdori
constructs clomping up an ordinary path to an ordinary Spyridon
street filled Eilwen with a dread beyond her capacity to express. She
felt as if the world itself had tilted, jolting her to her knees, and
she could no longer tell the difference between that and standing
upright.

Shivering, Eilwen crept backward, retreating to the safety of the
neighbouring fence as Arandras and Hesca reached the gate. The
golems followed, two dozen or more filing onto the street and clus-
tering around their master. Arandras glanced around, and Eilwen
was surprised to see an expression not of excitement or even determination but tightly-controlled distaste. Hesca muttered something
in his ear; Arandras gave her a sharp look, then nodded ungraciously and made a lead-the-way gesture.

They set off down the street, Arandras and Hesca leading the
rumbling mass of golems. Eilwen followed close behind, her awe
at the constructs tempered by a vast sense of relief. If Hesca had
indeed recruited the golems to the city's defence, then at one stroke
she'd not only given Spyridon its best chance of repelling the siege
but also rendered Clade's books irrelevant to anything beyond his
personal ambitions. Passers-by stopped and stared at their approach,
several gaping in wordless astonishment as others backed away shaking their heads and making signs of warding. Somewhere ahead of
the group, a panicked voice cried out in prayer.

"They've broken through!" someone shouted. "Gods have mercy!"

"No, they're here to help us," countered a man wheeling a handcart only a few paces from Eilwen. "They're going to fight for the
city!"

"Which is it, then?" called a large, curly-haired woman. "What
do you want with us?"

Hesca's response was obscured by a renewed burst of quavering prayer, but the thin cheer that greeted her words was unmistakable.

"Help at last!"

"Thank the gods!"

"Rip off their heads and shove them up their own cannons!"

The golems lumbered on, the crowd growing as they moved northward down the hill. People cheered and chanted, some running ahead to break the news to the next dozen people, others flocking around the golems with a mixture of wariness and excitement. One particularly bold or foolhardy youth grasped a golem's elbow, then raised his hand high with a triumphant laugh, and suddenly everyone was reaching out to touch their arms and hands and slap their backs.

A breathless group of students barged past Eilwen to join the crowd and she slowed her pace, wary of being caught up in the press. Spectators appeared at the windows of the taller buildings, watching the procession with various expressions of awe, suspicion, and delight. An elderly man knelt at the street's edge, his forehead pressed against the ground, his shoulders shaking. A carriage braked to a halt at the end of the block, horses tossing their heads at the noise, the driver gaping after the monstrous constructs.

The hill ended in a small dip, and for a moment Eilwen caught a chance glimpse of Arandras across the crowd. The man looked like he'd swallowed something foul and was struggling to keep it down. *He doesn't want to be here,* Eilwen realised. Yet there was nothing in his bearing that spoke of coercion. *A bargain, then? The might of the golems, in exchange for... what?*

The crowd rolled on. A cry of pain rose briefly above the din — perhaps someone had ventured too close and suffered a golem's weight on their foot — but it lasted only a moment. Even the boom of the cannons could barely be heard now. Eilwen was distantly aware that her knee was throbbing once more, but such details seemed to pale beside the magnitude of the crowd. A handful of people near the centre of the throng began singing the chorus of a well-known drinking song, the words altered somewhat in an attempt to fit the moment, and soon it seemed half the city was joining in.

Oh, we'll soon say farewell to the bastards outside
And when Donny comes looking, we'll hand him their hides!

The best kind of mischief is mischief denied
But when Donny's done laughing, we'll blow the house wide!

Northward they marched, their pace growing ever slower — and then, abruptly, they stopped. Eilwen stood on her toes, craning her neck to see where they had arrived. A narrow stone tower adorned with military red and grey stood a short distance ahead. The end of her journey, if she could somehow fight her way to the door.

So it was true. Somehow, Hesca had persuaded Arandras to the city's cause. She supposed it wasn't surprising. Everyone had their price. Perhaps all it had taken was for someone to ask the question who wasn't Clade.

The crowd continued to sing, apparently expecting the golems to march out and start tearing the besieging army apart at any moment. Eilwen turned away. At last she would be able to see whether Clade's concern for the city truly outweighed his own ambition. *Gods, I can't wait to see his face.*

Then she looked up, and there he was.

∽

Clade stared at the singing, cheering crowd in bewilderment. *The Oculus must have lifted the siege. What else could it be?* But no — cannons were still firing, and the air was still thick with the smell of spent powder, though the noise was all but lost beneath the crowd's din. *What, then?* The press of bodies stretched all the way to the command post to which Clade and Urjo were headed. Was that the focus of whatever was going on?

"Well, well," Urjo said. "All this for me? They really shouldn't have."

"Quite a turnout, isn't it?" a familiar voice said in seeming agreement, and Clade turned.

"Eilwen," he said. The woman seemed flushed, either from exertion or excitement. "What's happening?"

Eilwen gave him a peculiar look. "You don't see them?"

"See what?" The crowd, though impressive, was just a crowd — merchants and students, beggars and artisans, even several priests wearing the robes of the Dreamer or the Weeper. A row of soldiers stood outside the command post, apparently keeping the multitudes from getting too close, though Clade's view of the guards was obscured by something else, something larger but still human-shaped; and suddenly he saw them and wondered how he had overlooked them for even a moment.

Urjo swore. "By the Three."

"Arandras is here," Eilwen said, and Clade felt something twist within him, triumphant and despairing in equal measure.

"How many?" he whispered.

Somehow, Eilwen heard him. "Twenty or thirty," she said. "He just marched them out of his house and down to the command post. Hesca was with him."

Hesca. Clade gave a disbelieving laugh. The possibility that Hesca might actually persuade Arandras to help had never entered his thoughts. *Did she fuck him, too?*

"Agli was right all along. Gods." For once, Urjo's tone held no hint of mockery. "But you knew that, didn't you, Cale?"

Eilwen raised an inquisitive brow, but before she could speak a woman in the attire of a house-servant pointed at them in surprised recognition. "Look, it's the prince!"

A dozen heads turned in their direction.

"Prince Urjo!"

"He's here to command the attack!"

"Make way! Make way for the prince!"

An enthusiastic pack formed around them and began herding them into the larger press, those at the front bellowing the news of Urjo's presence and demanding the way be cleared. The prince responded with a beneficent smile, waving to onlookers as though he conducted such processions every day. Eilwen followed more cautiously, limping slightly on her bad leg, one hand raised to shield her eyes against the sun.

Thoughts whirling, Clade surrendered to the movement of the crowd. Arandras had brought the golems here. Did he truly mean to attack the Oculus, or was this something else — a defensive arrangement, or some kind of bluff? *If it's a sham, this crowd is going to be pissed.* But no, surely Arandras wouldn't sacrifice the secret of his golems for the sake of some ploy. What had he agreed to do, and what had Hesca given to persuade him to cooperate?

And how in the hells am I going to take the golems from him now?

The din and the press intensified as they neared their destination, and their pace fell to a crawl. Grasping hands reached past their self-appointed escort, one brushing Clade's hair, another catching hold of his sleeve for a moment before slipping away. He hunched his shoulders, his bad hand reaching by instinct to where his sword would have hung had he been wearing one. Madness, of course, to draw a blade in a crush like this, even had he been capable of wielding it; yet its absence left him feeling exposed nonetheless.

Then a shape loomed ahead, its pinprick eyes staring fixedly at the street down which they'd come, and Clade felt a shiver of recognition.

Their escort stumbled to a halt, each gazing at the golems in various degrees of awe. Even Urjo's smile faltered as he took in the ancient constructs. The nearest carried a flanged mace in its left hand and had come to rest holding the weapon upright like a torch. The whisper-thin strand of sorcery that connected the golem to its master stretched behind it, angling through the heavy stone walls to somewhere on the outpost's upper floor. Beyond any doubt, Arandras was here.

"Urjo! Share a drink with us!" A burly, pink-nosed man barged through the distracted escort, waving a half-empty tankard in an arc that narrowly avoided the prince's head. "To kicking the enemy's arse!"

Clade grabbed Urjo's arm with his good hand. "Move," he muttered, dragging the prince past the golems toward the cordon of soldiers encircling the outpost. "Prince Urjo is here," he called, locking eyes with a blunt-faced man wearing a battered helmet. "Let us in."

The man flicked his gaze over Clade's companions, his eyes narrowing in recognition when they landed on Urjo. "Let them through," he snapped, stepping sideways to make a space. "Just the prince and his party, no-one else."

Clade pushed Urjo through the gap and hurried after him, Eilwen close on his heels. Ahead lay the redoubt's narrow doorway, flanked by another two soldiers. "Hesca Matharan," Clade barked. "Where is she?"

"Upstairs, with the commander," came the reply, and Clade was inside and climbing the spiral stairs two at a time, his hand still locked around Urjo's arm. The stairs opened onto a wide, low-ceilinged room dominated by a great square table. On the other side of the table, half a dozen people stood frozen as though part of some wax tableau, lamplight glinting off no fewer than four drawn blades.

Clade skidded to a halt. Hesca stood with her arm wrapped around Piator Pronn's chest and her knife at his throat. Zann crouched beside her, his sword pointed at a contingent of three soldiers presumably loyal to Pronn. Two of those had their own swords drawn in counter-challenge to Zann, while the third hefted a bronze paperweight and glared at Hesca with murder in his face. On the other side of the subcommander stood Arandras, his expression that of a man who had just realised the folly of leaving one's only weapons standing in the street outside.

"Hello, Hesca," Clade said, tightening his grip on Urjo's arm. "Bad time?"

"Not at all." Only a slight shortness of breath betrayed Hesca's tension. "I was just explaining to our esteemed commander that his services are no longer required."

"Ah." Clade felt Eilwen slip into the room behind him and hoped she would have the wit to keep quiet. "Is it me, or has he not received your suggestion as agreeably as you might have wished?"

Hesca grunted. "Poor Piator. Doesn't want to send our soldiers out to fight. Doesn't want to send a squad of ancient killing machines out to fight. Doesn't want to step down. It's hard to fathom what in the hells the man does want."

"I daresay he wants to be the commander," Urjo offered. "Charm the ladies and nibble sweetmeats at all those lovely parties. It's a pleasant enough life if you can avoid the business of blood, isn't it, Piator?"

Despite the proximity of Hesca's knife, Piator Pronn managed a chuckle. "What are you talking about, Urjo? I don't think anyone else in Spyridon has heard my war stories more often than you."

"Ah, yes, the Acantha rebellion. But none of your stories ever seem to mention the soldiers you lost in that campaign. What was it, Piator? Thirty? Forty? How many men and women did it take for you to lose your nerve?"

Pronn scowled. "You don't want to do this, Urjo."

"You're right," Urjo said. "I don't. But not for the reasons you think." He extended his arm sideways, making Clade's grip on it obvious to everyone in the room. "The game is up, Piator. These fine people know all about the gold you've been sending my way." He shook his head in mock-reproach. "Stealing from your own army, Piator? I doubt even the most loyal soldier is going to forgive that."

The commander's face contorted in rage. "You gods-damned hypocrite! How dare you shake your head at me? The whole thing was your idea!"

Urjo gave an unruffled shrug. "Not this part. But here we are." He glanced to Zann and the other soldiers, who still faced each other with swords drawn, and sighed impatiently. "Did you follow that? Your commander just confessed to robbing you all, and the city to boot. How many of you feel like dying in defence of a traitor?"

~

The shouting began: first Piator, then Hesca, then Urjo and the soldiers and Clade until it seemed everyone in the room was bellowing something or threatening someone else. Arandras heard only noise. The idiocy of the whole situation was beyond belief, yet Arandras felt no surprise, just a weary disgust. Of course these people, charged with the city's defence, would choose this moment to bicker. Of course they would. It wasn't as if there was any other more productive gods-damned thing they might be doing instead.

Maybe we should just invite the Oculus in, Arandras thought as Hesca yanked Piator's head back by the hair, reducing the commander's invective to a strangled gasp. *Hand over the city and tell them they can do what they like so long as they leave the ordinary people alone. Weeper knows they couldn't do any worse a job than this lot.*

It would be so easy to slip down the stairs and away from this insanity, away from the blind self-interest of the powerful and the misdirected adulation of the rest. What did he care what happened to Spyridon? War was just one more proof of the fundamental stupidity of humankind. He should leave them to their squabbles and be done with it.

Except if he did that, he'd never be able to look Mara in the face again.

Why in the Weeper's name had he agreed to her request? It had seemed like the right choice at the time — though in truth it had barely felt like a choice at all — but now, watching the Spyridon army's finest minds quarrel like street brats, it seemed little short of lunacy. Yet agree he had, leaving him with only two alternatives: to renege on his commitment or to see it through.

The soldier brandishing the bronze paperweight feinted a swing, earning a contemptuous snort from Hesca's man. Out of patience, Arandras glanced through the window and reached out with his thoughts, trying to focus on just one of the golems gathered around the outpost. *Golem, can you hear me?*

The response was swift, calm, and singular. *I hear you.*

Pursing his lips, Arandras issued a series of commands. The hubbub outside shifted, all but masking the faint grinding sound of a golem lurching into motion. Then the door below crashed open, drawing startled reactions from Hesca and several of the others.

"What's that?" she snarled, yanking Piator's head back even further. "Friends of yours?"

One of the soldiers below gave an alarmed yelp. "Stop right there!"

"Get out of its way, you fool!" someone else shouted as a series of thumps sounded almost directly beneath the room. Then something thudded against the stairs and a large earthen head came into view.

Hesca shot a lethal glare across the room. "Arandras, what in the hells are you doing?"

Arandras ignored her. Step by ponderous step the golem ascended into the room, its shoulder and arm scraping the interior of the tight spiral. Several of the soldiers stared at the new arrival with varying expressions of cornered fascination, their disagreement momentarily forgotten. Clade, too, seemed caught by the golem's slow entry, his stiff expression unable to mask the flash of avarice in his eyes. Only Clade's companion appeared unmoved by the golem, her attention fixed instead on her employer.

Hesca tried again. "Arandras, this really doesn't help —"

"Shut up." Arandras glanced from face to face, not bothering to hide his contempt. "Piator Pronn, did you or did you not take the army's gold and give it to Urjo as part of some pathetic scheme cooked up between the two of you?"

Piator's hate-filled gaze settled on Urjo. "It wasn't like he says —"

"Did you. Take. The gold."

The commander gave a bitter smile. "Yes."

"And what would you like Hesca and the rest of us to do about it?"

Piator's gaze shifted to the golem, which had completed its ascent and now stood at the top of the staircase, blocking the sole exit from the room. A muffled cough sounded from somewhere beneath them, and Arandras was satisfied to see Piator's eyes widen with the realisation that those in the room below were listening to his confession.

"I'll step down," he said thickly. "That's what you want, isn't it, Hesca? To command this gods-damned siege? Fine. It's yours."

Arandras turned to the soldiers being held at bay by Hesca's lone ally. "And what do you three say to that?"

The nearest soldier seemed inclined to dispute the matter, but the other two regarded Piator with expressions of shock and anger. "You rat bastard," one of them spat. "We barely got the gates up for lack of coin, and you've been draining our coffers this whole time?"

"That was the circle's fault!" Piator said.

"How about the rest of you downstairs?" Arandras called. "Who do you say is your commander?"

There was a sound of whispers and muttered comments, then another, louder cough as the soldier responsible abandoned any attempt at stealth.

"I say Hesca," someone said.

"Are you mad?" a woman retorted. "That's mutiny."

"Hesca," said a third voice, followed by a fourth and a fifth. "Hesca. Hesca!"

Arandras gave another instruction and the golem stepped away from the stairs. Then he folded his arms and glanced pointedly at Hesca. *Over to you.*

Still with her knife at Piator's throat, Hesca summoned her man with a nod. "Strip his weapons, then lock him in one of the empties downstairs. You with the paperweight, find Cas and bring her here.

She's to arrange the guard on his cell."

"You can't do this," Piator protested as his swordbelt was pulled free. "I said I'd step down. Let me go!"

"I will," Hesca said. "As soon as the circle tells me to. Until then, you'd best get comfortable downstairs." A dagger and an eating knife joined Piator's sword on the floor. Two of the soldiers grabbed their erstwhile commander by the arms, and Hesca at last lowered her blade. "Take him." The soldiers marched him around the table and toward the stairs, Hesca following a pace behind. "I'll need a moment to speak to them," she said to Arandras, gesturing at the stairs and those waiting below. Though she offered no thanks, her tone held a matter-of-fact respect that hadn't been present before. "I'll return when I'm done."

A smattering of tentative boos sounded from the soldiers below as Piator was manhandled down the stairs. The cheers for Hesca were louder and more numerous, but to Arandras's ear they seemed somehow provisional, as though the cheerers still awaited some action from Hesca to elicit their full commitment.

They can tell she didn't topple Piator alone, he realised. *Even Urjo's support wasn't enough. The only reason she got her way was because I happened to be here.* The thought soured his stomach. *Which makes me what — a kingmaker, and Piator the golems' first victim? Weeper's tears, I should have told Mara no and just stayed put.*

As Hesca began to address the soldiers assembled below, Urjo shook his arm loose from Clade's grip and glanced around the room in satisfaction. "Well," he said brightly to no-one in particular. "I suppose that went about as well as could be expected."

~

Hesca's speech to the soldiers stationed in the command post was short and seemed to consist largely of exhortations to courage and unity against the Oculus threat. It amazed Eilwen that such platitudes could be expected to sway anyone, let alone a cohort of hard-bitten troops. Yet at the end of the new commander's oration, the gathered soldiers gave a resounding whoop and Hesca reappeared in the stairway with a hard smile on her face.

"My apologies for the delay," she said brusquely, speaking mostly to Arandras. "I'm having some maps brought up. The enemy has been largely static today. Seems they've found some positions they like."

Hesca and Arandras fell into a discussion about how the golems might best be deployed, whether they would fit through the sally ports, and what units they might target for maximum effect. Ordinarily, Eilwen would have listened with interest. History was being made here. News of ancient Valdori constructs marching into battle would soon fly to palaces and council chambers across Kal Arna. But she'd seen the hunger in Clade when the golem entered the room. It was a kind of passion she'd seen only a handful of times before — a window into the soul, a glimpse of the secret core around which one oriented one's life, and as reliable an indicator as she knew for what someone would choose when a decision could no longer be avoided.

As though drawn by her thoughts, Clade glanced across at her. Eilwen kept her gaze fixed on Hesca and pretended not to notice. If she spoke to him now, the signs of her knowledge would be all over her face. Though perhaps that wouldn't be a bad thing...

A portly youth in a crisp new uniform emerged from the stairs bearing half a dozen rolls of paper. "Your maps, subcommander." He flushed. "I mean commander. Sorry."

Hesca waved the slip away. "On the table, thank you." As the youth complied, Hesca turned back to Arandras. "The concentration of guns is greatest in two positions, both difficult to target with our defensive batteries. The first is on the eastern side. It's partly protected by a cluster of trees, but it's also some distance forward from the enemy's line. The other is to the north. Easier to approach, but closer to their camps. There's also their powder stores, but those are a long way back from the lines."

"Show me the eastern position," Arandras said.

Clade made a derisory sound. "You really think a few mercenaries can make a dent in one of *them?*"

Arandras glared. "Shut up, Clade." Prince Urjo stirred, giving Clade a shrewd glance for no reason Eilwen could fathom. "Better yet, leave. This has nothing to do with you."

"Oh, I think this has a great deal to do with all of us."

"Enough," Hesca snapped. "Clade, you can stay, but only if you remain quiet."

But Arandras folded his arms. "I want him gone." His gaze shifted to Eilwen. "Her, too."

The demand hung in the air. At last, Hesca sighed. "Clade."

Clade's brows drew together, and in the charged silence that followed Eilwen braced herself for an outburst of sorcery. Then, abruptly, Clade turned. "Come on," he snarled to Eilwen as he passed.

She followed him down the stairs, noting the long scrapes left by the golem on the inner spiral. Most of the soldiers that had congregated to hear Hesca's speech were gone, leaving the entry hall as sparsely populated as it had been on her way in. As she entered the hall, Clade grabbed her arm and drew her to one side, away from the few soldiers that remained.

"Did you get the books?" he said in a harsh whisper.

Eilwen shook her head.

"Then go back. Find them and bring them to me."

Eilwen pulled her arm free. "Why, exactly?"

Clade scowled. "What do you mean, why? Didn't you see that damn stone giant at the top of the stairs?"

"Of course I saw it. I saw Arandras preparing to do just what you want. Use the golems to defend the city."

"That's not the point."

"Really? Yesterday that seemed to be precisely the point."

"Those books are mine!" Clade hissed. "Arandras stole them from me."

"Well, the man himself is right here. When he comes downstairs you can take it up with him."

"Gods, are you dense? I don't want to argue with him about it, I want the books back!"

"That's right," Eilwen said softly. "You want the books back."

"What's that supposed to mean?"

"That's all you've ever wanted. The books. The golems. All this supposed concern about defending Spyridon against the Oculus — it was never real, was it?" She gave a mirthless chuckle. "Do you know, I think on some level I truly believed it was. Not for the city's sake, of course, but at least to deny the Oculus something they wanted. But even that pales beside your own gods-damned greed."

Clade stared at her. "You're wrong."

"I don't think so. But even if I am, it doesn't matter." Eilwen drew herself straight. "I'm not your hired thief, Clade. As of right now, I'm not your hired anything. Go steal the books back yourself if you want them so much. Or forget about the golems and spend the rest of your life dreaming up ways to get back at the Oculus for what you suffered. I don't care. I'm done."

Eilwen turned and strode toward the door, ignoring the curious looks of the soldiers on either side. Clade called after her, asking her to wait, but she ignored him. When she reached the door, he cracked. "Damn it, Eilwen, just listen to me!"

She smiled to herself and kept walking.

Outside, the crowd had begun to settle in. Someone had strung flowers into garlands and draped them over perhaps a quarter of the motionless golems. Street vendors worked their way through the press with shouted offers of food and drink. Though the guns continued to boom, this part of the city lay outside their range, and a relaxed, almost carnival air seemed to have established itself over citizen and soldier alike. Reinforcements had arrived, albeit of the most unlikely kind, and soon all would be well.

It was a fantasy, but right at the moment Eilwen didn't care. Her knee was throbbing, but she didn't care about that, either. Satisfaction filled her, warming her belly like liquor. And there was another feeling, too, one that took her several moments to identify.

Freedom, she realised, and laughed at the strangeness of it. The hells with the siege, she *was* free. The gods only knew why she'd waited so long to rid herself of the shackles Clade had offered. But they were gone now, and she'd be damned before she surrendered to such chains again.

Still smiling, Eilwen slipped past the soldiers and into the crowd.

CHAPTER 20

Surely the most terrible gift the All-God ever gave his creatures was the right to be wrong. What dreadful grace conceived of such indulgence?

— *Sermons and Expositions,* Sixth Volume

ARANDRAS LED THE GOLEMS THROUGH the darkened streets, the crowd flocking around them like gulls about a fishing sloop. Night distorted the senses, impeding visibility while magnifying sounds, giving Arandras the impression of being surrounded by a swarm of discorporate voices: an army of flitting ghosts come to fight alongside his ponderous earthen constructs.

Would that the ghosts could fight this battle alone, he thought as the torch of the soldier riding several paces ahead dipped left to indicate a turn. *Would that they needed nothing more from me than a word of direction. There is your foe! Defend your city!*

Another turn, and the gate tunnel loomed ahead, a dark void beneath torchlit fortifications. At least a dozen soldiers stood watch at street level, and more doubtless lurked behind the crenellations above. Someone in the military command had evidently heard the tales of the Oculus's first conquest and determined that Spyridon would not repeat Neysa's failure to keep its gates shut.

Their guide stood in his stirrups, waving the torch from side to side, and Arandras brought the golems to a halt. A sudden burst of scratchy laughter from somewhere in the crowd set his heart racing in his chest. *Damn ghosts. What a grand spectacle this must be for those staying safely behind the city walls.*

A door opened in the stone column beside the gate tunnel and a squad of soldiers emerged. They began pressing calmly but firmly into the crowd, forming a partial cordon around Arandras and the golems. More soldiers followed, creating a line between the gate and the crowd and slowly pushing the latter back. Such a manoeuvre would have been impossible amid the press earlier on in the day, but the crowd had thinned since nightfall and a channel to the gate was soon cleared, empty save for Arandras, the golems, and a scattering of soldiers.

"Open!" someone called softly from atop the wall; and the great gates at the end of the tunnel swung inward with a jarring screech.

Weeper's tears, why don't you just tell them I'm coming, Arandras thought, shivering as the slice of darkness between the two gates slowly widened. A distant band of firelight marked the position of the enemy line. The crosswise breeze carried the scent of smoke and potatoes, though the direction made it impossible to tell if the source lay within the city or without.

The gates jerked to a halt, still less than half open. Arandras took an unsteady breath. *Golems, form a column before the gate, two per rank.* The constructs immediately moved to obey, drawing cheers from the crowd and wondering curses from the less disciplined soldiers, but Arandras scarcely noticed. The foolishness of the task he'd assigned himself abruptly struck him full force. What was he thinking, to venture beyond the walls and lead an assault on the besieging army? This was a job for soldiers, not for him. Even Piator Pronn had declined to authorise such a mission, a decision which now seemed both wise and measured. Really, there was no way any-one could expect Arandras to go out there and take the battle to the Oculus. Even Mara had to see that.

The column stretched before him, a single golem standing un-paired in the final rank. The two in the lead looked to be all but past the gates already. *Come back,* Arandras wanted to say. *Come back inside.* Who was Hesca to ask this of him? Who was he to ask it of the golems? Small wonder the kings of old had invoked divine right to send their people to war. No other justification could bear such weight.

If he had been required to give the order verbally, he might not have managed it. But his link to his charges was blessedly, damnably unconstrained by speech.

Golems. Move out.

The column jolted into motion, Arandras trailing behind like the dung-sweeper at the end of a parade. The thick arch of the wall passed overhead; then he was out, the lamps and torches above casting squirming shadows at his feet. *Turn*, he instructed the golems, and the column veered onto the hard-packed earth beside the road as the gate screeched shut.

Blackness closed over them. Arandras peered futilely into the gloom, hunting for the first landmark Hesca had pointed to on the map: a bifurcated tree, its split trunk curving apart like a fountain frozen in wood. The bombardment had once again ceased at dusk, leaving him with only the city and the distant line of fires by which to gauge his position. A sudden longing filled him, a brief but intense desire for a companion against the dark; but strangely it was not Mara who filled his thoughts, nor even Tereisa, but Tiy.

An unseen stone caught his foot and he stumbled, catching himself on the golem at the column's rear. The darkness was all but complete now, the lights of the city and those of the besiegers equally useless for illuminating his immediate surroundings. Yet the golems marched on, their heavy footfalls unmarred by the scrape or crash of misplaced steps.

Golem, Arandras called, doing his best to direct the thought at the leftmost of the two leaders. *Tell me what you see.*

Earth and stone, the golem replied. *Fire and night. Cloud hides the sky. An owl flies east. Walls. Trees. Grass —*

Stop. Tell me about the trees.

A tree, tall and straight, leaves shifting in the breeze. A tree, wide and bare, unmoving. A tree, cleft in two, unmoving. A tree —

The tree cleft in two. Where is it?

Ahead and to the right, forty paces distant.

Arandras exhaled. *Lead us there.*

The column turned, but even with the city as a reference point, Arandras found it difficult to assess their change in course. The ground began to incline downward and Arandras shortened his stride, feeling for each step. The golems thudded on, untroubled by the slope; then, abruptly, they stopped.

A tree cleft in two, announced the golem, sounding for all the world like an excursionist's guide in some distant land. Arandras would have laughed at the incongruity of it but for the terror lurking in the pit of his stomach.

He continued forward as quickly as he dared, catching up to the golems and creeping past them to the front of the column. The gloom was so thick that he barely avoided striking his head against the tree in question. He reached out, feeling tentatively for the bifurcated trunk. Rough wood answered his grasp, curving past his head and out of reach. He ducked beneath the bough and around to the other side, feeling for the second stem; and there it was, bending away in what felt like a mirror image of the first.

From the split tree, the golems led Arandras across a patchwork of vacant pastures and fallow fields to a fence junction, the shell of an abandoned wagon, and a broken well, the second to last of Hesca's landmarks. As they crept through the empty land, time seemed to lose its meaning. Toward the end, Arandras found himself following the golems without question, his dread of the approaching task crowding out any inclination to second-guess their guidance.

A mound of earth, taller than it is wide, the golem announced, and Arandras edged past it and peered in the direction of the enemy line. The campfires were still some way off, many half-hidden by tents or other obstacles, though Arandras could see the shadows of soldiers patrolling the perimeter. Somewhere between the mound and the fires lay their target: a battery of cannons concealed amid a stand of trees. Hesca had not been able to tell him how many guns they might find, though her most conservative estimate had put the number above thirty.

Arandras swallowed hard. *Golem. What fire-barrels can you see?*

Fire-barrels. Five upon a ridge, chairs beside and behind. Four beside a pile of stones, their aim high. A multitude encircled by trees, uncounted, uncountable. Two near a fencepost, their mouths shattered.

The golem spoke on, listing every cannon perceptible to its uncanny sight. Chest pounding, Arandras forced the next question out. *The fire-barrels encircled by trees. How far are they?*

Thirty paces away.

For a moment Arandras wondered if he might simply instruct the golems to pick up the cannons and bring them back to Spyridon. But even if the golems could bear the weight, it would be impossible to manoeuvre the bulky gun carriages through the trees without someone in the camp noticing, and when that happened it would be far harder to make a clean retreat with guns and enemy soldiers in tow.

He closed his eyes. *Where are the nearest soldiers?*

A soldier passes water, fifty paces away. A soldier lies beneath a tree, fifty-five paces away. Three soldiers play dice by a fire, seventy paces away. A soldier weeps, eighty-five paces away.

That's enough. The absence of an immediate guard was a relief, though no doubt the golems would have plenty of company once they moved in. Yet still Arandras hesitated. Now that the moment was here, the wrongness he'd felt before the city gates returned like a physical blow. Who was he to command another living being to go out and destroy? Perhaps this was what lay at the heart of Piator Pronn's refusal to order a raid — a recognition, however belated in the man's life, of the absurdity of such pretensions. Perhaps he had at last found the courage to see those around him not as swords or hammers, but as men and women no different from anyone else within the city, or those without.

But there was a difference. The soldiers camped before him were here to conquer. And those in Spyridon had sworn to protect the city, freely and willingly. None of them would have begrudged Piator his right to send them into battle. Whereas he, Arandras, commanded beings whose capacity for choice had been stripped away. *They're killers already,* Mara had said to him; but if that were true, it was only because some previous master had valued their spirits so meanly as to trade them away for the sake of petty destruction — just as Arandras had come here to do.

And yes, he had his reasons, perhaps even good ones. Perhaps if he cared about Spyridon as Mara did he wouldn't find this so hard. Perhaps it truly was the right thing to do. Yet he couldn't shake the feeling that this deed, this act of coercion to inflict damage on another, was evil in some primal sense of the word, and its perceived necessity the malign root of everything hateful in the world.

If he had been alone, he would have thrown back his head and screamed at the sky. But the Oculus were right there; and the gods, despite the priests' pious vapidities, were not.

Golems, he called, and the word, though unspoken, filled his mouth with ashes. *Enter the trees and destroy the fire-barrels within. Defend yourselves as you must, but do not harm any soldiers unnecessarily.*

And in the privacy of his own thoughts he added, *Forgive me.*

Unburdened by doubt, the golems lumbered forward. Arandras hung back, allowing them to pass by before following at a distance. Their thudding footsteps seemed loud enough to be heard in Spyridon, let alone the enemy camp, but Arandras heard no voices raised in question and saw no alarm around the fires. A ragged laugh carried on the breeze from somewhere beyond, and with it the scent of oiled leather.

The first of the golems passed between the trees. A moment later, Arandras heard a splitting crash and the column slowed to a halt. Somewhere nearby a gruff voice shouted a question.

Report, Arandras sent, forgetting in his haste to narrow the command.

A wave of overlapping not-quite-voices responded. *Trees and grass and sky. My brothers and sisters around and below. We climb. An opening. Barrels without fire. Stakes and earth. My brothers climb.*

Arandras tried to sort through the answers. *Several of you fell into a spiked pit, is that it? And now you're climbing out?*

We climb.

The gruff voice spoke again, its tone one of command. Others answered, and a moment later Arandras saw a group of soldiers set out toward them. Resisting the urge to tell the golems to hurry — cajoling the constructs would achieve precisely nothing — Arandras edged backward, hoping he was as hard to spot in the gloom as the soldiers were to him.

The column of golems started forward once more. A single strike of metal on metal rang from the copse, like a bird calling tentatively to its flock. A second brassy clank answered, followed by a third;

then a raucous cacophony broke out, tearing the air with pounding and clanging as though from the Gatherer's own smithy.

Shouts of alarm sounded from the camp. Something flew into the air amid the trees, glinting darkly as it spun before crashing to the ground. Then came a wild ululation, and Arandras turned just in time to see a squad of shadowy figures plunge into the trees, their weapons high.

A scream pierced the din, followed by a howled curse, but the noise was so great that the sounds of battle could barely be heard beneath it. Arandras stared uselessly at the trees, torn between impatience and fear of leaving the job half done. Additional squads were assembling at the edge of the camp. Soon they would join their comrades, and any hope of minimising casualties would be lost.

The clangour eased for a moment, and Arandras heard a series of odd clinks like a pick-axe on stone: blades striking the golems. He clenched his teeth, wishing he could see what was happening. Surely the cannons had been rendered unusable by now, though the golems would continue their destruction until he told them to stop. Left to themselves, they might still be going by sunrise, breaking the remains into ever smaller fragments until they were too tiny to handle.

Golems, he called, reaching across the distance he'd put between them. *Do you hear me?*

We hear you.

Return to me, then continue to the wall and follow it around to the gate.

In an instant, the noise ceased. Golems emerged from the trees, little more than dark patches of moving shadow growing in size as they neared. A smaller figure followed a short distance, swinging ineffectively at the trailing constructs before giving up and retreating to the copse.

Exhilaration welled within Arandras, wild and powerful, pulling at him like a riptide. He fought it, resisting the impulse to exult in the destruction he had just wrought. This was what they had all been seeking — Agli, Feren, Clade, even the Quill — but it was *wrong,* no matter the insidious euphoria urging him to stride ahead, arms outstretched in triumph. There was no victory here, nothing that any sane person would willingly celebrate. If the gods looked down on this moment, surely they could do nought but weep.

They reached the wall. Arandras had the golems form a column once more, but this time he marched at their head, unwilling to deny his responsibility and compound his sin by trailing them as he had before. Voices called down to him as he led the golems around the embankment, but the moment was already too full and the words washed past him like smoke.

The wall jagged out and in, out and in. Arandras followed the tortuous path like a penitent pilgrim, so lost in his thoughts that he failed to realise he'd returned to the Anstice road until he stepped off it onto a patch of spongy grass. The city gates were already ajar, the space within a patchwork of torchlight and shadow. He led the golems inside, bracing for the expected cheers. But the crowd had dispersed in his absence — only a handful remained behind the cordon of soldiers, and they watched his return with a combination of uncertainty and residual enthusiasm, unaware of what had transpired.

Arandras brought the golems to a halt. As the gates began to screech shut, he turned to inspect the nearest constructs. For all the clinking blows of enemy swords, the golems seemed largely unscathed. One had a long scratch across its hip, and another had been scored behind its knees, but none of the damage seemed anything more than superficial.

Weeper's breath, he thought as he continued down the line, sorrow and regret momentarily eclipsed by wonder. *They're damn near unstoppable.* And he'd gone out there with just twenty-nine, leaving Tiy with Jensine so she could continue her work. What might the hundreds beneath Tienette Lake be capable of? No wonder the Valdori had dominated the continent.

When he reached the end of the line, it took him a moment to notice that something was wrong; but when he did, the realisation froze the blood in his veins.

He'd gone out with twenty-nine golems. Fourteen ranks of two, just like now, plus one at the end, alone and unpaired.

And now missing.

∼

Clade turned at the top of the street and watched the golems depart the command post. No doubt Arandras was ensconced somewhere between the clustered giants, directing their path with the same self-assured satisfaction he'd shown while taking down Piator Pronn. After everything Clade had done to procure Urjo's confession, Arandras had just strolled his damnable golem in and stared the commander down. If it hadn't been for Clade's efforts, the rank and file would never have accepted Pronn's removal — but had Hesca spared him a second thought? No. She'd sided with Arandras and dismissed Clade as easily and perfunctorily as the lowliest recruit in her command.

Which was, Clade had to admit, only sensible. In her position, he'd have done exactly the same. Hesca needed allies, both for her own sake and the city's, and in Arandras — or more specifically, his golems — she had the most powerful ally since the Valdori themselves. Of course she sought to attach herself to them. Only a fool would do otherwise.

So what does that make me? By his own logic, he ought to be trying to bring Arandras around to Clade's own fight against the Oculus. Except he knew already that such an effort was doomed to failure. Even if Arandras had the stomach for what Clade knew would be required, there was too much history between them, too much distrust for them to ever work together. Which left Clade with only one option, no less obvious than the first, the same goal he'd been pursuing this whole time.

Inevitably, Eilwen had seen past his obfuscation and divined his purpose. But she'd failed to perceive the wider context. Yes, he wanted the golems. Of course he did. But it had never been greed that had driven him — not in Anstice, not at the caverns, and not now. It had only ever been necessity.

And now, necessity and chance had combined to create an opportunity that would not come again.

He resumed his course, following the gently climbing road up the eastern side of the hill. Eilwen said she'd seen Arandras leaving his house, which meant the address Clade had obtained in Rhothe's Bar was correct. With Arandras occupied elsewhere, it would be a simple matter to slip inside, find the damn books, and recommence in earnest his efforts to claim the golems.

Even at night, the estate proved easy to find. Clade nudged the gate open, stepping cautiously onto the unlit path, and frowned. Light edged the windows — not just one or two, but half a dozen across several floors. He crept forward, alert for any sign of movement. All seemed quiet within. But it must have been several hours before sunset when Arandras set out. Surely he wouldn't have left the house with so many lamps burning.

A shadow passed before one of the windows, and Clade froze in mid-step. There was a pause, then the shadow passed back in the other direction. Whoever it was seemed to be pacing the room. Not a rival intruder, then, but someone who felt comfortable being there. A friend of Arandras's, waiting for him to return.

Carefully, Clade lowered his foot to the ground — but the path was not as wide as he thought. His boot caught the path's edge and he stumbled, his step slapping against the stone. Again he froze. For a moment, nothing moved. Then the shadow passed against the window once more, its pace unchanged, and Clade let out a slow breath.

He'd hoped to find the house empty, but a single occupant constituted only a minor complication. No doubt the rooms held plenty of timber furnishings. It would be simple enough to steer someone alongside one such object and then blow it apart. That done, the house would be Clade's to explore at leisure. Arandras would be gone for hours, and his return with the golems would hardly be stealthy.

He crept forward once more, stepping silently along the path. The only challenge now was how to get inside —

The grand front door swung open, revealing a tall silhouette holding a pair of long, curved blades. "Stop right there," the figure said, her voice low and hard.

Clade straightened, gesturing with his bad hand and opening the other to show he held no weapon. "I'm looking for a man named Arandras. I'm a friend."

The woman snorted. "Oh, I'm sure you are. Sadly, Arandras isn't here right now, so I'm afraid you'll have to piss off."

Clade risked a step forward. "Will he be back soon?" The

woman raised one of her cutlasses in warning, and Clade extended his hands sideways. "Perhaps I could wait inside?"

"No. And no. But if you give me your name, I'll tell him you were here."

Clade scanned the interior of the house. The door was timber, of course, though it seemed to have already received a binding, something simple against wear and rot. But inside he could see the edge of a staircase, its heavy wooden banister unmarked by sorcery. He edged forward. "Could I leave a message —"

Hissing, the woman swept her blade up so that the point was touching Clade's chest. "No closer," she snarled, eyes glittering dangerously in her dark face.

Something in the woman's glare tugged at Clade's memory. "I assure you, there's nothing to fear."

"Tell me your name," the woman said. "Or shall I say it for you?"

"No need for that." Affecting an air of wounded dignity, Clade reached for the first name that occurred to him. "I am Cale, and I am a friend to Arandras —"

"No, *Clade*, you're not." The woman raised her second blade, holding it high as if preparing to swing. "You'd best scamper back to the street before I decide to use these."

Ah, shit. Dark skin, twin blades. He should have recognised her earlier. This woman had been with Arandras at the caverns. But Clade had barely had anything to do with her at the time — Sinon had been the one to subdue her. Had he heard her name? He couldn't remember.

"All right," he said. "Fine. You know who I am. Then you also know that Arandras and I came to an understanding. We're not enemies."

The woman smirked. "A moment ago you were friends. Now you're just not enemies. I wonder what you'll be by the end of this conversation?"

Clade's gaze flicked back inside. The banister was too far away to do any damage, even if he could create a binding from here. He needed to manoeuvre her back inside. But how?

"Although when I say that," the woman continued, "there are really only two possibilities." She gave the first blade a push so that its tip pressed against Clade's chest. "Gone. Or dead."

Clade scowled. Whatever weaknesses the woman might have, he wasn't going to find them now. Better to make a show of submission and then look for another way in. "Fine," he snapped. "I'll leave."

"Yes, you will. And just so we're clear, I'm not alone in this house. My sorcerer friend is just upstairs." The woman's smirk widened to a grin. "So if you've got any clever ideas about what you'll do once you've put a safe distance between yourself and these cutlasses — by all means, give it your best shot."

A sorcerer? Drawing a breath, Clade opened his senses. A prickle from somewhere about the woman's waist marked the presence of a sorcery-enhanced blade. The front door throbbed dully behind her. Clade lowered his barriers further, welcoming the pain, and reached into the house. There was something there… something big…

Pain exploded in his head and he reeled backward, staggering to keep his feet. There *was* sorcery higher in the house, something complex but unfinished, surely the work of the sorcerer mentioned by the woman. But not all of it was unfinished. Something else was there too, something wonderful and beautiful, and Clade knew exactly what it was.

There was a golem in the house, and someone was building a spell with the construct at its heart.

Astonished and disturbed in equal measure, Clade stumbled back up the path and onto the street.

~

Arandras cast his thoughts beyond the wall, but the missing golem was nowhere he could sense. Hissing in frustration, he turned to the constructs before him. *Golems. One of you went out and did not return. What happened?*

Silence answered, the familiar blankness of a golem asked about the past.

Arandras muttered a curse. Such questions were futile, of course. But there was no way around it — *what happened* was the only thing he wanted to know.

He drew a breath, forcing himself to calm. *Golems, where are your nearest brothers and sisters beyond the group standing here?*

The response was immediate. *My brothers, above and below. Torches and lanterns. Walls of stone. Walls of earth. Stakes and sorcery. He stands. He lies. He is bound.*

Arandras considered. The brother above could only be Tiy. Sorcery, lanterns, stone walls. Which left the other... in the pit it had fallen into near the cannons.

Shit! Hadn't they told him they were climbing out? He spun around, flinging his arms out in exasperation, and narrowly avoided striking Hesca Matharan in the face.

If Hesca was perturbed by the near miss, she didn't show it. "What news?"

"The cannons are destroyed," Arandras said distractedly. He could turn around, take half a dozen golems out right now and retrieve their missing comrade. Except the Oculus would surely have found it by now. Stealth would be impossible — any rescue mission would inevitably result in casualties. *Abandon one of them to the Oculus, or else make the golems killers in truth. Weeper's tears, what a choice.*

"Did you meet any resistance?"

"Hmm?" Whoever might have it now, the missing golem was still bound to him. It would be impossible for the Oculus to gain mastery of it and send it against the city. And the risks of a rescue attempt could not be ignored. What if one golem was retrieved but two more were lost to some other trap? Perhaps the safer choice was to let it be, at least for now.

Hesca leaned forward. "I said, did you meet any resistance?"

"What? No. Nothing to speak of." He'd have to tell her about the golem's loss soon, but first he wanted time to think.

"And did you happen across any earthworks?" Hesca said. Arandras gave her a startled look, but in the dark Hesca seemed to mistake it for confusion. "Tunnels. Piles of earth. Anything to suggest their sappers have started digging toward the city."

"Oh. Not that I saw," Arandras said. "There was a spiked pit near the cannons, but that seemed more defensive than anything else."

Hesca rubbed the bridge of her nose. "What are they waiting for?" she muttered.

"It's black as pitch out there," Arandras said. "I might have passed within five paces of a tunnel and not seen it." He exhaled heavily. "Look, we'll find out tomorrow how badly we hurt them. I'm heading home."

"Fine." Hesca shot a glance over his shoulder. "You taking them with you?"

"Is there any reason I shouldn't?"

"It's up to you, of course," Hesca said. "Seemed like you didn't enjoy the parade earlier, though. You might want to leave them here until you're sure you're done."

Oh, I'm done, Arandras thought. But could he be certain? If an opportunity to retrieve the lost golem presented itself, but he had to fight his way across half the city first... He hesitated. "Will you be able to keep the crowds off them?"

"You have my word." Hesca crooked her finger at a nearby soldier. "And an escort home."

Arandras gave a weary nod. "All right."

Thankfully, his assigned companion shared Arandras's preference for silence over conversation. Arandras slouched through the empty streets, slowed by fatigue and a growing ache in his feet, but the man made no complaint, matching Arandras's pace and examining each doorway and intersection as they drew near, his snowy brows bunched in a permanent frown. On arrival at the estate Arandras offered his escort a grateful nod, to which he responded in kind. The man waited at the gate until the door opened and Arandras stumbled inside to find Mara striding from the other room with barely concealed relief.

"Arandras. You made it." She eyed him up and down. "Still in one piece?"

He shuffled past the smiling pouch-rat to the staircase and sagged awkwardly onto a step. "I'm fine," he said, waving his hand. "Just tired."

"Where are the golems?"

"Down by the gate. Mostly." He shook his head at her raised brow. "I'll tell you about it later."

"And the Oculus?"

"Down a few dozen cannons. I think."

Mara nodded slowly, but her expression was lost to Arandras's yawn. "Can I get you anything? A cup of water? Something to eat?"

The mention of food made him abruptly aware of the emptiness in his belly. He'd been so caught up in planning the raid that he'd missed dinner entirely. But while part of him suddenly wanted to scoff down a plate of whatever was closest to hand, a quiver in his stomach made him wonder if it would all just come up again. He shook his head. "Maybe some water."

Mara disappeared down the hall and returned with a clay cup and pitcher. "Drink," she said. "And then sleep. You look like you're going to nod off right there."

But despite his exhaustion, sleep refused to come. He lay on the thin bed and stared into the blackness, reliving the trek across the fields, the assault on the enemy's guns. Had he missed something, there in the dark — some signal that would have alerted him to the lost golem's plight? *I should have known,* he thought, as the clanking destruction wrought by the golems echoed in his thoughts. *Somehow I should have known.*

Though he had no awareness of drifting to sleep, his next sensation was of the sun's warmth creeping across his face. He sat up slowly, blinking against the light. The makeshift curtains they'd added to the room — cut from old sacks they'd found in the cellar — hung open beside the narrow windows, forgotten after his late return the previous night. Yawning, Arandras pushed himself to his feet. The sun had already climbed some distance above the horizon, but there was something odd about the scene outside. He shuffled to the window, wiping the sleep from his eyes, and tried to work out what was different.

The guns. They're not firing.

Faint sounds rose from beyond the estate: the call of street vendors, the clop of hoofs, even the chirping of birds — but the cannons both within and without the city were silent.

"Arandras." Mara stood in the doorway, tired but smiling. "How do you feel?"

He considered the question. "Exhausted. And hungry."

"The second of those is easily solved. Let me see what I can rustle up."

Arandras allowed himself to be led to the dining table and plied with an array of hardbread and preserved fruits. He ate slowly, pausing between mouthfuls to offer a brief account of the previous night's raid. Mara listened in silence, her triumphant grin at the cannons' destruction fading as he told of his discovery that one of the golems had been left behind.

"Gods," she said when he fell silent. "Is it... can you still reach it?"

Arandras shook his head.

"But it's still bound to you, right?"

"I think so," he said. He'd skipped confidently past that question the previous night, but now he found himself unsure. "I mean, there's no reason to believe it's not."

Mara seemed to hear his unspoken thought. "We'll get it back," she said. "We'll find a way. Gods know I owe you that much."

"Not me," Arandras said. "Them." He pushed away his empty plate and stood. "Where's Jensine? Best she hears this sooner rather than later."

Jensine received the news poorly. "Oh, that's wonderful. The Dreamer only knows where it is now, or where the rest will be when you get back to them." She gestured angrily around the boarded-up gallery, empty but for herself and Tiy. "I guess we'll do them one at a time, shall we? It's not like it takes me days to construct the binding. Oh, wait, it does."

"Don't worry. They'll be back before you're done." A thought occurred to him. "Though didn't you say your binding would be effective even if the golems were elsewhere in the city?"

"I said *maybe*. And I certainly didn't say it was a good idea." She folded her arms. "Do you really want their first moments of freedom to be at the edge of a battleground?"

Arandras swallowed. "No," he said. "You're right. They'll be here."

She glowered and he turned away, wandering across the room to the balcony. The sunlight was uncomfortably bright after the gloom of the gallery, and he raised a hand against it as he peered down at the view. It seemed the Oculus had pulled their guns back after the previous night's raid and were now hunkered down in their camp, leaving the defenders with nothing to shoot at.

Maybe they're pulling out. The thought lodged in his mind, tempting him with hope. It couldn't be that easy, could it? One raid, not even a fraction of the payback they'd earned for the pounding they'd given the city, and the Oculus were just going to turn around and go home? Surely their resolve was stronger than that. But then why halt their attack?

A hollow opened in his stomach. Perhaps the city was no longer their immediate goal. Perhaps, in the course of last night's raid, he had presented them with an even richer prize. Even now, the golem he'd left behind might be on its way back to Neysa with the besieging army soon to follow, there to reconsider their strategy in light of the new weapon that he, Arandras, had delivered to their doorstep.

He didn't want to believe it. *Weeper's breath, please don't let it be true.* But what other explanation was there?

A low rumble broke his thoughts. Confused, Arandras squinted at the sky. The few clouds were high and thin — nothing to suggest a storm. But there was something moving down by the wall, something large; so large that at first he could make no sense of it.

The rumble sounded again, and this time Arandras could feel the house shake beneath his feet.

"What's that?" someone called from inside. "What's happening?" But Arandras could do nothing but stare.

Weeper have mercy...

FOURTH INTERLUDE

To desire that a person or creature be fully and truly itself — this, and only this, is love.

— *Wisdom of the Pekratan Sages,* translated by Hila Sen

O N THE FORTIETH DAY AFTER he stopped eating, Nezhar saw the phoenix.

He woke before dawn, as he often did on the final day of an assignment. Sitting in front of the fire, prodding the embers back to life, he felt the first clutching pangs return to his stomach. The reserves of fat he'd been living off for more than a month were gone. His hands had been reduced to claws. Folds of skin hung from his belly like sheets drying on the line. With no alternatives left, his body now began to consume its own muscles and organs in order to keep him alive for another hour, another minute, another breath. Tonight he would eat, or else he would die.

Nezhar huddled by the fire, willing the flames to warm his chilled bones. The stars were beginning to fade, the approaching sun turning the thin eastern clouds a fiery orange. To the west, Spyridon had begun to stir, its lamps and torches dwindling in sympathy with the stars as the sky brightened. Nezhar sipped gingerly from his waterskin and listened to the distant chirps of birds greeting the new day. The air was calm and the morning fine. A perfect day for completing a contract.

Then he looked up, and there it was.

It soared above the trees, wings spread in a glide as it followed some current imperceptible from the ground. As it banked, the first rays of sunlight caught its plumes, sparking a brilliant, otherworldly incandescence. Gold and red flared from its wings, and its body was bronze touched with flecks of deep green. It seemed to Nezhar that it hung in the air, its sapphire crest just visible as it turned its proud head; then it vanished behind the trees, returning soundlessly to its nest in the rocks above.

Nezhar gazed after it, scarcely able to take in what he had seen. *Phoenix at dawn, the Weeper smiles.* A surge of energy filled him, blasting through the claws of hunger and the hundred different aches and pains that had accumulated during his time in the wilderness. The clarity of focus he had so painstakingly built up over the past forty days seemed to double in a heartbeat.

These are the moments we live for. The quote skimmed across his thoughts, ringing with a conviction fit for scripture. He took a breath and it was as though the entire hillside breathed in with him, his chest rising and falling as one with the fire, the trees, the earth beneath his feet. He had denied himself, disciplining his flesh so as to nurture the slender flame of his talent, and the Weeper had seen it and smiled upon him. Today was his day.

As the sun crested the hill behind him, Nezhar took up his position on the flat patch of earth facing the city. Cool air brushed his face, refreshing as a mountain stream. The scent of grass, woodsmoke, and eucalyptus filled his nostrils. Every sigh of shifting leaves and fragment of birdsong seemed to spread out around him, a landscape of sound to be explored at will. He could sense the energies held in balance by each rock, each twig, each crumb of dirt. And there, across the fields, crouched the city of Spyridon like a vast, misshapen excrescence.

He reached toward it, eager but controlled, cautious but unhesitating. Distance was no longer an impediment — indeed, it was a virtue, offering vital perspective on the task that now lay before him. Red sandstone at the city's summit marked the Library, the sun glancing off the fiery bricks in a fashion that might have awed him an hour ago but now seemed a poor imitation of the phoenix's majesty. It called to him, inviting him to narrow his view, focus on the upper windows or the thick load-bearing columns, and then push or pull or twist like a child with a dolls' house that displeased him.

But the Library was not his target today.

He moved lower, past the dark line of the Arcade, the expansive houses and grounds, the steep streets and variegated shops; then lower still, to the mess of buildings that spread like fungus from the base of the hill. Voices pulled at him, filling his ears with banal conversations and tedious complaints. He passed a singing Kharjik boy, a whooshing forge-bellows, a braying goat. Outward he moved, ever outward, until a thick skirt of earth and stone cut across his path with heavy finality.

The wall. He felt along its length, reaching out in both directions. It stabbed and retreated, jagging back and forth like the teeth of some ill-made saw. Nezhar spread his arms and leaned close. Had the wall been straight, he might have enfolded half its circumference, but as it was he could encompass only a portion of the barbed perimeter. He let out a breath and allowed his cheek to rest against an angled segment between two low towers.

It was enough. Oh yes, this was more than enough.

Arms wrapped about the distant city, Nezhar plunged deep into the waiting earth and began his spell.

CHAPTER 21

The principles men are prepared to die for and those they are willing to live by coincide all too rarely.

— Giarvanno do Salin I

THE WALL MELTED.

Arandras gaped at the impossible sight. For just a moment he wondered if he imagined the growing sag to the parapets, the drooping flagpoles atop the towers. Then, like cheese left out in the sun, the entire structure began to fall away.

A cluster of bastions at the farthest points of the star went first, the squared fortifications losing their shape as they sank into a strange, not-quite-liquid puddle. Their fall seemed to drag the connecting walls down with them, battlements tilting and bending in on themselves before dissolving into a shapeless grey mass. The initial rumbles gave way to an uncanny, sludge-like sound, as though inconceivable volumes of viscous mud were rolling down some vast slope, the earthy ooze doing nothing to conceal the panicked screams of those caught in its path.

The inexorable flow spread outward. Cannons and soldiers toppled from the wall or were simply absorbed by the liquefying earth. "Weeper have mercy," Arandras breathed, aghast. "Weeper save us." And as if in response to his prayer, it seemed to Arandras that the unearthly destruction began to slow. Another heartbeat and he was sure. The soldiers fleeing the collapse atop the battlements were outrunning it now, some pausing to look back as they sensed the danger ease. Behind them, the sinking wall seemed to be hardening, the surviving sections at either end forming a pair of misshapen ramps down to the puddled remains between them.

With a shaky breath, Arandras surveyed the damage. About a third of the wall between the north and east gates had fallen. Several structures built too close to the fortifications had buckled as they lost their main support, but as far as Arandras could tell, only the wall itself had suffered the unnatural melt. The thick, greyish line that marked the place where it had stood looked more like a road than anything else, or perhaps a river suspended in mid-flow, its height difficult to judge from this distance but likely to trouble only infants and the infirm.

"Gods," Mara muttered beside him, sick despair in her voice. "Who could do such a thing?"

Arandras shook his head. Never in his years with the Quill had he encountered anything like this, and if the histories contained any comparable account, he couldn't think of it right now. Was this the hand of Azador, the so-called god Clade had warned him about? Surely only the Valdori had ever approached this level of power.

"Not the Quill," Jensine said in a flat tone. "But there are others. Small cabals who pursue exotic forms of sorcery. Usually such methods are too costly or too unreliable, or both. But when they manage to get a binding just right…"

"What do you mean, costly?" Mara said.

Jensine shrugged. "Blood. Silence. Starvation. Could be anything. But I'll tell you one thing for sure. Whoever did this won't be repeating it any time soon."

Arandras gazed past the ruined wall. "I don't think that will matter." Like a kicked anthill, the Oculus army had sprung to life. Teams of soldiers were already returning cannons to their earlier positions and restoring their angles of fire, though a gap in the ring of artillery revealed the effects of last night's raid. As Arandras watched, one of the crews set off their gun, the uncalibrated shot arcing high but falling short of the city. Nearby, companies of heavily-armoured swordsmen began to mass at the camp's edge. "They're coming."

Mara grunted. "This is why they were waiting."

Another cannon fired, a low shot that sent the ball bouncing into the city where it crashed into some structure Arandras couldn't see. A series of booms followed in close succession from the north, past the destroyed section of wall; the attack, it seemed, was resuming on all sides. A group of uniformed figures scurried for cover as the enemy guns began to rediscover their range. Flaming cannonballs sailed through the space where the wall had stood, punching into the outermost buildings and prompting a fresh wave of shrieks.

"That's it, then," Mara said, her words heavy with defeat. "There's no defending a breach like that."

Jensine turned to Arandras. "What'll it be?"

It took him a moment to understand the question. "How much longer do you need?"

"To finish the binding? A few hours." She grimaced. "But it's getting harder to hold it all together. I know we talked about delaying if the weather isn't right, but I'm not sure that's still an option. If you want to do this, it'll have to be today."

Arandras cursed. Three infantry companies stood in formation outside the Oculus camp, with more assembling behind them. Several buildings at the outermost points of the star had been levelled and another was now alight, flames licking the rooftop beneath an ugly plume of black smoke. *Spyridon, city of learning,* he thought, the words coming to him from some half-remembered moment as though spoken by someone else. *The gods are at war with you now.* But it hadn't been gods, plural. Just one had been enough.

Abruptly, he turned away. "Keep working," he told Jensine as he swept past. "Whatever happens, don't let the binding slip."

"Arandras?" Mara called after him as he descended the stairs. "Hey, Arandras! What are you going to do?"

He ignored her and strode out the door, down the path, onto the street. Below, the Oculus cannons fired again and again, softening up the city as their soldiers marched closer. Elsewhere, still shielded by the wall near the north gate but beyond the range of his thoughts, the golems awaited his command. He set off at a run toward the golems, Mara's question ringing in his ears.

What are you going to do?

Arandras had no idea.

~

Eilwen flipped over the tile and grinned at Orval across the small table. "Five swords. Do you contest?"

"Only five?" Orval drew a pair of tiles from his hand and slapped them on the table. "Six swords," he said contentedly as Eilwen frowned at the stylised images on their faces: four blades on one, two on the other.

Her own hand offered ships and banners in abundance, but was woefully short on swords. "It's yours," she said in a mock-growl. "Tile or point?"

Orval considered the options: an additional tile for his reserve, face-down on this occasion and thus something of a gamble, or one of the small square tokens that represented a point toward victory. "Tile," he said at last. He picked up the piece and glanced at its face. "Oh, great. Like I need another of those."

"If in doubt, take the point," Eilwen quoted.

With an exaggerated scowl, Orval replenished his hand and moved his spent tiles and new acquisition to his reserve. "We'll see."

They'd found the tile set the previous evening in a cupboard near the dining hall. Eilwen had been an occasional player in her early days at the Woodtraders Guild, but she hadn't touched a tile for years and had been about to pass it over. Then Orval had picked it up and opened it in an offhand manner, which for him amounted to a keen expression of interest. They'd brought it back to their suite after dinner and played several rounds, Eilwen growing increasingly delighted at Orval's engagement with the game. With Clade out of the picture, her nephew's wellbeing had become her sole focus. Anything that might help her connect with him, or even just distract him from the siege, was worth its weight in silver.

"All right," Eilwen said, reaching for the supply of tokens. The cannons had been silent all morning, likely a result of whatever Arandras and his golems had got up to last night, though the respite was welcome whatever the cause. "It's first rise. Up go the stakes. The winner chooses either two points or one point plus a face-up tile." She drew a tile. "Huh. Seven banners."

Orval eyed the stakes. "Could be useful," he allowed, his casual tone belied by his lingering gaze on the tile.

Eilwen allowed herself an inward smile. *Boy's got a thing or two to learn about ruling his expression.*

A rumble sounded deep in the earth and Orval looked up, fear flitting across his face. "What was that?"

The room quivered as though shaken by a gust of wind, then fell still. The rumble faded, leaving a charged silence in its wake. Cautiously, Eilwen rose and approached the window.

"Was it them?" Orval said. "Is it an attack?"

Eilwen cocked her head. "Hush." A low whine from the alley beneath the window broke the silence; but there was another sound, stranger and more distant, like the sluggish flow of some impossibly thick river.

Orval stared at her, his hands braced against the table as though frozen in the act of getting up. "It's sorcery, isn't it? What else could it be?"

"I don't know." The whining grew louder, and Eilwen glanced down to see Jak standing almost directly below the window, ears flat and tail low, the dog's attention caught by something to the east.

"Do you think... could it have been cast by someone on our side?"

Eilwen dismissed the question with a shake of her head. "Stay here. I'll find out what I can and come right back." She fixed him with a stern expression. "Whatever you do, don't go outside. Understood?"

Orval nodded.

She ducked into the other room and crouched beside her bag, rummaging in its depths to find the wrapped bundle of the black amber egg. Slipping it into her pocket, she returned to the main room, pausing by the door. Orval still sat before the abandoned game, his brow knit with anxiety.

"Don't worry," Eilwen said. "I'll be back soon."

The street outside the boarding house seemed little different to what she'd become accustomed to over the past few days. Traffic was light but steady in the absence of new arrivals to the city, though there did seem to be a few more people about today, perhaps lured from their homes by the cannons' silence. The odd sound she'd heard from the window had faded or perhaps was harder to hear on the ground, obscured by intervening structures, the ordinary noise of the street, and the repetitive caws of a flock of gulls somewhere beyond sight.

Leaning against the building, she reached into her pocket and began to fumble with the wrappings. The beast stirred, lazily sniffing the air as it uncoiled within her. But the mystery of the tremor already occupied the parts of her that the beast customarily filled, and she found it easy to push it away. With a sharp exhalation, she reached beneath the wrappings and closed her hand over the cool, smooth egg. The presence of the distant army throbbed faintly at the edge of her senses; but nothing seemed out of the ordinary, at least not that Eilwen could discern — nothing that might explain the strange tremor.

A cannon boomed, shattering her concentration, and the calls of the gulls intensified. The beast opened a slitted eye in sudden alertness and Eilwen felt a chill run through her. *Those aren't gulls.* Pain-filled shrieks and screams of panic filled the air, unmistakable now as human. Passers-by cast worried glances eastward, some slowing in confusion, others hastening to the relative safety of their destinations.

A series of blasts split the air. Eilwen barely had time to register their source — *cannon fire from the north* — *so close!* — before a flaming ball whistled overhead and smashed into the building beside her. She leapt away, throwing her arms over her head as bricks and timber collapsed into the space where she'd been standing. A second crash followed, and Eilwen turned to see the roof sag inward along half the building's length. The lower floors groaned at the impact and the structure buckled, sending tiles and bricks cascading to the ground. Screams sounded behind her, but Eilwen scarcely heard them.

Gods have mercy. Orval.

She rushed forward, heedless of the tumbling debris or the prospect of further strikes. The alley she'd been looking into minutes before was choked with fallen masonry, forcing her to climb over the rubble as she neared their suite. "Orval! Can you hear me?"

Someone groaned nearby and she scurried toward the sound — but it was a woman, half-buried beneath a pile of bricks, a jagged cut across her brow spilling blood into her eye. *Not Orval.* Eilwen turned away.

"Orval! Where are you?" She stumbled toward their suite, or where it had been mere moments ago. The roof had fallen in, taking much of the building with it; but it seemed to Eilwen that the walls below her own suite still stood amid the wreckage of the upper floors. She clambered up a mound of tiles and broken timbers, searching for a place where she could hoist herself through a hole in the wall of the neighbouring suite. "Orval? Talk to me, damn it!"

Something moved in the debris beneath her feet. She backed away, almost losing her balance as she slid down the mound. Her heart in her mouth, she began dragging the broken beams aside. Grit stung her eyes and nose, but she dug on regardless. *Could be Orval... could be Orval...*

A moist object brushed her hand and she shrieked. Then a canine snout poked though the hole, followed by the rest of the animal's head. *Jak.* The dog pulled itself awkwardly through the opening, clearly favouring its foreleg as it stepped gingerly to the ground. It sniffed the ground, tail brushing from side to side, circling past Eilwen toward the heaped wreckage deeper in the alley.

Not Orval. Dry dust tickled her throat, and she gave a violent cough. *Please be alive. Please.*

A sudden scrabbling from the dog made her turn. Jak crouched before yet another pile of masonry, pawing and whining at a narrow hole near its base. Eilwen scrambled to the dog's side, her chest pounding. "Orval? Are you there?" She began tossing aside shattered bricks, digging through the snapped timbers and nail-studded boards with her bare hands. Jak climbed up beside her, yipping as she pulled debris from the hole.

She heaved aside a beam and Jak darted in, licking and whining. Beneath lay a cheek and a brow, the latter half-hidden by a curl of hair. *Orval.* Gasping, Eilwen bent to her work, clearing away wreckage to reveal a shoulder, an arm, a hip. Jak hunched down, pressing its nose into Orval's face. "I'm here, Orval," Eilwen said, repeating the words under her breath with every piece of rubble she lifted. "I'm here. I'm here."

She leaned closer, squatting awkwardly on her good leg to lift a block of cemented bricks from Orval's midsection. Her hands came away sticky with blood. *No, gods, please.* An ugly red stain marred the front of the boy's shirt: smaller than it might have been, but large enough to chill her. She looked away. *First things first.* If she couldn't free him from the masonry, nothing else would matter.

So intent was she on her task that she almost missed the low groan. She dropped the ragged beam she was holding and bent close. "Orval? Can you hear me?" He groaned again, his fluttering eyelids revealing crescents of white. "I'm going to get you out. You hear me? You're going to be all right."

She grasped his shoulders and heaved. For a moment he didn't budge, snagged perhaps on some jutting fragment, or maybe just too heavy for Eilwen to move. Then something shifted beneath him and he began to slide free of the pile, his voice rising in a cry of pain. Eilwen kept pulling. If his injuries were so bad that moving him made them worse, he was dead anyway. The thought was strangely calm, stripped clean by shock and necessity. The only way to save him was to get him out.

When his feet cleared the rubble she set him down, lowering him gently onto a relatively unlittered patch of ground. He blinked groggily, his eyes half-opening and closing. "Heard..." Orval breathed, then broke off, his mouth working. "Heard Jak."

"Jak's here," Eilwen said. The dog padded back and forth beside them, whining softly. "We're both here."

Orval tried to lift himself onto his elbow. "Where...?"

"Hush." Eilwen pressed him gently back down, and Orval subsided. "Just lie still."

She moved to his side, to the alarming crimson stain, and slowly reached out to grasp his shirt. As she did, her gaze fell on the cuts and scrapes covering her own hand. *Blood and blood,* she thought distantly as she lifted the hem of his shirt to reveal the flesh beneath. *Blood and blood...*

The gash was long and deep, but thankfully whatever had caused it seemed to have cut across his ribs rather than piercing them. Eilwen gave a shaky sigh and pulled the shirt back into place. *Still alive.*

"You're going to be all right," she said. "We're going to find someplace safe, and I'm going to get you some help, and you'll be fine.

Understand?"

Orval grunted, and his eyes moved down and up in what might have been meant as a nod.

"Good. Now, the first thing we need to do is get you out of the street." She paused, hating the question she was about to ask but knowing there was no other way. "Do you think you can walk?"

Orval grunted again. "Try."

"Good." Something pricked her eyes and she looked away, blinking rapidly. "That's good. Let's start by sitting up."

With the help of the alley wall and a conveniently sized length of timber they managed to manoeuvre Orval upright. Eilwen pulled Orval's arm across her shoulders, grimacing at the pain in her knee as she straightened beneath his weight. At Eilwen's instruction they took a tentative step, then another, Jak circling them in concern as they made their laborious way out of the alley.

A hospice wagon was already setting up as they emerged onto the street. "Injured citizens this way," called a young man with a clerk's bearing as behind him two physicians prepared to receive patients. "You, madam," he said, catching sight of Eilwen and Orval. "Are you a citizen?"

"My nephew," Eilwen said, staggering toward the wagon. "He needs help."

"Of course." The man opened a loosely-bound folio. "Your names, please."

"I, uh." Eilwen grasped for a name that might satisfy the man — an old trading partner, perhaps, someone she'd dealt with on one of her Woodtrader-sponsored journeys to Spyridon. "Wetha. Wetha Sorn."

The man flipped a page. "And what are your parents' names, Wetha?"

"Ah." Eilwen stared at the man stupidly. "I don't know."

"I see." The man essayed a tight but not entirely unsympathetic smile. "You're welcome to wait until the citizens are seen to, madam. The physicians will make every effort to attend to your nephew, provided we're not called away. Wait over there by the street lamp, if you would."

Eilwen opened her mouth to argue, but the man had already

turned to speak to a heavyset woman whose cheek and neck were smeared with blood. *Provided we're not called away, indeed.* The boom of the cannons continued unabated, as intense a barrage as any she'd heard up to now. Every hospice and wagon in the city would be turning non-citizens away soon. The chances of finding help before then were slim at best.

With cloth and water she could start tending to Orval herself. But she couldn't do anything out in the street. Eilwen cursed in frustration. *A damn roof over my head is all I need. Is that so much to ask?*

But there was no-one in Spyridon who might take her in, no-one she even knew...

Except for one person.

Ah, hells. After what she'd said to him, she'd be lucky to get through the front door. But what choice did she have?

Resignedly, Eilwen steered Orval around and began stumbling down the street in search of a carriage.

～

Clade paced the length of his suite and contemplated the ruin of his plans.

The list of his failures since arriving in Spyridon was depressingly long. He'd lost the Library's prized book. He'd lost Hesca's interest and likely her patronage. If Arandras's golems had ever been in the balance, he'd lost them as well. And now, it seemed, he'd lost the city.

The angle from the window was too low to see what had happened, but it was clear that something had gone profoundly wrong. Until this morning, his view had been dominated by one of the squat towers that watched over the city's new wall, its banners fluttering in the sea breeze. Now that tower was gone. Clade could only assume that the wall itself had somehow been brought down, a theory that found additional weight in the renewed bombardment and the answering screams. If so, it was only a matter of time before Spyridon fell.

Clade was not especially concerned for himself. If the Oculus repeated the pattern they'd established at Neysa, he'd have little trouble leaving the city as soon as the siege was over. And if not, well, his own particular talents meant that any stray plank or piece of furniture could serve as a weapon. He'd want to lie low during daytime — no need to risk being seen by a former colleague who just happened to be carrying Azador — but on the whole he anticipated little trouble extracting himself from the city when the time came.

No, what stuck in his craw was the fact that *Azador had won*. Clade had thrown himself into Spyridon's defence as soon as he'd learnt of the approaching threat, and it had made no difference at all. He'd struck no blow against the god. Azador had brushed him aside without even realising he was here. And he still had no idea why the Oculus wanted Spyridon or Neysa in the first place.

And to top it all off, the one ally he'd managed to win in the past year had thrown his friendship in his face and abandoned him. It seemed Eilwen had forgotten all he'd done for her in those early months, the help he'd offered against that feral part of her that wanted only to kill. Whatever control she'd regained was because of him; yet she'd walked away as though he were nothing more than a casual acquaintance she no longer desired.

It would be satisfying to simply dismiss her. What benefit was there to keeping her around, assuming she could even be persuaded to stay? Yet the matter was not so straightforward. For one thing, her own grievance against Azador ran deep. In time, he might still find a way to channel that grievance to his own advantage. More important, however, was the damage she might do if she chose to oppose him.

The fact was that he'd trusted her. How many months had they travelled together? Nine? Ten? He'd revealed things to her that nobody else knew. On more than one occasion they'd discussed his plans to bring down the god of the Oculus — never in great detail, true, but enough to harm him if she desired it. Put plainly, she was a liability, and Clade had no desire to give the Oculus any more weapons against him than they already had.

Which meant that when all this was over he'd need to seek her out, determine whether she could still be used; and, if not…

A rapid knock on the door broke his thoughts. "Clade, are you in there?" someone called urgently, and his brows rose as he recognised the voice. "Open up!"

He slid the bolt and pulled the door open to reveal a bloodied and bedraggled Eilwen, her arm wrapped around an equally dishevelled youth who seemed barely capable of standing. *Not done with me after all, then?* She staggered in as soon as the door opened, clumsily lowering the boy to the floor where he collapsed in a heap, his eyes rolling back in his head.

Eilwen rose, fixing Clade with a steely glare. "We need help."

"And just who in the hells is 'we'?" Clade asked.

"This is Orval," Eilwen said, her expression an odd mixture of defiance and vulnerability. "My nephew."

"Your *what?*"

"He travelled with me from Neysa. I was supposed to get him away from the gods-damned Oculus." She stepped closer. "I told you I had family here. I told you I needed to get them out. But you insisted I stay. You owe me."

"*I* insisted...?" Anger and incredulity welled up within him. "I told you to send your family away! Don't blame me for your own choices."

"Send him away with who? He's a boy, Clade! I couldn't just parcel him up and post him off to the next city!"

A low whine issued from the open doorway. A thin, miserable-looking dog crouched just beyond the threshold, perhaps hoping its pitiful display would yield a scrap of food. Clade slammed the door in its face.

"You want help?" he said. "Fine. You'll have it as soon as you complete your assigned task. Go to Arandras and get my books back."

"Oh, for the gods' sake. What is it with you and those books? And why are you so sure that Arandras has them? I mean, why would he want them?"

It was a challenge not to gape at her in disbelief. "You're asking why Arandras would be interested in a book about golems?"

"Golems he already has! He knows how to communicate with them. He knows how to control them. And I don't know if you were paying attention yesterday, but it looked to me like he was hating every minute of it. Gods, his expression when he brought those things out of his house was like someone reaching into a bucket of shit. So what exactly do you think either of those books is going to tell him that he's interested in knowing?"

Clade blinked in surprise. It was true that beneath his impatience, Arandras had seemed strangely subdued at the command post. Clade hadn't thought much of it at the time. The man had been preparing to lead a military assault. A degree of fear was to be expected. But now that he considered it, there'd been more to Arandras's demeanour than simple trepidation. Even the crowd's euphoria had left him untouched. Most people would have been hard-pressed to resist a smile at being cheered through the streets, but Arandras had just stood there scowling like a man who'd been robbed.

Yet when Clade had approached Arandras's house, he'd sensed sorcery — sorcery with a golem at its heart...

Clade felt a chill run through him. *Gods and demons.* It couldn't be. Yet given the man's recalcitrance, it made a perverse kind of sense. *He's trying to find a way to destroy them.*

He must have spoken the thought aloud. Eilwen looked at him in shock. "Are you sure?"

"You tell me," Clade retorted, but with little expectation of an answer. His thoughts were already racing ahead. "Stay or go, I don't care. But if you're still here when I get back, I'm going to expect your assistance. Understood?"

Eilwen hugged her arms around her body. "What are you going to do?"

"I'm going to stop him," Clade said. "And you're going to help me."

CHAPTER 22

He would not grant them victory until they submitted to his call, surrendering their freedom for the sake of their brothers, and marched into Meddig, helms bright and banners raised to the heavens, to die.

— Prophet Samoval the Fourth, *Warriors of the All-God*

ARANDRAS HURRIED THROUGH THE CITY, his thoughts ranging ahead as far as he could stretch them. *Golems. Are you there? Answer me.* The incessant barrage of enemy guns seemed to have finally sent the city mad. Every corner he turned revealed a new, wildly different scene: a street choked with panicked locals, or one entirely bare; a uniformed squad quick-marching to some assigned rendezvous, or a pair of soldiers with bloodied faces staggering into an alley; a gang of street children shrieking excitedly as they flew past, or a pair of small feet protruding horribly from beneath a tumbled-down wall. Arandras hastened on, some part of his mind reducing each new location to a simple dichotomy of avenues and obstacles while his thoughts reached ever outward.

Golems. Are you there? Can you hear me?

When the reply came, it was faint but clear. *We hear you.*

Come to me.

He stumbled to a halt, blinking at his surroundings. Between the shops on one side of the road was a small park, in truth little more than a ragged lawn and a handful of trees, the space currently occupied by perhaps a dozen adults and half again as many children. Several stared about them in slack-faced shock, while others clung to their companions and gave muffled sobs or murmured encouragements. A flat-nosed Halonan woman with braided hair noticed Arandras and pulled her two boys close as though he might try to snatch them from her grasp. Too spent to do anything more than shake his head, Arandras turned away, his steps carrying him toward the edge of the city where the once-proud wall now ended in a misshapen slope of unnaturally smooth earth.

A makeshift barrier of broken carts blocked the end of the street, though if the army had raised it they'd neglected to keep it manned. Arandras edged past an upturned barrow, gazing at the malformed wall in something akin to awe. A low shelf at the wall's base showed where the stone had puddled and spread, creeping outward like melting ice before inexplicably hardening once more. What remained held none of the usual texture of stone. More than anything, it resembled an uncanny form of glass, opaque and barely reflective but with the characteristic smoothness and small imperfections Arandras had seen in windows from Chogon to the Library.

He pressed his hand against the strangely flat surface. *This is stone,* he thought, and felt a wave of vertigo rush over him. What must it be like, to look at the basic substances of the world and see not constraints but possibilities to be rearranged at will? Was this what the Valdori had been: gods in all but name, no longer held back by anything save their own imaginations? What did one become when the earth itself could no longer resist one's command?

The tramp of heavy footfalls announced the golems' arrival. Arandras closed his eyes and leaned his head against the wall. The moment seemed primed with some insight he couldn't quite grasp, deeper than sorcery or theology, one that reached to the heart of what it meant to live in a world that suffered men and women to change it. A world charged with dizzying arrays of possibilities, yet collapsing with every passing moment into the tyranny of the real.

"Gods be praised!" came a voice from somewhere nearby. Arandras looked up. A grey-haired soldier wearing an officer's braid stood before him, open relief on her face. "The enemy will be here in minutes. We need you out there right now."

It took Arandras a moment to recollect himself. "The enemy. Right." He hadn't intended to fight, exactly — except that part of him must have intended that very thing. Why else bring the golems to this place? He performed a quick head count — all that he had left by the gate still present, thank the Weeper — then peered along the wall, but the view through the gap was obscured by smoke and fallen houses. "Is there a vantage point nearby?"

The officer gestured at the remains of the wall behind him. "The end's just down that way. It's a bit steep, but the footing is solid."

Arandras turned. "You want me to *climb* it, like it's a Weeper-damned ramp?" But then, why not? He grimaced his acceptance. "Lead the way."

The officer departed at the base of the slope, leaving Arandras to clamber up the fallen wall alone. Though the wall's thickness made for a wide path, the surface was uncomfortably slippery. Arandras climbed in a half-crouch, his hands stretched ahead and to the sides to catch himself in case he stumbled, his skin itching with the conviction that each step made him a more inviting target to the Oculus archers below. As he ascended, rough ridges began to grow along the edges of the wall, higher on one side than the other, providing handholds to speed his progress and shielding him from the view of those below. Only as the outer ridge reached the height of his knee did he realise that it was in fact the wall's parapet, or what was left of it, its jagged form an echo of the battlements that had once stood tall enough to shield a soldier's entire body.

From the ground, the wall had seemed little higher than the Trattasi estate house. The view from the top seemed twice as high. Arandras crouched behind the battlements, peeking out as a squad of archers rushed to his side from further along the wall and began setting arrows to their bows. This section of wall extended out to a star point and seemed to run almost perpendicular to the wide gap in the city's defence. The Oculus cannons had fallen silent here, no doubt to avoid hitting the half dozen companies that had assembled a short distance away. As Arandras watched, a shout went up, shockingly loud despite the distance, and the gathered soldiers began charging toward the city.

A row of defenders had formed a short distance behind the

wall's remains, likely with the intention of turning the topography of ruined buildings and piled rubble to their advantage, but even Arandras could see that they were hopelessly outnumbered. *This is where Spyridon falls. Right here, right now.*

Unless I do something.

He could sense the golems below his position, lined up where he had left them like performers awaiting their cue to take the stage. Arrows hissed down as the charging soldiers entered bowshot range; but the missiles were few, and fewer still hit their mark. Someone called an order and a section of the defensive line shuffled backward, breaking apart at what looked like an overturned vegetable stand and reforming behind it.

Arandras drew a breath. He had no right, no standing, no authority to instruct the golems to defend the city. No argument could justify it. But he had already committed that sin, already selected it from the vast mass of possibilities and etched it into the fabric of the world. Would a second transgression be any worse than the first?

Golems, he sent. *Take up positions in front of the defenders and prevent the enemy soldiers from entering the city. Use force as you must to deny the enemy passage, but do not unnecessarily injure or kill.*

Swifter than he would have expected, the golems spread across the opening in the wall. Some of the defenders recoiled at their approach, though others who were quicker on the uptake gave a scrappy cheer. Yet as the constructs positioned themselves in a loose, widely-spaced row, the scale of the breach became clear. Three times as many golems would not have been enough to plug this hole. The enemy could not be kept out.

The charging soldiers reached the edge of the puddled earth that had once been the wall. In the last moments before they struck, the golems dropped to a crouch and spread their arms; and Arandras thought the Oculus vanguard hesitated in its final steps as though suddenly unsure of the reception that awaited them.

Then the wave of attackers broke over the improvised reef of golems, and all was chaos.

Cries, grunts, and the clash of steel filled the air. Enemy soldiers piled against the golems or slipped through the spaces between them. But the defenders had crept closer to their unexpected allies, gathering behind the gaps in the golems' line to form killing zones thick with Spyridon steel.

A fresh wave of soldiers reached the city and piled into those ahead of them. A few managed to clear enough space to hack ineffectually at a golem, but for the most part the crush of humanity seemed too great for swords. And in the channels left by the golems, enemy bodies were beginning to form their own barrier. A surge near the centre of the line saw a knot of Oculus blades succeed in breaking through; but as Arandras watched, a reserve detachment swept in, encircling the invaders and cutting them down as a smaller group peeled off to bolster the defence.

It's working. Weeper's breath, it's actually working. The attackers' momentum was gone, and the defensive line had barely shifted. Several of the golems began swinging their arms forward to throw soldiers into the legs of their companions. Elsewhere, enterprising defenders stabbed and sliced around and below the golems' thick limbs, their enemies unable to defend themselves for the crush.

From somewhere in the press came a barked command, the order echoing rapidly along the line — and suddenly the Oculus were turning and running. A cheer went up from the defenders, some hurling taunts at the enemy's back while others raised their arms in triumph. Arandras sagged back against the battlement, panting for breath as though he'd been swinging a sword himself.

Golems. Report your condition.

I stand. I am undamaged. I remain functional. The answers streamed back, but they were fewer than Arandras expected. He straightened in alarm, gazing down at the battleground where the defenders had now turned to the messy business of killing the enemy's wounded. But none of the golems he could see appeared to have suffered significant harm, and none of the responses spoke of anything more substantial than scratches.

Perhaps the golems at the end of the line were simply too distant to have heard his command. Probably that was all. Still, he should check and make sure.

Crouching, Arandras began his descent. The smoothness of the stone that had so impeded his climb now aided him, allowing him to slide down the slope while using his hands to control his speed.

As the battlements on either side shrank he pressed his hands flat against the stone, wincing as bumps and knots jagged against his palms, then grimacing anew as the irregularities disappeared entirely for the final stretch before he reached the ground.

Bodies littered the earth, the stench of gore and loosed bowels all but overwhelming. The nearest golem stood only a few paces away, its arms and torso daubed red. Arandras swallowed hard. Ordering the golems not to kill was fine as far as it went, but he'd still forced them to participate in this mad butchery. To feel lives snuffed out, to see bodies broken open against their own earthen forms. *Will they thank me, when I free them? Will they understand the necessity that drove me to this end? Or will they consider this abomination to be normal — just one more activity in which free beings may choose to indulge?*

A series of dull booms sounded somewhere nearby — an important noise, he knew, but one disconnected from his present horror. *Cannons,* some distant part of him realised. The cannons were firing again...

Something hard and violent smashed into the golem before him. Arandras reeled backward, arms raised to shield his face. The golem teetered back a step, then collapsed to the ground. A cry sounded in Arandras's head, a primal expression of shock and pain unlike anything he had heard before.

I... am wounded...

Stunned, Arandras stared at the ruin before him. The golem's chest seemed to have caved in. Its pinprick yellow eyes flickered, then faded. On the ground beside it lay a cast iron sphere still wreathed in sorcerous flame — the instrument of the golem's doom.

Yet the voice in his head did not go away.

I am... wounded. I... am wounded.

Arandras stepped closer, his gaze intent on its face. It eyes were empty, lifeless. The golem was dead.

Except some part of it would not die. Could not die.

Its voice sounded in his head, over and over, relentless as the waves on the shore.

I am... wounded...

∽

The guards outside the command post offered no objection as Clade swept past. Either he had been seen in Hesca's company often enough to be accepted as one of her aides or the dark urgency that drove his steps forestalled any questions. He strode inside, paused at the stairs to weigh the likelihood of finding Hesca in the room above or the chambers below, and elected to climb.

His guess proved correct. The subcommander — no, the commander, now — stood with folded arms beside the great square table as an officer with drooping whiskers moved a cluster of tokens across a map of the city. Clade peered at the display, noting the painted wooden army surrounding the wall and the gap in the city's own line of cannons where the disaster he'd half-glimpsed from his suite had apparently claimed entire batteries. Miniature soldiers in Spyridon grey and red stood in the breach, opposed by twice as many black-stained figures — yet for some reason the officer was moving the enemy soldiers away.

"Do you think they'll try again today?" Hesca asked.

"It's an hour since midday. There's time." The officer shrugged. "Or they might like their chances better after dark."

"All right." Hesca's gaze fell on Clade, but she spoke on without interruption. "Tell the captains to stay alert, and get as many of our archers as possible around that section of wall. I'm going down there to talk to Arandras." The officer departed with a nod, and Hesca turned to Clade. "Something you want?"

"It's about Arandras. He..." Clade trailed off. "What did you just say?"

"Arandras and his golems just saved our collective arses. We'd have Oculus in the streets right now if it wasn't for him." Her mouth twitched in the hint of a smile. "If you're here to tell me he's agreed to help, you're too late."

"What? No, I..." Clade shook his head. "Are you sure?"

"Pretty damn sure," Hesca said, and there was a lightness to her tone that Clade hadn't heard since their first exchange at the massage parlour. "I'm headed down there now. Want to see for yourself?"

"It's a ruse," Clade said. "It must be. Listen, Hesca, you don't know him."

"And you do? Seems you two aren't exactly the best of friends."

"I never said we were. But I know him, and I can assure you that Arandras has no intention of permanently enlisting his golems in your army. In fact, I have reason to think he's planning to destroy them."

Hesca's face went still. "How you do you know that?"

"Be*cause*…" Grimacing, Clade glanced away. The truth was that he didn't know, only suspected. But on some deep level, it felt true. "You were with him yesterday. Did it look to you like he was enjoying himself?"

"You came to this conclusion based on his *looks?*"

"All right, forget how he looked. What did he say? Did he set any limit on his assistance?"

"Yes," Hesca said. "And he's already surpassed it."

Clade exhaled in frustration. "Why are you defending him?"

"What do you want me to say? Arandras agreed to help, and that's what he's done. He's helping right now. I very much hope he'll continue to help. But even if he doesn't, what on the All-God's own earth makes you think I can do anything about it?"

"You persuaded him to do this much —"

"Bah." Hesca waved dismissively. "I was lucky. Truth is, I don't think his decision had anything to do with me. But whatever his reasons, I'm grateful. Those golems have already saved Spyridon once —"

"But he's going to destroy them —"

"I don't care! All I care about is this city! For the All-God's sake, what will it take to get that through your skull?"

The intensity of her words struck Clade like a blow to the gut. He'd spent hours weighing her motives and pondering her words to find the meaning concealed beneath them, and the answer had been precisely what she'd told him at the beginning. *I am an honest soldier.* And so she was. *You're a tool, nothing more.* And so she had treated him. *And if you, or Piator Pronn, or anyone else does anything to threaten my city, I will find out about it, and I will hunt them down.* And so she had done, and Pronn's commander's braid now hung from her shoulder.

Unexpectedly, he laughed. She'd wanted to defend Spyridon. He'd wanted to defeat the Oculus. Their goals had been the same, or near enough. *That morning in Hesca's house. Each of us trying to seduce the other into doing what we were going to do anyway.* Their dance had been perfect in its absurdity.

She must have seen something of his thoughts on his face. Her expression softened, her lips curling in an echo of his own amusement. "Doesn't happen often, does it?"

And somehow he could guess at her thought, too. *To find one's mistrust... misplaced.* "No," he said. "Not often."

"The circle has all but collapsed," she said, as if that were somehow relevant. "Feren's locked herself in the Library. Urjo's off somewhere drinking himself into a stupor. The All-God only knows where Ernst is."

"There's still you," Clade said.

She gave him a searching look. "So there is."

"Perhaps you'll drive the Oculus off. Establish a new circle."

She glanced away, and Clade realised she had been hoping to hear something else. *We,* not *you.* "Perhaps I will."

Perhaps. But at this point, probably not. Spyridon was lost. Even Hesca had to see that. All that remained to Clade now was to ensure that the golems were not lost with it.

He nodded once, and she returned the gesture. No point in lengthy farewells. If there'd ever been anything personal between them, it lay buried beneath the demands that had animated them. What could they say?

Yet as Clade paused at the top of the stairs, Hesca looked back at him, her auburn hair soft about her face. A wordless moment passed between them, and Hesca smiled faintly, the expression wistful and inviting and mocking all at once.

Clade took a breath. "You never did tell me how you got that scar."

"No, I didn't." Hesca's smile turned barbed. "Now piss off. I've got a war to win."

~

Take cover! Arandras screamed, flinging the words at the golems strung across the breach in the wall. Perhaps he spoke them as well; but if he did, the sound was buried beneath thunderous booms from the enemy guns. A ball punctured the roof of the house directly behind him, sending tiles skittering to the ground and Arandras scurrying for the illusory safety of its neighbour. Soldiers in grey and red streamed past, faces streaked with blood and dust, many adopting a crouched jog as they fled the field. Only a few spared a glance for the crippled golem sprawled in the intersecting street; but those who did seemed to falter for a moment before raising their shoulders higher and breaking into a flat run.

Its inflection shifted subtly with each recitation, just enough to make Arandras sure the words were not merely a sorcerous echo but a genuine utterance of the ruined construct. *I... am wounded,* it said, as matter-of-fact now as if reporting on the weather; yet the surge of pain and astonishment Arandras had sensed as the missile struck seemed to haunt the golem's statements, infusing its emotionless delivery with a depth of unfathomable loss.

"You can't stay here!" someone shouted. Arandras glanced around and saw the officer that had greeted his arrival gesturing urgently back the way he had come. "Get behind the wall!"

He almost laughed. Of course it was no longer safe. Did the woman think he couldn't see? *Golems,* he called, reaching blindly for those at the far end of the breach, hoping they were near enough to hear him. *Golems! Come to me!*

I am... wounded, replied the crippled golem. Beyond it, inhumanly large figures emerged onto the debris-choked streets and began striding toward him. As the first few drew near, he instructed two of them to hoist their injured companion onto their shoulders. Then he turned toward the waiting officer and the shelter of the wall.

Come to me. Follow me.

"There's a square about fifty paces that way," the officer said as Arandras approached, pointing to a side street as though directing sorcerous constructs was something she did every day. "Should be large enough for you all to wait out the bombardment. I'll keep you informed of the enemy's movements..." She caught a glimpse of the broken golem, borne aloft by its fellows like a Kharjik prince, and trailed off. "Gods preserve."

"We're not staying," Arandras said.

"What?" The officer pulled her gaze back to Arandras. "What

does that mean?"

"Just what it sounds like." Arandras stepped around the officer without breaking stride. "We're done."

"No, you can't leave." The officer scrambled to catch up. "We need you. Please, we need you right here."

"Tough."

"Stop walking, damn it!" The officer interposed herself in Arandras's path, forcing him to halt. Soldiers looked around, their attention caught by the note of desperation in her voice. "Do you hear what I'm saying? Without you fighting for us, Spyridon will fall!"

"I hear you," Arandras snapped. "Now hear me. That golem" — he pointed at the construct's impacted chest — "is not dead. *It's still there.* Do you have any concept of what that means?"

The officer blinked in obvious confusion. "But it's not really alive, is it? In the end it's just earth and sorcery."

"No, it's not!" Arandras shouted. But as the officer's expression hardened, he realised there could be no explanation — not here, not to these people whose lives and homes depended on the falsity of what he knew to be true. For if the golems were mere objects, nothing could be more obvious than that they should serve in the city's defence; but if they were more, if in truth they were unwilling conscripts in someone else's war and capable of suffering a fate more horrific than death — then, indeed, someone was doomed, and the only question was who.

"We need you," the officer repeated, the simple entreaty of one clinging to the only truth they knew. "Please."

Arandras exhaled. Spyridon had its army to fight for it; its commanders, its circle. The golems had only him. "I'm sorry."

Her face twisted in disbelief. "You're *abandoning* us?"

And this was his reward: the thoughtless expectation that help once given would continue to be provided. "You were never mine to abandon."

He moved to pass, and her hand dropped to her sword hilt. She stared at him, her cheeks flushed, her gaze rich with threat. Then she glanced over his shoulder, and the intensity of her challenge slipped away.

Once more he tried to step past her, and this time she let him go.

"Bastard," she snarled after him. "Traitor!" The golems trailed after him, stomping past her on both sides, but she pursued her harangue as though he and she were alone. "May the hells swallow you! Every death that comes now is on your head!"

A clod of dirt whizzed past his ear. Another struck his shoulder. Arandras glanced around to see several of the soldiers that had witnessed their exchange stooping for ammunition or gesturing in anger. "Rat! Turncoat!"

Grimacing, Arandras instructed the golems to form a barrier around him. There were fewer of them than there should be — perhaps some had been too distant to hear his command after all? But there was no going back for them while the Oculus bombardment continued. Jensine's spell would free them, same as the rest, just so long as they remained unhurt. *Please let them be unhurt.*

Rocks clattered against the golem bodies surrounding him, insults filled the air, but none of that mattered to Arandras now. Jensine had been right. Sending the golems into battle had been a fool's choice. Shamefully, losing one of their number during the raid hadn't made that clear to him. But there was no gainsaying the horror of the ruined golem that now rode the shoulders of two others directly before him. Only a monster could ask another being to bear such a cost.

He laboured up the hill beneath the afternoon sun, to Jensine and the golems' freedom.

◇

Eilwen wrapped the strip of cloth around Orval's midsection, grimacing at the hitch in his breath each time she pulled the bandage taut. She'd washed the wound as best she could and had been encouraged to find her initial assessment confirmed. Though deep, the cut had damaged flesh only. The side of Orval's ribcage had prevented a worse injury. Assuming she could find a fleshbinder in the coming days to ward off infection, there was every reason to expect that it would heal.

Less reassuring were the bruises that covered her nephew's chest and back, several of which had already turned distressing shades of green and yellow. Eilwen was no physician, but she suspected that at least one of Orval's ribs was broken. His lungs seemed undamaged — Eilwen could hear no congestion, at any rate — but she had no way to know if any other hidden part of him had been injured in the crush.

She fastened the bandage with a pin and sat back to study her handiwork. Orval sat propped against the wall of Clade's suite, eyes shifting beneath closed lids in what Eilwen hoped was simple sleep. Gods preserve, if Den could see them now. *I should never have agreed to take Orval away from Neysa. He'd have been safer where he was.*

Tears stung her eyes, and she wiped them angrily away. Self-flagellation wouldn't get her anywhere. Orval needed her.

She crawled to the corner of the room, grimacing at the pressure on her sore knee, and retrieved her dagger from where she'd discarded it across Clade's partially destroyed bedsheet. *More bandages.* At some point Orval would need his dressings changed, and if she prepared them now it would be one less thing to do later. The extra water she'd brought up had acquired a coppery taint and could do with being replaced, but she had removed her boots shortly after arriving at Clade's suite and had no desire to pull them on again just yet. At least she'd had her purse on her belt when she stepped out of the boarding house — the reward of a lifetime's habit of keeping her valuables close to hand. The silver she'd taken from Neysa meant she wouldn't have to worry about food or shelter for a while.

Assuming the city doesn't collapse around our ears, that is. Even if she'd had some way to miraculously sneak past the besieging army, Orval was in no shape to travel. If the rumours she'd heard from the carriage driver were true and the wall had indeed been breached, there was nothing left to do but wait for Spyridon's likely fall, hope for the victorious Oculus to show the same restraint they had at Neysa, and get Orval to the first fleshbinder who would see him. Really, the sooner the Oculus managed to force their way in, the better off she'd be. Not that there was anything she could do about that, either. All she could do now was wait.

It was almost a relief. No more efforts to influence matters beyond her control. No more balancing Orval's needs against demands issued by Clade or her own petty desire to strike back at the Oculus. Family was what mattered.

A low groan sounded, little more than a barely-voiced exhalation. "What… happened…?"

"Orval?" Eilwen dropped the partially cut bandages and scrambled to the boy's side. "Oh, thank the gods."

Orval swallowed. "Something fell…"

"The boarding house was hit. The cannonball must have struck a supporting beam. I had to dig you out." She grasped his shoulders. "But you're going to be all right, you hear me? I'll make sure of it."

"What about…" He coughed, his face twisting in a pain-filled wince; but when he tried again his voice was stronger. "What about Jak?"

"Jak's fine," Eilwen said. "He led me to you. Showed me where to dig, then followed us here. Shall I fetch him in?" Not waiting for his response, she stood and opened the door. "Clade won't mind. Actually, he probably will, but he'll just have to deal with it." She looked up and down the hallway, but the dog was nowhere to be seen. "Bound to be around somewhere. I'm sure he'll be back soon."

"Cl… Clade?"

She turned to see Orval struggling upright, his face grey with pain. "Hey, easy now," she exclaimed, hurrying across and wrapping an arm around him for support. "Standing can wait. Here, sit at the table. I'll pour you some water." Orval yielded, sitting heavily in the proffered chair, and she reached for the pitcher of drinking water. "Clade is my employer, remember? Only not any more. We've… parted ways."

Orval accepted the mug and took a tentative sip. "This is his place?"

Eilwen nodded. "He wasn't thrilled to see us, in truth, but don't worry about that. I'll work something out."

"He's coming back?" Orval said, and Eilwen thought she heard a slight quaver in his voice.

"Sooner or later." She sat beside him, close enough that their arms were touching. "There's no need to worry. Clade hates the Oculus as much as we do, so we're all on the same side."

Orval made a noise that might have been meant as a grunt of assent but trailed off in a groan.

The sound filled her ears like a declaration of her own failure.

Eilwen loosed a voiceless sigh. "Gods, Orval, I'm sorry I put you through this. You were right. We should never have stayed here. I know I keep saying it, but I really am going to make this right. I promise."

Orval drew a breath. "There's something..." He trailed off. "They said I couldn't tell anyone. They said..."

The door swung open, and Orval flinched. Clade entered the suite, an odd expression on his face, part determination and part... melancholy? Eilwen shook her head. Surely she was mistaken.

"Still here, are you?" Clade's gaze rested briefly on Orval before flicking to Eilwen. "Come with me. We've got work to do."

Eilwen folded her hands. "What kind of work?"

"You'll find out soon enough." Clade gestured impatiently. "Fetch your things. Your boy will still be here when you get back."

So that was the way he wanted it. She turned to Orval. "We'll talk when I get back, all right?"

Orval nodded slightly, his gaze fixed on Clade, his expression unreadable.

"Right." She stood and made for the adjoining room where her discarded boots lay on the floor. "Just give me a moment here," she called back to Clade.

One boot, then the other, the second more awkward with the pain in her knee. What else? Just the dagger she'd been using to cut bandages. She returned to the main room, stomping her good leg to check the tightness of her lacing — and froze.

Clade stood before her, his face a picture of surprise. Behind him stood Orval, barely upright, his arm wrapped around Clade's chest. And in his other hand, the glint of Eilwen's dagger pressed against Clade's throat.

CHAPTER 23

We do not choose which cares to take up, only which cares to deny.

— Daro of Talsoor

ORVAL SWALLOWED, COUGHED, AND SWALLOWED again. "Nobody move," he croaked.

"Orval?" Eilwen blinked, trying to make sense of the scene before her. "What are you doing?"

"Shut up!" Despite their difference in height, Orval's weight had dragged Clade down enough for him to speak almost at the level of the taller man's ear. "Your name is Clade Alsere, right?"

Clade allowed the enquiry to hang in the air for a moment. "Would denying it do me any good?"

"Answer the question!"

"Yes, I'm Clade." He glanced around the room — looking, Eilwen guessed, for objects that might serve as the basis of some improvised spell — but by chance or design, Orval had positioned Clade between himself and the table in the room's centre. "Who are you, boy? Should I know you?"

Orval's grip tightened. "You betrayed the Oculus, didn't you?"

Clade raised an eyebrow. "'Betrayed', is it?"

"Orval, what's going on?" Eilwen began.

"*They've got Vess!*" Orval cried. "They said... they said..."

Something stirred in Eilwen's belly. "Who's got Vess?"

"The Oculus! Somehow they knew you were there. In Neysa, I

mean."

"Knew *I* was there?" An image from the governor's arrival flitted through Eilwen's mind: the sorcerer atop the harbourmaster's tower, Azador behind its eyes. The beast uncoiled, sniffing the air. "You need to start making sense, Orval. Right now."

"It was a couple of days after you arrived," Orval said. "I was coming home — me and some friends had been watching the ships come in on the canal — and they grabbed me right off the street. It wasn't even dark! I thought I was going to disappear, like Vess." He blinked, and Eilwen saw moisture on his cheeks. "They took me someplace, I don't know where. And they started asking me questions."

"About me," Eilwen said.

"Yes." Orval heaved a breath, and Eilwen saw Clade tense as though preparing to burst free... but the dagger at his throat refused to drop. "At first. Then it changed. They asked if you were still in contact with someone called Clade, and where he was, and what he was doing. Only I couldn't answer them because you hadn't told us anything. Then they said..." He gave Eilwen an agonised look. "They said if I ever wanted to see Vess again, I had to do exactly what they told me."

"Which was?"

Unexpectedly, Clade spoke up. "Oh, come on. It's obvious, isn't it? Attach himself to you so that he could get to me." He glanced sidelong in Orval's direction. "I have to give you credit, boy. You're the third they've sent after me, and you've managed to get further than the others. But did you ever wonder why the Oculus were so keen to see me dead?"

"Doesn't matter," Orval said. "If you die, Vess comes home."

Clade chuckled. "That's not going to happen, boy. Once Azador gets its claws into someone, there's no prying them loose. We wouldn't be standing here otherwise."

"That's what it was," Eilwen breathed. A second memory unfolded: the siege barely a day old, Orval turning away in despair and disbelief, Eilwen helpless to console him. *You don't understand.* But it wasn't the Oculus army that had prompted the reaction. It was something else: the name of Eilwen's employer. "You didn't expect to actually find him, did you? You thought the whole thing was a false trail."

Orval's face screwed up. "I was going to ask if I could leave with you. I thought if it looked like I was trying, then Vess might be all right. Then they came to our house, and I thought… I thought…"

A scornful expression formed on Clade's face, blessedly hidden from Orval's view by their position, and Eilwen guessed he was thinking the same as she. What better way for the Oculus to persuade Orval's parents to let him go than by threatening him? Even so, she had to ask. "Did your mother and father know about this?"

"No. I don't know. I don't think so."

"Gods, Orval. Why didn't you tell me?"

"How could I, after what you said?" He stared at her in anguish. "Don't you remember? You said you'd rather die than take one copper duri from them. You wouldn't have helped. You would have just…"

Let Vess die. No need to speak the words aloud when the silence fairly shouted them. The beast roared its denial — anything for family! Eilwen gasped, caught on the twin prongs of Orval's accusation and the beast's lust for blood. *No,* she thought, unsure for the moment which of the two she was rejecting. *No more death. No to all of it. No!*

And still the dagger pressed against Clade's throat — pressed, but did not cut. Orval's gaze locked on hers, and behind his pallor and desperation she at last saw what she should have seen from the beginning. *Fear.* The boy was terrified, caught like her between two impossible alternatives, but without the capacity to see beyond them. Death had been thrust into his hands, and he saw no means by which he might release it.

The beast howled within her, willing Orval to take up what had been given him and turn it against his foes. It was the only choice. It was what Eilwen herself had done…

No.

"Orval," she said, willing her voice to calm. "This isn't the way."

"Tell me, then." Anger filled his voice; but she knew now what lay beneath it, could almost hear the flare of hope as he grasped for some other possibility. "What is the way?"

"Let Clade go, and I'll free Vess myself."

Orval stared. "You."

"Me."

"Alone."

Eilwen took a breath. "Yes."

"How?"

"I'll work it out."

Fresh tears tracked down Orval's cheeks. "Why?" he whispered.

"Because she's family. Like you."

Orval drew a shuddering breath. The dagger tumbled from his fingers, its point striking the floor just beside Clade's booted foot. Clade wrenched himself free, sending Orval stumbling against the wall. The youth sank to the floor, head bowed in pain or exhaustion or relief, or a mixture of all three.

"Bastard," Clade snarled, rounding on Orval as though the boy were a disobedient dog. "How dare you threaten me?"

"Oh, shut up," Eilwen said, and Clade turned in surprise. "It's what the Oculus does, isn't it? Figure out how to twist people to serve its own ends? You of all people should appreciate that."

Clade's eyes narrowed. "You have something you want to say?"

Eilwen stooped to retrieve her dagger. "No. You?"

If it occurred to him to thank her, he gave no sign of it. "We need to go," he said. "Follow me."

She glanced to Orval. The boy sat against the wall, knees drawn up and head down, his breaths slow but regular. She wanted nothing more than to sit beside him and tell him that she understood, to begin rinsing away the accretion of fear and shame. But there would be time for that later. Above all else, her nephew needed shelter, and this was its price.

"Fine," she muttered. "Let's go."

As she trailed Clade out to the street, she reflected that perhaps it was just as well he hadn't thanked her. As sure as all the hells, there was no way she could have told him that he was welcome.

~

Arandras barged into the house, the golems trailing behind him. "Jensine! Tell me you're ready."

A clattering on the floor above answered him. Mara descended the stairs in a rush, the relief on her face unmistakable. "You're all right. Thank the gods." Something over his shoulder caught her gaze and she pulled up short. "What happened?"

Golems marched through the door, the first two carrying their wounded brother between them by its arms. The ruin of its body was even starker from side-on as the compression wrought on its torso became jarringly clear. "Cannon," Arandras said shortly, turning from the horrific sight and wishing he could as easily close his ears to the construct's endless report. *I am... wounded.* The words echoed in his thoughts as though the city itself were crying out.

"Arandras." Mara grasped him by the arms, and he turned reluctantly to face her. "What happened?"

He couldn't meet her eyes. "It's dead," he said. "Except... part of it isn't. Part of it's still there."

Mara shifted, her gaze returning to the crippled golem. "Is it in pain?"

"It was. Maybe it still is." Arandras exhaled. "It keeps saying the same thing over and over, like it's caught in that moment and can't get free. But if it can't die, then what? It's just going to stay like that forever?"

"You didn't know this could happen," Mara said, and there was an odd note in her voice. "None of us knew."

"I can't send them out again," Arandras said. "Not if it means facing... that."

Mara released his arms. "What about the others?"

Arandras heaved a sigh. As he neared the estate, he'd paused in a quiet stretch of street to assess his losses. Five golems had been left behind, either too distant at the time to hear his command to follow, or... "I don't know." He glanced in the direction of the stairway. "Is Jensine ready?"

"Just about." Mara stepped back. "She's waiting for you."

The landing above the stairs was quiet, the doors to the balcony closed. The air seemed charged in some indefinable way — an effect of the sorcery, perhaps, or maybe just his own anticipation. He entered the gallery cautiously. Tiy stood alone in the empty space, its back to Arandras. "Jensine?" he called softly, squinting in the gloom.

Slender fingers of light stretched across the gallery from the cracks between the boards, the crosswise pattern accentuating the broader shadows. "Are you here?"

"Took your time," came a strained voice from the near corner. Jensine sat on simple chair, her shoulders hunched, her attention focused on a point about a foot in front of Tiy. "Hope you've been to the privy. If you still want to do this, it's now or not at all."

"Now sounds good to me," Arandras replied. He stepped forward, then froze at a hissed exhalation from Jensine.

"Slowly," she said. "Try not to agitate the air." She took a laboured breath. "Are the golems here?"

"Most of them."

"Bring them in. Line them up... in front of the boards. Make sure you leave some space around Tiy."

Arandras gave the command. "I had to leave a few down by the wall. This will free them too, right?"

"Only one way to find out." Jensine tensed as the first of the golems lumbered into the room. "Now, I'll need you to move in front of Tiy. Not too close — maybe two paces distant. Then we'll connect you up..."

Not too close turned out to be a precise location just beyond the golem's reach. Arandras stood facing his charge while Jensine worked whatever final steps were required to complete the binding. The light angling through the boards moved across the room, then faded. At some point Mara appeared bearing a pair of mirrored Quill sparkers, apparently obtained from one of the house's many unused rooms — a form of light, Arandras surmised, that would preserve the stillness and quality of the air by minimising both smoke and heat currents.

Sunset came and went. The booms of the cannons had continued through the dusk, but as night fell they began to ease. The cool light threw the planes of Tiy's face into sharp relief, and Arandras found himself wondering if the golem had any conception of what was about to happen.

Tiy, he said. *Do you hear me?*

I hear you.

You will soon be free — you and all of your brothers and sisters in this room. Do you understand?

"Hey," Jensine said sharply. "Whatever you're doing, stop it."

"I was just talking to Tiy."

"Don't. You can chat all you like when we're done."

Arandras fell silent. There'd been no response from Tiy anyway.

"All right," Jensine said slowly. "We're almost ready. Just let me tie off these last threads…"

There was a short exhalation from the direction of the stairs. "Shit," Mara said.

"Mara?" Arandras craned his neck, unable to see past Tiy to the room beyond. "What is it?"

Mara shuffled into the room, a chagrined expression on her face. And behind her, holding a blade to the side of her neck, stood a man both instantaneously recognisable and utterly out of place.

"Hello, Arandras," Clade said, glancing around the room with an expression of unrestrained self-satisfaction. "Looks like I got here just in time."

~

Getting into the house proved easier than Clade expected. The front gate was unlocked, and though the door was not so fortuitously unsecured, it was a simple enough matter to break a sitting room window in time with a cannon blast, swing the frame open and climb inside. The room, though not exactly bare, seemed more sparsely ornamented than he would have expected in a house such as this. As Eilwen clambered in behind him, Clade's gaze fell on the only thing that seemed out of place in the thin lamplight: a slender book seemingly forgotten on a side table.

He picked it up and caught the faint scent of spices as he flipped through the pages. His lexicon. Stolen at the same time as the other, far more precious volume. So Arandras *had* arranged the theft, just as Clade had thought. He jammed the book in a pocket and glanced around the room, but the second volume was nowhere visible. Upstairs, perhaps. The grand sorcery he'd sensed before had grown — indeed, if he judged correctly, it was now all but complete. Time was running out.

He beckoned Eilwen closer. "Our target lies above," he

murmured. "Follow me."

Clade opened the door and emerged in a carpeted hallway. There were at least two other people in the house besides Arandras: the dark-skinned woman who had met him earlier and the sorcerer responsible for the binding. The sorcerer would undoubtedly be found close to their work, but it was possible that either Arandras or the woman might be lurking downstairs.

They crept down the hallway to the foot of the stairs, where a stuffed animal the height of his knee regarded him with an incongruous smile. If it hadn't been for the unfinished sorcery pressing down on Clade's awareness, he might almost have thought the house empty. Then a voice spoke somewhere on the floor above. "Whatever you're doing, stop it."

Now, Clade mouthed to Eilwen and began to climb, pulling a knife from his belt and holding it low and close so as not to give off an inadvertent reflection. As he neared the top he saw the dark-skinned woman standing at a nearby doorway, her attention caught by something within the room. *Just stay right there,* he thought as he cleared the stairs and began edging closer. *One more moment...*

He pounced. "Don't move," he muttered, pressing the knife against her neck.

She stiffened, then went slack. "Shit," she said.

Someone called a question from the other room, but Clade ignored it. "We'll just leave these here," he said, pulling the first of her cutlasses free. "No sudden moves. You don't want to finish up on the end of your own blade, do you?" He dropped the second cutlass on the floor behind him. "There. Inside, now."

She walked obediently forward, leading him into... a boarded-up gallery? Clade glanced rapidly around the room. Golems lined the gallery's outer side, creating a wide space in the middle presently occupied by a single golem — and behind it, in the midst of the unfinished binding, Arandras himself.

"Hello, Arandras," Clade said. "Looks like I got here just in time." A stocky woman with unkempt hair stood a short distance from Arandras and the chosen golem, her shoulders bowed beneath the weight of some invisible boulder. *The sorcerer.* "No tricks from you, if you don't mind. Believe me, I'll know."

"Clade." The expression on Arandras's face lay somewhere between fury and disgust. "What in the hells are you doing here? This has nothing to do with you."

"No, of course not. What possible interest could anyone else have in such masterworks as these?"

"Just put down the knife —"

"*Shut up.*"

Arandras swallowed and fell silent, and it was all Clade could do not to laugh out loud. Gods, but it felt good to be on this end of the knife for a change. Between Hesca's overenthusiastic underlings and Eilwen's brat nephew, he'd begun to develop a keen appreciation for the bargaining possibilities inherent in a hand's length of steel.

"You stole my books," Clade said conversationally.

Arandras's eyes narrowed. "Do you mean the one you killed Onsoth for? Not sure I'd consider that particular volume to be yours."

"Ah. So I suppose you returned it to the Library right away, did you?"

"Are you really here to argue about a book?" Arandras said. "If it's not too much trouble, perhaps you could come back tomorrow."

"Yes, I can see you're very busy," Clade said. "And what a travesty it would be, to destroy such marvellous work…" He trailed off, frowning. Arandras hadn't moved since Clade's entrance, not even to step back or shake his head. Sorcery filled the space around him; but it was more than that, Clade could now see. The binding was *connected* to him, and not only to him but also to the golem — indeed, tendrils of the unfinished spell snaked out along the links that tied each of the golems to their master. Whatever this was, it was more than simple destruction. He reached closer, trying to grasp the pattern; but as he did so, the binding rippled beneath his questing thoughts and the stocky woman gave a strangled gasp.

"If you want to collapse that spell," the woman said through gritted teeth, "and risk killing us all, then by all means do that again. Otherwise, keep your hands to yourself."

"What is this?" Clade demanded. "What are you doing?"

"The golems were people once," Arandras said quietly. "Somewhere inside, they still are. We're going to free them."

Clade gave a disbelieving laugh. "Are you mad? Those things are *two thousand years old —"*

Movement, a sudden twisting down and away. Clade lunged after the dark-skinned woman, grasping for her ponytail only to feel it slip through the unresponsive fingers of his crippled hand. *No!* Desperate, he kicked out and felt his boot connect solidly with a fleeing ankle. The woman tripped, crashing face-first to the floor, and Clade swooped, digging his knees into her back and abdomen as he returned the knife to its place against her neck.

"That… was foolish," he gasped. "Do that again… and you'll regret it."

A grinding footfall sounded nearby. Clade looked up to see a golem step toward him from the edge of the gallery, its pale, pinprick eyes fixed on his position.

"Let her go," Arandras said.

Clade chuckled. "You're going to free them, are you? Just *not yet.*" He shook his head. "Tell me, Arandras, what are you going to do for muscle when you don't have an army to push people around with?"

"Let her go," Arandras said again.

"*No.*" The intensity of his own grin surprised even Clade. "You forget. We've played through this little scenario before."

Hesitation. "What do you mean?"

"You remember," Clade said. Eilwen had told him what had happened, there at the mouth of the cavern — how Arandras had yielded at last, agreed to surrender the golems in exchange for his friends. "She was there, wasn't she?" he said, pressing his weight against the dark woman's back. "And now here we are again. Only this time, you don't have to give up the golems to keep her alive. It could be that all you have to do… is *not* give them up. I wonder what you'll choose?"

Arandras said nothing.

"I know you, Arandras. You don't like threats, do you? Can't bear the thought of someone else telling you what to do. Hells, I had that much figured out the first time around. So let me be very clear that this is not a threat. Think of it as a negotiation. I realise there are limits to what I can ask you to do, even for her sake. Most people in your position would do anything I told them. But not you."

He chuckled. "I respect that, you know. She mightn't, but I do."

Arandras stirred. "She does, actually."

"Is that so? Have you discussed that, the two of you? 'This is how far I'll go to keep someone from slitting your throat, but no further?'" Clade paused, but Arandras had lapsed back into silence. "Well, no matter. In any case, I know you have limits, and I've got a pretty fair idea of where they are. And so long as nobody else does anything stupid" — he dug his knee further into Mara's prone form — "I'm confident we'll be able to reach a mutually satisfactory outcome."

"What do you want?" Arandras growled.

"To start with, I'd like this binding dismantled." He shot the sorcerer a sharp look. "Nice and easy, if you don't mind. And please, no triggering it 'by accident'. I'm afraid that would not bode well for your friend's throat —"

Something sharp tickled the small of his back. "Enough talk."

Clade twisted around, squinting in the dim light to see who stood behind him. Was there someone else in the house that he'd missed? "Stand down, or your friend dies," he said.

A figure moved sideways into view. Eilwen gazed down at him, the dark woman's cutlasses in her hands.

"She's not my friend," Eilwen said.

〜

All through the journey to Arandras's house, Orval's anguished face filled her thoughts. They broke in, gained the stairs, interrupted whatever grand binding Arandras had commenced, and still Eilwen could think only of her nephew's torment at the hands of the Oculus.

Then she opened her eyes to find the same tired nightmare playing out again.

A woman — Mara — lying on the floor, Clade's knife at her neck. Arandras and another woman trying to disguise their horror as Clade began issuing demands. And Eilwen herself, standing by and watching it happen.

No more.

Mara's cutlasses filled Eilwen's hands eagerly. She reached out, pressing the tip of one against Clade's back. "Enough talk."

Clade glanced back, more impatient than concerned. "Stand down, or your friend dies."

"She's not my friend." A lie? Perhaps. Just what was necessary to disarm Clade's snare, nothing more.

"Eilwen?" Now the concern began to show, albeit clothed in anger. "What are you doing? Put that down."

"You first." A strange calm filled her, unlike anything she had experienced before. The beast was there too, but it simply watched without demand. "Let her go."

"Damn it, Eilwen." He glanced across the gallery, taking in the boards and the golems standing before them, then scowled and turned back to her. "Put that down or I kill her."

Eilwen shrugged. "Kill her, then."

Clade glared in impotent rage.

"You never really left, did you?" Eilwen said. "Deep down, you're still one of them."

"What, the Oculus? How can you even suggest that? I hate Azador as much as you do!"

Eilwen waved the free cutlass dismissively. "Not that."

"Then what?"

"This," she said. "What you do. It's just the same." She pointed the cutlass at Mara. "Vess." At Arandras. "Orval." At Clade. "Azador."

"That's completely different —"

"No. You violate people. Turn their love into a weapon against them. Tear them apart with it."

"*Everyone* does that, you fool! That's how the game is played!"

Eilwen swung the cutlass back toward Arandras. "He doesn't." She hadn't paid much attention to the argument between Clade and Arandras, but enough of what they'd said had sunk in. "He wants to let the golems go. Release them. Is that right?"

"It is," Arandras said.

"Gods, you are all such fools," Clade said. "Yes, this is what the Oculus do. And guess what? Their army is about to march right into this city. *This is what works.* You can spout all the sanctimonious bullshit you like and it'll get you exactly nowhere. You want to win? This is how!"

As if to punctuate Clade's assertion, a single cannon blast sounded from somewhere beyond the gallery. The beast stirred, roused by Clade's words, and Eilwen felt her preternatural calm begin to slip. *This is what works.* The violence done to her family, Orval's suffering — all of it waved away, just like that. Such was the nature of power. There could be no end to it. One could only hope to avoid it, or if that failed, to avenge whatever wrongs one endured.

A rasping laugh jolted her from her thoughts. "You're right," Mara said, the words muffled by the floor.

"There, you see?" Clade said. "This one's got more sense than the rest of you put together."

"You're right," Mara repeated, taking advantage of a loosening in Clade's grip to turn her head. "If your goal is to win."

Clade tensed, and though his back was to Eilwen, the scowl in his voice was unmistakable. "You'd rather lose, would you?"

"Not me," Mara said. Her eyes flicked to Arandras. "Him. He doesn't want to lose. But he doesn't want to win, either."

Arandras stared at Mara, his expression unreadable. Clade shifted. "Then what in the hundred hells does he want?"

"To change the game."

The words settled over Eilwen like fragrance. She breathed them in, drawing them deep, and felt the beast lay its head on its paws. *No more.* Her own resolution, made for her own sake as much as Orval's. So Clade and the Oculus wanted to pursue their monstrous contest? Let them. She was done.

"Foolishness," Clade snarled. "There is no other game."

"Perhaps," Mara said. "But that's what he wants. And that's why…" She broke off and a look passed between her and Arandras, too deep for Eilwen to decipher. "That's why," she whispered.

❦

Arandras grunted as though struck. Mara's words seemed to peel him open, pinning his soul for display like the exhibits that had filled the gallery before the owner's hurried departure from Spyridon. *That's why… what?* The implied meaning loomed before him, too large and fragile for words. She *knew* him, saw deeper into his tangle of desires than he saw himself, yet despite that — or perhaps, most frightening of all, *because* of it — she... what? *Loved* him?

"Listen to me," Clade said, but Arandras scarcely heard him. The enormity of her words was too much, their implication too momentous, and he shied away; yet some part of him could not let them go. How could he not have known? Yet how could it be true?

"No," Eilwen said. "I'm done listening. Drop the knife."

Clade hissed, his fingers tightening about the hilt. A bead of blood gathered at Mara's neck and slid down the side of the blade. Mara gazed at him, her face pressed against the floor, and it seemed to Arandras that her look held both recognition and bitter amusement. To reach this moment at last, only for it all to end here...

"Eilwen —" Clade began.

Eilwen gave the cutlass a twist. "Drop it. Now."

The moment hung, and it seemed the whole world stood on the edge of the blade at Mara's throat. Clade grimaced, the muscles at his neck and wrists cording with tension. The blade fell...

... and clattered away onto the floor. Clade raised his empty hand in grudging surrender, shifting sidewards to ease the pressure on Mara's back. Swallowing, Mara hauled herself free. From her place by the wall, Jensine heaved a shuddering sigh. "Thank the gods," she breathed.

"Do it," Eilwen said, and Arandras realised she was speaking to him. "Finish the spell. Release them."

"You'll pay for this," Clade spat, the cutlass point still prodding his back.

Arandras drew a breath. Mara was standing now, her fingers rubbing at the thin smear of blood on her neck. A cannon boomed, then another, and Arandras looked away. Suddenly he wished Mara were anywhere else, unable to hear him pronounce an end to her city's final hope.

"Jensine," he said softly. "Whenever you're ready."

Jensine squared her shoulders. "Right," she muttered. "Just let me check that nothing's slipped or shifted. If you could all please hold still."

She lapsed into silence, her lips moving soundlessly as she traced over the spellcraft that was invisible to everyone else in the room, save perhaps Clade. Despite his ire, the former Oculus sorcerer seemed to have accepted his loss for the moment, waiting with no sign of anything more than impatience for Jensine to be done. Perhaps the risk of meddling with another sorcerer's binding was simply too great.

"All right," Jensine said at length. "This should only take a moment." She paused. "You might want to hold your breath."

Why? Arandras had time to wonder. Then the spell struck.

A draught whispered past his cheeks, sliding toward the space between himself and Tiy. For a moment everything before him seemed to thin, as though the world itself were losing substance. Then a rush of air filled the gallery, blasting the boards inward to shatter against the assembled golems. Arandras felt an alarmed cry rise from several constructs simultaneously — then silence.

Golems, he thought, reaching out with a habit borne of the past year. *Tiy. Can you hear me?*

The golems gave no response.

He groped toward them, feeling for the presence at the edge of his awareness that he'd become so accustomed to. But there was nothing there, only emptiness.

"Golems," he said in Old Valdori, stepping closer to study the construct before him. "Tiy. Are you there?"

Tiy stood motionless, the pinprick orange of his eyes glowing sightlessly over the top of Arandras's head.

Unease crept into him. "Tiy. Look at me. Show me you can hear me."

"What happened?" Mara strode across the room, her gaze fixed on Jensine. "Did something go wrong?"

"What? No!" Jensine seemed to be struggling to stand, but the conviction of her words was clear. "It worked. Everything worked."

"Then what happened? Why aren't they moving?"

"I don't know." Jensine leaned against the wall, breathing heavily. "What can you sense, Arandras? Is there still a link?"

"No." Arandras tapped a finger against Tiy's forearm. "There's nothing. Nothing at all." He tried again, this time with an open hand; then, a fist.

Tiy did not move.

"They're gone," Arandras said.

CHAPTER 24

To demand of the All-God that wrongs be righted is the height
of insolence. So the Tabernacle tells us. But what if the reverse
is true? What if your burning discontent — the very thing that
seems to drive you so far from the god — is nothing less than your
divine inheritance?

— Barais neb-Ohel, *A Theodicy*

CLADE KNELT ON THE STONE floor and felt the pressure of
the sword point in his back ease ever so slightly. The boards
that had walled off the gallery lay in splintered fragments
on the floor, including several almost close enough to touch. Arandras and his companions clustered around the golem in the middle
of the room, their attention for the moment directed away from him.

He leaned forward, measuring the distance to a wicked-looking
sliver almost as long as his forearm — too small to ground a binding of any significance, but eminently serviceable as a weapon. The
blade point followed him, its weight light but steady. He drew a
long, calming breath. *Not yet.*

"Are you sure they're gone?" said the sorcerer. "I mean, look at
their eyes."

The other woman nodded. "Jensine's right. Remember when we
discovered them in the cavern? Their eyes were completely dark."

For just a moment, Clade had been the one holding the knife.
Despite the magnitude of the disaster he'd sought to avert, the
world in that moment had felt right in a way he'd barely experienced

since ridding himself of Azador. Then the fates had turned on him yet again, and now he huddled on the floor, forced to watch as his grand project crashed and burned.

Galling as it had been to stand there as Eilwen's brat nephew held a dagger to his throat, it had at least reminded him of one thing. Any attempt to fight Azador by eliminating its people was doomed to failure. Orval clearly had no desire to kill, yet the Oculus had found a way to motivate him all the same. No doubt many of the soldiers outside the city would rather have been anywhere else — yet here they were, and soon the city would fall before them. He could fight them, he could kill them, but Azador would always find more; and in the end, the sheer weight of numbers would overwhelm him.

The alternative was the same as it had always been: to separate Azador from the people that served it, just as he had done for himself, and ultimately to drive Azador away and reclaim the Oculus from its dark master. And the key to all of that — essential on every front — were the golems standing motionless before him.

"It was him," the dark-skinned woman said, turning suddenly on Clade. "He must have interfered somehow."

"No." The sorcerer, Jensine, placed her hand on the other woman's arm. "Mara. It wasn't him. I would have known."

Their attention swung away once more. The blade at his back shifted lower, pulling his shirt tight against his shoulders. Clade eyed the sliver of wood lying just out of reach.

Not yet.

Curious, he stretched out his thoughts, reaching for the space where the binding had been. Emptiness answered. The spell, whatever it had been designed to do, was gone. The damage wrought in the moment of completion might have indicated failure, yet Clade had sensed no connection between the binding and the boards that now lay broken on the floor. Perhaps that had simply been a side-effect, unrelated to the substance of the spell. Which had been... what?

We're going to free them, Arandras had said moments before the spell, and it appeared he'd been sincere. The man seemed genuinely perplexed at the golems' lack of response. Yet the binding had centred on Arandras himself, using him as a kind of conduit into the complex weave of the golems' own sorcery, presumably in an attempt to simultaneously lift some check in each of the bound golems.

"What about the others? The ones you left by the wall. Can you sense them?"

"No, but that doesn't mean anything. The distance is too great."

Clade reached toward the golem Arandras had moved toward him: a pale-eyed construct with an open-faced helmet sculpted onto its head and a mace in one mammoth hand. Once before he'd traced the lines of sorcery within a golem, marvelling at the richness of its binding. At the time, he'd been so driven by his need to escape Azador that he hadn't stopped to consider the presumption of his plan. But now, as he immersed himself once more in the wonder that was a golem's sorcery, the depth of his earlier arrogance — and that of Arandras and Jensine now — struck him like a blow. His own bland confidence at his ability to isolate the golem's spirit in a binding had been bad enough. But what Arandras sought to do — to reshape the sorcery that gave the golems life — revealed a level of hubris that could only be described as mad.

Yet as he followed the singing whorls through the construct's body, something tugged at the edge of his thoughts — something *different,* something that hadn't been present in that other golem back in the cavern... or the absence of something that had...

Realisation came, stunning for its simplicity.

It's not bound.

They'd been unmistakable in the cavern, even beautiful in their way despite what they represented. But the slender shoots of sorcery that had once bound the golems to Arandras... were gone.

Hope surged through him. Heart racing, he formed the words and pressed them toward the golem. *I command you. I am Clade Alsere, and I command you. Obey me.*

A heartbeat. Two. Then the golem turned its head to look directly at Clade and dropped to one knee. *Clade Alsere. I obey.*

"Hey!" Mara called. "Did you do that?"

Get up, Clade instructed, barely able to contain his exultation. *Come here.*

"No," Arandras said as the golem lumbered forward. "Weeper, what's it doing?"

The golem lurched to a halt, its heavy foot smashing the sliver of wood before Clade to a pulp. Behind him, Eilwen murmured a reverent curse, and the blade fell away from his back.

Now.

~

Arandras watched in horror as Clade leapt to his feet and darted behind the golem. "Nobody move!" Clade called, and the triumph in his voice cut Arandras to the bone.

Tiy, he thought, pushing the words urgently at the golem standing motionless before him. *I am Arandras. Know me as your master. Know me.*

Tiy knelt, and the confirmation of what had happened filled Arandras with despair. *I know you.*

"Oh, gods," Jensine said.

"I said, don't move!" Clade's golem strode menacingly toward Eilwen, who stumbled backward, Mara's cutlass clattering to the floor.

"Enough." Arandras sent a command to Tiy, and the golem stepped into the other construct's path. A heavy clank rang out as they collided, the knee of Clade's golem striking Tiy on the upper leg. Tiy crowded close, wrapping its arms around the other golem, and Arandras turned to the nearest of the constructs at the gallery's edge. *Know me.*

Clade bellowed in frustration. His golem shoved back, the wrestling constructs filling the room with a horrible grinding scrape that set Arandras's teeth on edge. The third golem knelt with a thud, and Clade whipped his head around. He locked eyes with Arandras, his face contorted in a grimace. "By all the gods, why are you *always in my way?*"

Arandras gave him a cold stare as the third golem climbed to its feet. "Enough," he said again, the word little more than a whisper. Without turning, he narrowed his focus to his re-bound servant. *Golem. Restrain the man directly in front of me.*

But as the construct moved to obey, Clade's golem grasped Tiy by the shoulders and thrust it away, sending it stumbling past Eilwen to crash into the wall. Clade whirled, sprinting for the stairs, his golem following as though in pursuit. *Stop them!* Arandras sent, and the third golem lunged for its fleeing brother. But its foot skidded on one of Mara's cutlasses and it stumbled, crashing to its knees, leaving Arandras to watch helplessly as Clade and his golem clumped down the stairs and out of the house.

He swung away. "*Damn* it."

"Is everyone all right?" Mara said.

Arandras ignored her. "You," he said softly, advancing on Jensine. "You botched the spell. You were supposed to *free* them. Instead you released my binding, allowing Clade, of all people, to steal one from under my nose!"

Jensine sagged against the wall, exhausted. "I'm sorry. Dreamer, Arandras, I'm so sorry." She exhaled. "I told you from the start. The sorcery in those things is beyond me. There's not a man or woman alive who could say what even a fraction of it does. But I thought I could make it work if I could just make sense of the right pieces."

"At least we know how to unbind them now," Mara said. "Could be useful."

"Could be, if selling them was something we were even remotely considering," Arandras snapped.

"Or if we're able to retrieve the one Clade just walked out of here."

Arandras ran his hand over his face. "You're right. It could help."

"If we know where he's headed, we can go after him…" Mara trailed off, and it took Arandras a moment to realise why. Eilwen was gone.

"Well, that's just wonderful," he said.

"At least she left my swords," Mara said, retrieving her cutlasses from the floor. One of the blades was wider than the other, the metal bent and flattened near the hilt where the golem had trodden on it. "Or what's left of them."

Arandras turned away, his gaze falling on the row of golems still standing along the outer side of the gallery: quiescent, unbound, subject to no-one's orders. It was freedom of a sort, he supposed. Perhaps, if they were left long enough, the glow of their eyes would fade and they would fall dormant, just as he had found them nearly a year ago.

The prospect of turning around and leaving them, of relinquishing the responsibility he had so blithely assumed that day in the cavern, filled him with an unexpected longing. The burden of another being's life, even enclosed in a shell of earth and sorcery, was too great for one soul to bear. It was, he realised, no longer merely the golems' freedom that he sought. It was his own.

But the promised relief at leaving them here was illusion, nothing more. In this state, the golems were *vulnerable* — to Clade, to the Oculus, or to anyone else who might come along and recognise them for what they were. Only by binding them once more could he prevent someone else from subjecting them to an even greater slavery.

It took only a fraction of an hour, but to Arandras it felt interminable. Without the dais in the cavern, each golem had to be bound individually, and each one felt like a betrayal. *I am Arandras Kanthesi. Know me as your master.* Even in his thoughts, the words burned; but the golems paid no mind to his anguish, each kneeling before him as it yielded once more to his will. When he approached the one that had been injured, he paused for a long moment, loath to open himself once more to its distress. Yet to cast it aside now would multiply the injustice of his actions. *Know me,* he told it; and something flickered within, reaching toward him from some incalculable depth, then fading as the familiar refrain began once more. *I... am wounded.*

"What about the others?" Mara said when he was done. "The ones that got left behind?"

He looked a question at Jensine, who simply shrugged. "The effect might not have reached them. I don't know." Her mouth twisted as though tasting something sour. "But I'm pretty sure we mentioned them when Clade was here. If he heard, he might be down there right now."

Shit. Some corner of Arandras's mind jumped in alarm, but the weight of his failure was so great he could barely manage a nod. "I'll go," he said.

Mara's voice stopped him halfway to the stairs. "Want some company?"

The look she'd given him from beneath Clade's knife filled his thoughts. *That's why.* He closed his eyes. It was too much to think about, too much to make sense of. It was all just too much.

"It's fine," Arandras said. "I'll take Tiy."

He sent a command, and the golem obeyed. Together they descended the stairs and emerged into the night.

~

The sorcerer slumped against the wall before Arandras's fury, fatigue etched in the lines of her face, and began a halting apology. Eilwen edged backward, knee screaming at her slow, silent footfalls, then turned and slipped away. Clade had left the house only moments before, but Eilwen emerged on the dark street to find him and the golem gone. Cursing, she broke into a painful half-trot. Chasing after the man she'd just held at sword-point was about the most foolish course of action she could imagine, but she had no choice. Orval was still in Clade's suite, alone and unwell, and she'd be damned before she abandoned her nephew to Clade's vengeance.

The night was clear, the stars' brightness only slightly diminished by the intermittent streetlamps, the air fresh with the scent of the sea. Eilwen toiled grimly down the hill, straining her senses for any sign of Clade or his new slave, but to no avail. Perhaps they'd gone a different way. Perhaps when she arrived at the suite they'd already be there...

No more. She'd sworn it twice this evening: once as she talked Orval down, and again in defiance of Clade's outburst. *No more death.* It was this, she realised, that lay at the heart of the peculiar calm she'd experienced, a calm that still nestled within her despite the urgency of her chase, as though some missing piece at her soul's core had at last been filled. Her knee ached, her breath laboured in her lungs, and her worry for Orval made her stomach churn — yet somehow, despite everything, she'd never felt more alive.

I won't let him have you, Orval, she thought as she pounded around a corner and saw Clade's building loom before her. *I'm coming. Just hold on.*

She charged inside, the violence of her entry tearing the door from its fragile lock and sending it crashing against the wall. The suite was much as she had left it, the ruined bedsheet still puddled in the corner, the pitcher of water on the table still half full. Clade wasn't here, nor his golem — and neither was Orval.

Anxiety mounting, she strode to the bedroom; and there was Orval, sprawled fully-clothed on the pallet, his face cast into shadow by the lantern burning fitfully behind him. She rushed to his side, her fingers questing at his neck for a pulse. Clammy flesh answered her touch, and beneath it a skittering rhythm that filled her with fear. She brushed his cheek, turning his face toward her, and felt her throat tighten. Even in the wavering lamplight it was clear that the boy's pallor had worsened markedly in the short time she'd been away.

Gods. Orval.

His eyelids flickered, and he let out a breathy moan. "Mother?"

Eilwen swallowed. "No." She took his hand. "It's your Aunt Eilwen. Remember?"

"Aunt..." Orval's eyes opened fractionally, then drooped shut again. "Feel strange. Cold... hot."

A whine sounded from the doorway. Eilwen turned to see Jak pad across to the other side of the pallet, its ears and tail down, and press its nose into Orval's hand.

The ghost of a smile flitted across Orval's face. "Jak. You're here."

"Orval..." Eilwen closed her eyes. This was far worse than a few bruises and cracked ribs. Something was badly wrong, something internal: the sort of thing that even a Quill-trained fleshbinder would struggle to set right. *He's dying,* a voice whispered in her thoughts, and she felt a hollow open up within her. After everything they'd gone through, despite all she'd done, Orval was dying.

No. Not despite. Because.

Wild plans filled her head, each more implausible than the last. She would drag Orval down to the barracks and demand the attention of an army medic. She would go back to Arandras's house and beg Jensine's assistance, never mind that the woman had likely never so much as set a bone in her life. She would find Clade and force him to help, somehow...

Orval's hand twitched in a faint squeeze. "'M sorry."

Eilwen squeezed back, gently. "What about?"

"Sorry I drank all that... you know. Before." He sucked in a mouthful of air. "Shouldn't've."

It took Eilwen a moment to fill in the missing word. *Ale. Cider. Whatever it was.* "It's fine," she said. "It's nothing. I'd already forgotten."

"You won't tell Father?"

Another squeeze, to cover the hitch in her breath. "I won't tell."

As if to supplement Eilwen's assurance, Jak withdrew its nose and gave Orval's hand a wet lick. The smile flickered across Orval's face once more. "Mmm. Tickles."

Eilwen stood unsteadily and stumbled toward the other room and the remains of the bedsheet. *You're sorry? Gods, I should be apologising to you. I could go for quite a while.* But there would be time for that later, if Orval recovered — and if he didn't...

She collected the bedsheet, grabbed the pitcher off the table, and shuffled back to the bedroom. Drawing her dagger, she cut a strip of cloth and dipped it in the water, then laid it across Orval's brow. "Is that better?" she asked. "I can take it away if it's too cold."

"No," Orval said, and she paused, not sure of his meaning. He exhaled softly. "Better."

"Good," Eilwen said, sitting once more beside the pallet. If it were possible, he seemed even greyer than a moment ago. "That's good."

Orval's fingers shifted as though trying to grasp something. "Aunt Eilwen."

"What is it?"

The fingers twitched again. "Stay."

Eilwen took his hand. Tears spilt down her cheeks, but somehow she kept the quaver out of her voice. "I'm not going anywhere."

⁓

Clade loped down the empty streets, the golem — his golem! — at his heels. It hovered at the edge of his thoughts, silent but attentive, its presence oddly reminiscent of another, far less welcome companion from Clade's past. But the fetor of Azador's greed had been enough to make him gag, whereas the golem seemed devoid of any emotion at all. It simply abided; waiting, Clade assumed, for some fresh instruction to obey.

Experimentally, he gave it one. *Tell me what you see.*

A street paved in stone, its lanterns alight, the golem responded. *The master runs. Windows, bright. Windows, dark. Doors. A mouse. A rosebush, budding. A cracked pot —*

Enough. A poor question, perhaps — too open-ended to be useful. He tried again. *Tell me your name.*

Golem.

Did your former master address you as such? Or is that how you think of yourself?

The construct did not reply.

Clade frowned, unsure what to make of the non-answer. It was possible that he'd simply phrased the question incorrectly — Old Valdori was difficult enough to read, let alone speak. But he would have ample opportunity to delve into such questions in the coming days. Right now he had more pressing matters to attend to.

He slowed to a walk. The golem matched his pace, presumably in response to his earlier command to *follow.* Arandras's companion had mentioned other golems, somewhere near the wall — perhaps abandoned under fire, perhaps left behind to bolster the city's defences. But Clade thought it unlikely that Arandras would voluntarily omit any of his local contingent from the ceremony just past, and so he had made his way here to the breach in the wall, the most probable site by far for any disorderly retreat. Perhaps he would find nothing, or perhaps the unbinding wrought by Jensine had failed to reach all the way to the wall; but any prospect of adding to his solitary golem could not be passed up.

The guns had fallen still for the night, but Clade could hear activity somewhere ahead: scraping and clattering, impatient commands and muffled curses, and an occasional deep thump. Construction work, he guessed — likely a futile effort to raise some sort of barricade before tomorrow's inevitable assault. He eased forward into streets unlit by lanterns or windows, the moonlight picking out the damage in the buildings around him: a holed roof; a dented wall; a broken door. Something caught at his foot and he stumbled, almost tripping over a block in the middle of the road. No, not a block, a ball: one of the missiles flung into the city by the artillery beyond. He stepped past it, following the street around a bend and into devastation.

With no light to aid him but that of the moon, it was hard to tell where one heap of rubble ended and the next began. Ragged walls jutted from the ruins like growths, and for a moment it seemed to Clade that he beheld some otherworldly farm in which structures might be cultivated from fields of masonry. He shivered, awed by the totality of the destruction before him. Whatever purposes these buildings had once served, they were now indistinguishable from one another, reduced to their component parts as effectively as cattle beneath the butcher's knife.

A faint orange glow caught his eye, jarring for its warmth beneath the pitiless moonlight. A golem crouched not a dozen paces from where he stood, its pinprick gaze illuminating part of the broken brick wall behind which it sheltered. Clade stepped tentatively toward it. If it was aware of his approach, it did nothing to show it. But for its eyes, it might easily have been mistaken for a peculiarly-posed statue.

He drew to a halt with two paces still between them. The golem seemed intact, as far as he could tell: both arms were plainly undamaged, and though its bulk hid one of its legs, its position showed no sign of favouring a missing limb. Its binding, too, seemed undamaged. Clade reached toward it, feeling for the sorcery tying it to Arandras — but the familiar, hated strand was nowhere to be found.

Corralling his excitement as best he could, Clade withdrew his senses and straightened. *Golem,* he sent. *I am Clade Alsere. Obey me.*

There was a thump from the direction of the late-night construction, then a grinding noise as the golem swivelled its head toward him. *Clade Alsere,* it replied, its words ever so slightly deeper and slower than those of the first golem. *I obey.*

Clade clenched his fist in triumph. Two golems, now, with more to be found. He glanced up and down the rubble-choked street, peering in the dim light for anything resembling a golem's bulk. Perhaps Arandras had been forced to separate them, stringing them across the breach to defend the Oculus assault. If so, any remaining golems would likely be arranged in a rough line...

He found one lying flat behind a row of foundation stones, and two more partly buried amid smoking detritus. Near the end of the breach he found another, its right leg torn off at the hip. He tried to bind it anyway, but the golem stared dumbly at the sky and offered no response. After several attempts, he left it and moved on.

Five, he thought, listening to their grinding movements and heavy tread as he passed the end of the breach, the wall's dark bulk rising once more at the city's edge. Barely a drop in the bucket against the hundreds Arandras had led out of the cavern; yet if he'd imagined this night a year ago — himself free from Azador, master of the constructs that now marched behind him — he would have deemed it a success beyond reckoning. He'd defied not one but three Oculus assassins; and now, at long last, he was in a position to strike back.

"Clade." Arandras stepped from the mouth of an alley, a solitary golem at his side. He glanced past Clade, his expression hardening as he took in the gathered constructs. "If you wanted your own golems so badly, you could have just asked."

Clade eyed Arandras warily. The alley behind him was dark, and large enough to conceal a dozen or more constructs. "I rather think you'd have suggested I take a tour of the hundred hells."

"So I would," Arandras said. "To be honest, I'm more than a little tempted to tell you that right now."

Clade raised a brow. "But...?"

"You know I'll find you." Arandras gestured with his chin. "Find them. Take them back."

"So... you're not taking them now?"

Uncertainty flickered in Arandras's expression, and Clade smiled.

Surround them, Clade ordered, and the golems strode forward. Arandras stumbled back, evidently realising his mistake; but as he turned, two of Clade's golems stomped past to block his retreat, the rest forming a ring around him and his companion.

"Well, well," Clade said softly. He walked to the edge of the ring, smiling in at a pale-looking Arandras. "What a remarkable turn of events."

Arandras folded his arms. "Really? Seems to me we've been here before."

"Oh?" Clade considered him. "Ah. The caverns. You think that if I didn't kill you then, I'm hardly going to kill you now, is that it?" He paused. "Or perhaps you're thinking of later. Perhaps you're thinking about how you had me at — what would you say, at golem-point? Is that a word? But you spared me, so now you imagine I should do the same."

"Both good arguments," Arandras said. "I was thinking of the first one, mostly. But you missed a part." He fixed Clade with a cold stare. "That's the part where I've got the Weeper only knows how many golems at my beck and call, and you really don't want to be responsible for me giving them a dying command."

Clade returned the stare. He'd seen perhaps two dozen golems in the house — too far away for Arandras to reach from here, by his own admission. *Assuming they're still there. And assuming he doesn't have others seeded around the city.*

"You're bluffing," Clade said.

Arandras shrugged. "Am I?"

"Yes," Clade said. "I think you are. But it doesn't matter."

"And why might that be?"

Clade loosed a breath. "I never wanted to be your enemy, Arandras. It was you who sought me out. You who tried to kill me. Even here, just a few days ago, I came to you seeking your help, and how did you respond? By breaking into my house and robbing me. This... antagonism, whatever it is — it's all you. All I've ever done is look to defend myself."

"You killed Tereisa," Arandras growled.

"Azador killed Tereisa. I served it, just as your golems serve you."

"And now I want to free them," Arandras returned. "Just as you freed yourself."

"No. You want to evade the responsibility to *do something* with the gift you've been given. Throw away the opportunity to make a difference — and for what? You think you can undo whatever the Valdori did to create these things? You think you can unbind what they bound? Unkill what they killed? *You?* You're a child compared to them. Hells, you're not even a sorcerer. *I'm* a child. You're a damned vegetable."

Arandras shook his head. "You're wrong."

"No, I'm not. And let me tell you something. I am going to take these golems, all five of them, and I am going to put them to work." He pointed at the wall, at the army camped on the other side. "The

Oculus have to be stopped. You could do it tonight if you wanted to, but you won't. So I'll have to do it more slowly." He stepped closer. "And if you ever come after me — if you ever try to 'take these golems back' — know that I will have them destroy themselves before I give them up. So if you really care as much for them as you claim, you'll make damned sure you stay the hells away."

Arandras glared. "This isn't over."

"You'd better hope it is," Clade said. "You spared me once. Now I'm returning the favour. We're square. Seems like a good way to leave it, wouldn't you say?"

"What?" Arandras choked back a laugh. "You graciously decline to kill me with my own damn golems, and you call that *square?*"

"Not your golems." Clade sent a command, and the two blocking the alley stepped aside. He smiled. "Mine."

CHAPTER 25

If a man loved his wife the way the gods love the world, he would
not remain married for long.

— Kassa of Menefir, *Solitude*

ARANDRAS OPENED THE DOOR OF the estate house and
stepped inside, Tiy close behind. Despite the lateness of
the hour — past midnight by now, probably — lamps still
burned both in the entry hall and on the upper floors. Exhausted, Arandras pulled the door closed behind him and began a final
climb of the stairs.

The gallery was much as he had left it: boards torn from their
place and shattered on the floor, golems arrayed with their backs
to the destruction like errant sentries. He left Tiy with the others
and climbed on, following the trail of lamplight to the upper room
where he found Mara and Jensine on the settee gazing out to the
darkened city.

Mara glanced across as he entered the room. "Find them?"

"No," Arandras said. "Clade got there first."

"Dreamer's bloody daughters." Jensine bowed her head. "I should
have known freeing them wouldn't be that easy. I'm sorry."

As though in echo, Clade's words returned to Arandras. *You
think you can unbind what they bound? You're a child compared to
them.* He swallowed. "It wasn't just you," he muttered. "Ah, hells,
Jensine. It's not your fault."

"What now?" Mara met his gaze, and he saw the hope flare to life behind her eyes. "There's still time."

"I can't, Mara. I'm sorry. Not at the price of…" He took a breath. "And I can't keep them here, either. Not with the city about to fall." He didn't want to go on, but to not tell her would be even worse. "I have to leave. Tonight."

Mara gave a thin smile. "I see."

Arandras reached out a hand. "Come with me."

Slowly, Mara shook her head. "I can't," she whispered.

"Why?"

"You already know." Mara's tone was gentle, almost calm. "This is my city. I won't abandon it."

Arandras tried to smile, tried to understand. "You think you can keep the Oculus out?"

"No," Mara said. "But Spyridon won't stop being my home just because of them. And the battle won't end just because…" She trailed off, then snorted. "Besides, I took a contract. I'm stuck watching this house for the next fifty days, give or take, or until Master Trattasi returns to release me. Couldn't leave if I wanted to."

Arandras looked away. "What happened tonight, with you and Clade…" He hesitated, unsure what he wanted to say and wishing that Jensine were elsewhere to give him a chance to say it. "What you said. It, uh, made me realise…"

Mara smiled, and the way the lamplight glinted in her eye told him everything he needed to know. "It's about time," she said.

"So…?"

She shrugged. "Seems we'll have to wait a bit longer, won't we?"

Arandras exhaled soundlessly. "I guess so."

"I, uh…" Jensine glanced from Arandras to Mara and back again. "Not to interrupt, but did I hear you say that you're planning to bust past all those disturbingly well-armed men and women down there?"

With an effort, Arandras turned his gaze to Jensine. "You want to get out before they get in?"

"Please." She turned to Mara. "I wish you'd come, too. A conquered city is no place to be."

"I'll be fine," Mara said. "Really."

Jensine stood and pulled Mara to her feet for an embrace. "Be well, then."

"I will."

They broke apart, Jensine rubbing at her eyes. "I'll fetch my things," she said. "See you downstairs."

She bustled out, leaving Arandras and Mara facing each other. He blinked, unable to speak, the jumble of words that lay within his grasp utterly inadequate to the moment.

Mara leaned close and kissed him on the cheek. She smelled of leather and blade oil and Kharjik spices, a combination of scents uniquely hers.

"Go," she whispered. "Prove him wrong. Prove them all wrong." She took his face in her hands, her gaze and scent and words filling his senses so that his entire world seemed to hold only her. "Find a way to change the game."

~

They were, it turned out, all damaged. None were as badly hurt as the golem Clade had failed to bind, but each of the five had suffered harm, ranging from scratches and dents to chipped blades and crushed toes. Clade paraded them beneath the streetlamp, inspecting each in turn, his withered hand thrust into the pocket of his greatcoat. It seemed every ally he managed to attract, even temporarily, was broken in some way. Eilwen had been lamed both within and without by her previous confrontation with the Oculus. Even Hesca had her scars.

Broken, all of them. Just like me. Each had run up against the sharp edges of the world and been battered by the encounter — a small foretaste, perhaps, of the ultimate destruction that came to all. Perhaps that was the reason for the contempt such wounds sometimes attracted. Perhaps those who mocked cripples did so in the hope that by scorning the tokens of mortality they might somehow outrun death.

Yet the thread joining his allies was strangely appropriate, even if they failed to understand it themselves. Eilwen had seen only his ambition, mistaking his immediate goals — obtaining the golems, for instance, or even defeating Azador — for ends in themselves. Perhaps it was to be expected. She'd never known the Oculus as anything other than what Azador had made it. If he'd tried to explain, she'd probably have laughed in his face.

Azador grieves for the fallen Empire. Azador longs for its restoration. That is the purpose for which the Oculus exists. The beginning of that credo he now knew to be false, but the final part shone no less brightly than it had on the first day he'd recited the words. Restoration of the Empire — its healing, its grace — and with it, renewal. And who better to bring about that renewal than those who bore the ills of the world in their own person — those who understood, deeply and profoundly, the petty tyrannies of hardship that the Oculus had once sought to defeat?

His hand, clawed and unresponsive, pressed against his thigh through the fabric of his clothes. He'd found ways to work around the impairment, learnt anew how to eat and dress and piss, but the resentment he felt every time he beheld the useless lump of flesh had only grown. It was *wrong*, the world writ small; and although there was nothing he could do about his hand, the wider world might yet be redeemed.

To that end, Clade would lie, cheat, steal, kill, and do anything else that might help him tear down Azador and return the Oculus to its true path. And now, at last, he had the means.

He considered the row of constructs, pinpoint eyes gleaming in their shadowed faces. If Hesca were here, he had no doubt what her counsel would be. *Join us. Drive the Oculus away. Defeat their design.* Would five golems be enough to turn the tide of the siege? Perhaps they would, if properly deployed. But Clade had seen the damage wrought by the enemy's cannons. With two or three unlucky shots he might lose the better part of tonight's windfall. Half a dozen would see him back where he started.

Or he could flee the city. It was the safer option, no doubt. He'd have time to learn the golems' capabilities, time to ponder how they might best be deployed. And it would put some distance between himself and Arandras, just in case the man failed to heed Clade's warning and decided to pursue him after all.

As decisions went, this was one of the easier ones.

To his suite, then, to collect his things — but no. Arandras knew where he was staying, as shown by his theft of Clade's books;

and if he'd forgotten, Eilwen would no doubt be on hand to remind him. The prospect of returning only to be overpowered by Arandras's other golems was too dismal to entertain. *Perhaps I should have killed him when I had the chance.* But then, of course, *all* the golems would have been freed from their binding, not just those within range of the sorcerer's spell. Far better, for now, to leave them idle in Arandras's care than risk them falling into the hands of someone else — the Quill, say, or Azador itself.

Well. There was little enough in his suite that he'd miss. His lexicon he'd retrieved from Arandras's house, and his coinpurse was safely attached to his belt. The other book, the one he'd killed Onsoth for, was still missing and must now be given up as lost. Everything else could be easily replaced at the first village he found. And with the golems now at his disposal, he suspected he wouldn't have too much trouble replenishing his silver.

He chose a street that skirted the hill and set off northward, the golems marching behind. The breeze from earlier in the evening had dropped off, leaving the city cool and still. As he rounded the hill's north side, his nostrils alerted him to his destination: the sewer tunnel that passed below the northwest wall before curling around to empty in a swamp on the westward shore.

It took some time to locate an entrance to the sewer, but eventually Clade found a short alley that terminated in a heavy iron gate. Two soldiers in grey and red barred the way; but at the sight of the golems and on hearing Clade's tale of a midnight raid, they readily gave him leave to pass. He accepted the offer of a torch and descended the stairs, stepping gingerly onto the slick side path as the golems splashed into the main channel.

The stench filled his nose, defying all efforts to obstruct it. Yet as Clade edged down the passageway, he found himself smiling beneath the cloth he pressed to his face. With the constructs that now waded beside him, he at last had the means not only to strike back at Azador but to free others from its grasp. Others like him. Many, no doubt, would revile him as Rathzange had, but surely some would seek him out once they heard of the freedom he offered.

Soon, he might have allies in truth. Allies who understood both the struggle and its necessity. Allies who, like Clade, would do whatever it took to win.

His smile broadened, and as he followed the tunnel down its barely-perceptible incline, he imagined himself welcoming sorcerers to his cause, each newcomer filled with gratitude for their freedom and eager to do his bidding in the war against Azador.

It would be good to no longer be alone.

～

The sky had just begun lightening to deep, pre-dawn blue when Arandras led the golems down to the breach in the wall. Jensine marched beside him, her bag slung over her shoulders, still subdued after the failure of her sorcery — or perhaps just tired. Though the city was beginning to stir, most of the houses behind the breach were deathly still. Lamplight glimmered in only a handful of windows and the streets were bare, save for the occasional soldier heading toward the front line or coming back the other way. More than one passing soldier gave a weary cheer at the sight of the constructs, but Arandras ignored them all, passing half-collapsed buildings and rubble-choked alleys as he made his way steadily eastward.

He heard the chatter of voices just before he turned the corner and saw it: a crude barricade stretching across the line of the fallen wall, waist-high at best, most of it little more than a row of hastily repositioned wreckage. A knot of soldiers stood a short distance away, sheltered from the enemy by the remains of some shop or house, their braids of rank glinting by the light of a single lamp. One of them murmured in surprise, prompting the entire group to turn in Arandras's direction; then a woman detached herself from the group and strode across.

"So," she said as she drew near, and Arandras recognised Hesca, her eyes alight with hope. "Come to fight after all?"

Arandras pursed his lips and gave a single shake of the head.

The hope in Hesca's expression faded. "No," she said in flat resignation, her gaze locked to his. "You're leaving."

"I am," Arandras said.

Hesca sighed heavily. "Well," she muttered. "I suppose that makes it easier, in a way."

"Makes what easier?"

She waved the question away. "Never mind."

Arandras glanced at the makeshift barricade. "That won't keep them out, you know. Their cannons will cut through it like butter."

"Thank you for your expert assessment," Hesca said with a hint of her old sharpness; then she sighed again, deflating like a spent bladder. "Best you just leave."

She led them to a narrow opening in the barricade: a choke-point, Arandras guessed, through which enemy soldiers were to be funnelled. They passed through in single file, Arandras first, followed by Jensine, then the golems, the two carrying their damaged brother turning sideways to clear the passage. When the final golem emerged, Arandras looked back for a last farewell to Hesca, but the commander was already walking away.

They turned north, hugging the barricade and then the star-shaped wall. The eastern sky was growing brighter. Soon they would be visible to the enemy's spotters.

Soon we'll be gone.

At the fourth point of the wall's star, he called a halt. The Oculus line was thinner here, and from what he could see and his recollection of the briefing at the command post, the terrain was largely free of fences and other obstructions.

He sent a command to the golem nearest Jensine and it dropped to a crouch, its back sloping before her, its arms wide. "Climb on," he said.

Jensine gave the golem a wary glance. "What?"

"Climb onto its back." She looked at him askance, and Arandras shrugged. "Or do your best to keep up. Your choice."

Gingerly, Jensine clambered onto the golem's back and wrapped her arms around its neck. At Arandras's direction, the golem drew its own arms over her calves and slowly straightened.

"Comfortable?" Arandras asked.

Jensine rolled her eyes. "Oh, just peachy."

As the glimmer on the eastern horizon grew brighter, Arandras repeated the procedure, this time with himself and Tiy. Though smooth, the golem was not slippery, and Arandras was able to climb to a point behind Tiy's shoulders without much trouble. His stomach lurched as Tiy lifted itself upright; but as Arandras settled into position, so too did his viscera, and he glanced appreciatively from his new height at the golems around him.

Form up, he commanded. *Jensine and myself in the middle, the rest of you in a ring around us.*

Wordless, save for the one that would never be silent again, the golems obeyed.

He glanced across at Jensine. "Ready?"

Jensine glared. "Dreamer, but you ask stupid questions some-times, don't you?"

Golems. Arandras took a breath. *Run.*

They set off at a swift jog, pounding over the packed earth, forc-ing Arandras to cling to Tiy's head to avoid being thrown clear. The wind plucked at his shirt, the scents of city and sea falling away to be replaced by the smell of campfires and the faint whiff of latrines. They thundered down a slight incline, then up again, trees and bushes whipping past at tremendous speed. A long, jolting moan sounded beside him, and Arandras risked a glance to see Jensine clutching her golem for dear life, her face locked in a rictus of terror.

Shouts of alarm rose before them; then they were crashing into the besiegers' camp, tents and cookfires transformed in an instant to flapping canvas and scattered embers. A dull clink at the edge of the ring marked an attempt by some particularly brave or foolish swordsman to bring down one of the golems; but the sound was followed by a snap and a cry of pain, and then that too was behind them and they were through, running over open fields as the sounds of chaos gradually receded in their wake.

Only when the fields gave way to orchards did Arandras allow the golems to slow. They drew to a halt behind a row of apple trees, the morning sun angling through branches dotted with unripe fruit.

"Gods have mercy," Jensine said slowly, her voice thick. "Let us never do that again."

Exhaling, Arandras closed his eyes. "No argument here."

"Put me down, will you?"

Arandras complied; but as he turned his attention to his own position, he heard unexpected words fill his mind.

A relic, Tiy said beneath him. *A relic.*

Arandras froze, waiting for Tiy to continue, but the golem said nothing. At last he ventured a question. *What relic?*

A relic, Tiy repeated. *The master. Darkness to light. We emerge.* There was a moment's pause, then Tiy spoke again. *A relic. A girl lifted high.*

Arandras blinked. *Two* memories, the first describing — what? Arandras himself, leading the golems from the cavern? And a second memory to go with the first. A girl lifted high. No, not a girl — Tiy's daughter. Lifted high, then, must mean... what?

He shifted uncomfortably, his legs caught against the golem's side, and exhaled in realisation. *Lifted high, just like me.* A memory of Tiy carrying his daughter on his shoulders.

Arandras climbed awkwardly down, grimacing at the wobble in his legs as he reached the ground. *You're still in there,* he sent, stumbling around so he could look Tiy in the face. *Still there. I hear you.*

"Gods," Jensine said, lying flat on the ground. "Gods and demons. Never again."

Arandras reached up to Tiy's face. *I haven't forgotten. I won't give up. I'll find a way to free you. I swear it.*

Tiy gazed back and said nothing.

～

In the cool, grey hour before dawn, Orval died.

Eilwen sat by his sleeping form, her hand covering his as his shallow breaths slowed, hitched, and fell still. She sat there as his fingers cooled beneath hers, waiting for the next breath — whether his or her own, she could not tell.

Eventually she rose. The litany of her failures bubbled up within her, clamouring for attention, but she paid them no mind. Orval was dead. What else was there to say?

As she trailed toward the window, Jak stirred on the other side of Orval's pallet. The dog pawed at Orval, whining softly, then cocked its head questioningly at her. She turned away. Whatever the dog was asking, the answer was no.

No, he won't wake.

No, I can't help.

No, it's not right.

No, no, no.

She looked out the window. Dawn had broken, the sun casting slantwise shadows across the street. Clade would likely return soon, and Eilwen doubted he'd arrive in a forgiving mood. While Orval had lived there'd been no question of leaving Clade's suite, no matter the risk; but now...

Eilwen turned. Her nephew lay as though still asleep, Jak disconsolate beside him. To leave him like this seemed cruel beyond measure, not least to Den and Irilli, but what could she do? At this point in the siege, she might be waiting days before a priest or a gravedigger could attend to him; and none of it would matter anyway if Clade returned before she was done. Better to go while she could.

She bent over and kissed Orval on the forehead, his flesh cool beneath her lips. "Farewell," she whispered. "May the gods smile upon you."

It took only moments to gather her possessions. She hesitated at the door, part of her unwilling to leave him even now; but as she glanced back at what remained of her nephew, Jak rose and limped to her side. The dog gazed at her silently, its tail brushing the floor; then it stepped forward and pressed its moist snout into her hand.

"All right," she said softly, scratching the back of its head with her knuckles. "Let's go."

As the first cannon blasts of the day boomed over the city, Eilwen found herself retracing her steps of the previous night, limping up the hill to the Trattasi estate house. By the time she stood outside its door the sun had climbed high enough to raise a sweat and her knee felt ready to buckle.

An unfamiliar man answered her knock: young, thin, with messy hair and a squint that made her feel like a sheep at market. "Who are you?"

"My name is Eilwen," she said, bemused by the stranger's presence. "I, uh, was here last night..."

There was movement inside, and a moment later Mara appeared beside the man. "It's fine, Druce," she said. "I know her." The man grunted and disappeared inside. "So," Mara said, glancing at Jak with faint amusement. "I see you found a friend."

"You, too."

"What, Druce?" Mara chuckled, but something about it seemed forced. "He won't stay, I shouldn't think. Or maybe he will, if his news is accurate."

Eilwen swallowed. "Can I come in?"

"Well, that really depends, doesn't it?" Mara said. "What happened?"

Eilwen opened her mouth, then closed it again. The matter was too big for explanations. Nothing she could say could come close to encompassing its weight, its awful finality. "Orval," she said. "He…"

Understanding flickered in Mara's gaze. "Clade?"

Eilwen shook her head.

"Have you seen him?"

She shook her head again.

Mara's expression softened. "All right," she muttered as she stepped aside. "But if that dog makes a mess, you'll be the one cleaning it up."

"Hey." Druce's voice floated down from somewhere above them. "You'd better come see this."

They trooped upstairs. At the top, Eilwen glanced reluctantly to the gallery — but the golems were gone, leaving only the broken boards around the gallery's outer edge as witness to the night's events.

"What is it?" Mara asked, joining Druce on the balcony and shading her eyes against the sun.

Druce pointed.

A single rider had emerged from the city and now stepped cautiously toward the enemy line; and in the rider's upraised hand, a large white flag bearing a single horizontal line.

Mara gave a deep sigh. "Surrender."

"Told you," Druce said.

Eilwen turned away, overcome with exhaustion. Her failure was complete. No matter what she did, the Oculus simply marched on, grinding anything and anyone that stood against them into the dirt. *Gods, I should have just stayed in Neysa. Or with the Woodtraders.* Her head drooped to her chest. Had she done a single thing right since Havilah called her into his office that evening after her return to Anstice? If so, she couldn't think of it.

She became aware of someone standing nearby — Mara, looking almost as worn as Eilwen felt, yet watching her with something close to sympathy. "Bad day, huh?"

Eilwen choked back a wild laugh. "You could say that."

"Yeah." Mara took a breath. "Still. Could have been worse."

Eilwen shook her head.

"Last night," Mara said. "There was a moment when I thought… it was going to be worse. And it would have been, if you hadn't been there."

Eilwen glanced sideways. There, just inside the gallery, was the place she'd held the blade to Clade's back. The place where she'd talked Clade down. *She's not my friend.* Her own words echoed in her ears, and she looked away. "Um. What I said —"

"Was just what you needed to say." Mara grasped her arm. "Truly. I would have said exactly the same."

"Oh." The woman's lips quirked in a half-smile, and Eilwen felt its reluctant answer on her own face. "Well. That's all right, then."

"If you need a place, you're welcome to stay here," Mara said. "Arandras and Jensine are gone, so it'll be just us, and maybe Druce. There's plenty of food, and with luck the bastards out there will be too busy disposing of the city's best and brightest to give us much attention."

A lump formed in Eilwen's throat. "Thank you," she said. "But I can't. There's something I need to do."

Orval was dead, but her promise to him was not.

Let Clade go, and I'll free Vess myself.

Why?

Because she's family. Like you.

Mara gave her a close look. "Is it the sort of something that needs you to be out there roaming the streets while the Oculus lay claim to the city?"

Eilwen considered. "No. Not really."

"A few days, then?"

"All right." She exhaled in a rush, gratitude and weariness overcoming her last defences against Mara's kindness. "I'll stay a few days."

"Good."

A cough sounded from the balcony; then Druce called out, his voice tight. "Here they come."

The satisfaction fell away from Mara's expression. She turned and stalked to the balcony, Eilwen trailing behind.

Even though she knew what she would see, the glare of the eastern sun defeated her eyes for several moments. Then she saw them, formed up in columns, marching across the torn fields to claim their prize.

A distant screech of hinges sounded, carried to them by some trick of the breeze as the free city of Spyridon opened its gates to the soldiers of the Oculus.

EPILOGUE

Fools claim the world is as it should be, and devils whisper that it
should be as it is. In the wide spaces between lie all the sorrows of
humankind.

— Vissbronaumi, *On the Tragedies*

O N THE TWELFTH DAY AFTER he resumed eating, Nezhar
took ship from Port Gallin.

It was a shock to find himself among people again.
The noise and stench and endless movement assaulted his senses,
pulling his fragmented attention in a hundred directions at once.
This was the part he hated most, as the glory of his grand binding,
already fading from memory, was trampled into the mud by the
grunts and bellows of a slack-jawed, arse-scratching populace.

It would pass, of course. It always did. A month from now he'd
be comfortably ensconced in some well-appointed bordello with his
choice of whore for company, enjoying the rewards of his success
here in Spyridon. But none of that made the present moment any
easier.

Squinting against the glare, Nezhar surveyed the ships tied up
to the sun-bleached wooden piers. The far end of the docks had
been set aside for Oculus vessels, but most of those spaces were
empty, the ships in question patrolling the waters beyond the harbour, away on assignment, or yet to arrive. Just now only two ships
were anchored in the restricted area: a three-masted carrack with a

prow carved to resemble a wildcat's head, and a smaller vessel with a single mast and a row of empty gun ports.

By all accounts, Spyridon's fall had been relatively bloodless. It seemed that most of the ruling circle had already fled or gone into hiding before the Oculus triumph, and although the commander of the army, one Piator Pronn, had been found locked in a cell and promptly executed, the city's figurehead monarch had somehow contrived to disappear shortly after the surrender. In some districts, contingents of the defeated army had been granted leave to resume their function of keeping the peace; but here on the docks, as at the Library and other key locations, the soldiers wore the hard smiles and rough armour of the conquering mercenaries.

The public end of the docks was more densely populated, though even here more than half of the berths lay empty. Nezhar could see several high-prowed traders, their triangular sails rigged in the Kharjik fashion; a multi-decked behemoth from Tan Tahis, its painted forecastle a riot of colour; and even a Jervian longship, as far from home as it could get without leaving the continent entirely. The latter had just arrived, and as Nezhar watched, a trio of mercenaries stepped aboard, presumably to compare the ship's cargo to its manifest and extract whatever duties the Oculus had seen fit to impose.

A wave of fatigue washed over him, draining the strength from his legs, and he reached unsteadily for a nearby rail. Though he'd been eating again for more than a week, he was still a long way from recovering his full vigour. The number of people recoiling from his gaunt visage had declined in recent days, but that meant only that his appearance had begun to shift from *death warmed over* to *underfed pauper*. And even that impression lasted only so long as nobody asked him to speak.

The weakness passed. Nezhar released the rail and forced himself to stand straight. Mere thinness mattered little, and the appearance of poverty was easily remedied with hard silver, but no captain would grant him passage if they thought him diseased.

Nezhar opened his bag, reaching past the hand-axe and his other gear for the item he needed only now that his isolation was over: a writing slate tucked into a pocket in the bag's side. Slate in hand, he walked slowly to a Kharjik vessel being loaded with crates and barrels. A dark, leathery woman with a pale green kerchief on her head looked up at his approach. "Get lost," she said, scowling and waving her arm. "You won't find no charity here."

Nezhar wrote the word *Captain?* on the slate and held it out.

"What's that?" The woman squinted in displeasure. "Captain? That's me, and I'm telling you to piss off."

Nezhar wiped the slate and wrote again. *Sailing west?*

"You're a sharp one, aren't you? Where else would we be headed, across the Endless Sea?" The captain folded her arms. "If you want to work for passage, forget it. I've got rats below deck that look healthier than you."

Nezhar reached into his bag and hefted a jingling pouch.

The captain's brows rose. "Well, now. That's a whole other bill of goods. Where are you headed?"

Erelah, Nezhar wrote.

She frowned. "We're not going that far into the bay. But you could leave us at Alba, if you like. Twelve scudi for a hammock in the hold. Another ten if you want to share our food."

He shrugged in acceptance. Either city would serve. The Hungry Men had contacts in Alba and Erelah both, trusted agents who could relay messages to their hideaway: an old cloister deep in the mountains separating Sarea from the Kharjik Empire.

"Right, then." But the captain hesitated. "You one of them religious types? Vow of silence or something?"

Nezhar stepped close and opened his mouth wide.

Most people flinched the first time they saw the blackened ruin of Nezhar's tongue; but the captain merely studied it with something approximating cool interest. "That's a thorough-looking job," she said, a slight wrinkle in her nose the only sign of distaste. "Who'd you cross to earn that?"

He shrugged again. His crimes lay so far in the past that they hardly mattered now, and he certainly wasn't about to dredge them up for the benefit of a nosy captain. *Father,* he wrote — his standard lie, calculated to replace suspicion with sympathy.

It worked. The captain glanced away, her expression softening ever so slightly. "We sail in an hour," she said. "If you've got any belongings that need fetching, best you see to them now."

Nezhar shook his head, and the captain waved him aboard.

Rather than venturing below to claim a space in the hold, Nezhar found an out of the way spot by the rail with a view of the open water to the south. A heavily armed warship tacked eastward, its colours still those of Spyridon but its command now held by the Oculus — an unthinkable possibility even a month ago, but now nothing less than plain fact.

Because of him.

Perhaps he'd been hasty, that first day without food. Transcendence came in many forms, but there was something unique about moments like these. To stretch out one's hand and set the world on a new course — how many people could claim such a thing? If the gods had been real, then for a moment Nezhar could have counted himself among them. No doubt the more credulous had already attributed Spyridon's fall to some divine whim, be it rage, retribution, or simple neglect. And now, like a god in truth, Nezhar would slip quietly away — and nobody, not even this weather-worn captain, would have the slightest notion of his significance, or how momentous this ordinary ship's departure became by virtue of his presence.

Once more, then. When he was done with his whores and the wines he could not savour, he would return to the cloister and advise Sehv and the other elders of his willingness to accept another assignment. It would be small, no doubt; trifling compared to what he had achieved here. But within the confines of whatever drama he was called upon to alter, the taste of it would be the same. And there was nothing in the world that Nezhar relished more.

He stood by the rail for a long time, gazing past the horizon as the ship eased from the harbour and slipped out to sea.

About the Author

Like every child, Matt Karlov was raised on stories of the impossible, from the good parts of *Sesame Street,* to *The Hobbit,* to *Watership Down* and beyond. As Matt grew older, he had the good fortune to retain his taste for the fantastic, which soon developed into a deep love of speculative fiction in its many guises. He has been struggling to make room on his shelves for new books ever since.

Matt has been a software designer, a web developer, and a business analyst. He lives in Sydney, Australia. *The Lordless City* is his second novel.

Visit www.mattkarlov.com to discover more about Matt's writing and the world of Kal Arna.

CPSIA information can be obtained
at www.ICGtesting.com
Printed in the USA
BVHW072143120819
555663BV00009B/312/P